AMULET

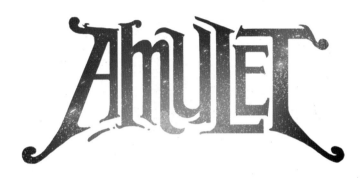

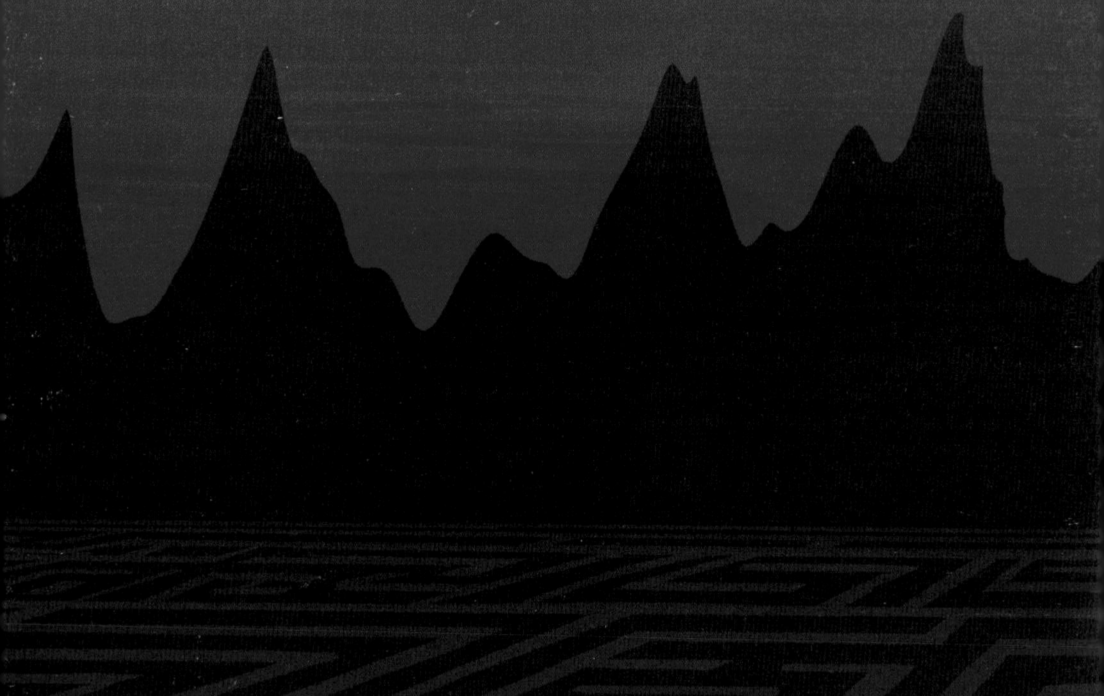

Library of Congress Control Number: 2015936071
ISBN 978-0-545-83966-2 (hardcover)
ISBN 978-0-545-43316-7 (paperback)

10 9 8 7 6 5 4 3 2 16 17 18 19 20
First edition, March 2016
Edited by Cassandra Pelham
Book Design by Kazu Kibuishi and Phil Falco
Creative Director: David Saylor
Printed in the U.S.A. 88

This book belongs to:
Ashton Mead

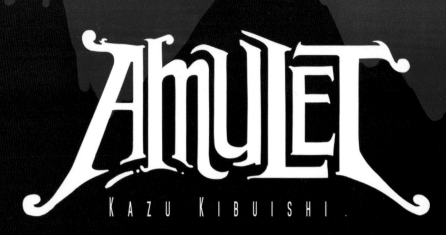

AMULET

KAZU KIBUISHI

BOOK SEVEN
FIRELIGHT

AN IMPRINT OF

SCHOLASTIC

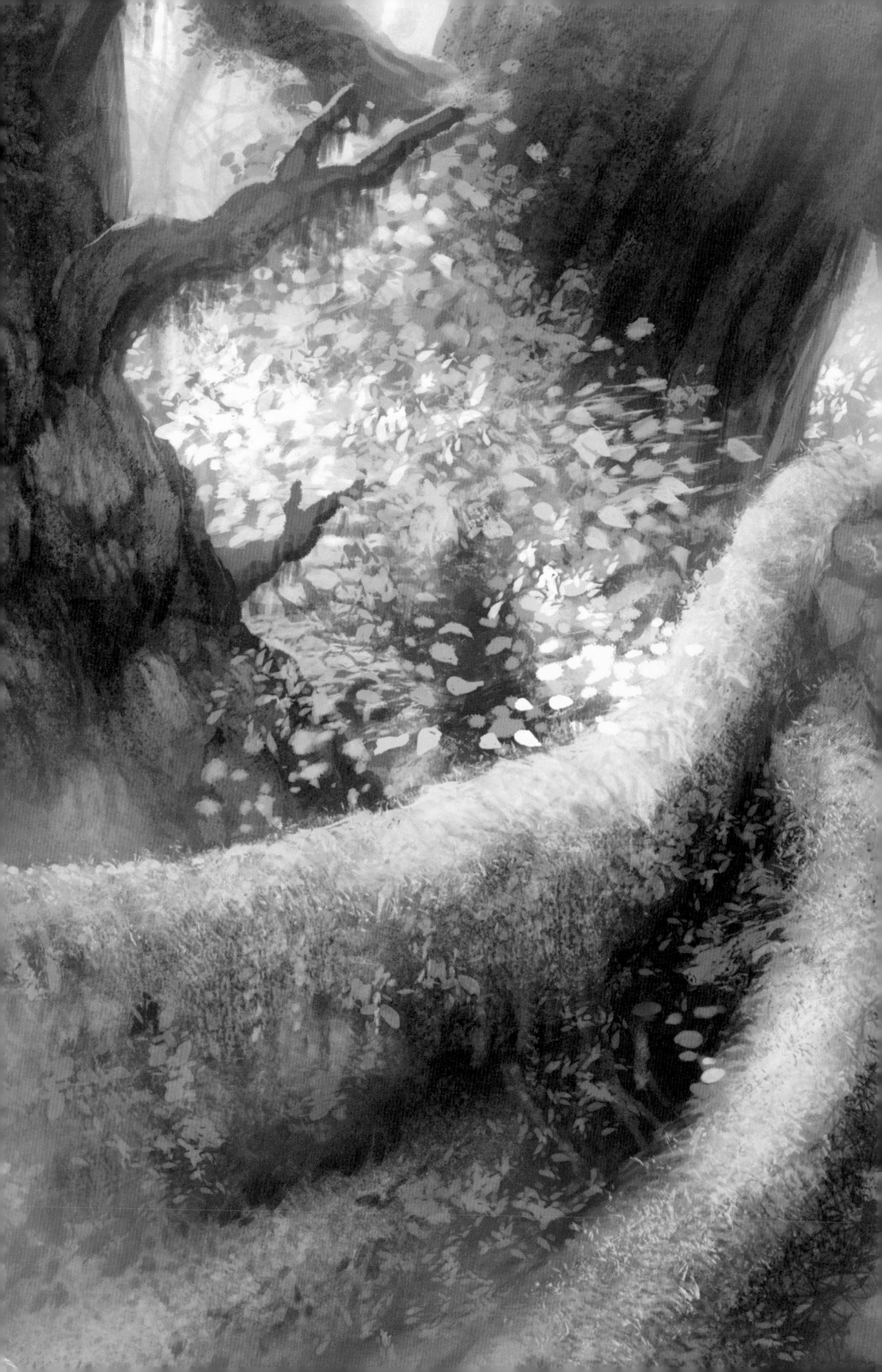

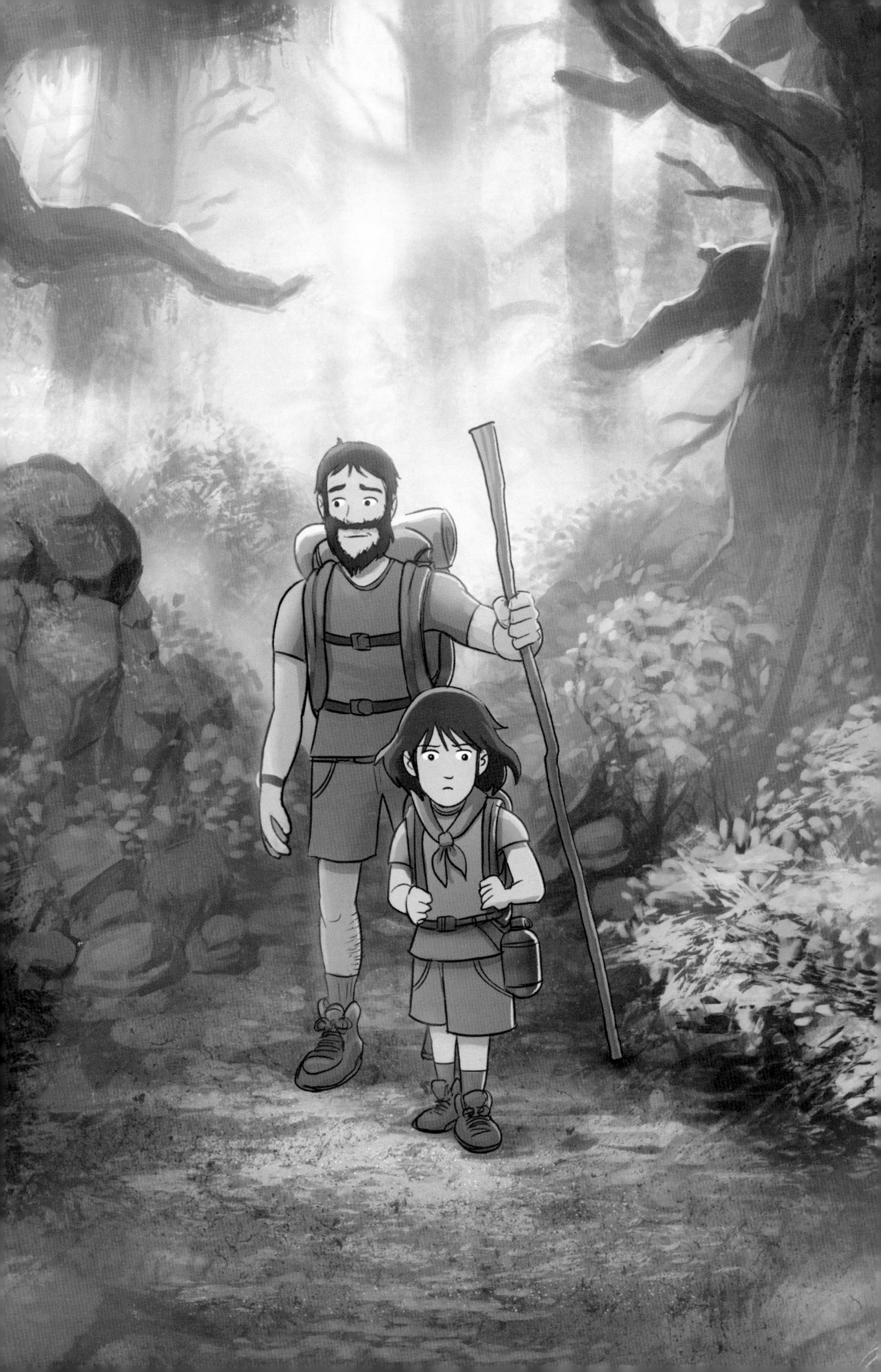

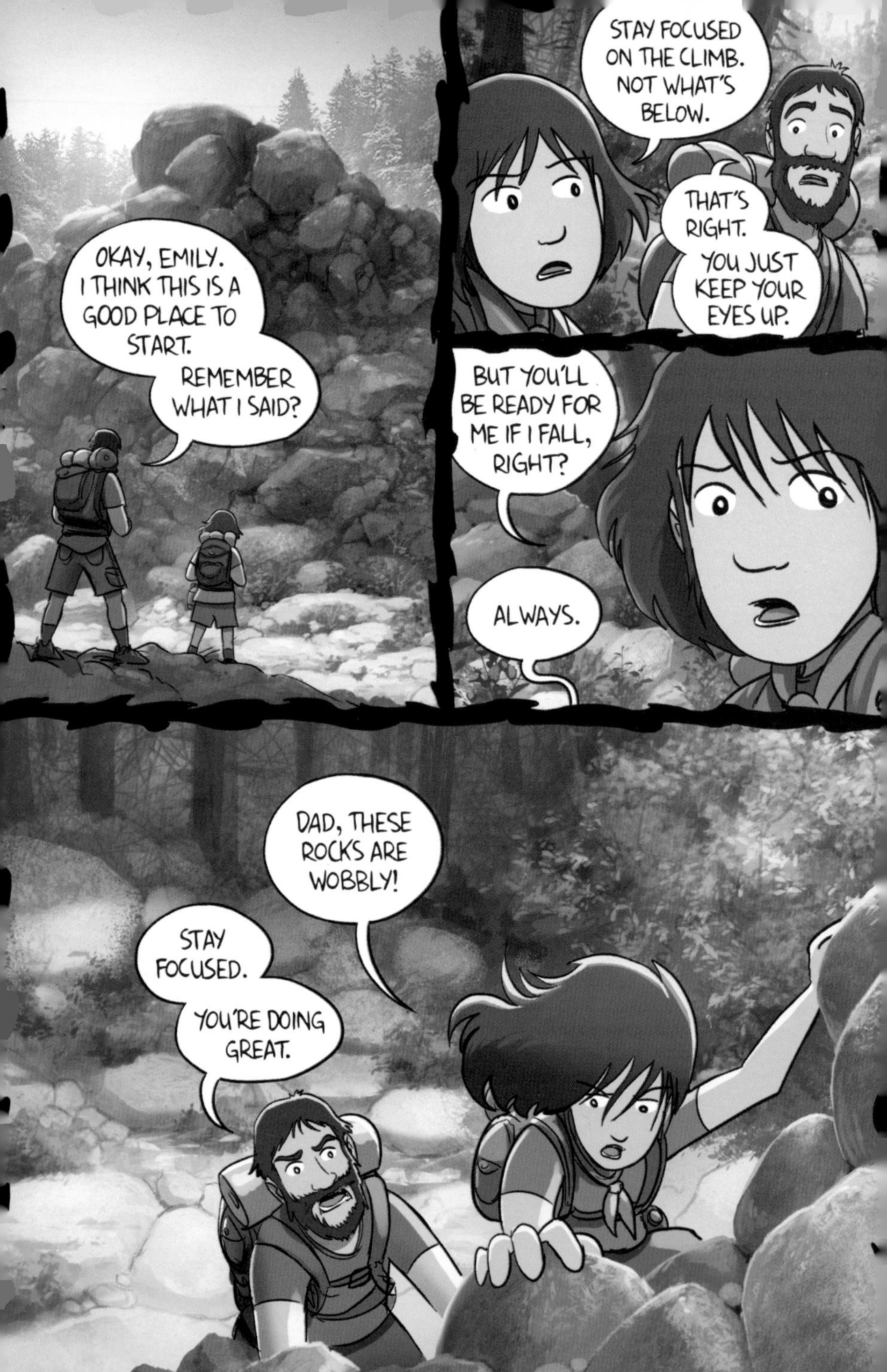
OKAY, EMILY. I THINK THIS IS A GOOD PLACE TO START.
REMEMBER WHAT I SAID?
STAY FOCUSED ON THE CLIMB. NOT WHAT'S BELOW.
THAT'S RIGHT.
YOU JUST KEEP YOUR EYES UP.
BUT YOU'LL BE READY FOR ME IF I FALL, RIGHT?
ALWAYS.
DAD, THESE ROCKS ARE WOBBLY!
STAY FOCUSED.
YOU'RE DOING GREAT.

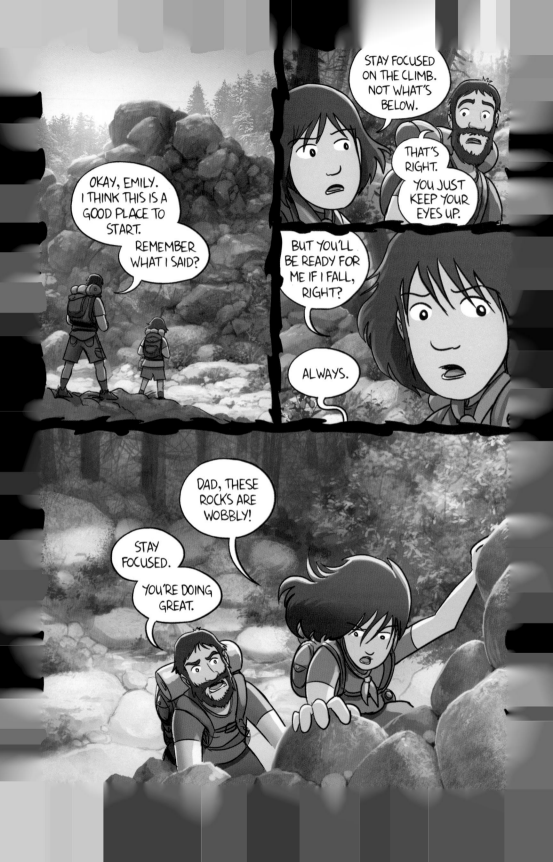

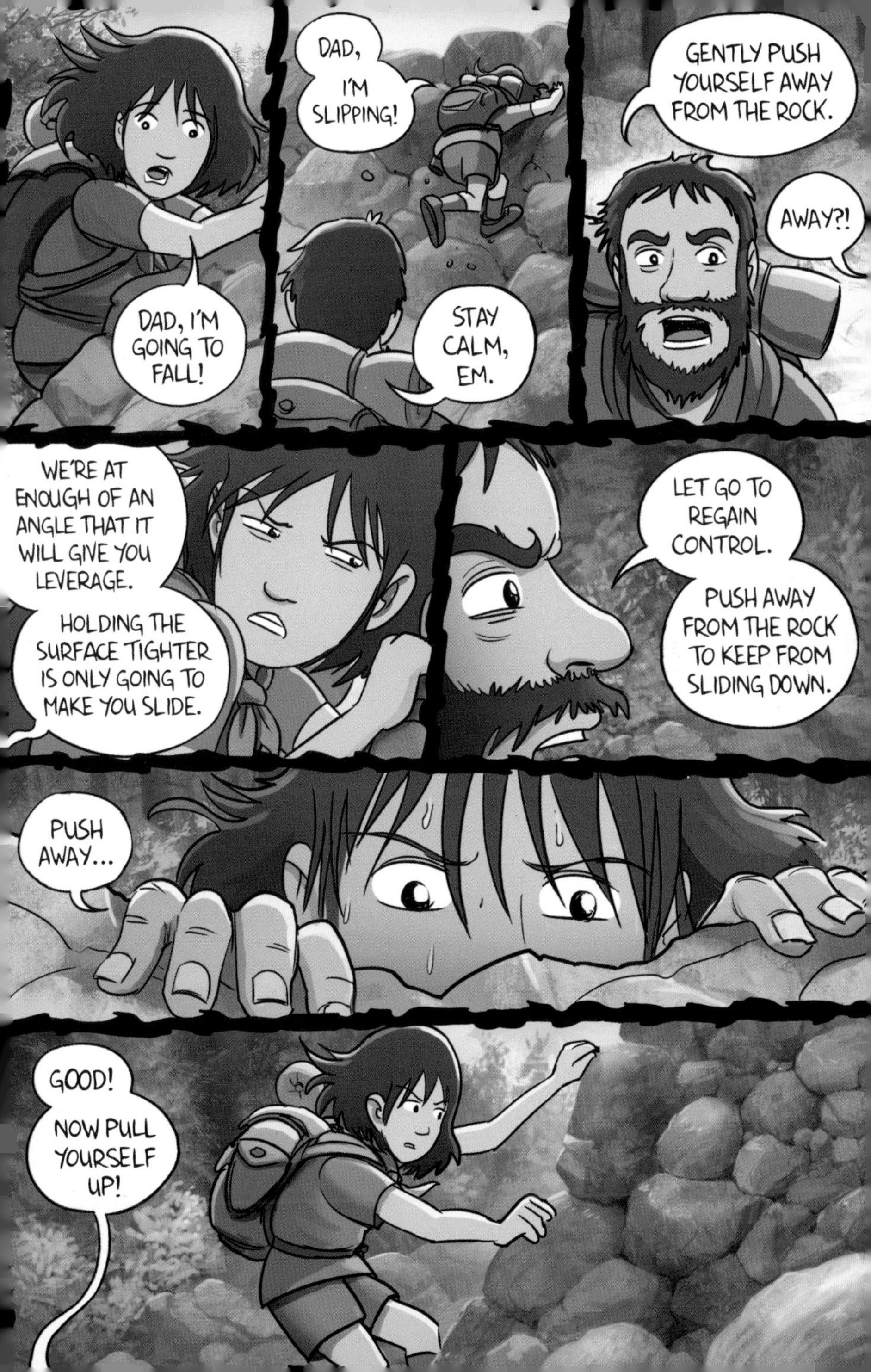
DAD, I'M GOING TO FALL!
DAD, I'M SLIPPING!
STAY CALM, EM.
GENTLY PUSH YOURSELF AWAY FROM THE ROCK.
AWAY?!
WE'RE AT ENOUGH OF AN ANGLE THAT IT WILL GIVE YOU LEVERAGE.
HOLDING THE SURFACE TIGHTER IS ONLY GOING TO MAKE YOU SLIDE.
LET GO TO REGAIN CONTROL.
PUSH AWAY FROM THE ROCK TO KEEP FROM SLIDING DOWN.
PUSH AWAY...
GOOD!
NOW PULL YOURSELF UP!

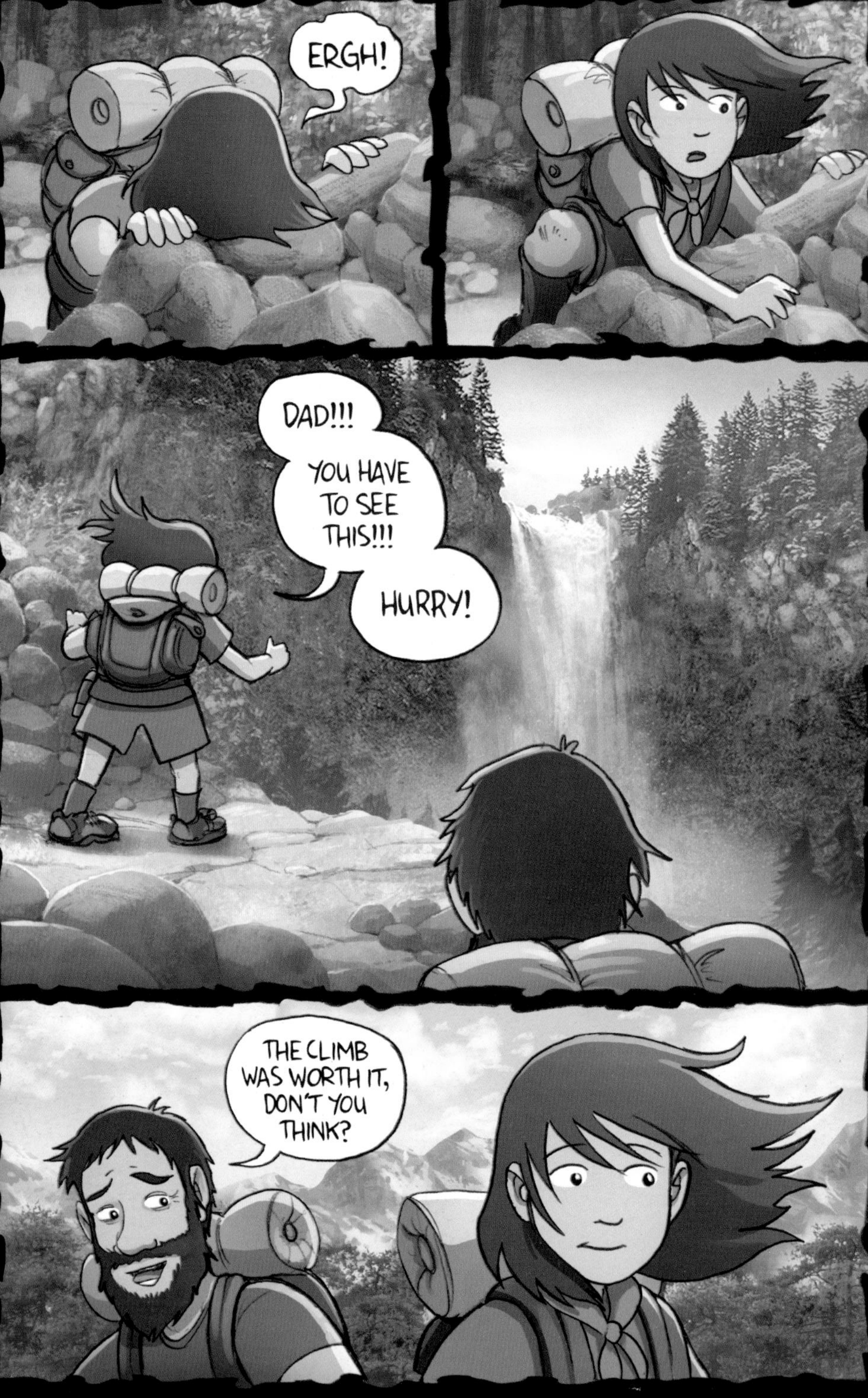
ERGH!
DAD!!!
YOU HAVE TO SEE THIS!!!
HURRY!
THE CLIMB WAS WORTH IT, DON'T YOU THINK?

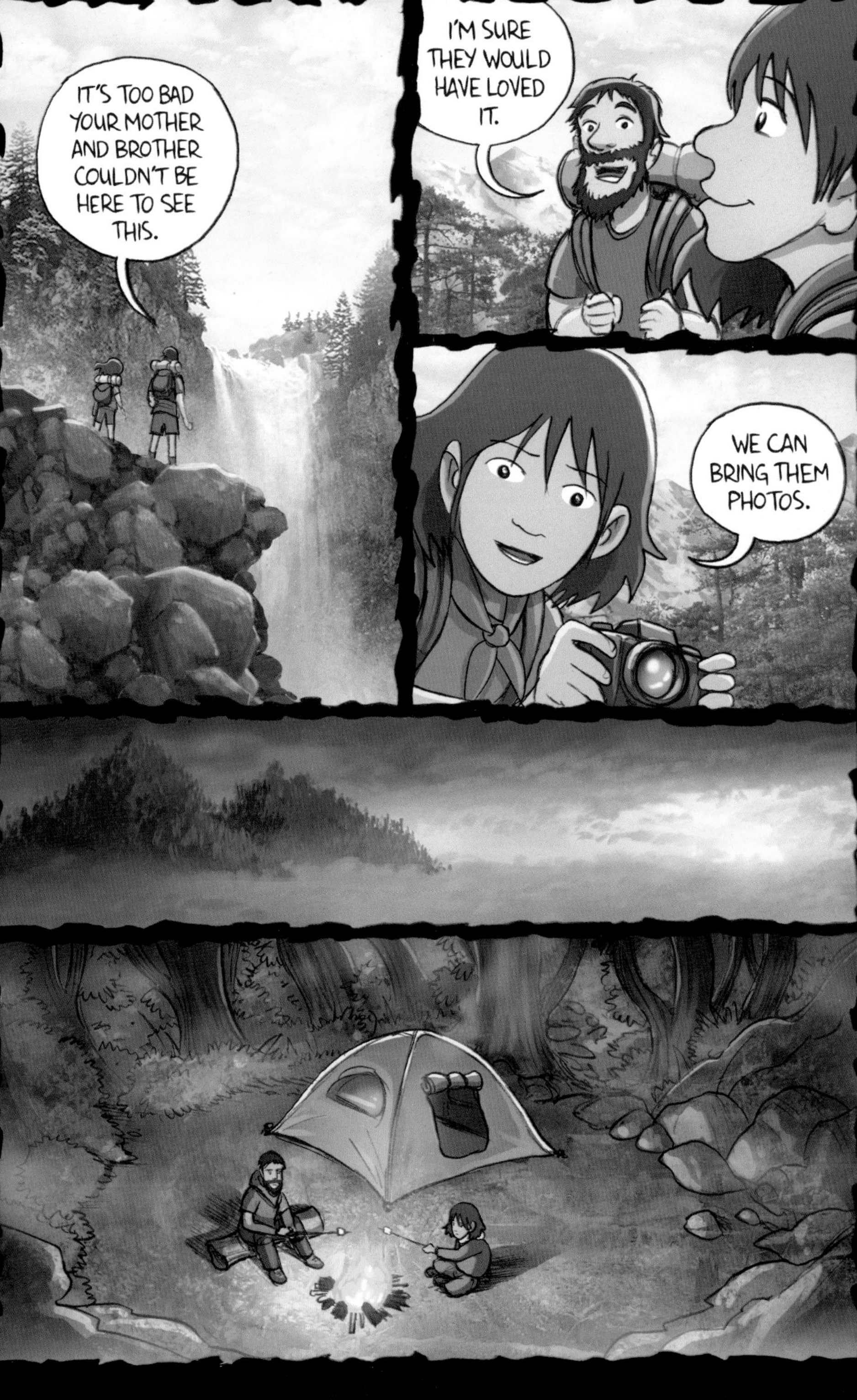
IT'S TOO BAD YOUR MOTHER AND BROTHER COULDN'T BE HERE TO SEE THIS.
I'M SURE THEY WOULD HAVE LOVED IT.
WE CAN BRING THEM PHOTOS.

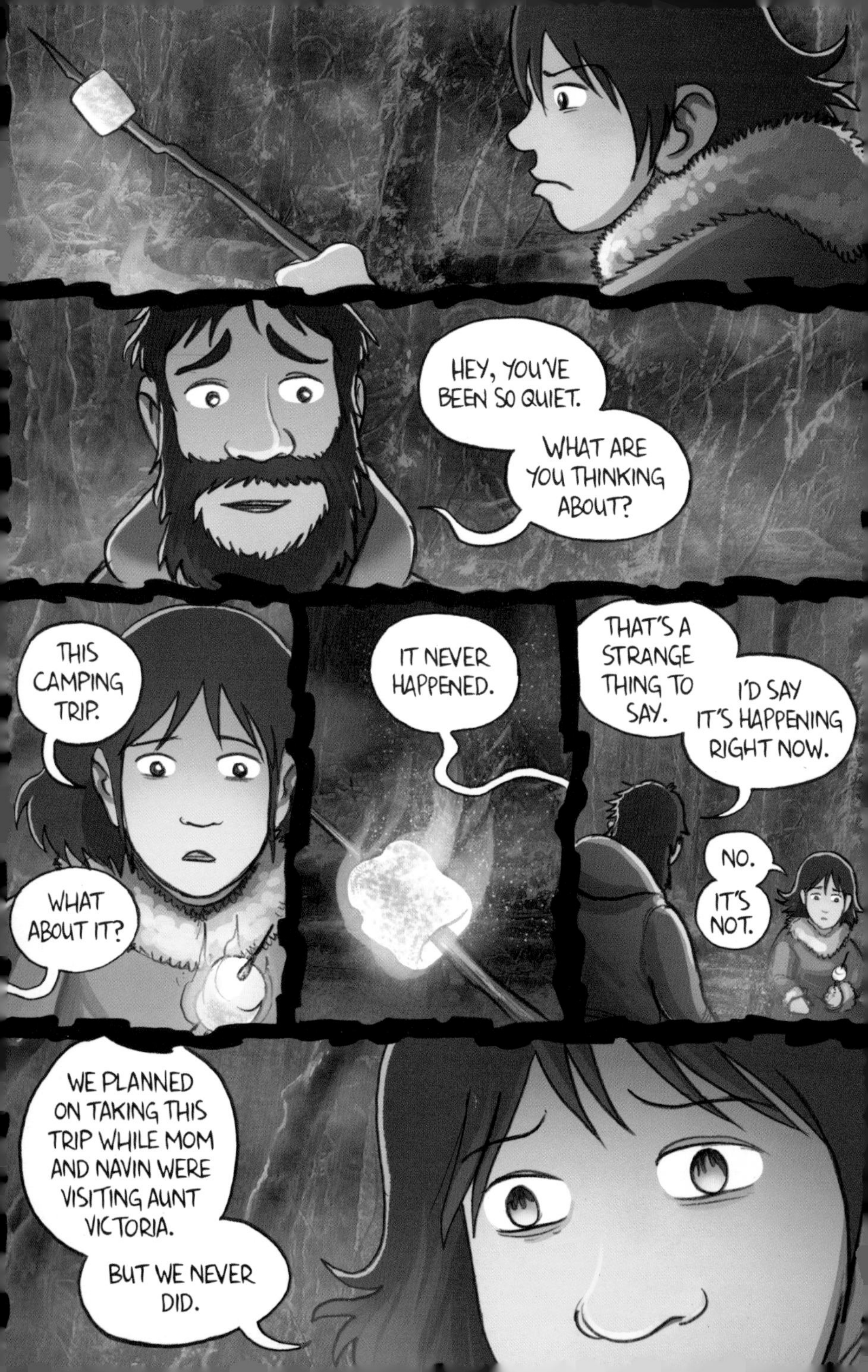
HEY, YOU'VE BEEN SO QUIET.
WHAT ARE YOU THINKING ABOUT?
THIS CAMPING TRIP.
WHAT ABOUT IT?
IT NEVER HAPPENED.
THAT'S A STRANGE THING TO SAY.
I'D SAY IT'S HAPPENING RIGHT NOW.
NO.
IT'S NOT.
WE PLANNED ON TAKING THIS TRIP WHILE MOM AND NAVIN WERE VISITING AUNT VICTORIA.
BUT WE NEVER DID.

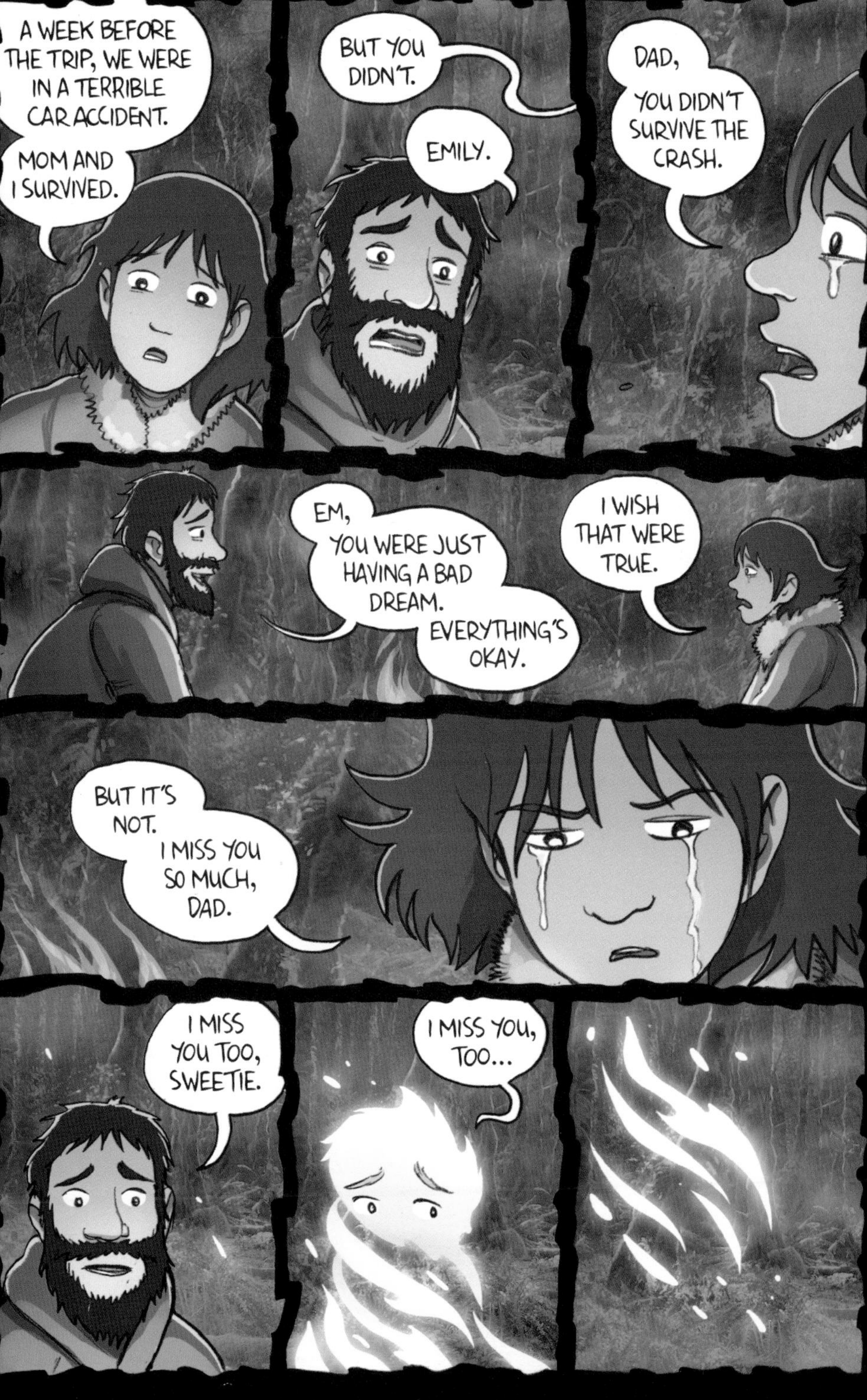
A WEEK BEFORE THE TRIP, WE WERE IN A TERRIBLE CAR ACCIDENT.
MOM AND I SURVIVED.
BUT YOU DIDN'T.
EMILY.
DAD,
YOU DIDN'T SURVIVE THE CRASH.
EM,
YOU WERE JUST HAVING A BAD DREAM.
EVERYTHING'S OKAY.
I WISH THAT WERE TRUE.
BUT IT'S NOT.
I MISS YOU SO MUCH, DAD.
I MISS YOU TOO, SWEETIE.
I MISS YOU, TOO...

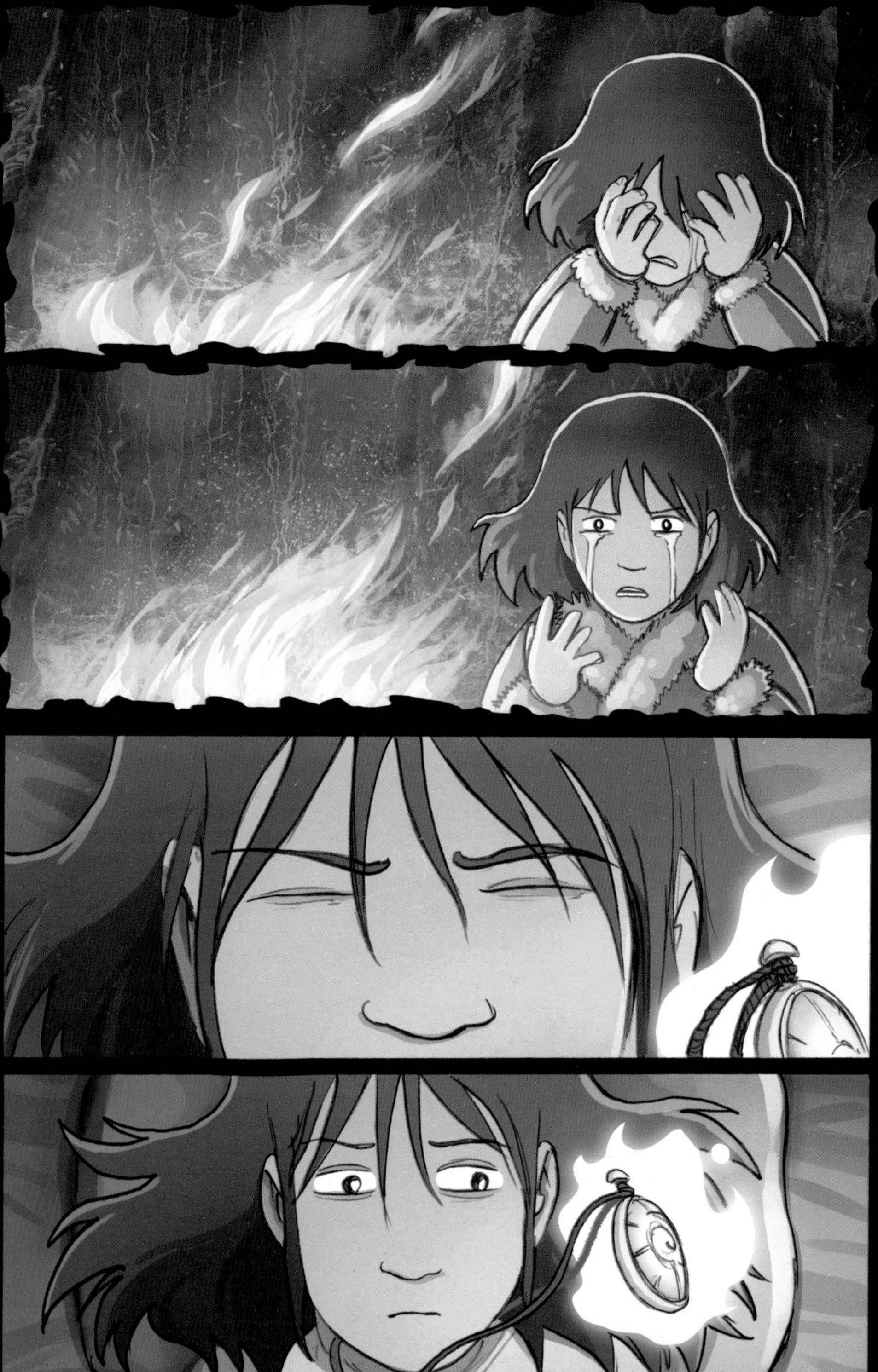

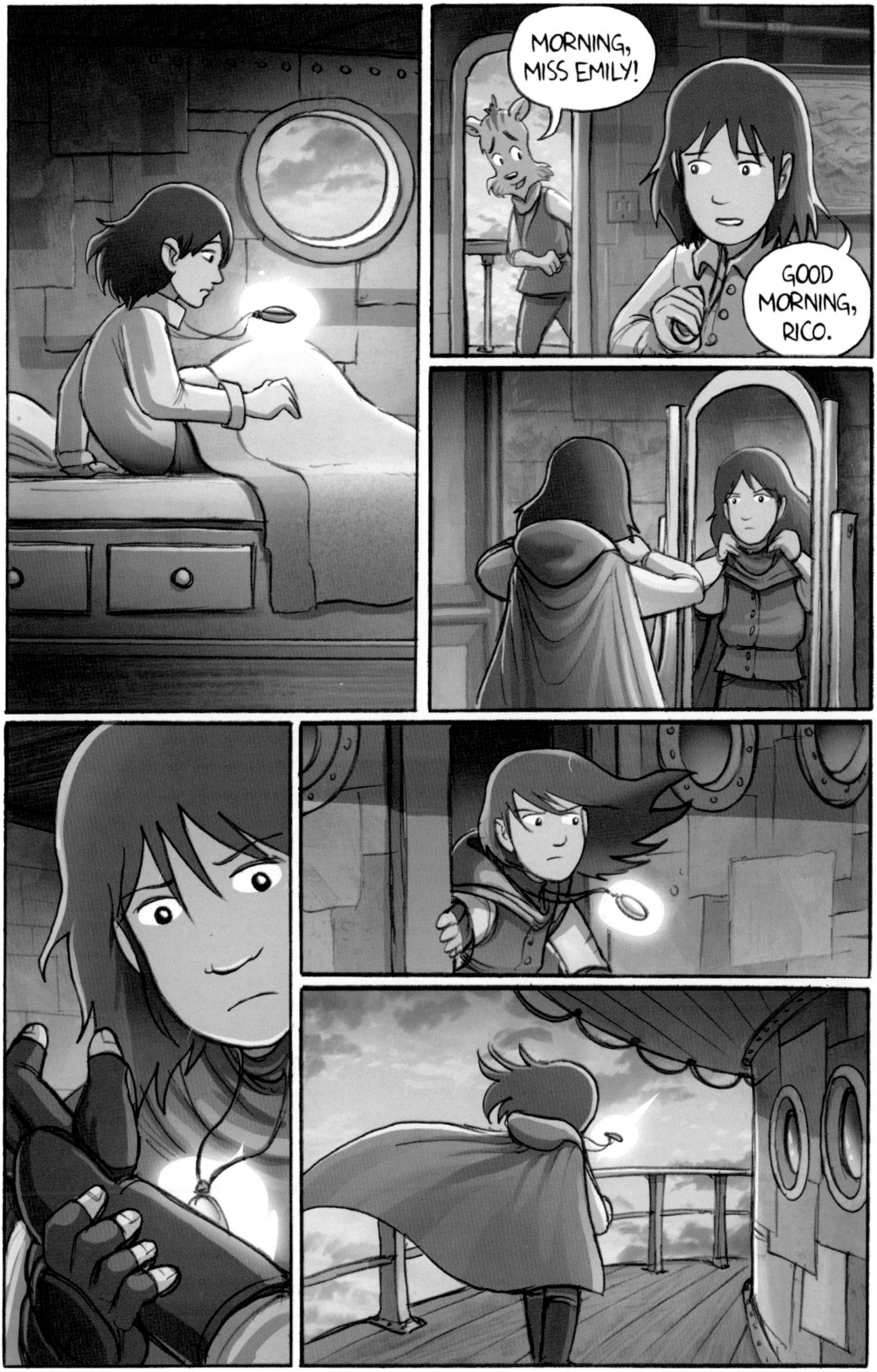
MORNING, MISS EMILY!
GOOD MORNING, RICO.

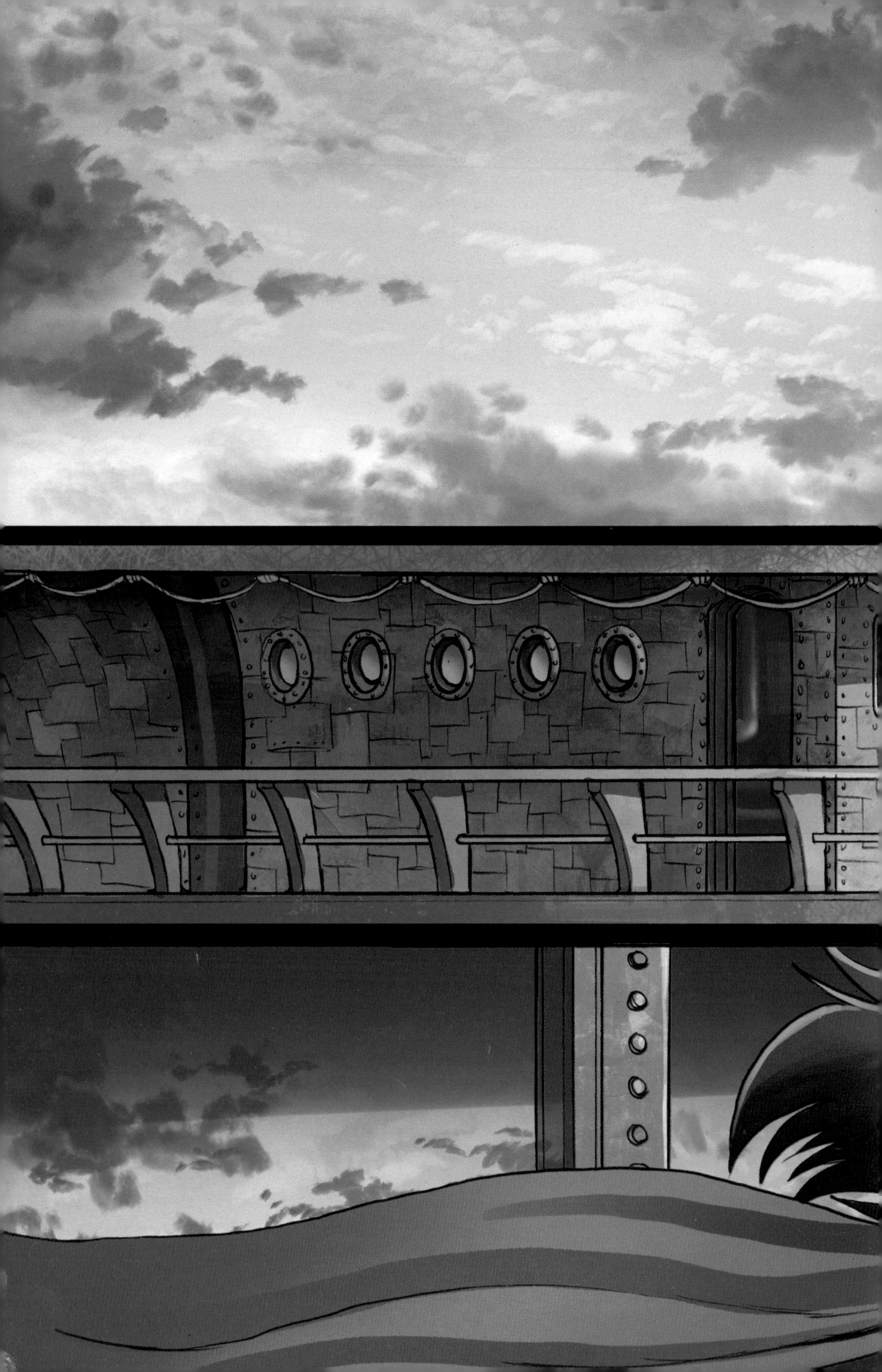

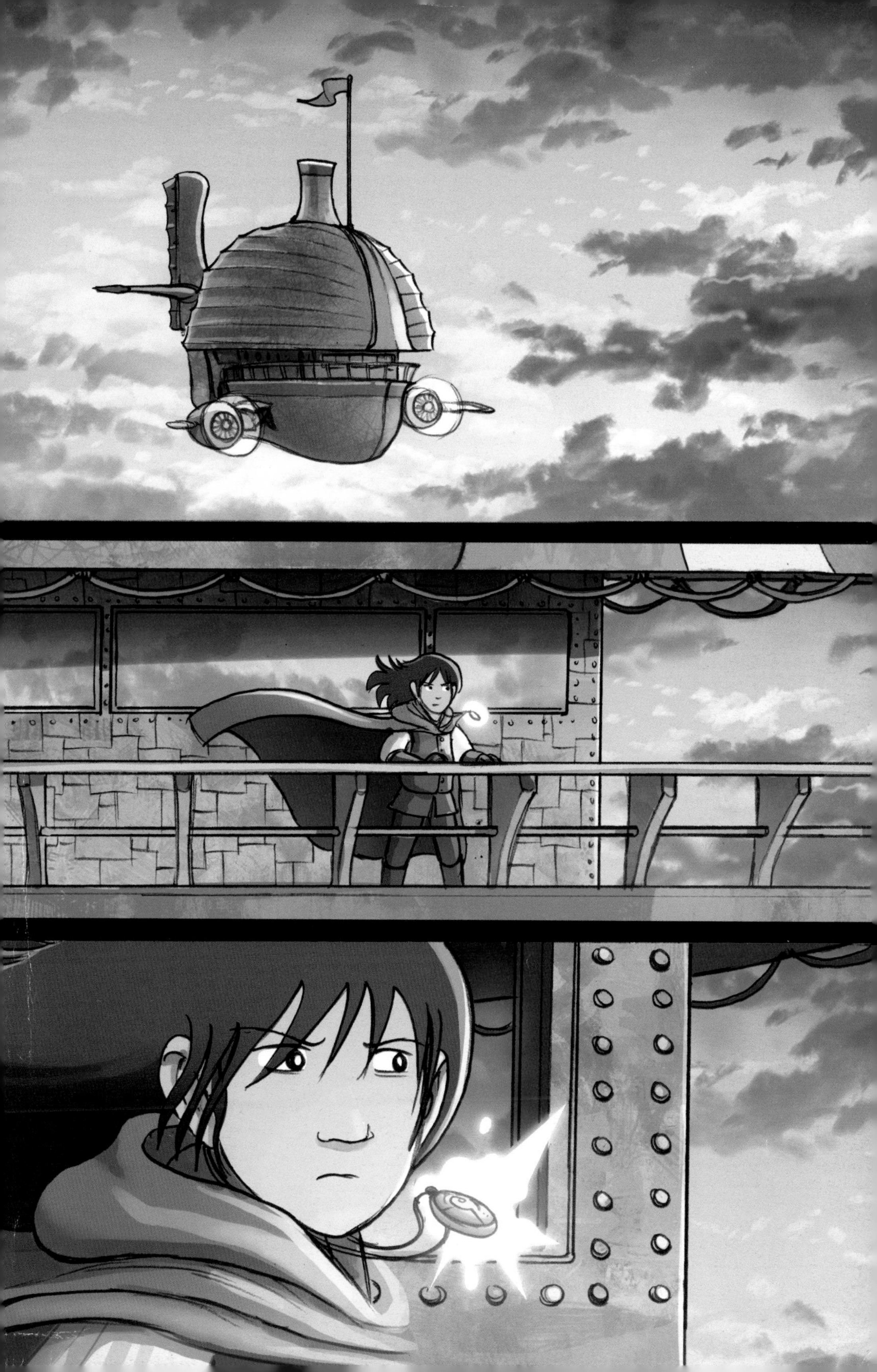

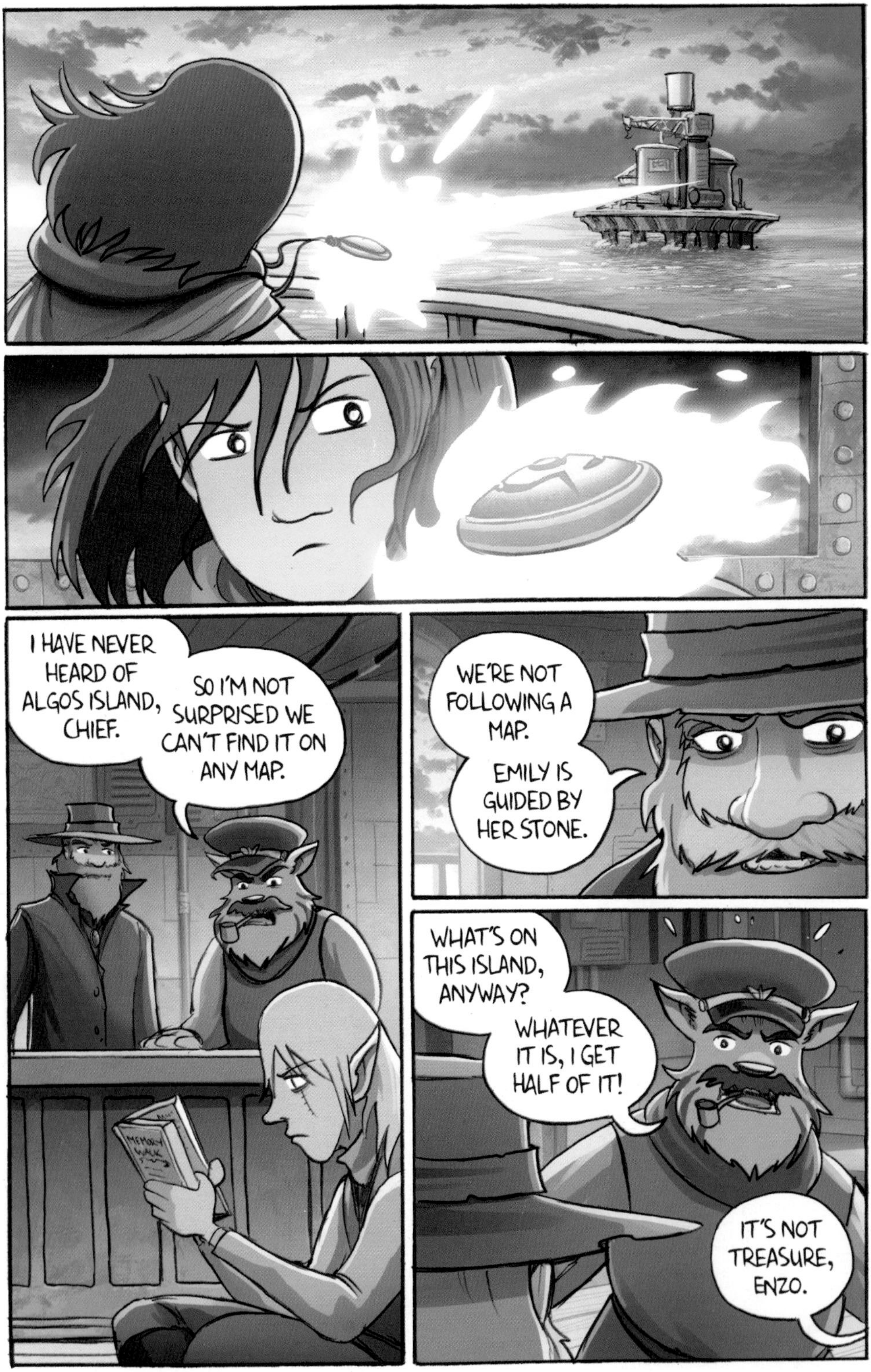
I HAVE NEVER HEARD OF ALGOS ISLAND, CHIEF.
SO I'M NOT SURPRISED WE CAN'T FIND IT ON ANY MAP.
WE'RE NOT FOLLOWING A MAP.
EMILY IS GUIDED BY HER STONE.
WHAT'S ON THIS ISLAND, ANYWAY?
WHATEVER IT IS, I GET HALF OF IT!
IT'S NOT TREASURE, ENZO.

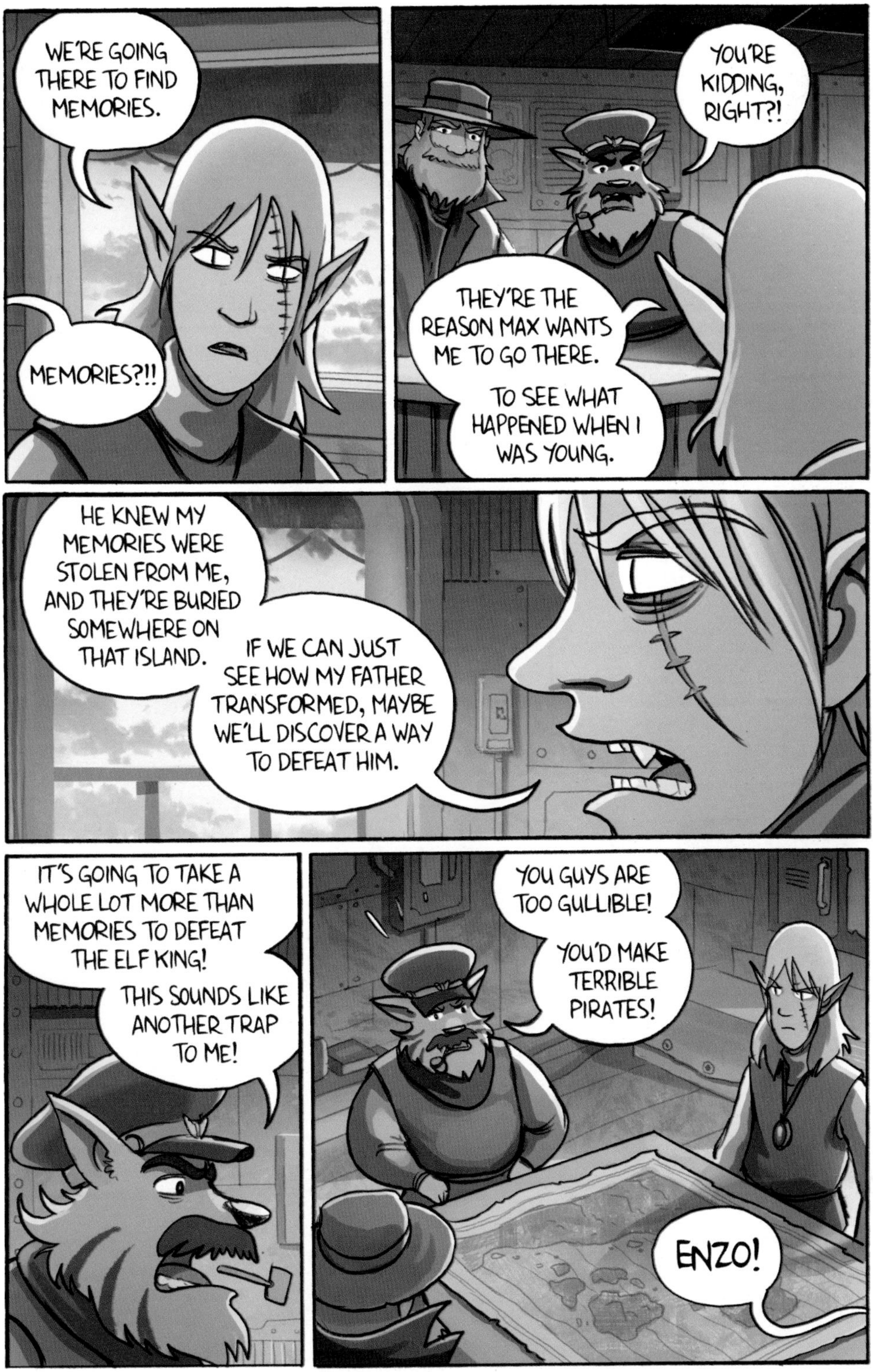
WE'RE GOING THERE TO FIND MEMORIES.
MEMORIES?!!
YOU'RE KIDDING, RIGHT?!
THEY'RE THE REASON MAX WANTS ME TO GO THERE.
TO SEE WHAT HAPPENED WHEN I WAS YOUNG.
HE KNEW MY MEMORIES WERE STOLEN FROM ME, AND THEY'RE BURIED SOMEWHERE ON THAT ISLAND.
IF WE CAN JUST SEE HOW MY FATHER TRANSFORMED, MAYBE WE'LL DISCOVER A WAY TO DEFEAT HIM.
IT'S GOING TO TAKE A WHOLE LOT MORE THAN MEMORIES TO DEFEAT THE ELF KING!
THIS SOUNDS LIKE ANOTHER TRAP TO ME!
YOU GUYS ARE TOO GULLIBLE!
YOU'D MAKE TERRIBLE PIRATES!
ENZO!

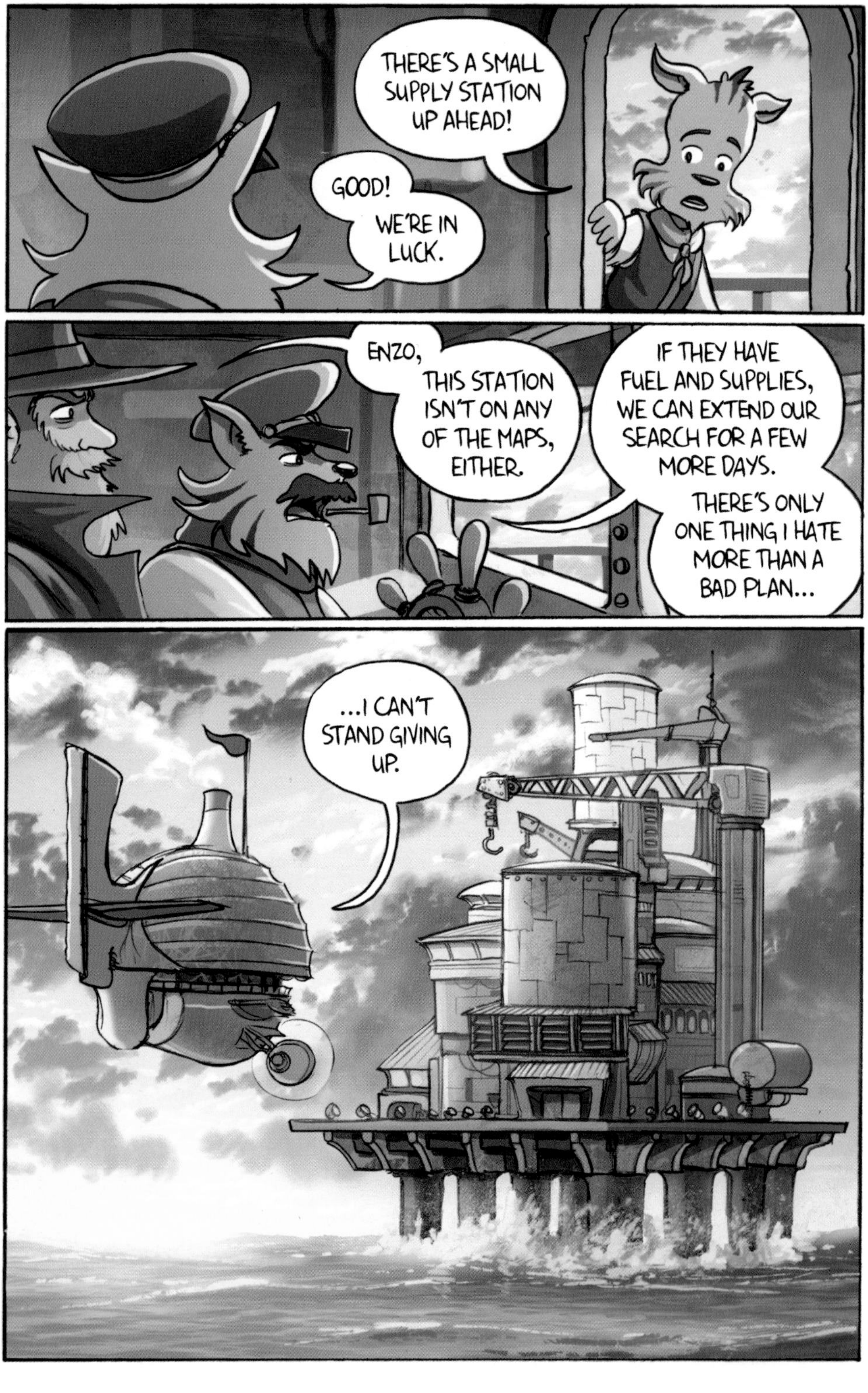
THERE'S A SMALL SUPPLY STATION UP AHEAD!
GOOD!
WE'RE IN LUCK.
ENZO,
THIS STATION ISN'T ON ANY OF THE MAPS, EITHER.
IF THEY HAVE FUEL AND SUPPLIES, WE CAN EXTEND OUR SEARCH FOR A FEW MORE DAYS.
THERE'S ONLY ONE THING I HATE MORE THAN A BAD PLAN...
...I CAN'T STAND GIVING UP.

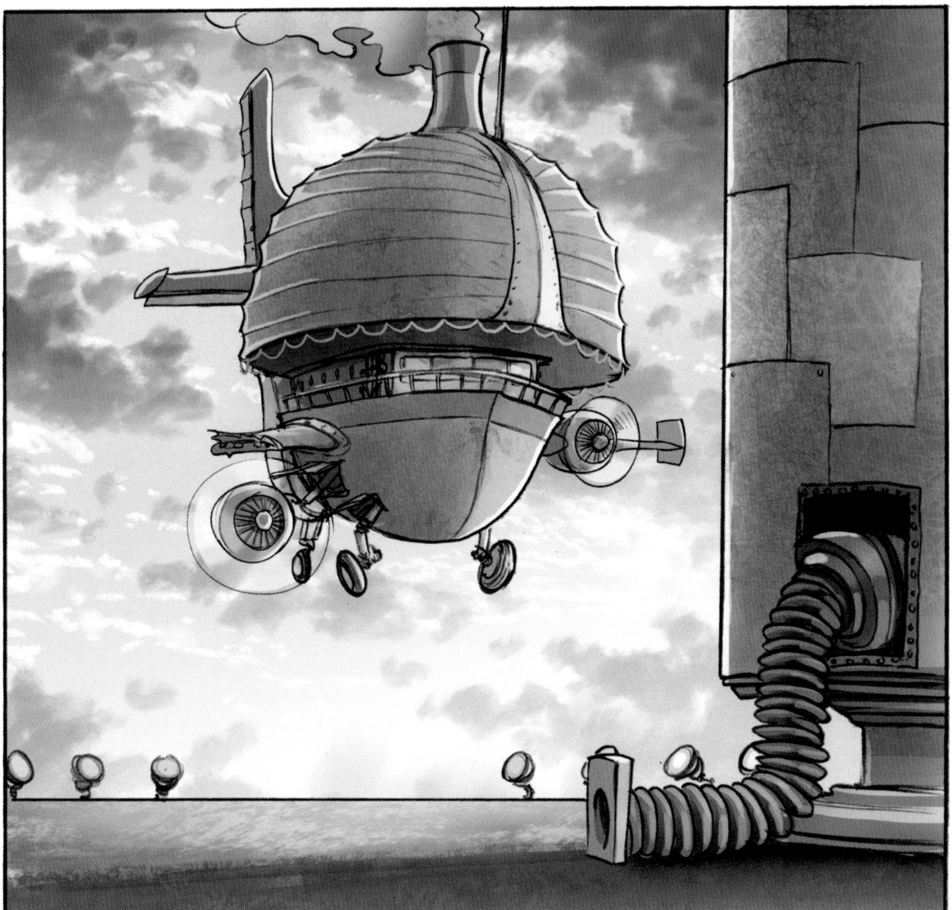

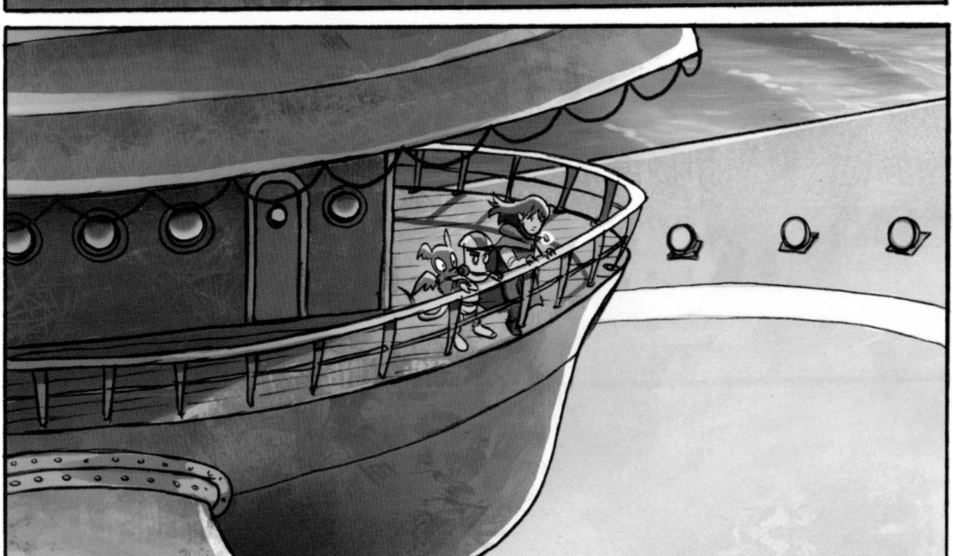

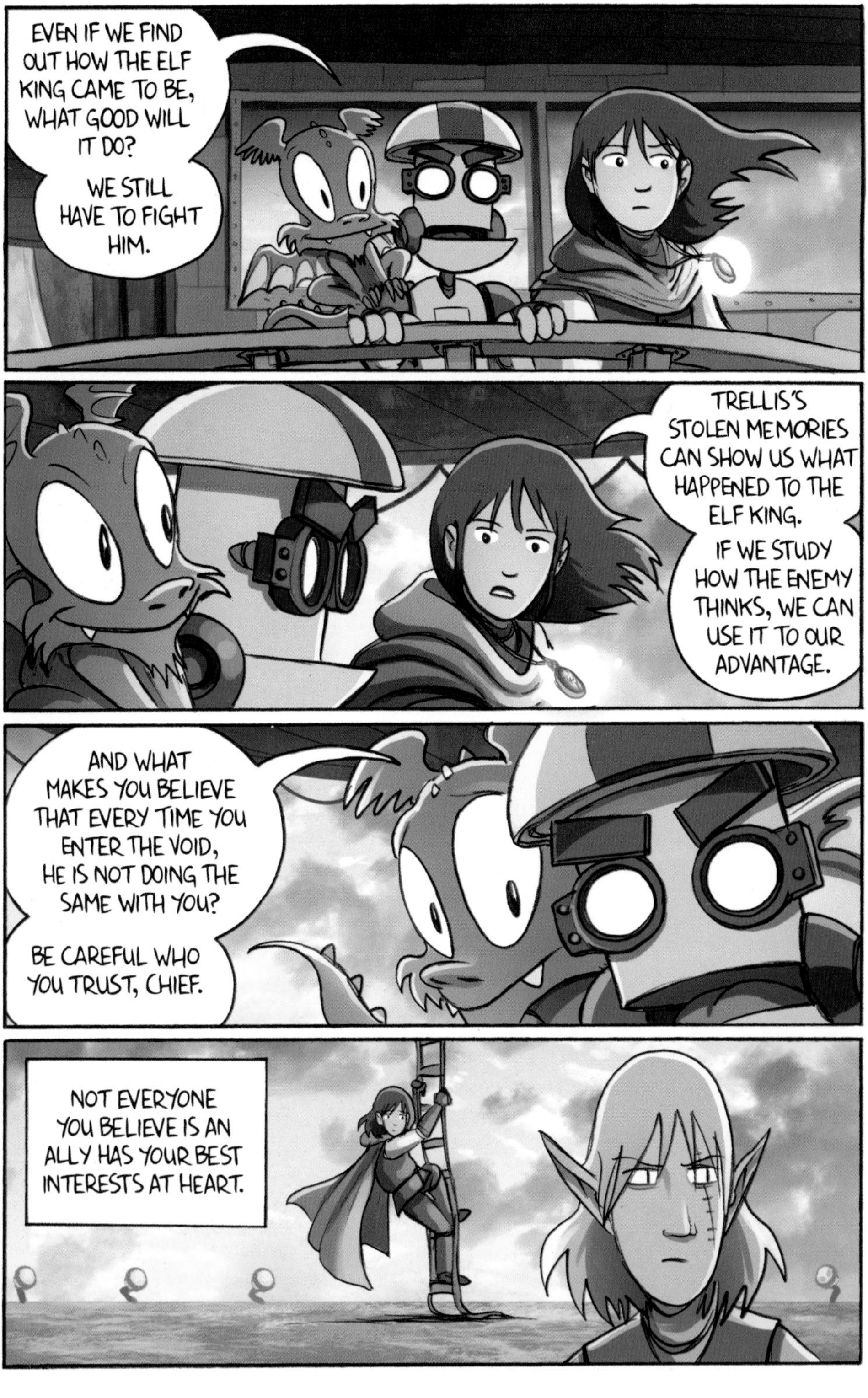
EVEN IF WE FIND OUT HOW THE ELF KING CAME TO BE, WHAT GOOD WILL IT DO?
WE STILL HAVE TO FIGHT HIM.
TRELLIS'S STOLEN MEMORIES CAN SHOW US WHAT HAPPENED TO THE ELF KING.
IF WE STUDY HOW THE ENEMY THINKS, WE CAN USE IT TO OUR ADVANTAGE.
AND WHAT MAKES YOU BELIEVE THAT EVERY TIME YOU ENTER THE VOID, HE IS NOT DOING THE SAME WITH YOU?
BE CAREFUL WHO YOU TRUST, CHIEF.
NOT EVERYONE YOU BELIEVE IS AN ALLY HAS YOUR BEST INTERESTS AT HEART.

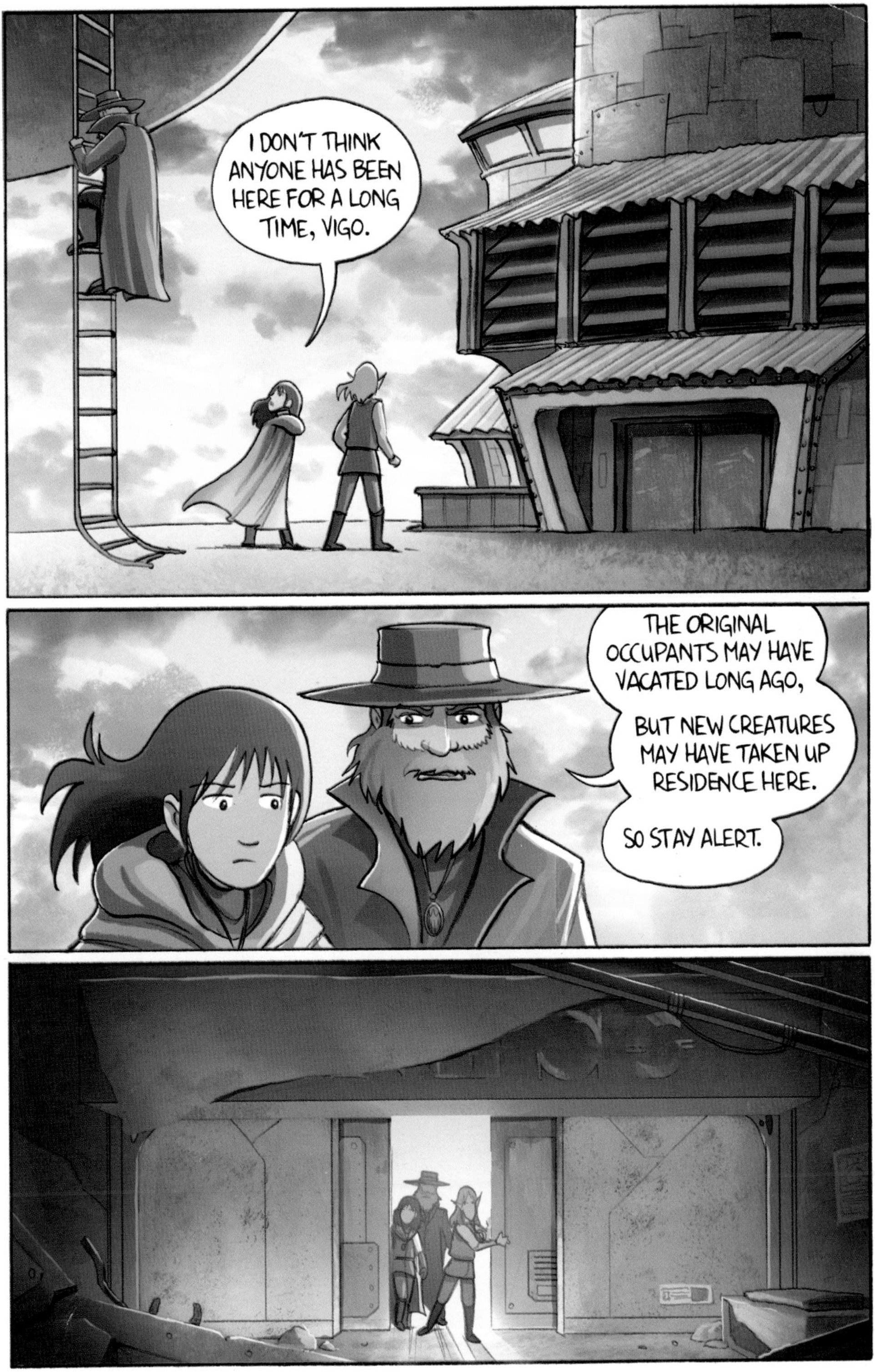
I DON'T THINK ANYONE HAS BEEN HERE FOR A LONG TIME, VIGO.
THE ORIGINAL OCCUPANTS MAY HAVE VACATED LONG AGO,
BUT NEW CREATURES MAY HAVE TAKEN UP RESIDENCE HERE.
SO STAY ALERT.

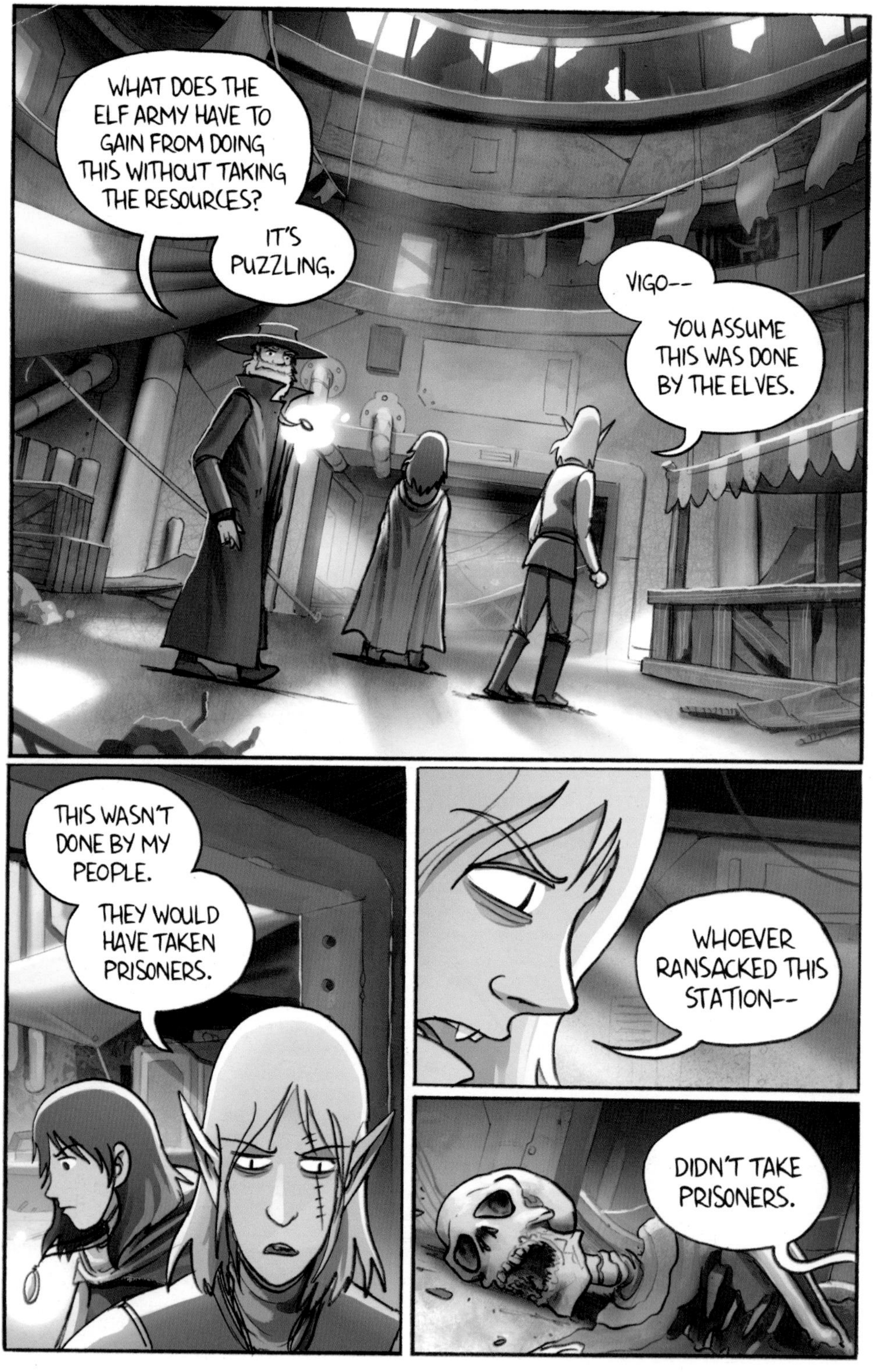
WHAT DOES THE ELF ARMY HAVE TO GAIN FROM DOING THIS WITHOUT TAKING THE RESOURCES?
IT'S PUZZLING.
VIGO--
YOU ASSUME THIS WAS DONE BY THE ELVES.
THIS WASN'T DONE BY MY PEOPLE.
THEY WOULD HAVE TAKEN PRISONERS.
WHOEVER RANSACKED THIS STATION--
DIDN'T TAKE PRISONERS.

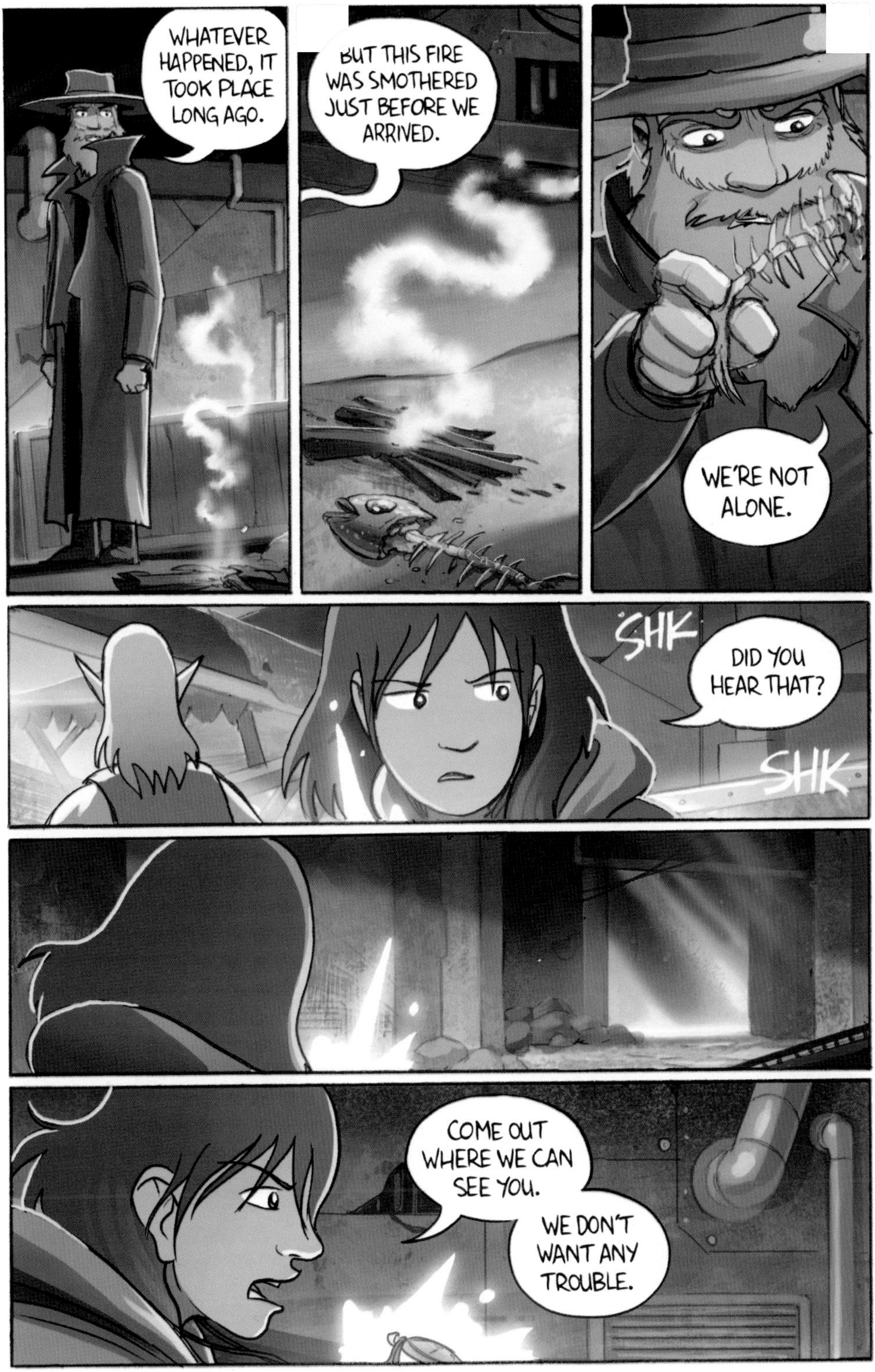
WHATEVER HAPPENED, IT TOOK PLACE LONG AGO.
BUT THIS FIRE WAS SMOTHERED JUST BEFORE WE ARRIVED.
WE'RE NOT ALONE.
SHK
DID YOU HEAR THAT?
SHK
COME OUT WHERE WE CAN SEE YOU.
WE DON'T WANT ANY TROUBLE.

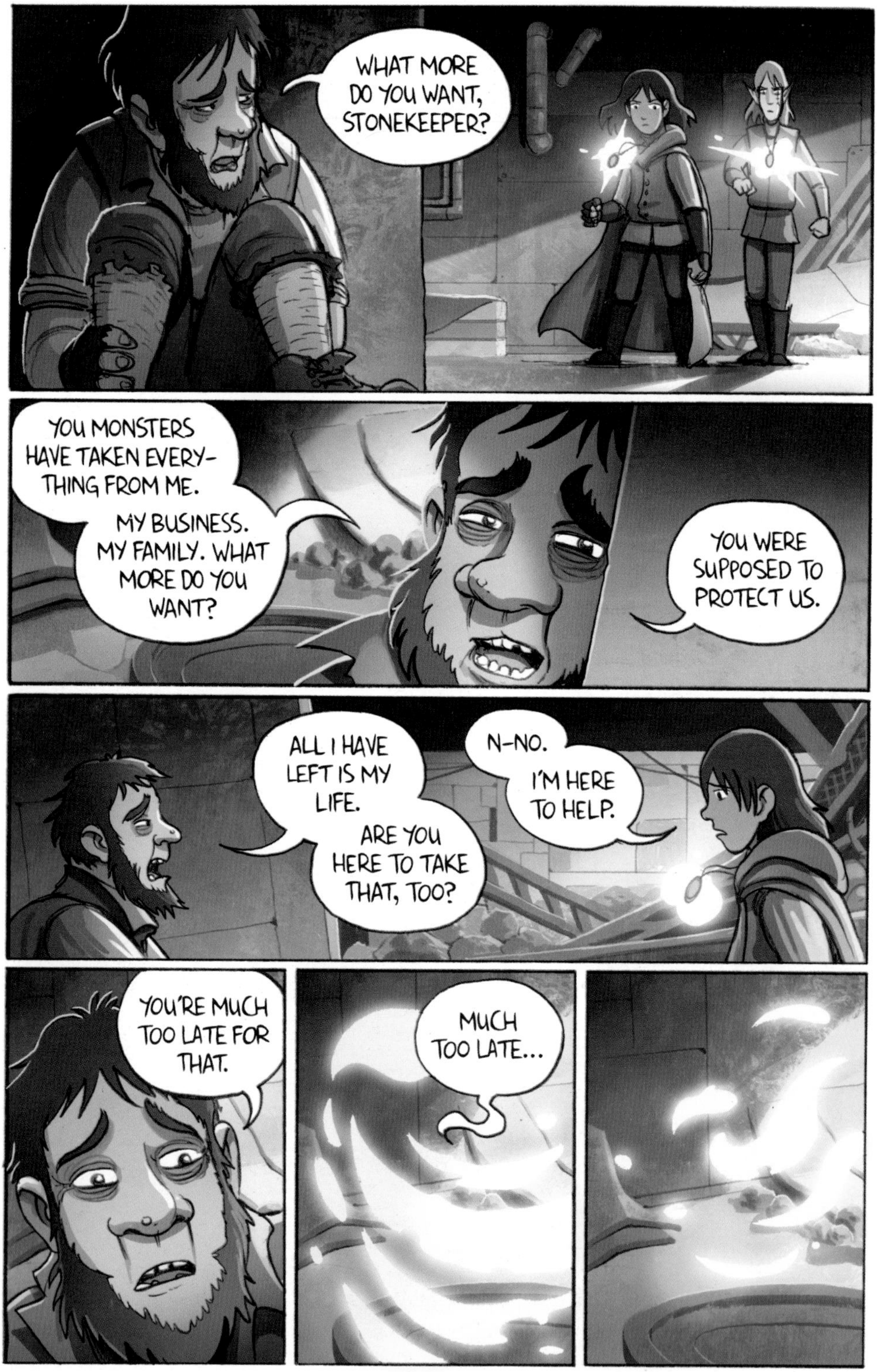
WHAT MORE DO YOU WANT, STONEKEEPER?
YOU MONSTERS HAVE TAKEN EVERY-THING FROM ME.
MY BUSINESS. MY FAMILY. WHAT MORE DO YOU WANT?
YOU WERE SUPPOSED TO PROTECT US.
ALL I HAVE LEFT IS MY LIFE.
ARE YOU HERE TO TAKE THAT, TOO?
N-NO.
I'M HERE TO HELP.
YOU'RE MUCH TOO LATE FOR THAT.
MUCH TOO LATE...

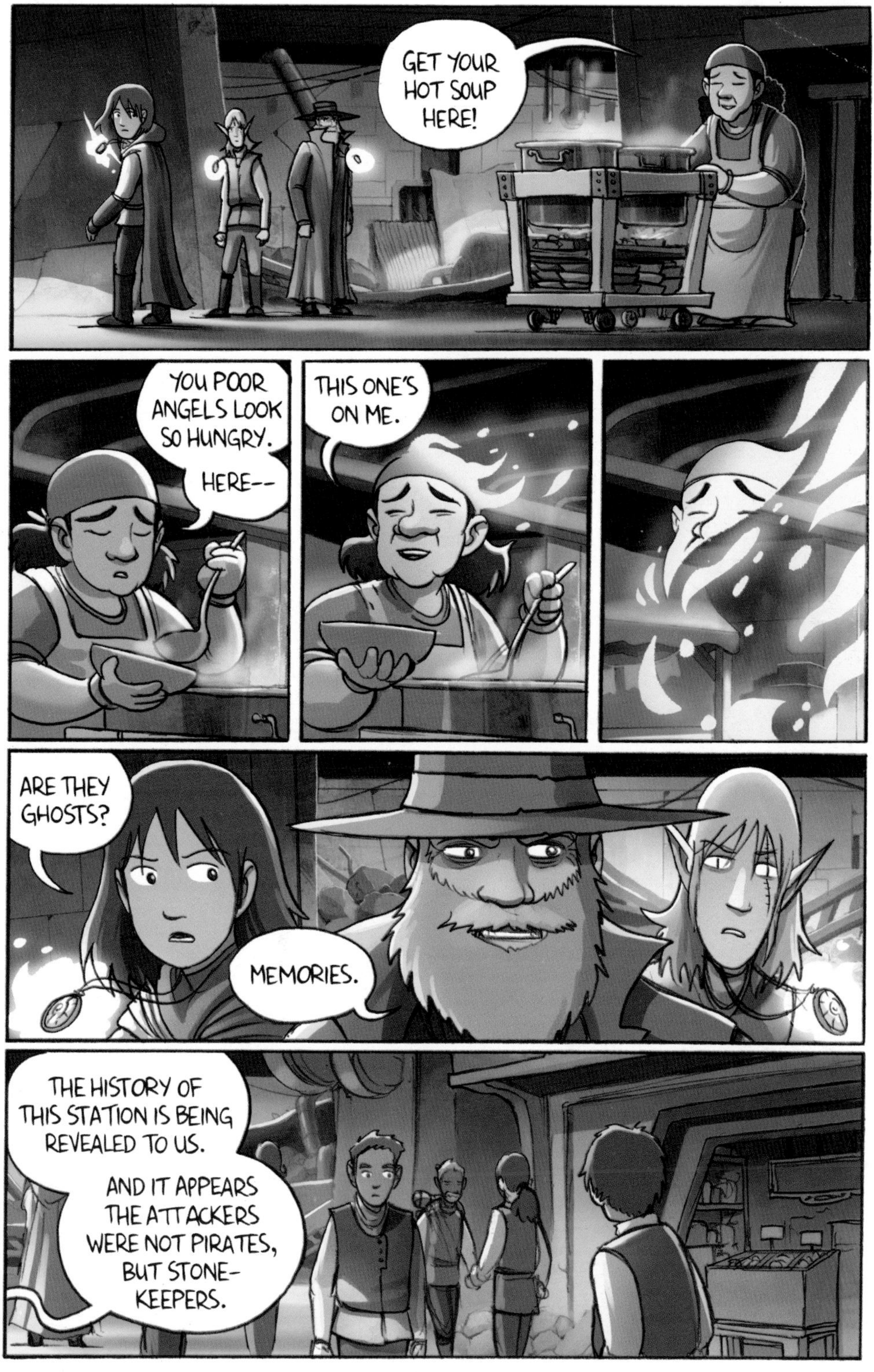
GET YOUR HOT SOUP HERE!
YOU POOR ANGELS LOOK SO HUNGRY.
HERE--
THIS ONE'S ON ME.
ARE THEY GHOSTS?
MEMORIES.
THE HISTORY OF THIS STATION IS BEING REVEALED TO US.
AND IT APPEARS THE ATTACKERS WERE NOT PIRATES, BUT STONE-KEEPERS.

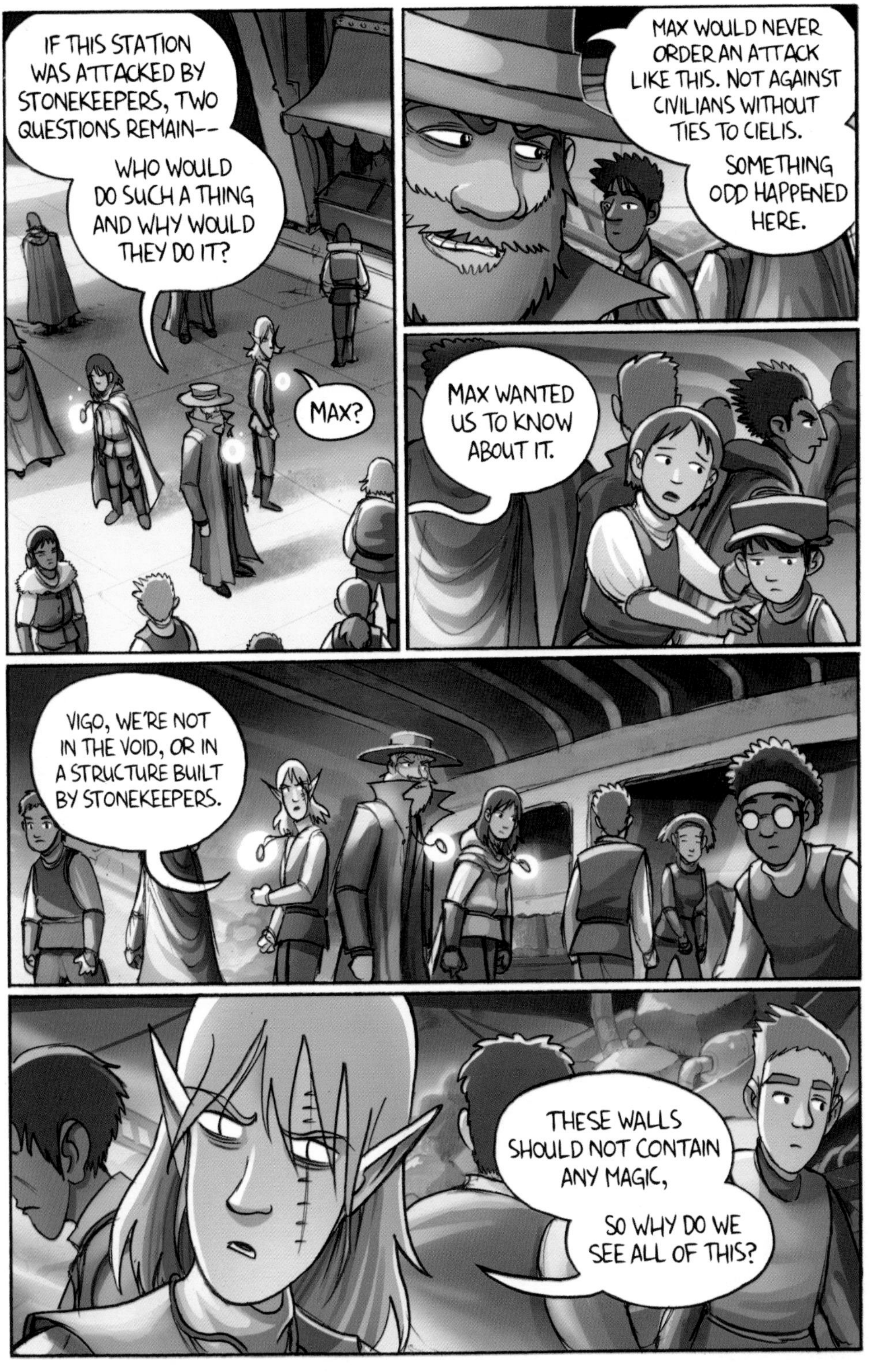
IF THIS STATION WAS ATTACKED BY STONEKEEPERS, TWO QUESTIONS REMAIN--
WHO WOULD DO SUCH A THING AND WHY WOULD THEY DO IT?
MAX?
MAX WOULD NEVER ORDER AN ATTACK LIKE THIS. NOT AGAINST CIVILIANS WITHOUT TIES TO CIELIS.
SOMETHING ODD HAPPENED HERE.
MAX WANTED US TO KNOW ABOUT IT.
VIGO, WE'RE NOT IN THE VOID, OR IN A STRUCTURE BUILT BY STONEKEEPERS.
THESE WALLS SHOULD NOT CONTAIN ANY MAGIC,
SO WHY DO WE SEE ALL OF THIS?

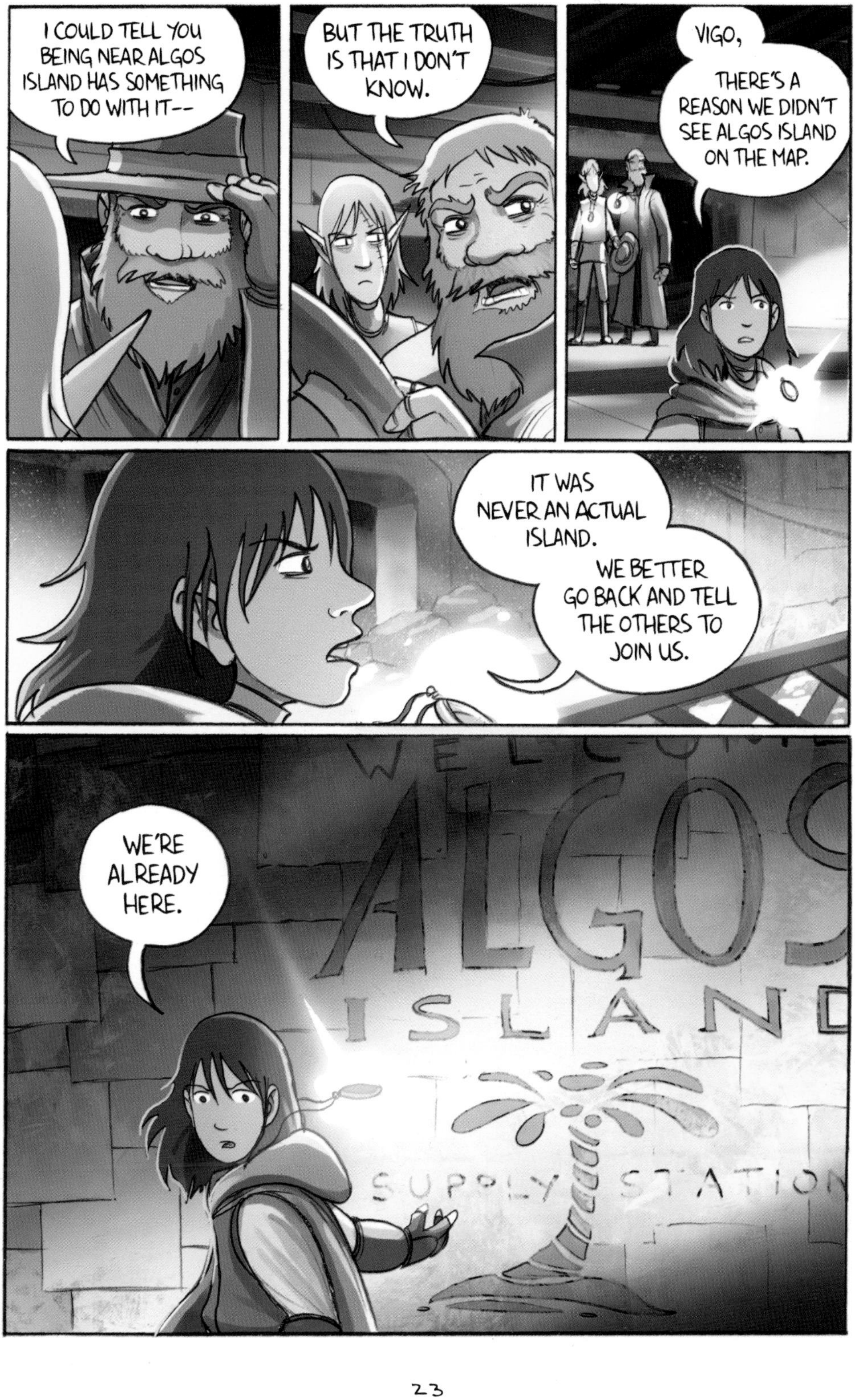
I COULD TELL YOU BEING NEAR ALGOS ISLAND HAS SOMETHING TO DO WITH IT--
BUT THE TRUTH IS THAT I DON'T KNOW.
VIGO,
THERE'S A REASON WE DIDN'T SEE ALGOS ISLAND ON THE MAP.
IT WAS NEVER AN ACTUAL ISLAND.
WE BETTER GO BACK AND TELL THE OTHERS TO JOIN US.
ALGOS
ISLAND
SUPPLY STATION
WE'RE ALREADY HERE.

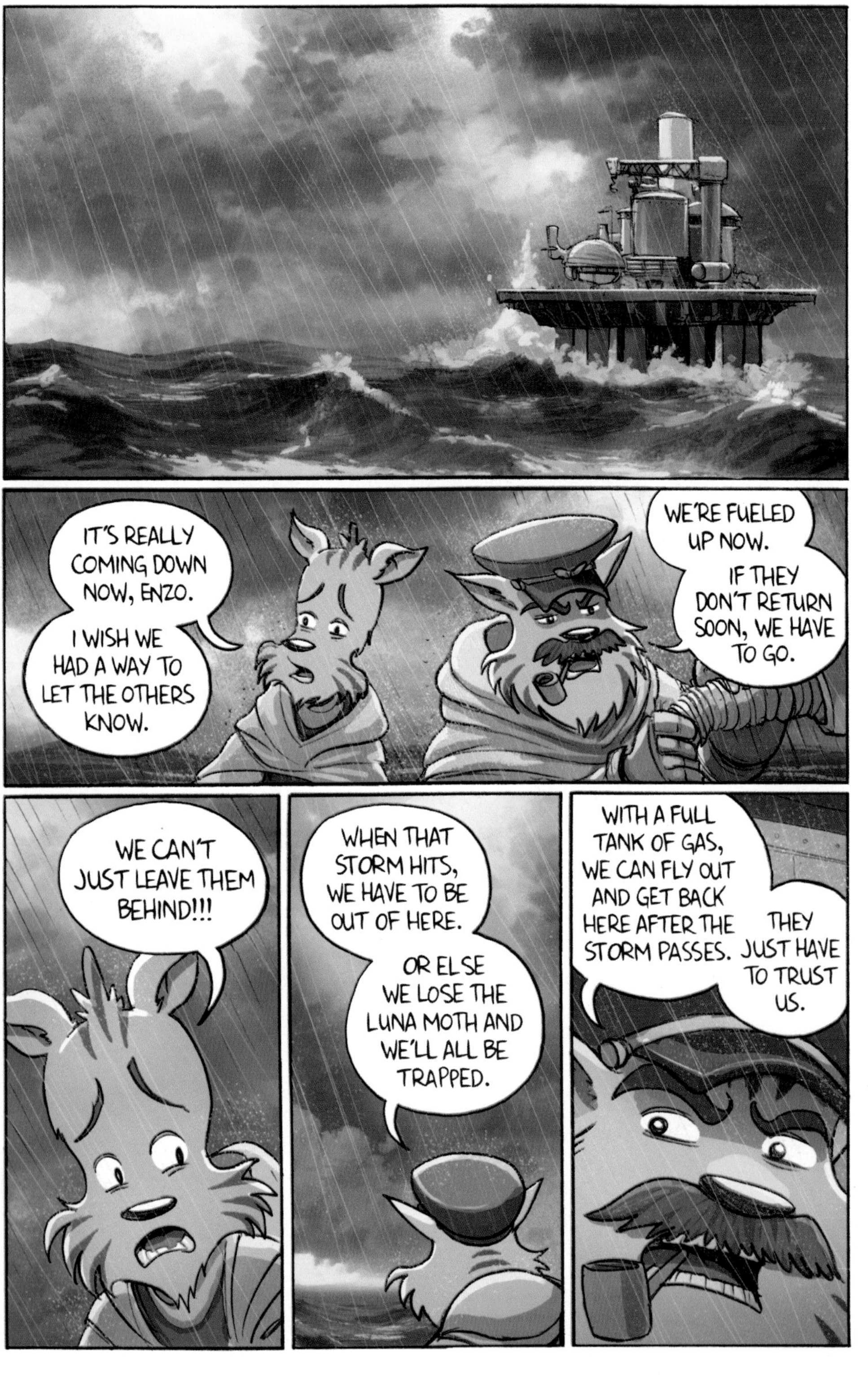
IT'S REALLY COMING DOWN NOW, ENZO.
I WISH WE HAD A WAY TO LET THE OTHERS KNOW.
WE'RE FUELED UP NOW.
IF THEY DON'T RETURN SOON, WE HAVE TO GO.
WE CAN'T JUST LEAVE THEM BEHIND!!!
WHEN THAT STORM HITS, WE HAVE TO BE OUT OF HERE.
OR ELSE WE LOSE THE LUNA MOTH AND WE'LL ALL BE TRAPPED.
WITH A FULL TANK OF GAS, WE CAN FLY OUT AND GET BACK HERE AFTER THE STORM PASSES.
THEY JUST HAVE TO TRUST US.

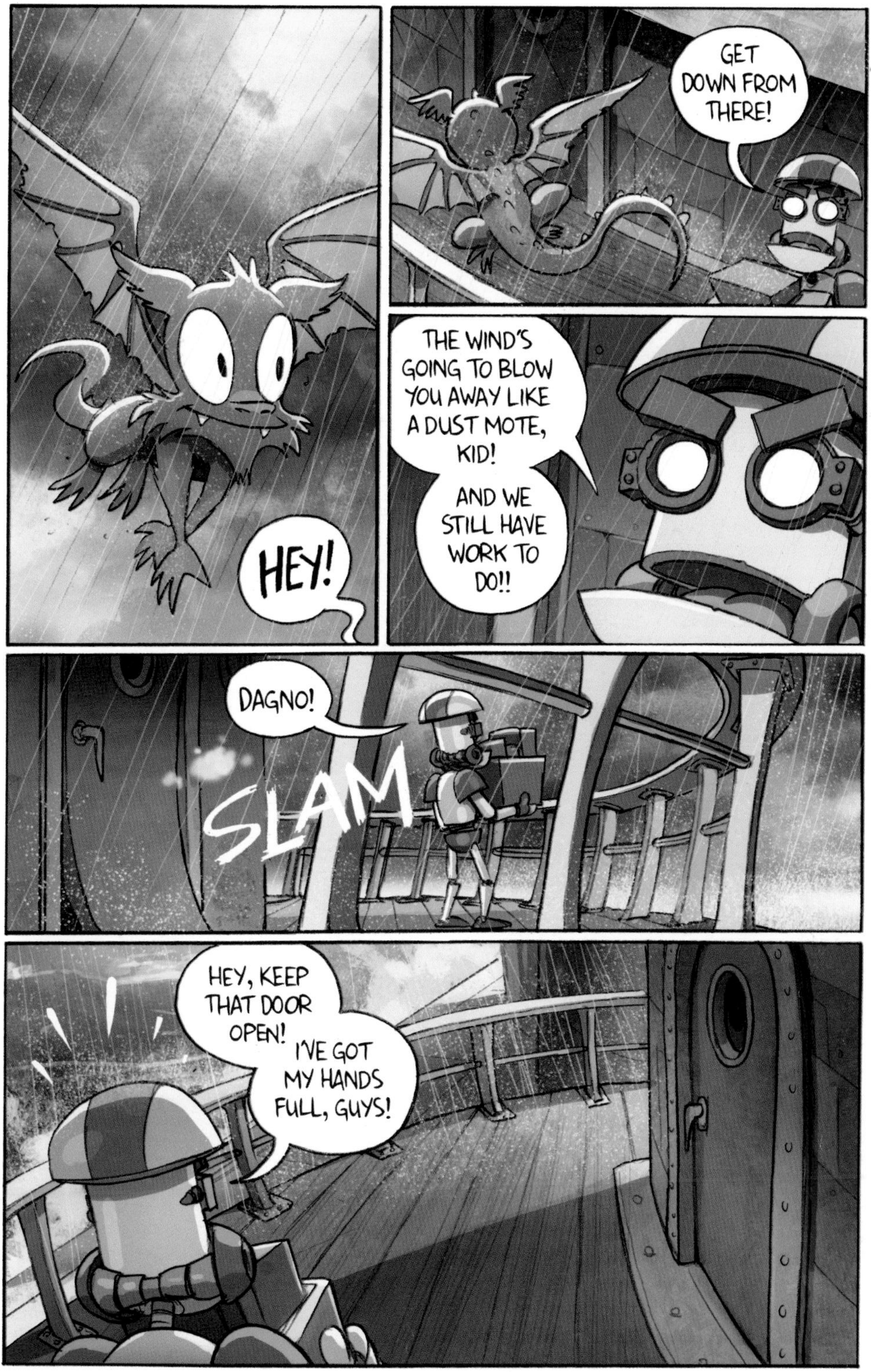
HEY!
GET DOWN FROM THERE!
THE WIND'S GOING TO BLOW YOU AWAY LIKE A DUST MOTE, KID!
AND WE STILL HAVE WORK TO DO!!
DAGNO!
SLAM
HEY, KEEP THAT DOOR OPEN!
I'VE GOT MY HANDS FULL, GUYS!

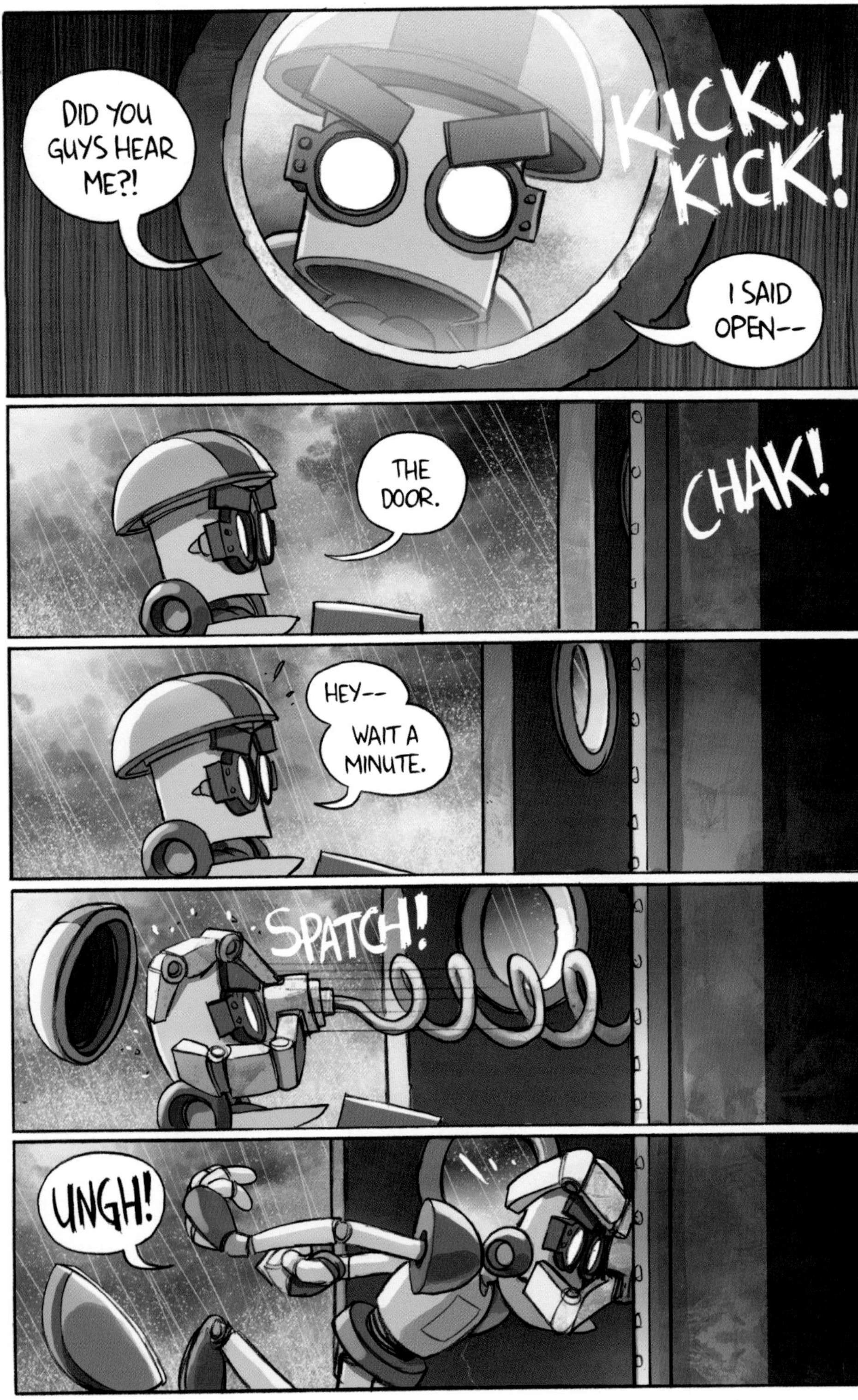
DID YOU GUYS HEAR ME?!
KICK! KICK!
I SAID OPEN--
THE DOOR.
CHAK!
HEY--
WAIT A MINUTE.
SPATCH!
UNGH!

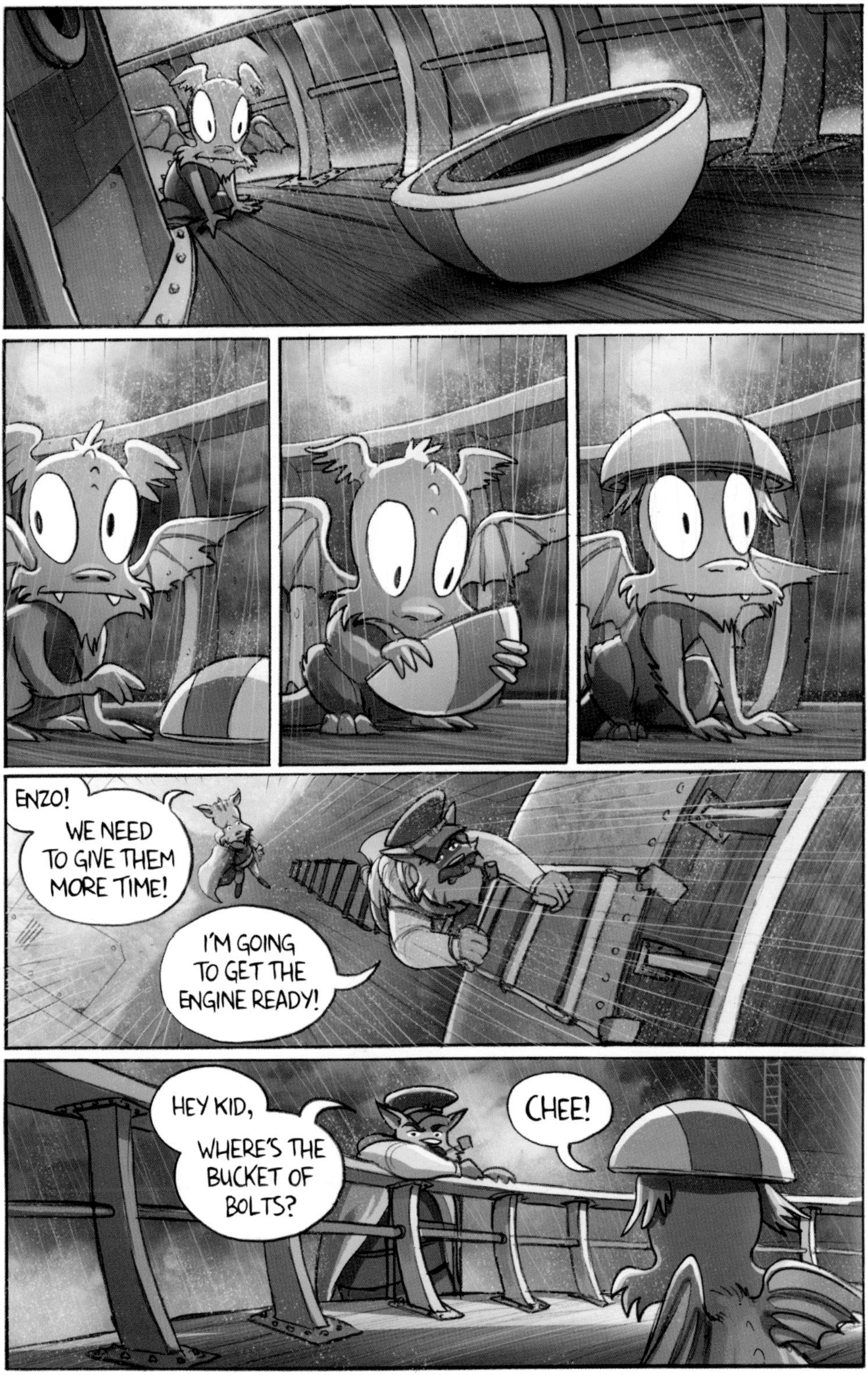
ENZO!
WE NEED TO GIVE THEM MORE TIME!
I'M GOING TO GET THE ENGINE READY!
HEY KID,
WHERE'S THE BUCKET OF BOLTS?
CHEE!

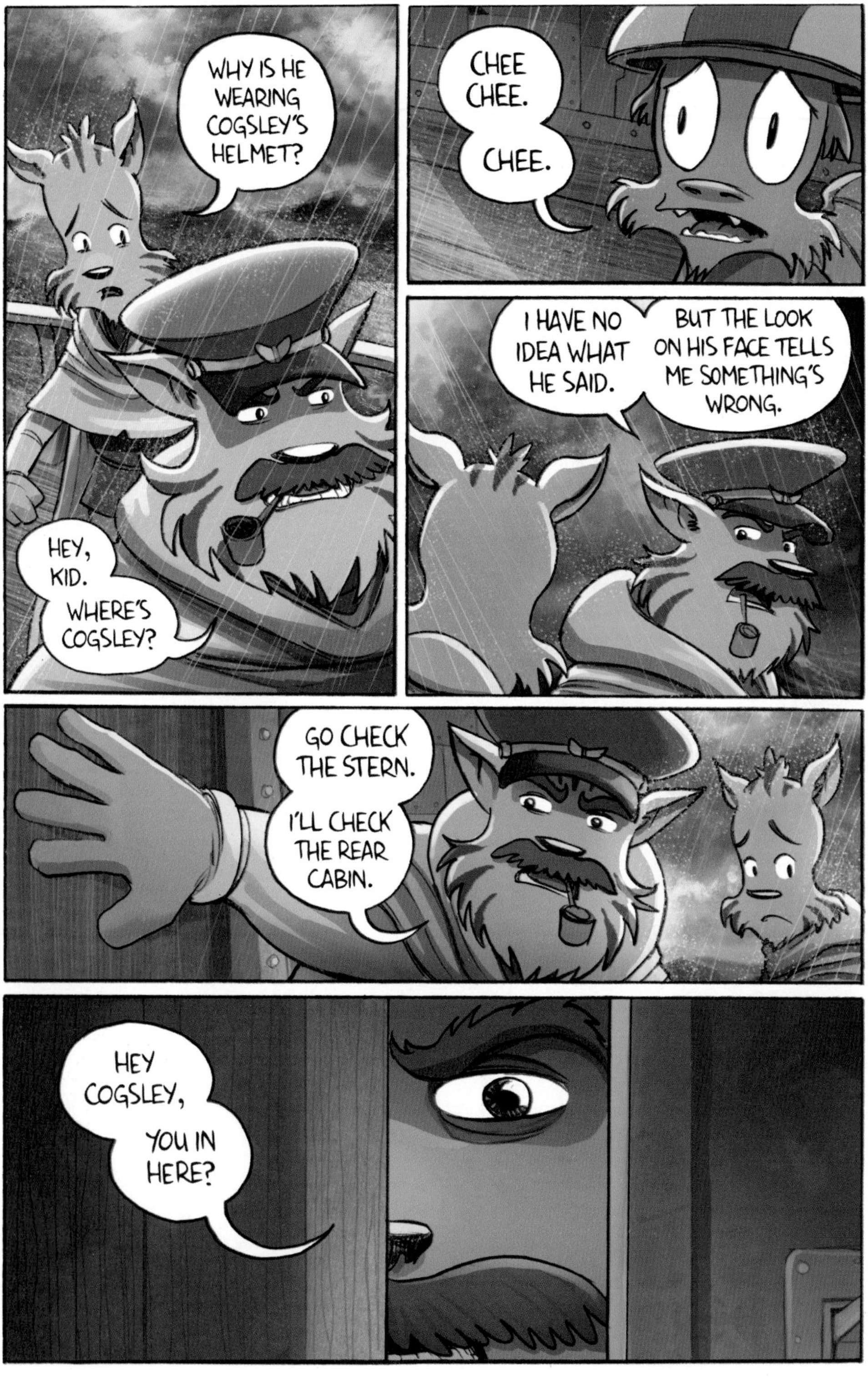
WHY IS HE WEARING COGSLEY'S HELMET?
HEY, KID.
WHERE'S COGSLEY?
CHEE CHEE.
CHEE.
I HAVE NO IDEA WHAT HE SAID.
BUT THE LOOK ON HIS FACE TELLS ME SOMETHING'S WRONG.
GO CHECK THE STERN.
I'LL CHECK THE REAR CABIN.
HEY COGSLEY,
YOU IN HERE?

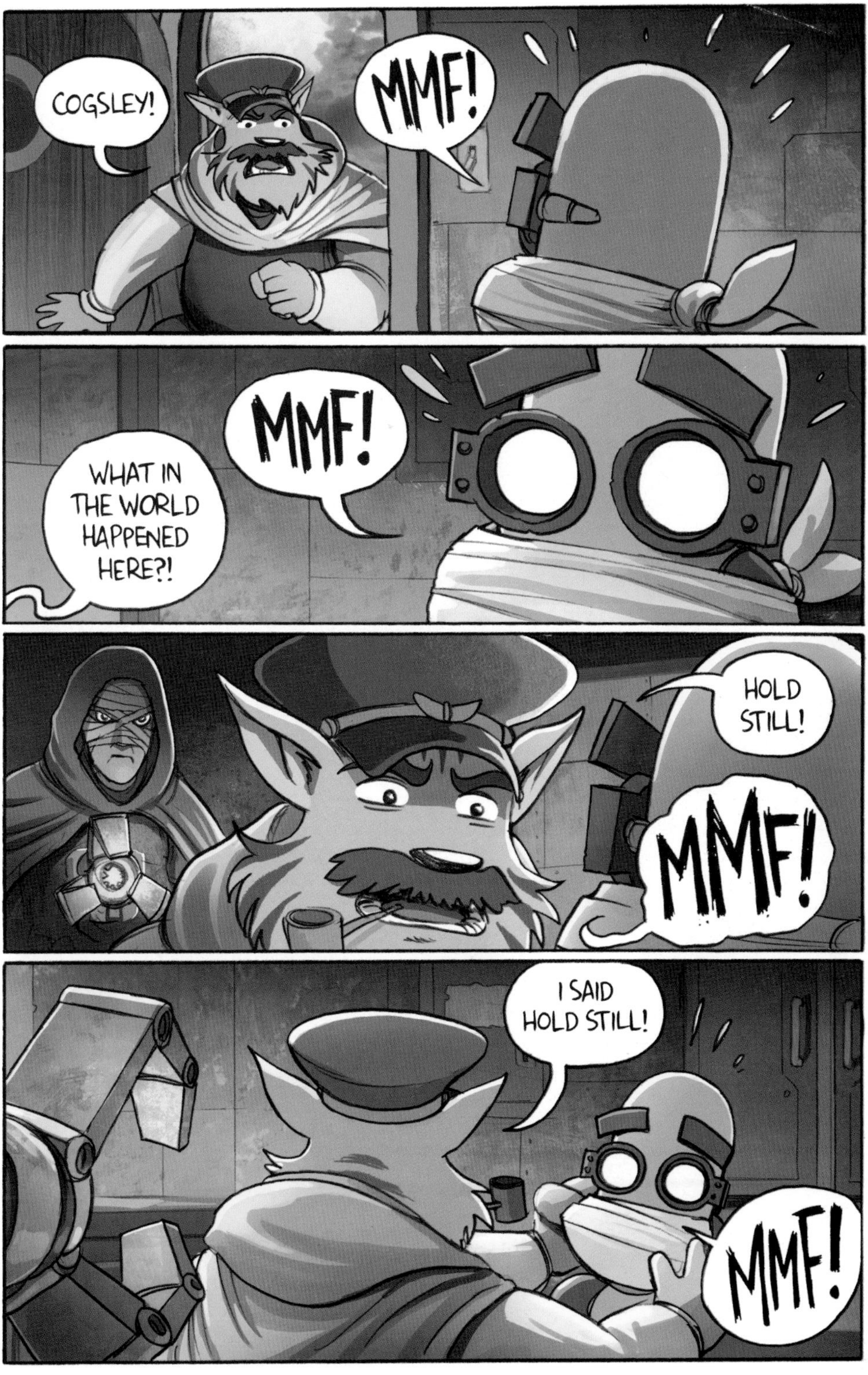
COGSLEY!
MMF!
MMF!
WHAT IN THE WORLD HAPPENED HERE?!
HOLD STILL!
MMF!
I SAID HOLD STILL!
MMF!

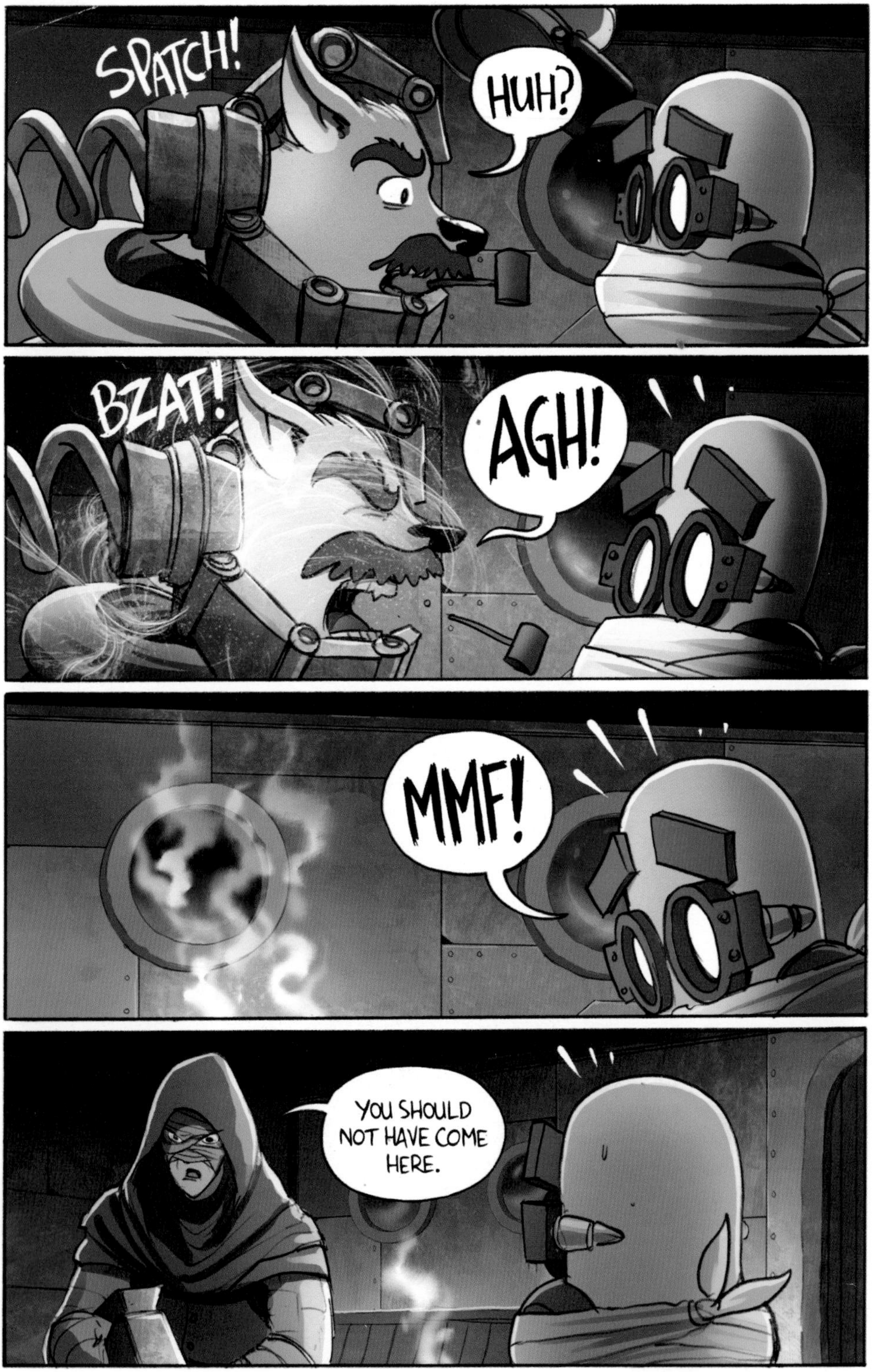
SPATCH!
HUH?
BZAT!
AGH!
MMF!
YOU SHOULD NOT HAVE COME HERE.

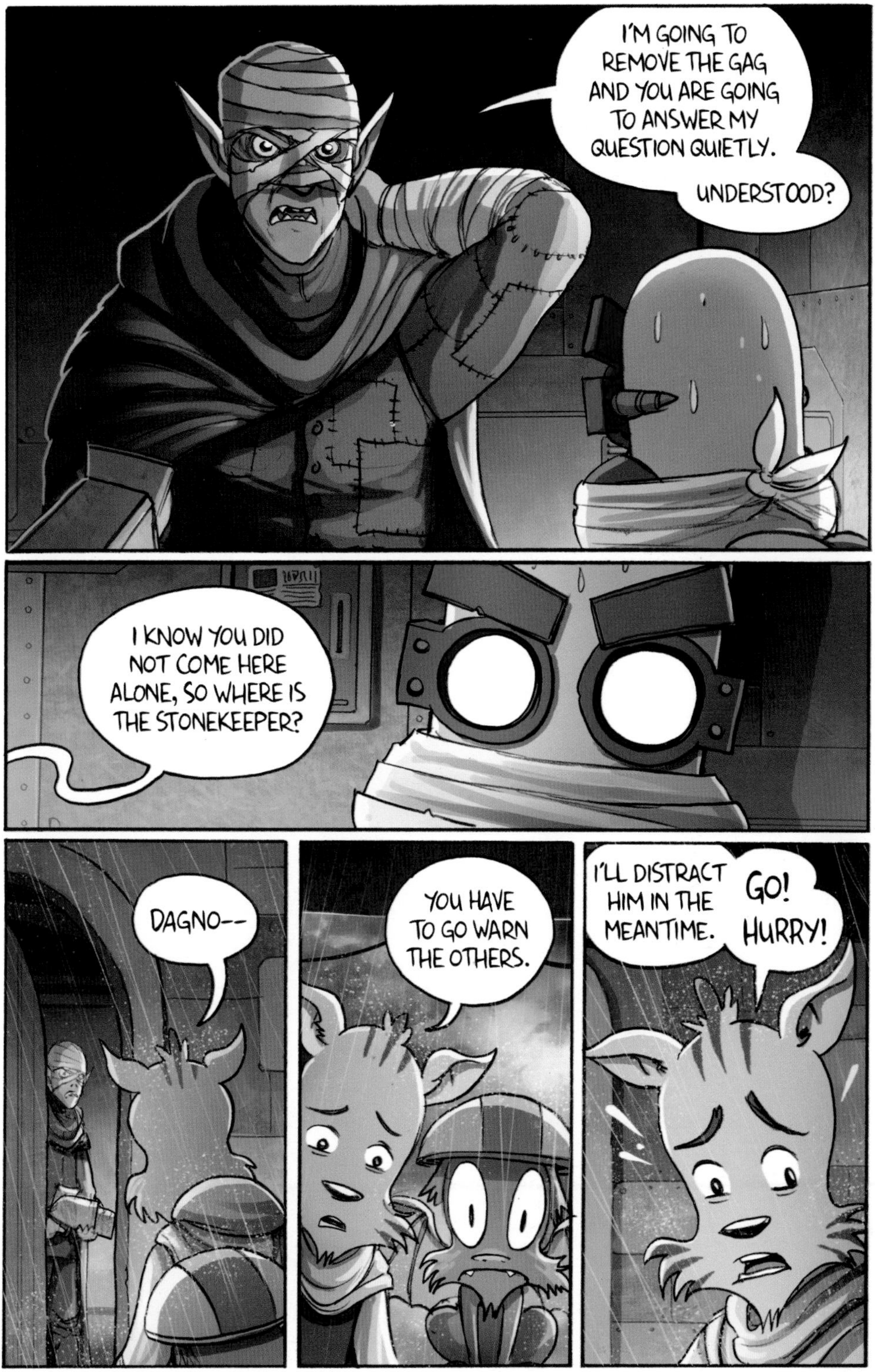
I'M GOING TO REMOVE THE GAG AND YOU ARE GOING TO ANSWER MY QUESTION QUIETLY.
UNDERSTOOD?
I KNOW YOU DID NOT COME HERE ALONE, SO WHERE IS THE STONEKEEPER?
DAGNO--
YOU HAVE TO GO WARN THE OTHERS.
I'LL DISTRACT HIM IN THE MEANTIME.
GO! HURRY!

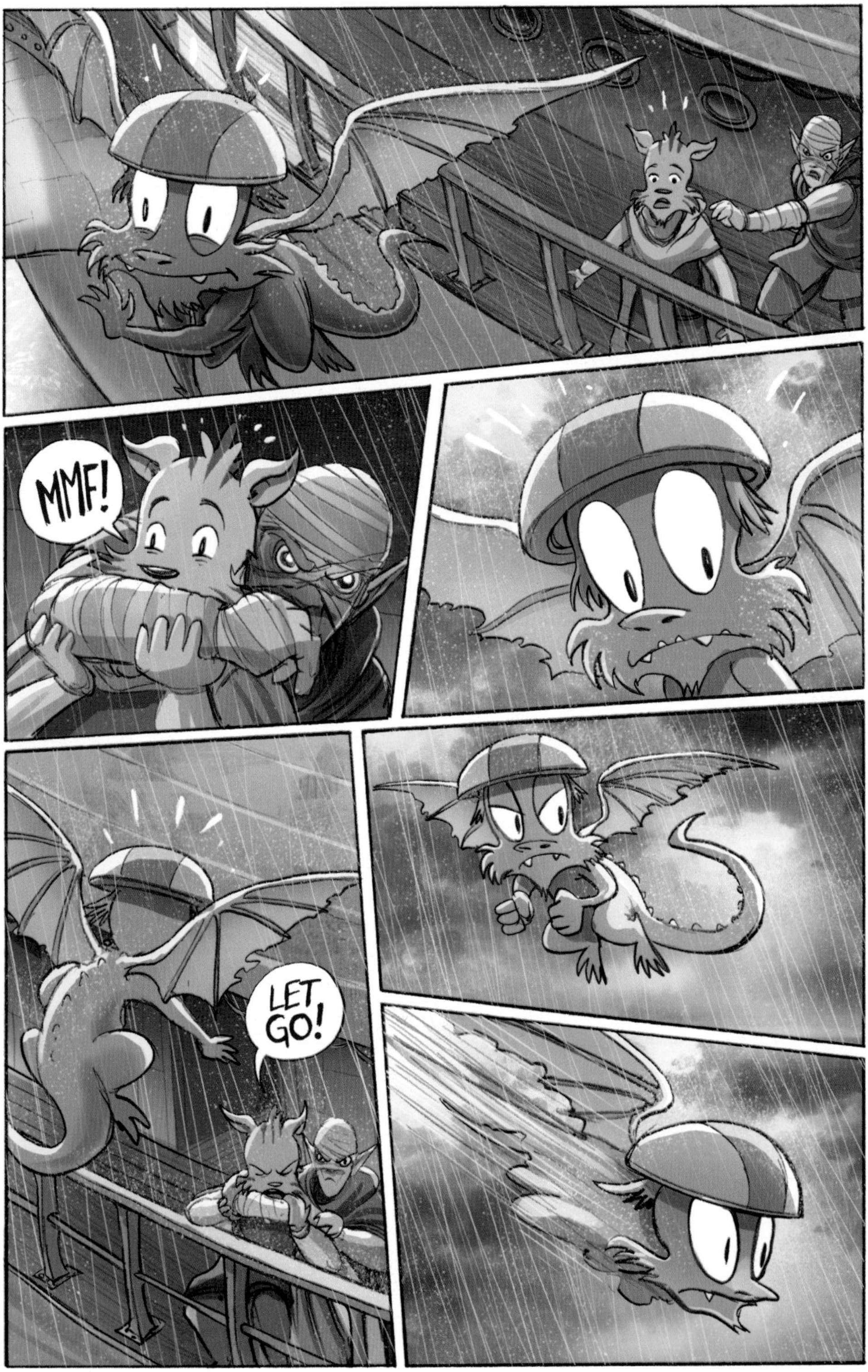
MMF!
LET GO!

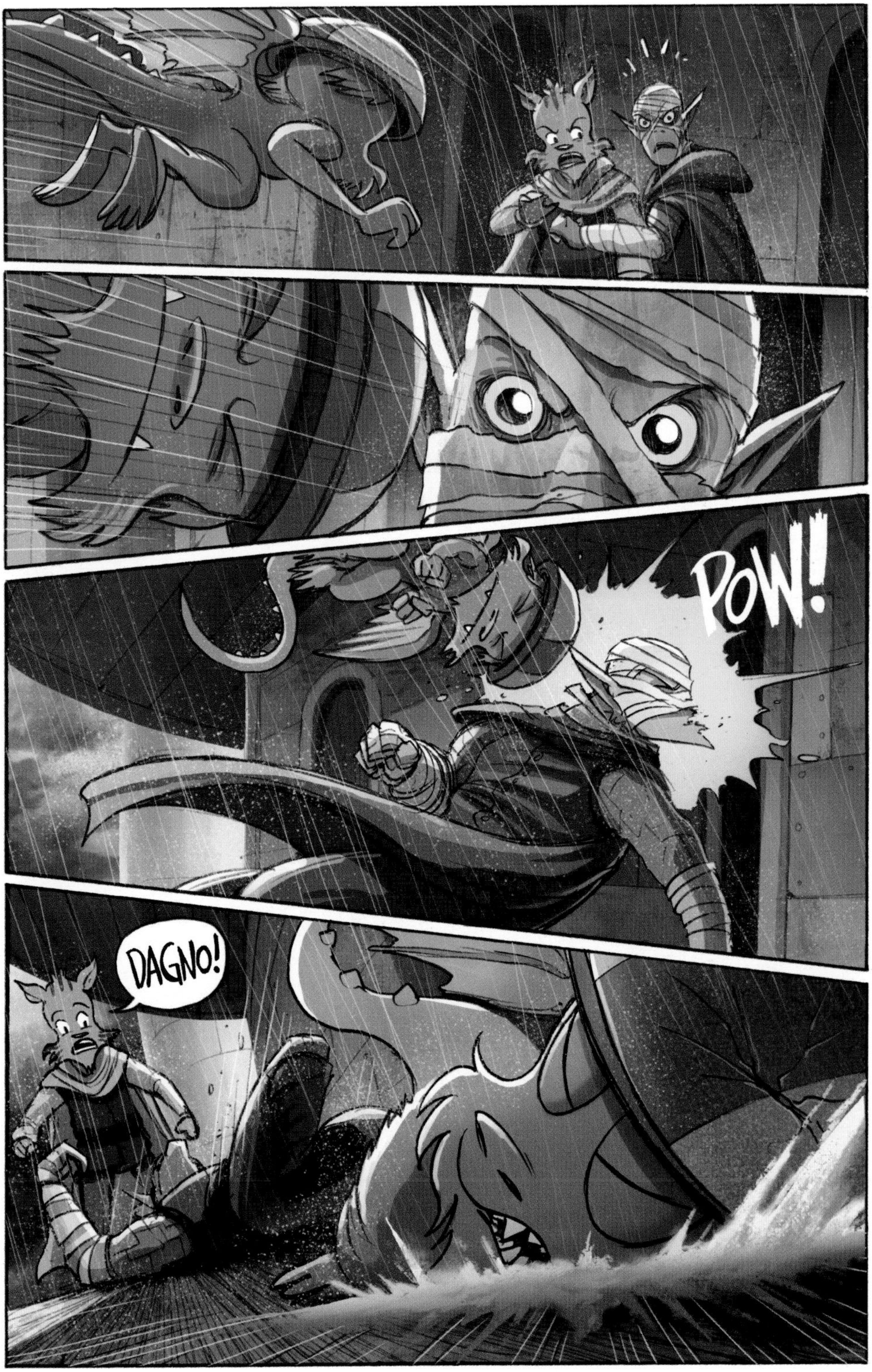
POW!
DAGNO!

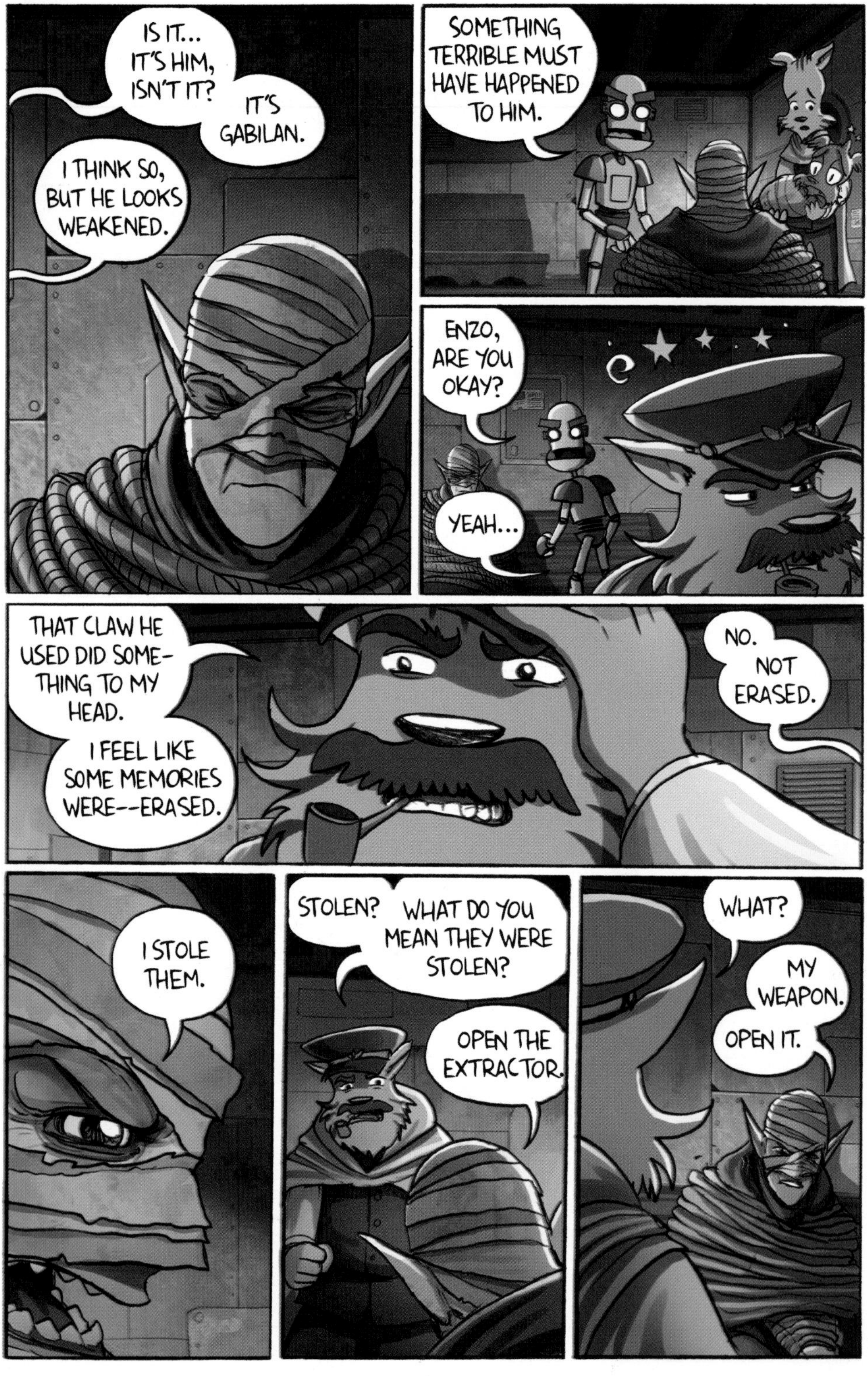
IS IT... IT'S HIM, ISN'T IT?
IT'S GABILAN.
I THINK SO, BUT HE LOOKS WEAKENED.
SOMETHING TERRIBLE MUST HAVE HAPPENED TO HIM.
ENZO, ARE YOU OKAY?
YEAH...
THAT CLAW HE USED DID SOME-THING TO MY HEAD.
I FEEL LIKE SOME MEMORIES WERE--ERASED.
NO. NOT ERASED.
I STOLE THEM.
STOLEN? WHAT DO YOU MEAN THEY WERE STOLEN?
OPEN THE EXTRACTOR.
WHAT?
MY WEAPON.
OPEN IT.

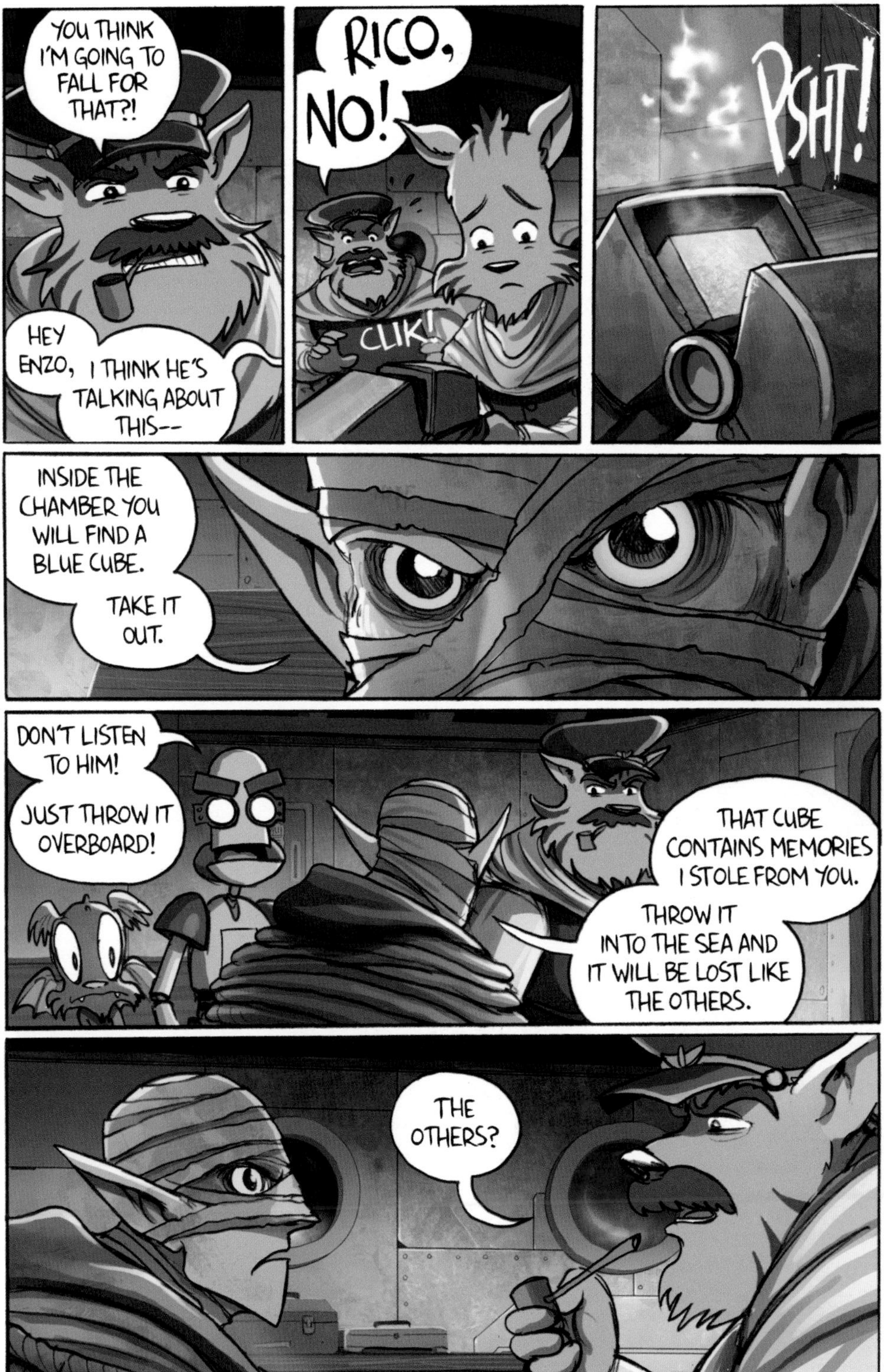
YOU THINK I'M GOING TO FALL FOR THAT?!
HEY ENZO,
I THINK HE'S TALKING ABOUT THIS--
RICO, NO!
CLIK!
PSHT!
INSIDE THE CHAMBER YOU WILL FIND A BLUE CUBE.
TAKE IT OUT.
DON'T LISTEN TO HIM!
JUST THROW IT OVERBOARD!
THAT CUBE CONTAINS MEMORIES I STOLE FROM YOU.
THROW IT INTO THE SEA AND IT WILL BE LOST LIKE THE OTHERS.
THE OTHERS?

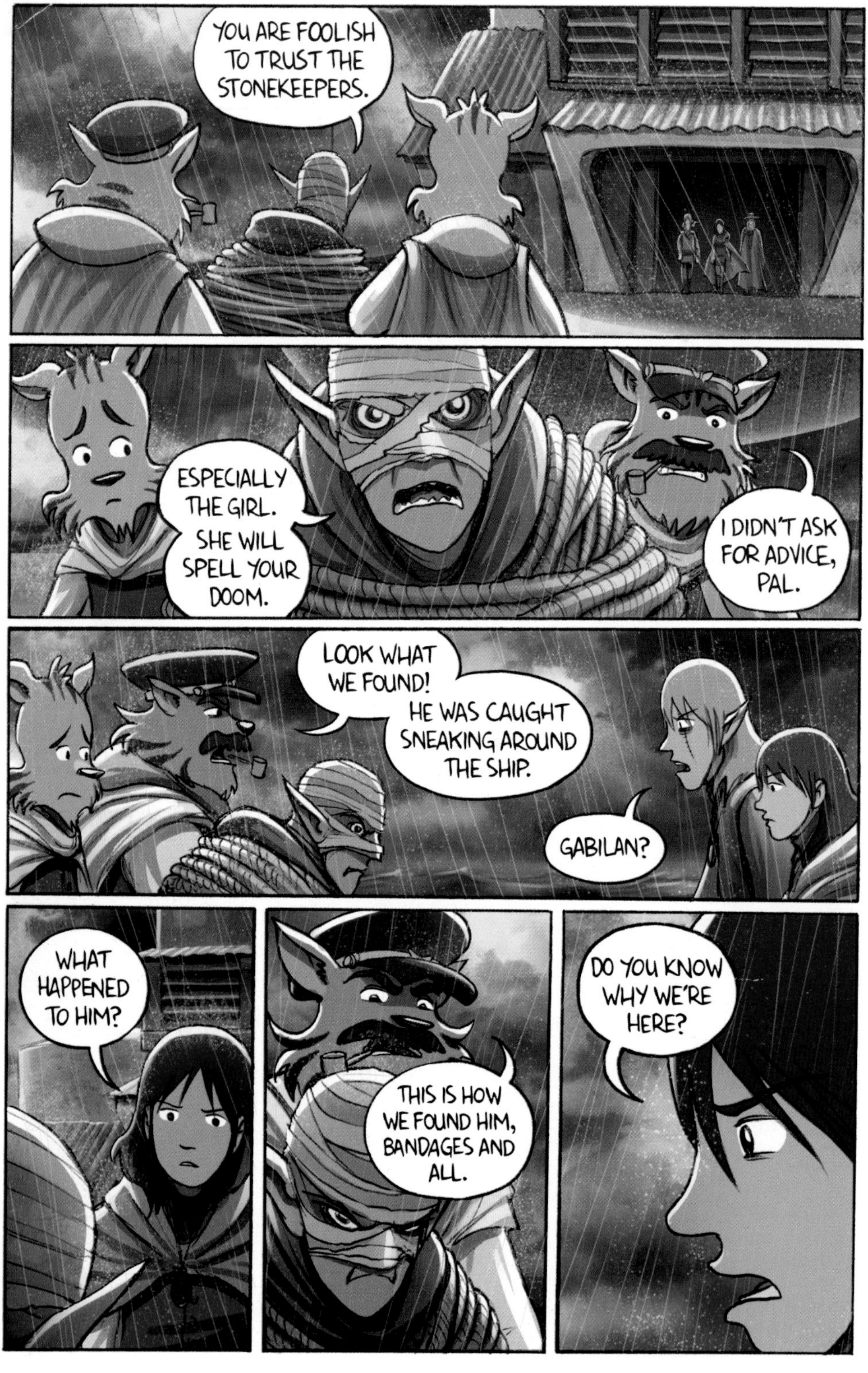
YOU ARE FOOLISH TO TRUST THE STONEKEEPERS.
ESPECIALLY THE GIRL.
SHE WILL SPELL YOUR DOOM.
I DIDN'T ASK FOR ADVICE, PAL.
LOOK WHAT WE FOUND!
HE WAS CAUGHT SNEAKING AROUND THE SHIP.
GABILAN?
WHAT HAPPENED TO HIM?
THIS IS HOW WE FOUND HIM, BANDAGES AND ALL.
DO YOU KNOW WHY WE'RE HERE?

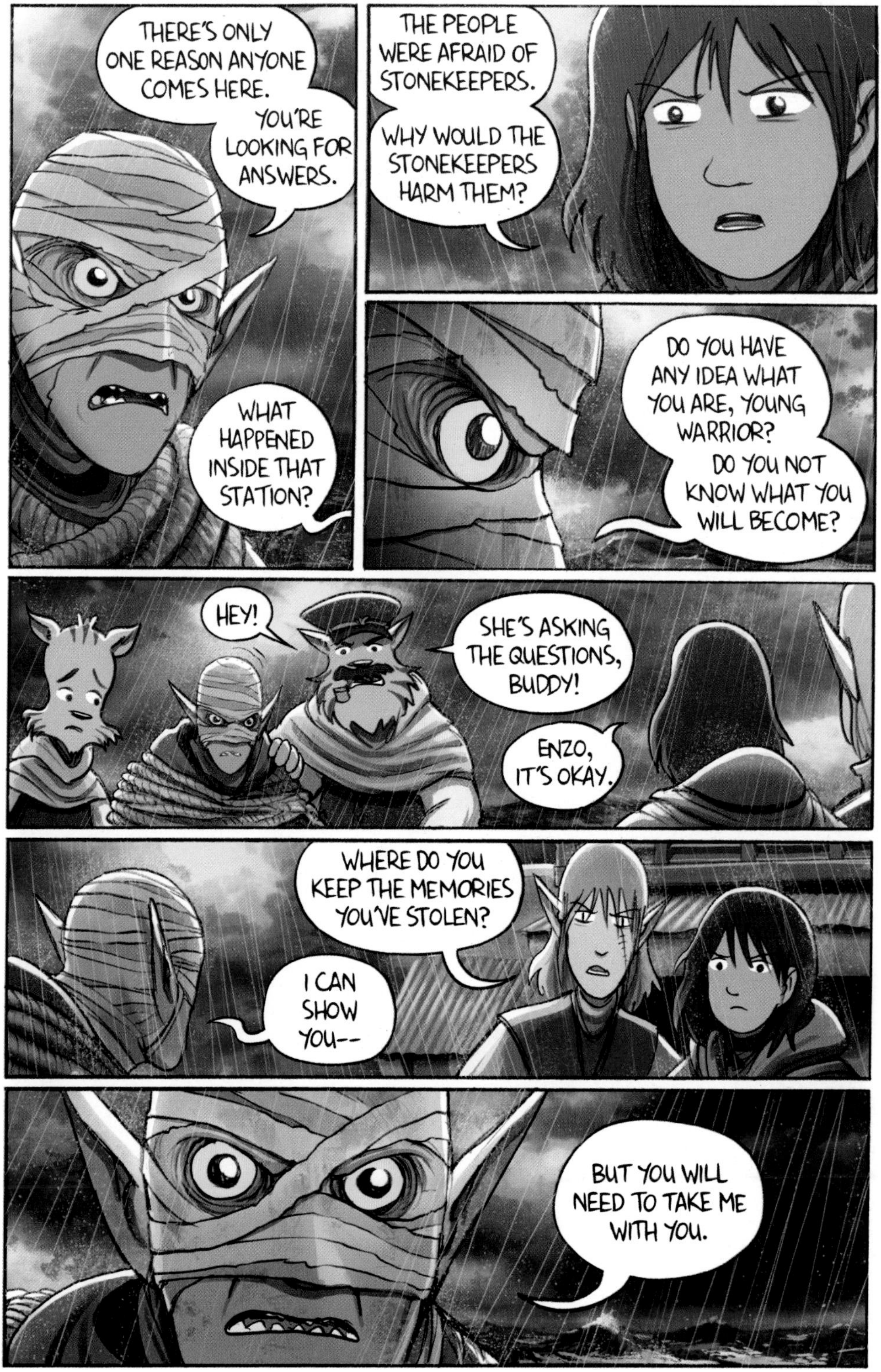
THERE'S ONLY ONE REASON ANYONE COMES HERE.
YOU'RE LOOKING FOR ANSWERS.
WHAT HAPPENED INSIDE THAT STATION?
THE PEOPLE WERE AFRAID OF STONEKEEPERS.
WHY WOULD THE STONEKEEPERS HARM THEM?
DO YOU HAVE ANY IDEA WHAT YOU ARE, YOUNG WARRIOR?
DO YOU NOT KNOW WHAT YOU WILL BECOME?
HEY!
SHE'S ASKING THE QUESTIONS, BUDDY!
ENZO, IT'S OKAY.
WHERE DO YOU KEEP THE MEMORIES YOU'VE STOLEN?
I CAN SHOW YOU--
BUT YOU WILL NEED TO TAKE ME WITH YOU.

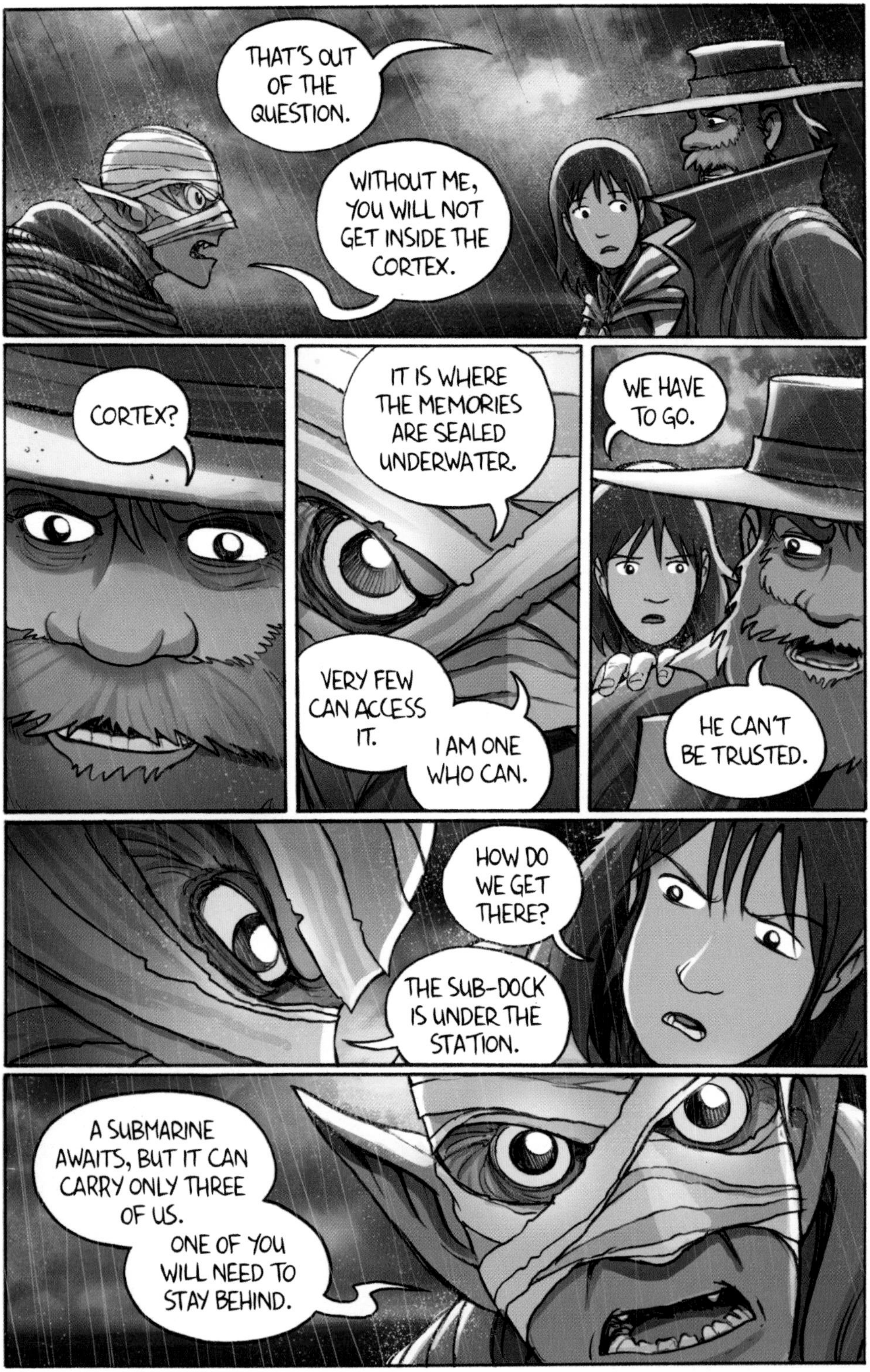
THAT'S OUT OF THE QUESTION.
WITHOUT ME, YOU WILL NOT GET INSIDE THE CORTEX.
CORTEX?
IT IS WHERE THE MEMORIES ARE SEALED UNDERWATER.
VERY FEW CAN ACCESS IT.
I AM ONE WHO CAN.
WE HAVE TO GO.
HE CAN'T BE TRUSTED.
HOW DO WE GET THERE?
THE SUB-DOCK IS UNDER THE STATION.
A SUBMARINE AWAITS, BUT IT CAN CARRY ONLY THREE OF US.
ONE OF YOU WILL NEED TO STAY BEHIND.

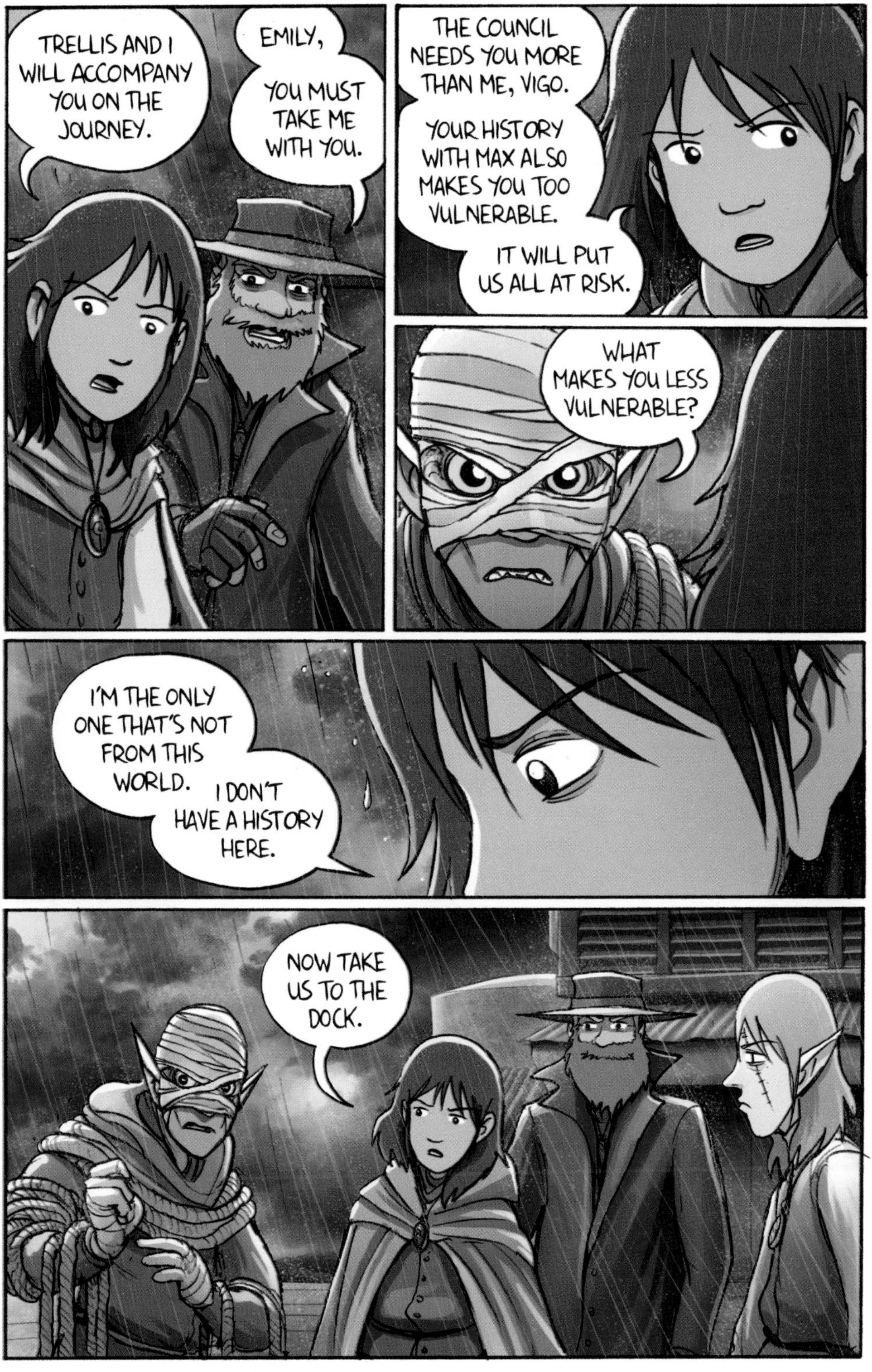
TRELLIS AND I WILL ACCOMPANY YOU ON THE JOURNEY.
EMILY,
YOU MUST TAKE ME WITH YOU.
THE COUNCIL NEEDS YOU MORE THAN ME, VIGO.
YOUR HISTORY WITH MAX ALSO MAKES YOU TOO VULNERABLE.
IT WILL PUT US ALL AT RISK.
WHAT MAKES YOU LESS VULNERABLE?
I'M THE ONLY ONE THAT'S NOT FROM THIS WORLD.
I DON'T HAVE A HISTORY HERE.
NOW TAKE US TO THE DOCK.

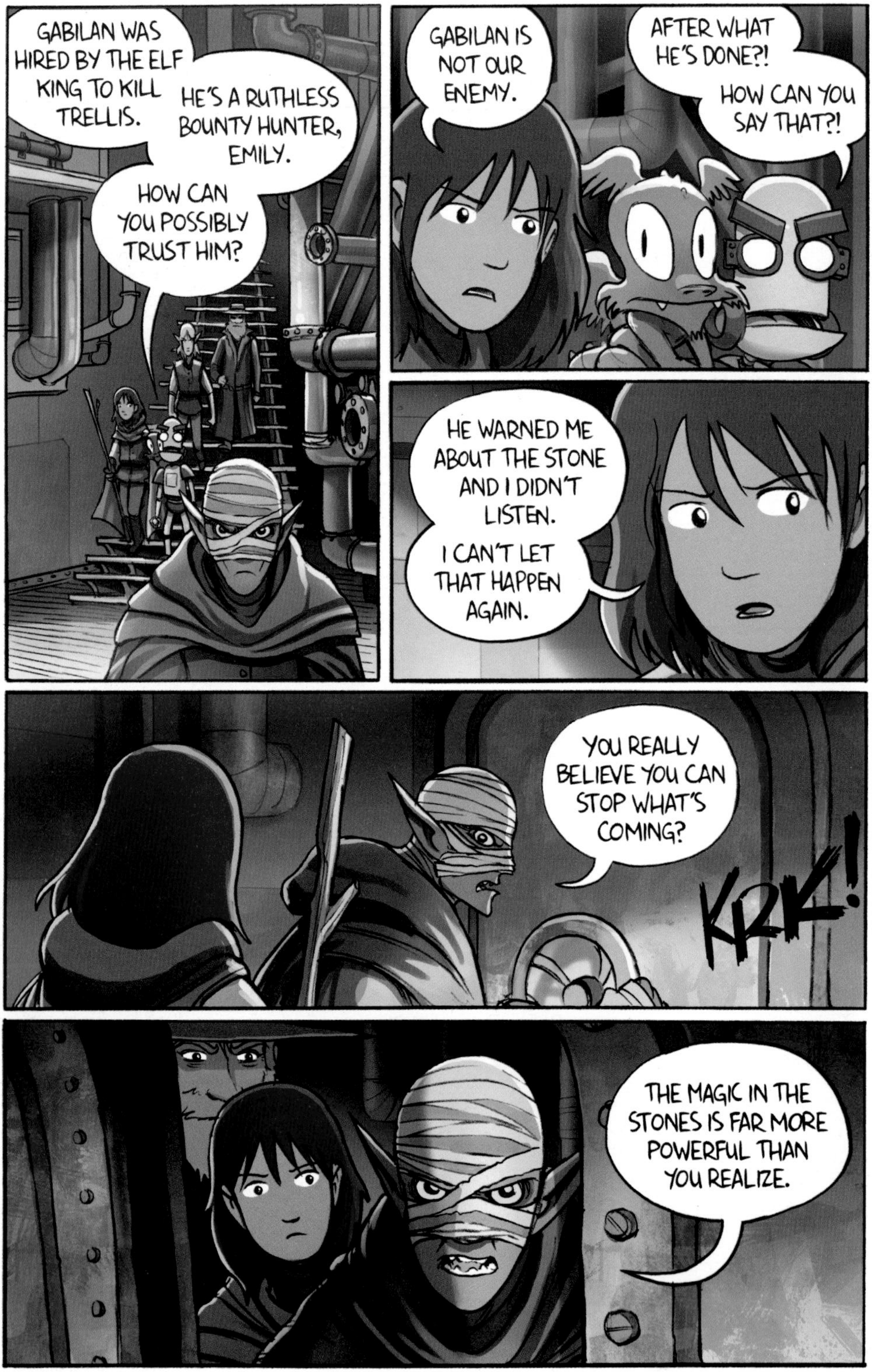
GABILAN WAS HIRED BY THE ELF KING TO KILL TRELLIS.
HE'S A RUTHLESS BOUNTY HUNTER, EMILY.
HOW CAN YOU POSSIBLY TRUST HIM?
GABILAN IS NOT OUR ENEMY.
AFTER WHAT HE'S DONE?!
HOW CAN YOU SAY THAT?!
HE WARNED ME ABOUT THE STONE AND I DIDN'T LISTEN.
I CAN'T LET THAT HAPPEN AGAIN.
YOU REALLY BELIEVE YOU CAN STOP WHAT'S COMING?
KRK!
THE MAGIC IN THE STONES IS FAR MORE POWERFUL THAN YOU REALIZE.

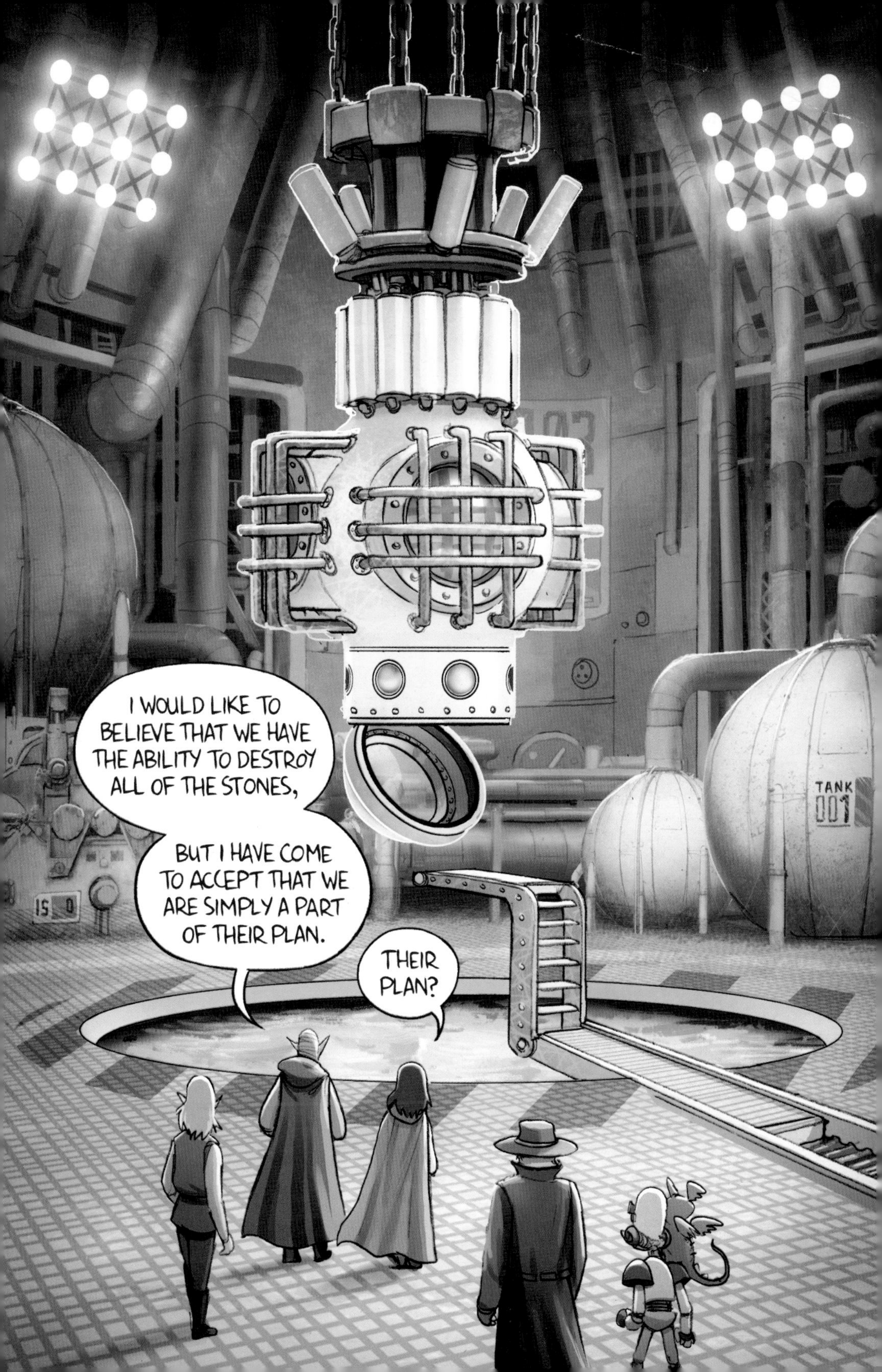
I WOULD LIKE TO BELIEVE THAT WE HAVE THE ABILITY TO DESTROY ALL OF THE STONES,
BUT I HAVE COME TO ACCEPT THAT WE ARE SIMPLY A PART OF THEIR PLAN.
THEIR PLAN?
TANK 001

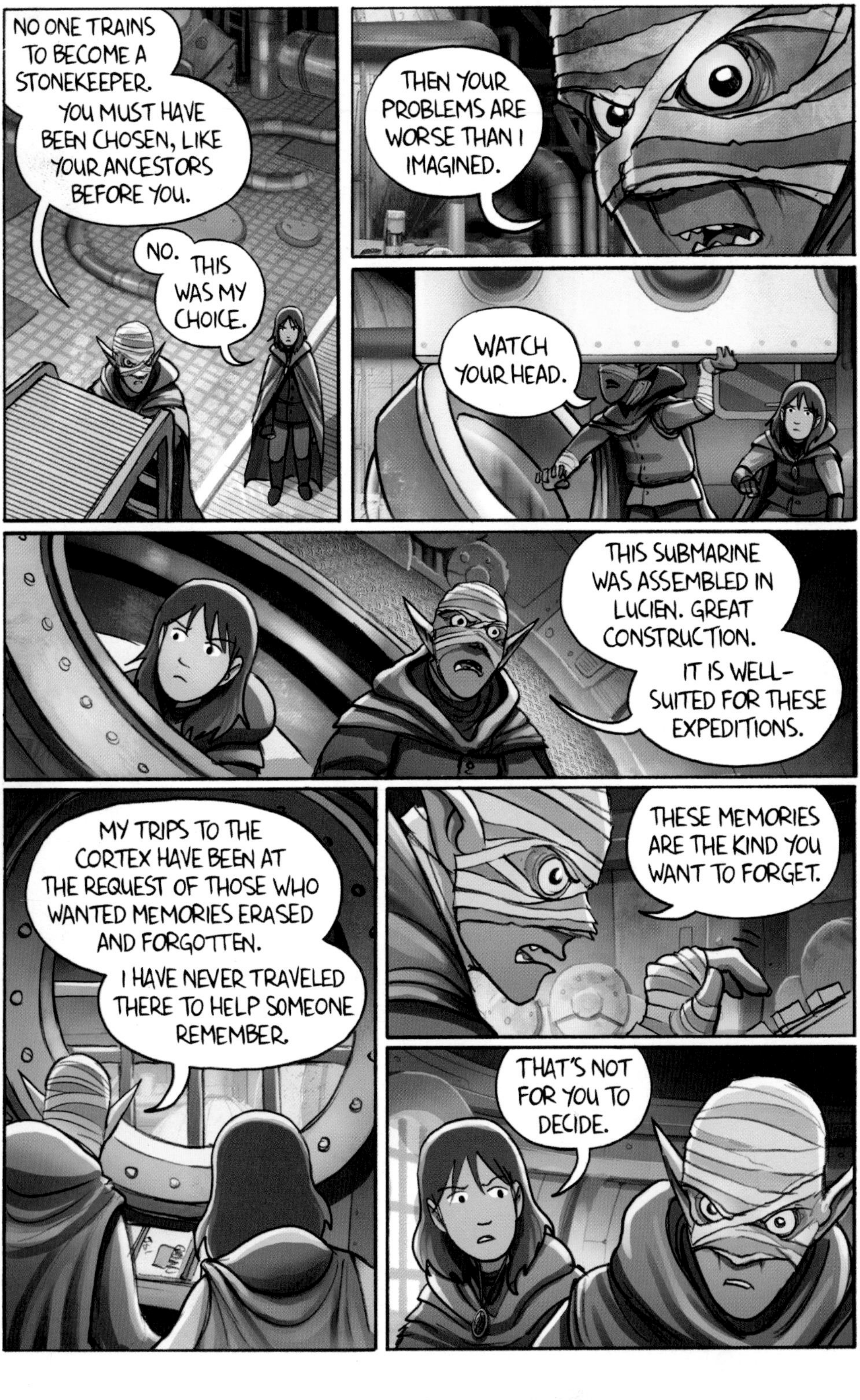
NO ONE TRAINS TO BECOME A STONEKEEPER.
YOU MUST HAVE BEEN CHOSEN, LIKE YOUR ANCESTORS BEFORE YOU.
NO.
THIS WAS MY CHOICE.
THEN YOUR PROBLEMS ARE WORSE THAN I IMAGINED.
WATCH YOUR HEAD.
THIS SUBMARINE WAS ASSEMBLED IN LUCIEN. GREAT CONSTRUCTION.
IT IS WELL-SUITED FOR THESE EXPEDITIONS.
MY TRIPS TO THE CORTEX HAVE BEEN AT THE REQUEST OF THOSE WHO WANTED MEMORIES ERASED AND FORGOTTEN.
I HAVE NEVER TRAVELED THERE TO HELP SOMEONE REMEMBER.
THESE MEMORIES ARE THE KIND YOU WANT TO FORGET.
THAT'S NOT FOR YOU TO DECIDE.

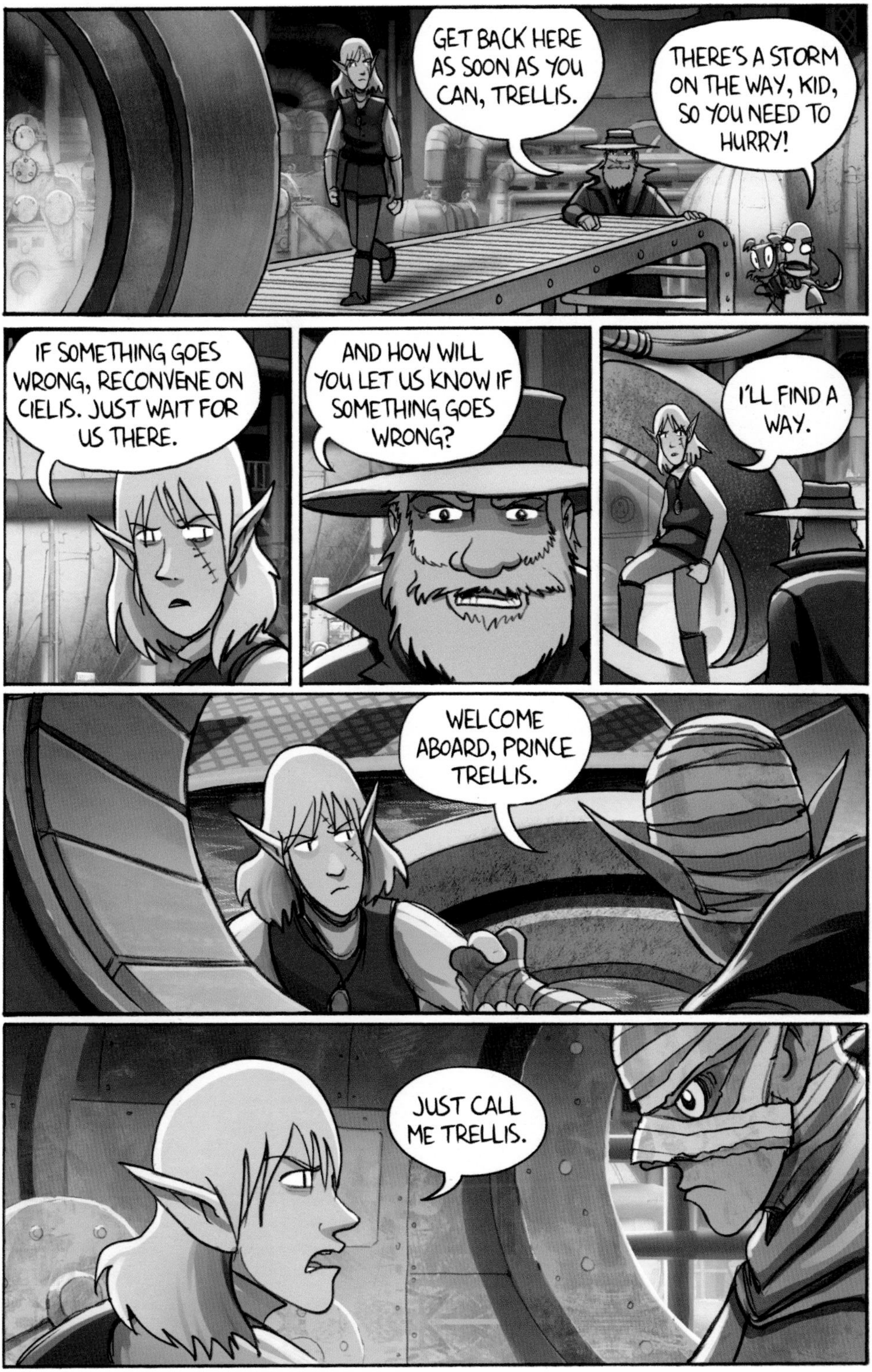
GET BACK HERE AS SOON AS YOU CAN, TRELLIS.
THERE'S A STORM ON THE WAY, KID, SO YOU NEED TO HURRY!
IF SOMETHING GOES WRONG, RECONVENE ON CIELIS. JUST WAIT FOR US THERE.
AND HOW WILL YOU LET US KNOW IF SOMETHING GOES WRONG?
I'LL FIND A WAY.
WELCOME ABOARD, PRINCE TRELLIS.
JUST CALL ME TRELLIS.

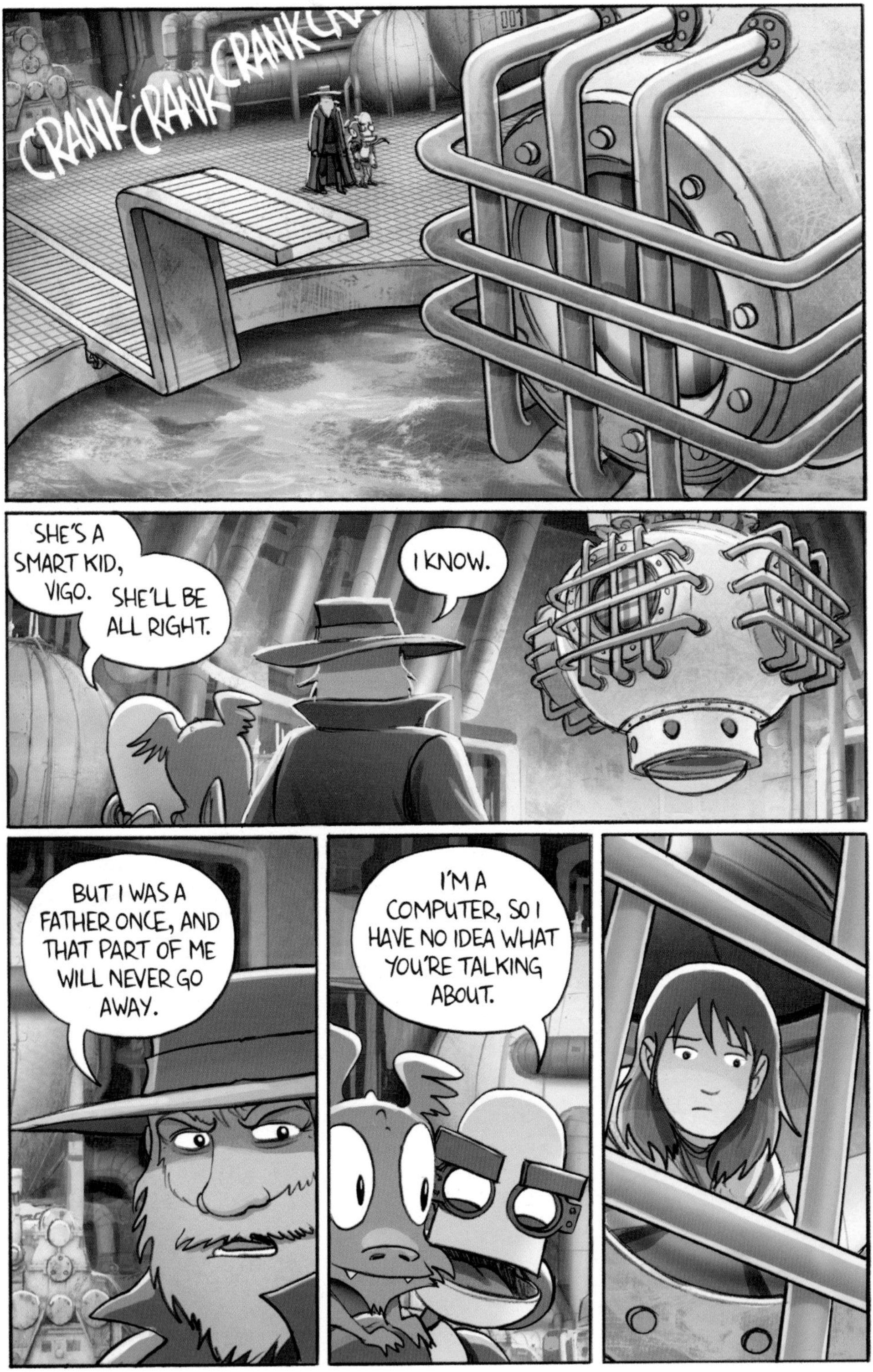
CRANK CRANK CRANK
SHE'S A SMART KID, VIGO.
SHE'LL BE ALL RIGHT.
I KNOW.
BUT I WAS A FATHER ONCE, AND THAT PART OF ME WILL NEVER GO AWAY.
I'M A COMPUTER, SO I HAVE NO IDEA WHAT YOU'RE TALKING ABOUT.

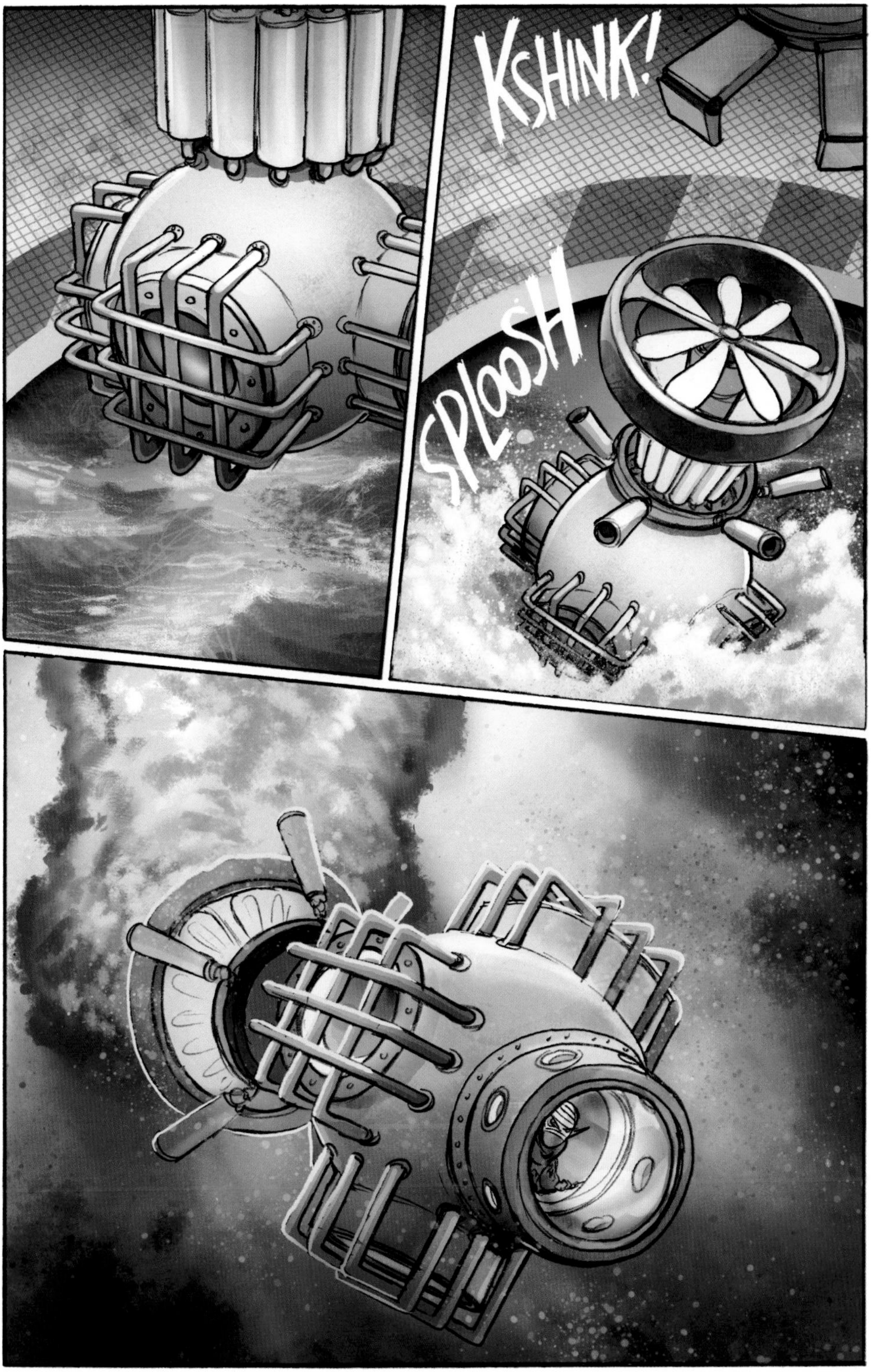
KSHINK!
SPLOOSH

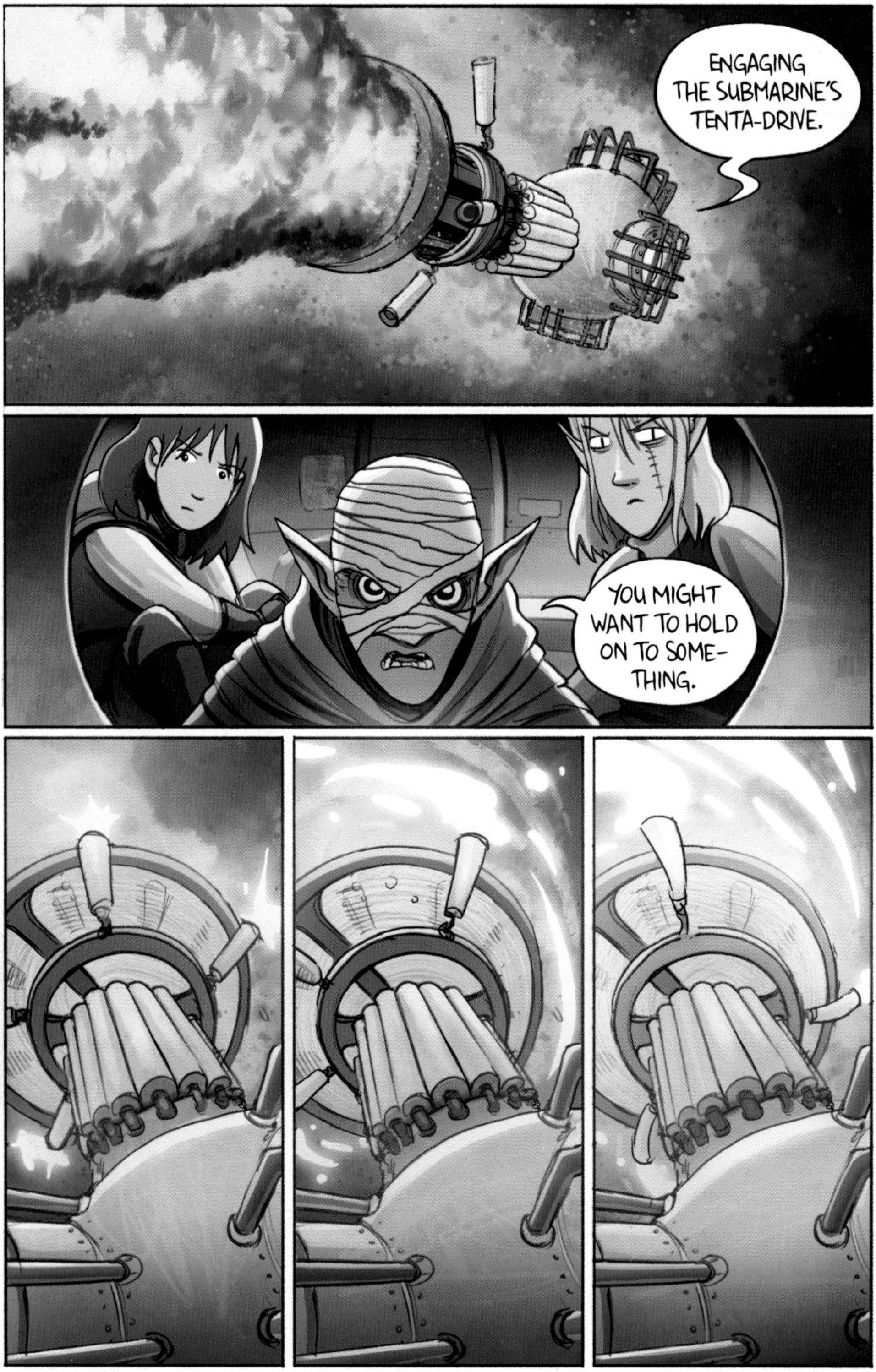
ENGAGING THE SUBMARINE'S TENTA-DRIVE.
YOU MIGHT WANT TO HOLD ON TO SOME-THING.

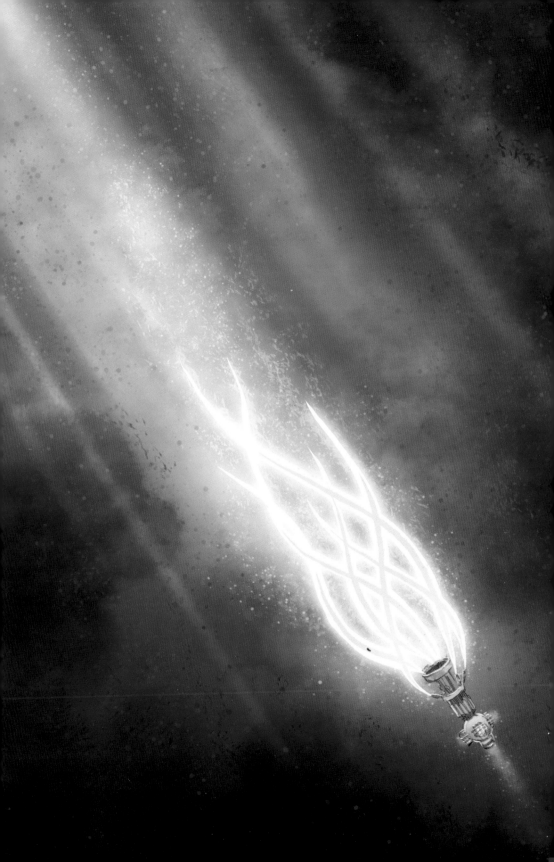

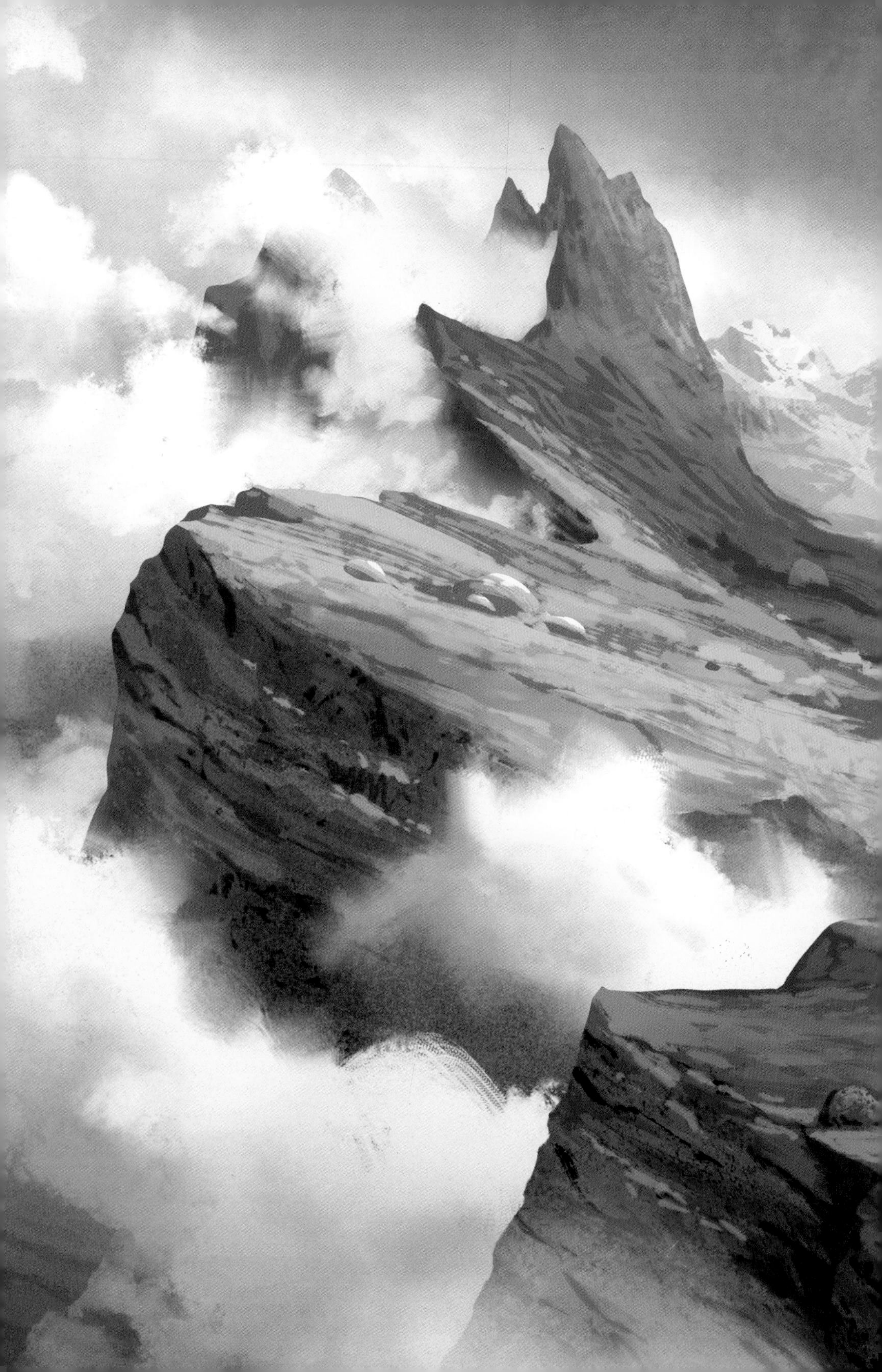

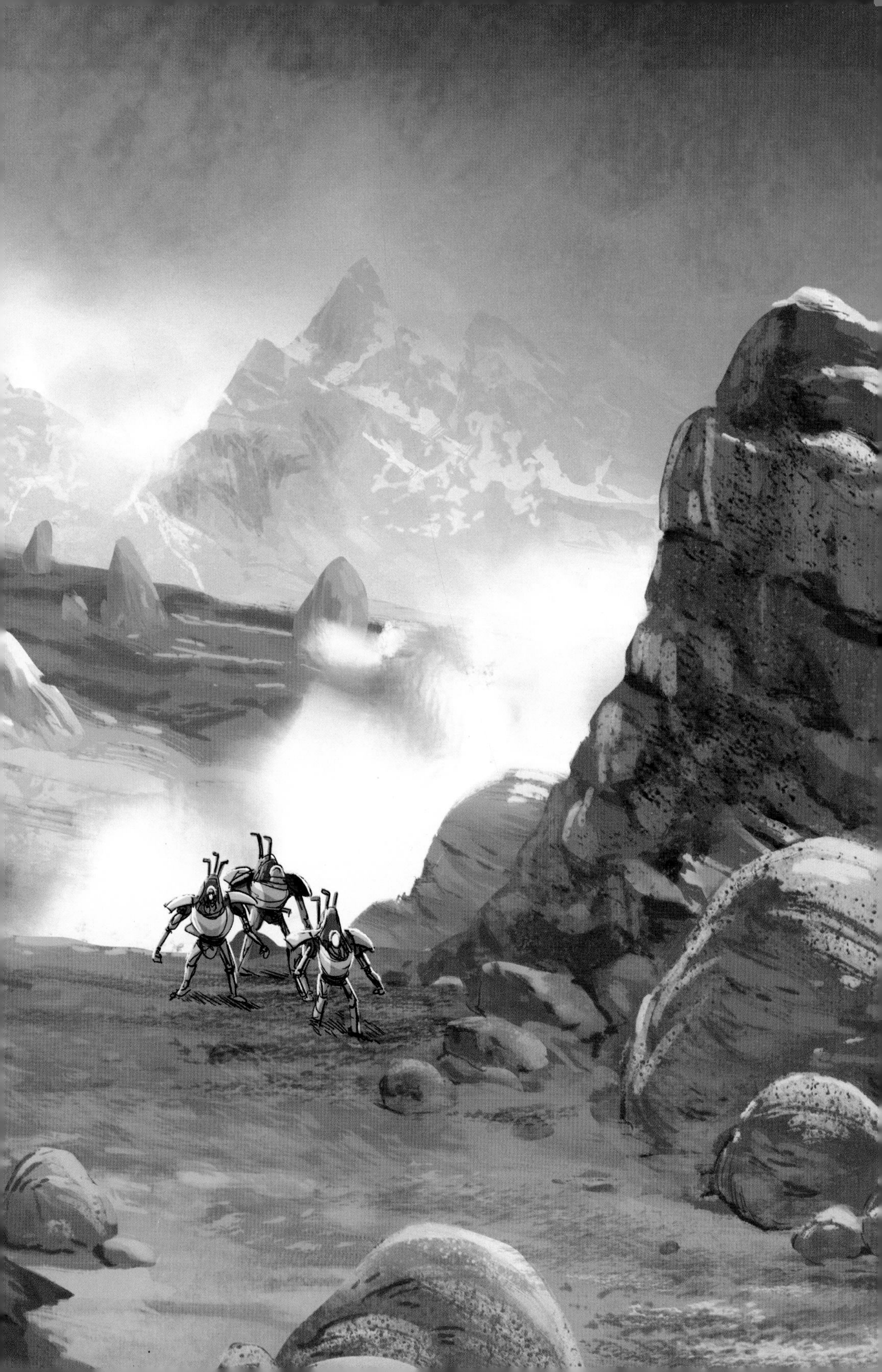

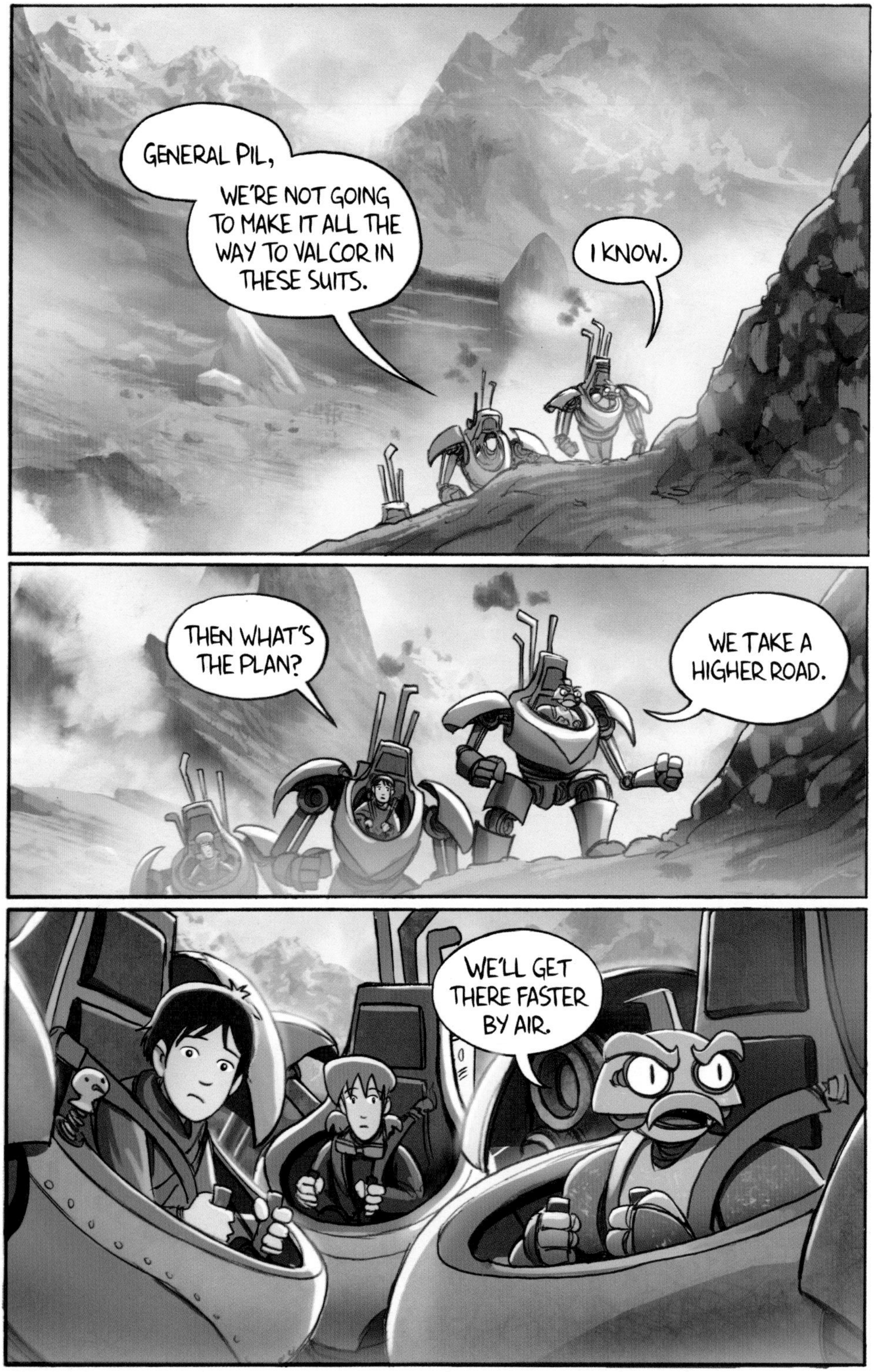
GENERAL PIL,
WE'RE NOT GOING TO MAKE IT ALL THE WAY TO VALCOR IN THESE SUITS.
I KNOW.
THEN WHAT'S THE PLAN?
WE TAKE A HIGHER ROAD.
WE'LL GET THERE FASTER BY AIR.

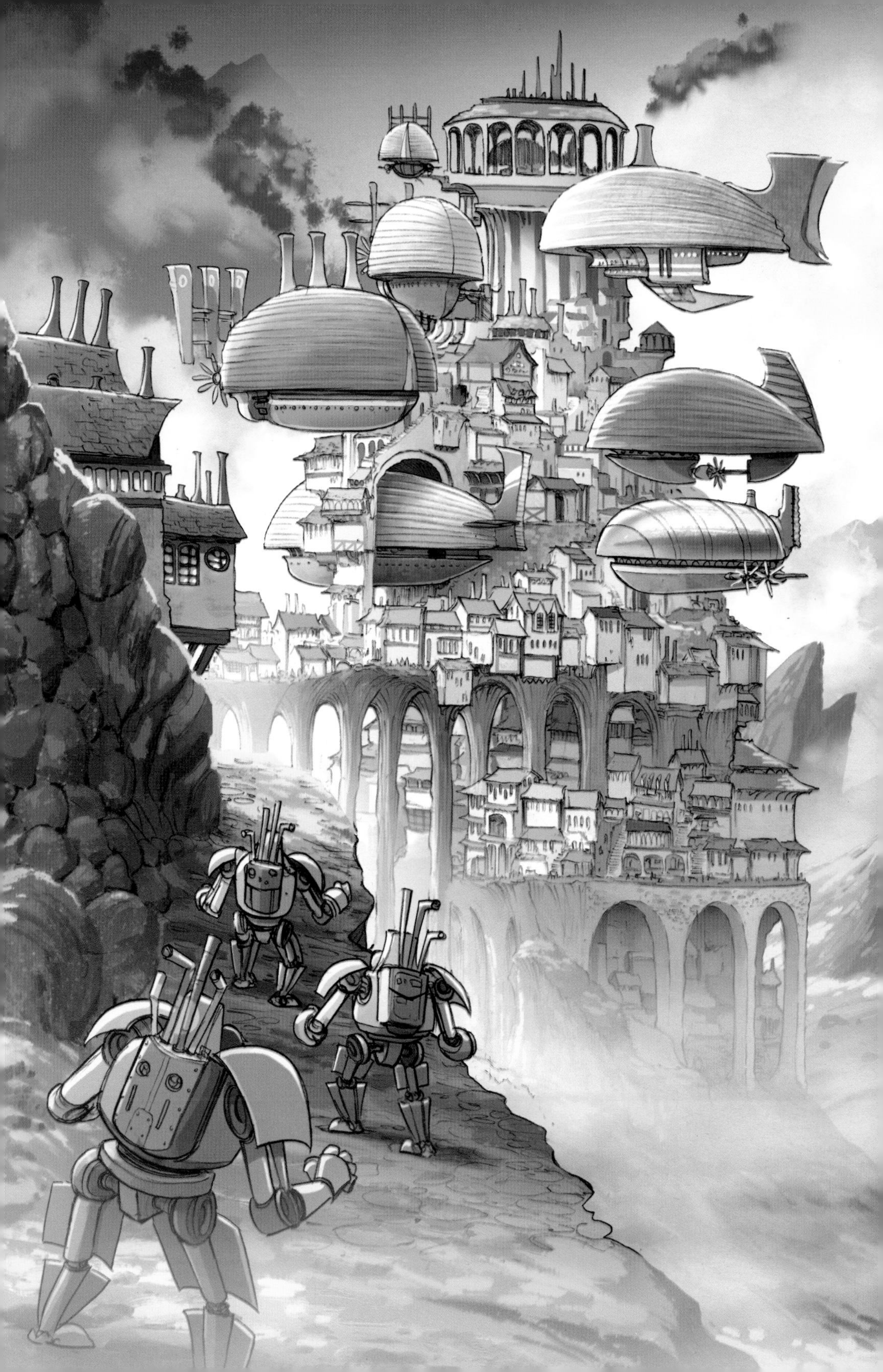

GENERAL, WE DON'T HAVE MONEY FOR TICKETS.

NOT TO WORRY!

WE'LL SELL THESE SUITS FOR A GOOD PRICE.

WE PROMISED YOUR PARENTS WE'D BRING THESE BACK IN ONE PIECE.

BAH!

WHO ARE YOU GOING TO GET TO BUY THESE SUITS ANYWAY?

I USED TO SELL ALL SORTS OF THINGS TO TRAVELERS IN LUCIEN.

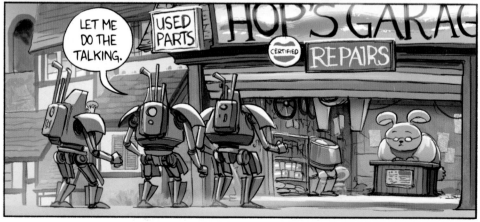

LET ME DO THE TALKING.

USED PARTS

HOP'S GARAG

CERTIFIED

REPAIRS

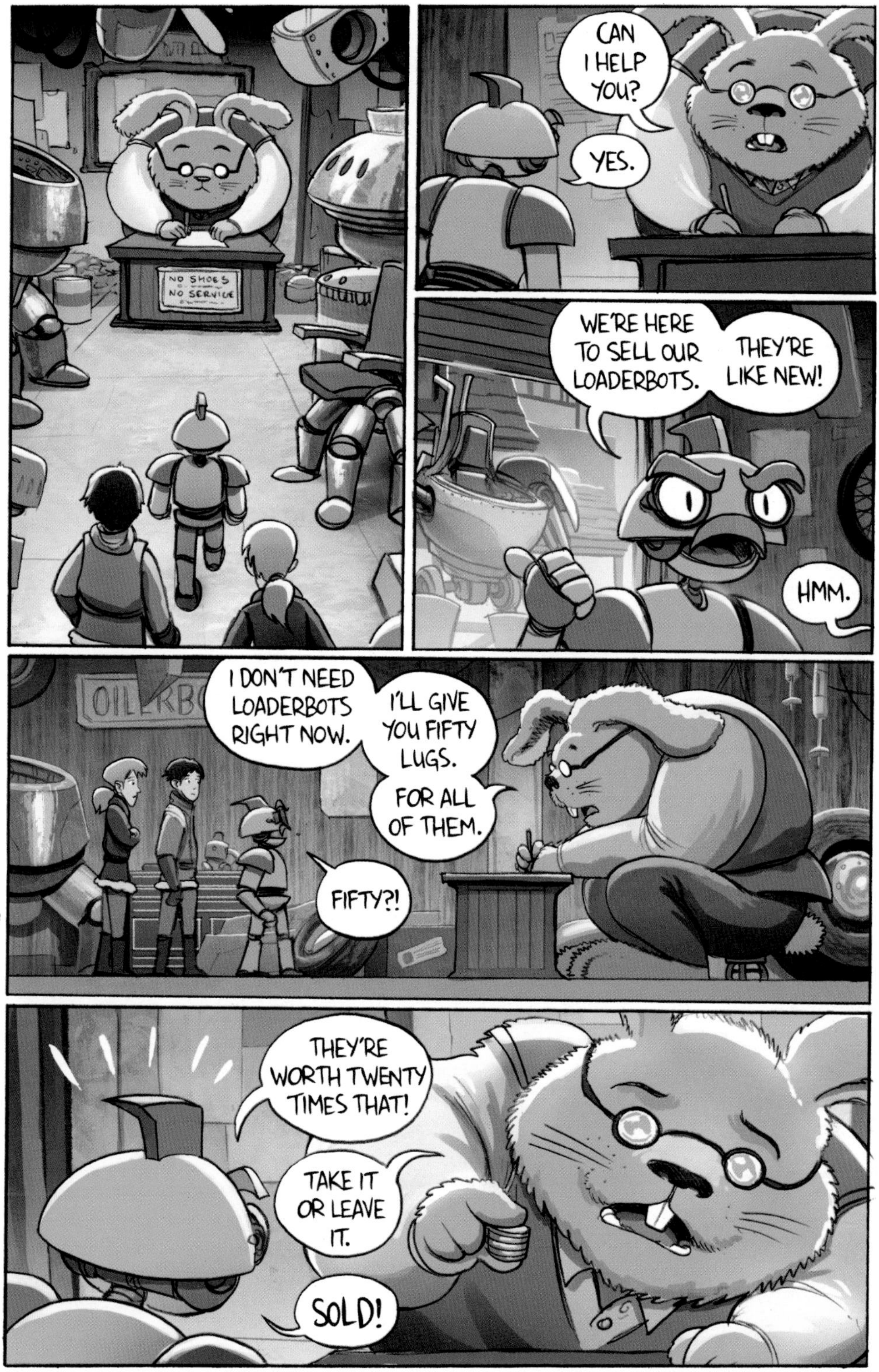
NO SHOES NO SERVICE
CAN I HELP YOU?
YES.
WE'RE HERE TO SELL OUR LOADERBOTS.
THEY'RE LIKE NEW!
HMM.
OILERB
I DON'T NEED LOADERBOTS RIGHT NOW.
I'LL GIVE YOU FIFTY LUGS.
FOR ALL OF THEM.
FIFTY?!
THEY'RE WORTH TWENTY TIMES THAT!
TAKE IT OR LEAVE IT.
SOLD!

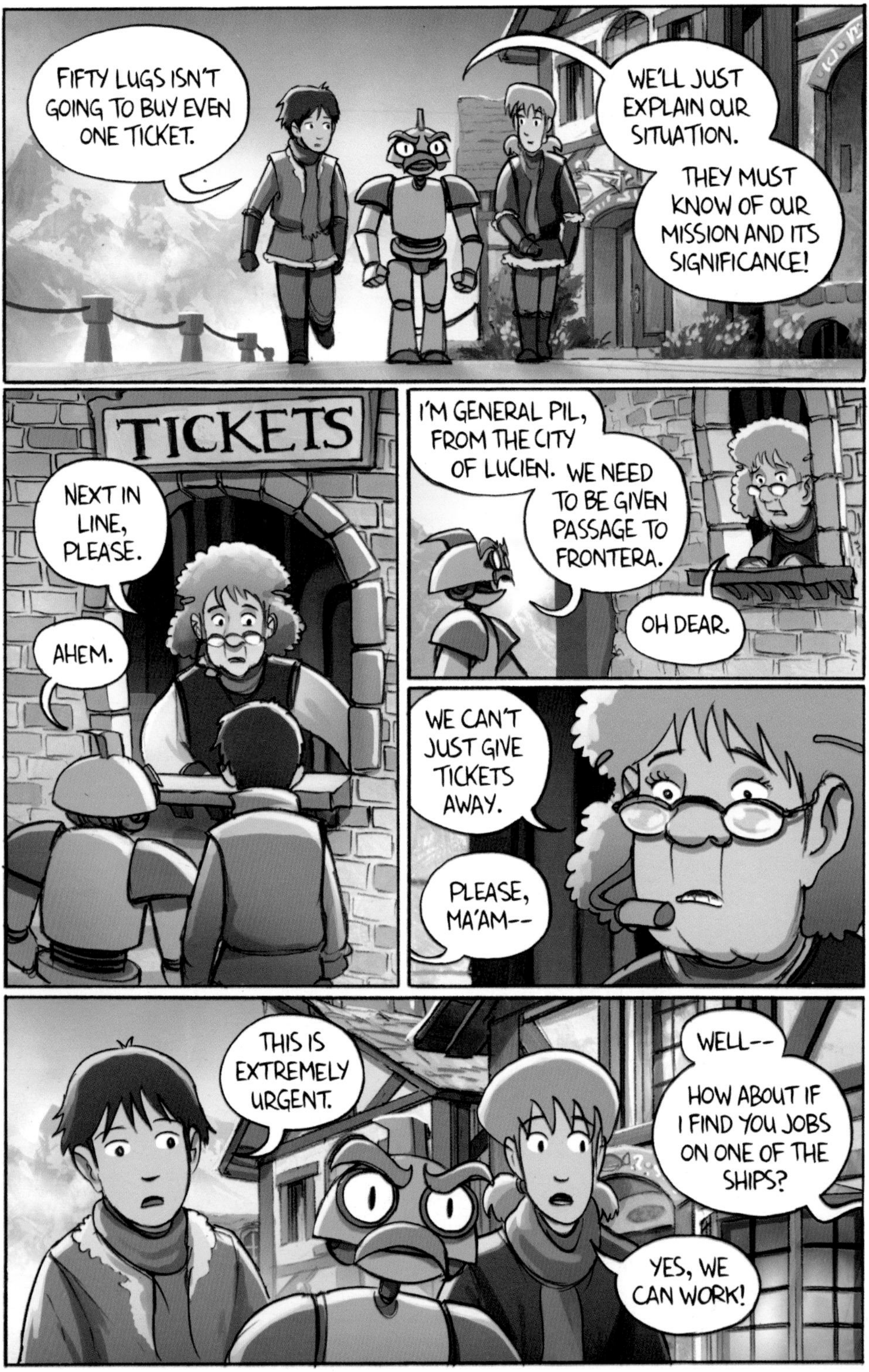
FIFTY LUGS ISN'T GOING TO BUY EVEN ONE TICKET.
WE'LL JUST EXPLAIN OUR SITUATION.
THEY MUST KNOW OF OUR MISSION AND ITS SIGNIFICANCE!
TICKETS
NEXT IN LINE, PLEASE.
AHEM.
I'M GENERAL PIL, FROM THE CITY OF LUCIEN. WE NEED TO BE GIVEN PASSAGE TO FRONTERA.
OH DEAR.
WE CAN'T JUST GIVE TICKETS AWAY.
PLEASE, MA'AM--
THIS IS EXTREMELY URGENT.
WELL--
HOW ABOUT IF I FIND YOU JOBS ON ONE OF THE SHIPS?
YES, WE CAN WORK!

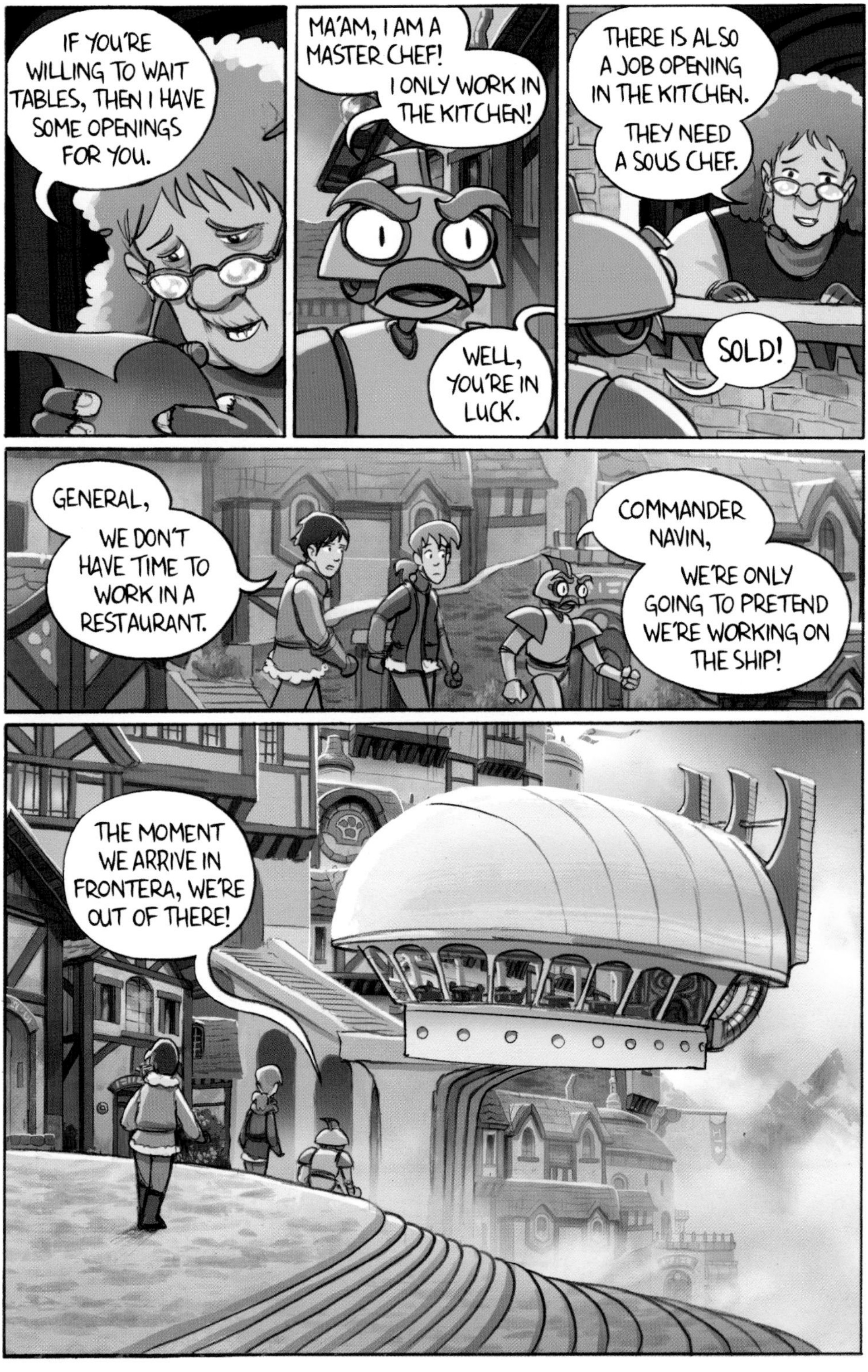
IF YOU'RE WILLING TO WAIT TABLES, THEN I HAVE SOME OPENINGS FOR YOU.
MA'AM, I AM A MASTER CHEF!
I ONLY WORK IN THE KITCHEN!
WELL, YOU'RE IN LUCK.
THERE IS ALSO A JOB OPENING IN THE KITCHEN.
THEY NEED A SOUS CHEF.
SOLD!
GENERAL,
WE DON'T HAVE TIME TO WORK IN A RESTAURANT.
COMMANDER NAVIN,
WE'RE ONLY GOING TO PRETEND WE'RE WORKING ON THE SHIP!
THE MOMENT WE ARRIVE IN FRONTERA, WE'RE OUT OF THERE!

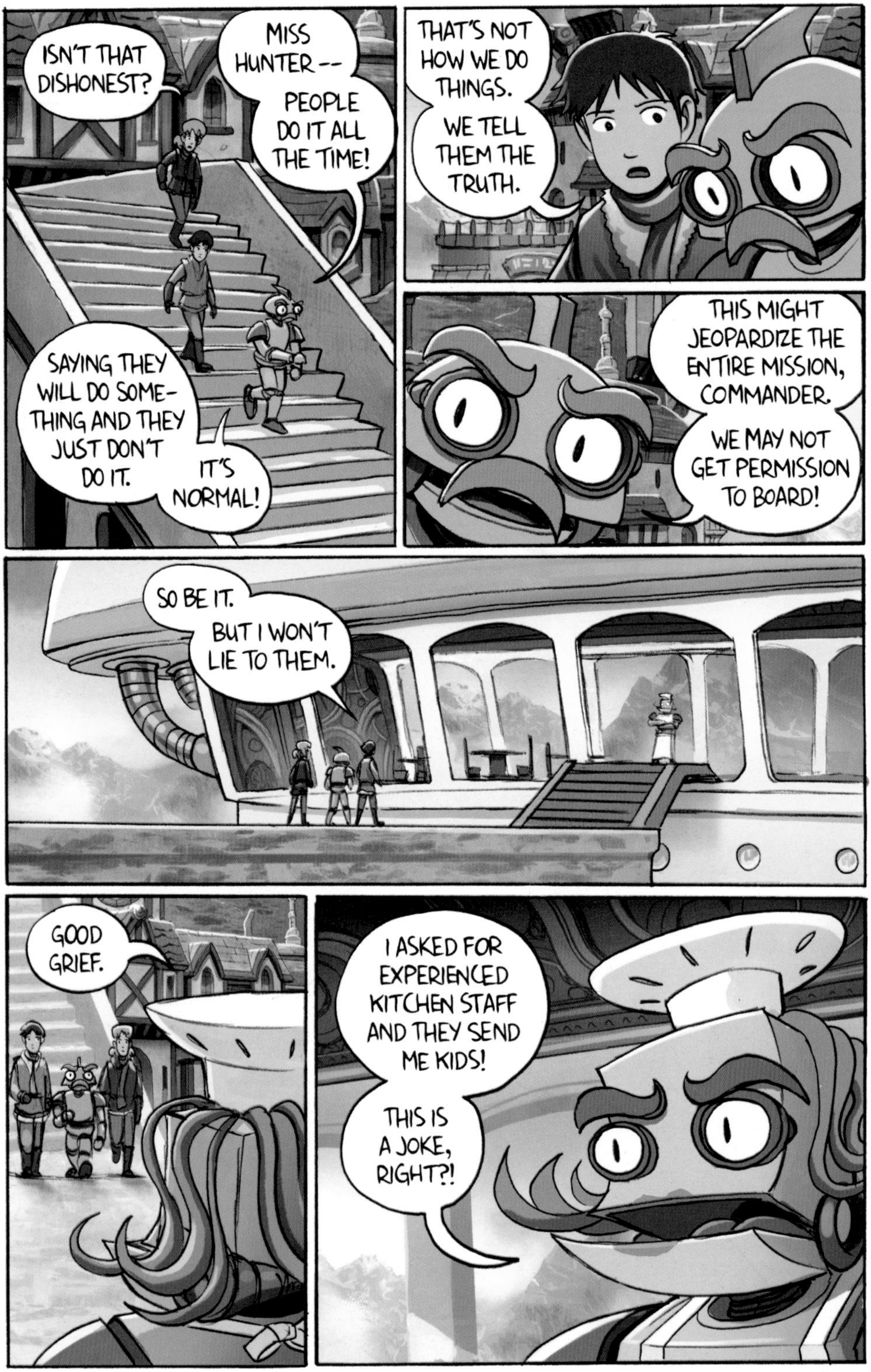
ISN'T THAT DISHONEST?
MISS HUNTER --
PEOPLE DO IT ALL THE TIME!
SAYING THEY WILL DO SOME-THING AND THEY JUST DON'T DO IT.
IT'S NORMAL!
THAT'S NOT HOW WE DO THINGS.
WE TELL THEM THE TRUTH.
THIS MIGHT JEOPARDIZE THE ENTIRE MISSION, COMMANDER.
WE MAY NOT GET PERMISSION TO BOARD!
SO BE IT.
BUT I WON'T LIE TO THEM.
GOOD GRIEF.
I ASKED FOR EXPERIENCED KITCHEN STAFF AND THEY SEND ME KIDS!
THIS IS A JOKE, RIGHT?!

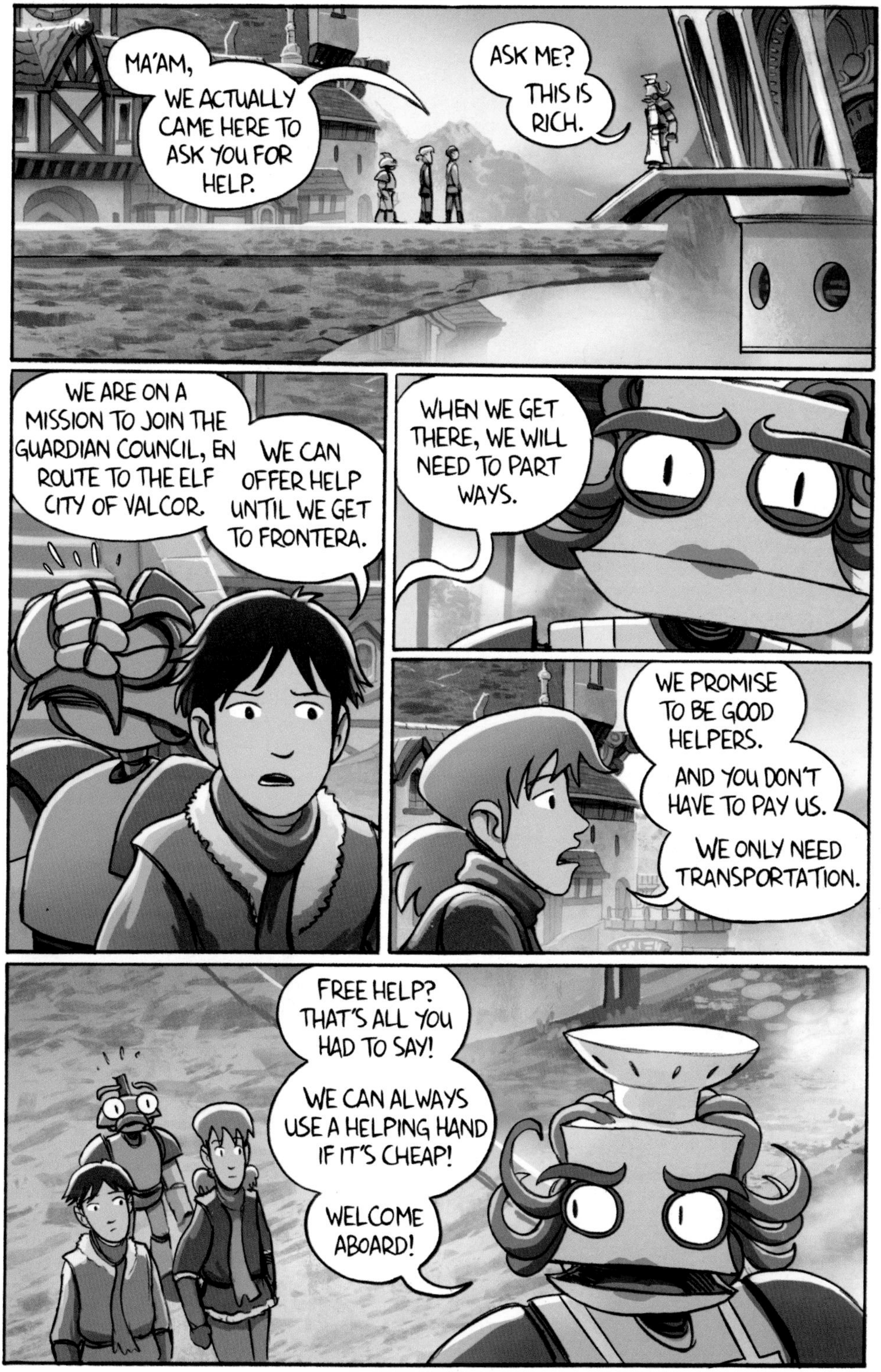
MA'AM,
WE ACTUALLY CAME HERE TO ASK YOU FOR HELP.
ASK ME?
THIS IS RICH.
WE ARE ON A MISSION TO JOIN THE GUARDIAN COUNCIL, EN ROUTE TO THE ELF CITY OF VALCOR.
WE CAN OFFER HELP UNTIL WE GET TO FRONTERA.
WHEN WE GET THERE, WE WILL NEED TO PART WAYS.
WE PROMISE TO BE GOOD HELPERS.
AND YOU DON'T HAVE TO PAY US.
WE ONLY NEED TRANSPORTATION.
FREE HELP? THAT'S ALL YOU HAD TO SAY!
WE CAN ALWAYS USE A HELPING HAND IF IT'S CHEAP!
WELCOME ABOARD!

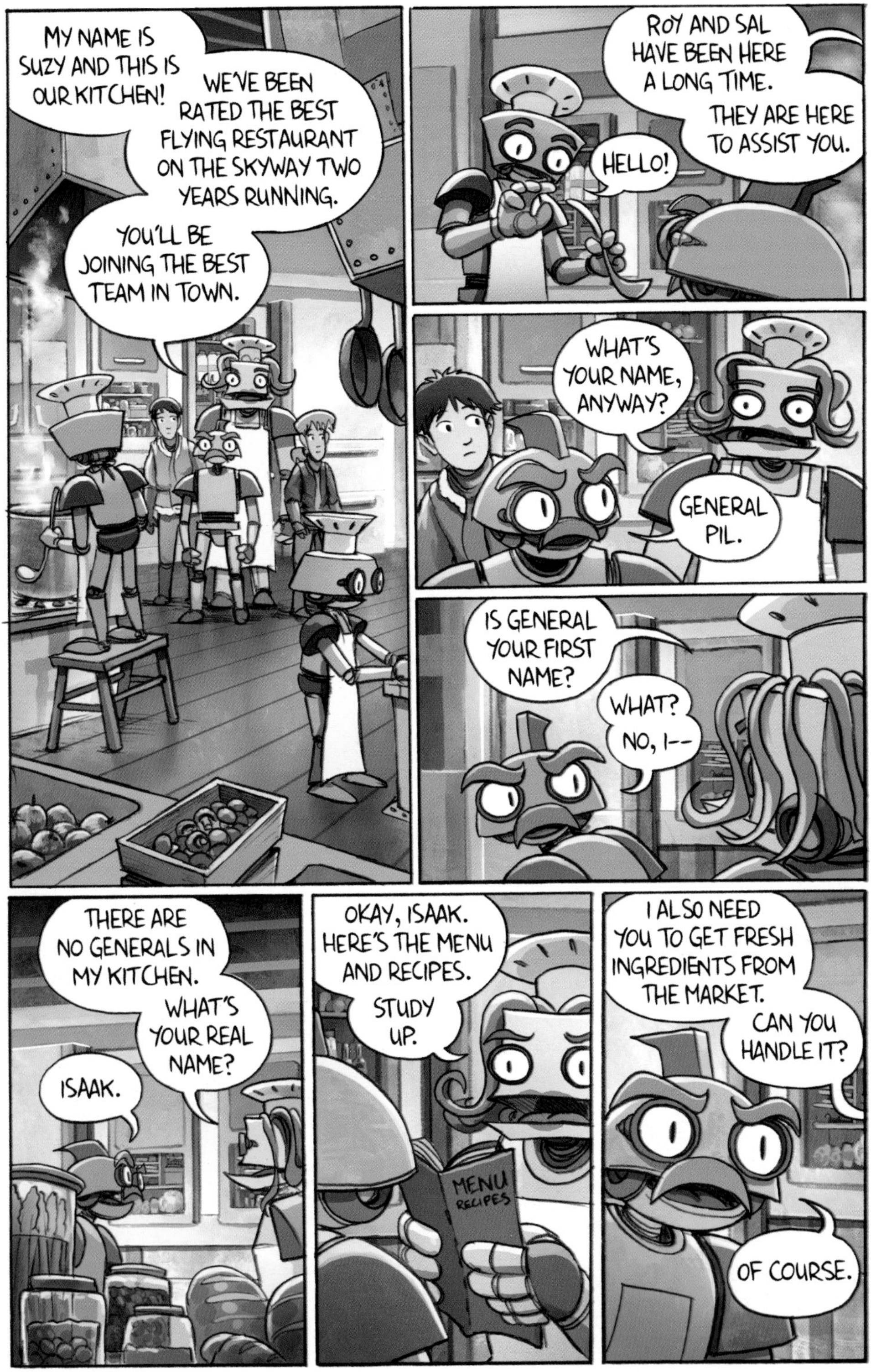
MY NAME IS SUZY AND THIS IS OUR KITCHEN!
WE'VE BEEN RATED THE BEST FLYING RESTAURANT ON THE SKYWAY TWO YEARS RUNNING.
YOU'LL BE JOINING THE BEST TEAM IN TOWN.
ROY AND SAL HAVE BEEN HERE A LONG TIME.
THEY ARE HERE TO ASSIST YOU.
HELLO!
WHAT'S YOUR NAME, ANYWAY?
GENERAL PIL.
IS GENERAL YOUR FIRST NAME?
WHAT? NO, I--
THERE ARE NO GENERALS IN MY KITCHEN.
WHAT'S YOUR REAL NAME?
ISAAK.
OKAY, ISAAK. HERE'S THE MENU AND RECIPES.
STUDY UP.
MENU RECIPES
I ALSO NEED YOU TO GET FRESH INGREDIENTS FROM THE MARKET.
CAN YOU HANDLE IT?
OF COURSE.

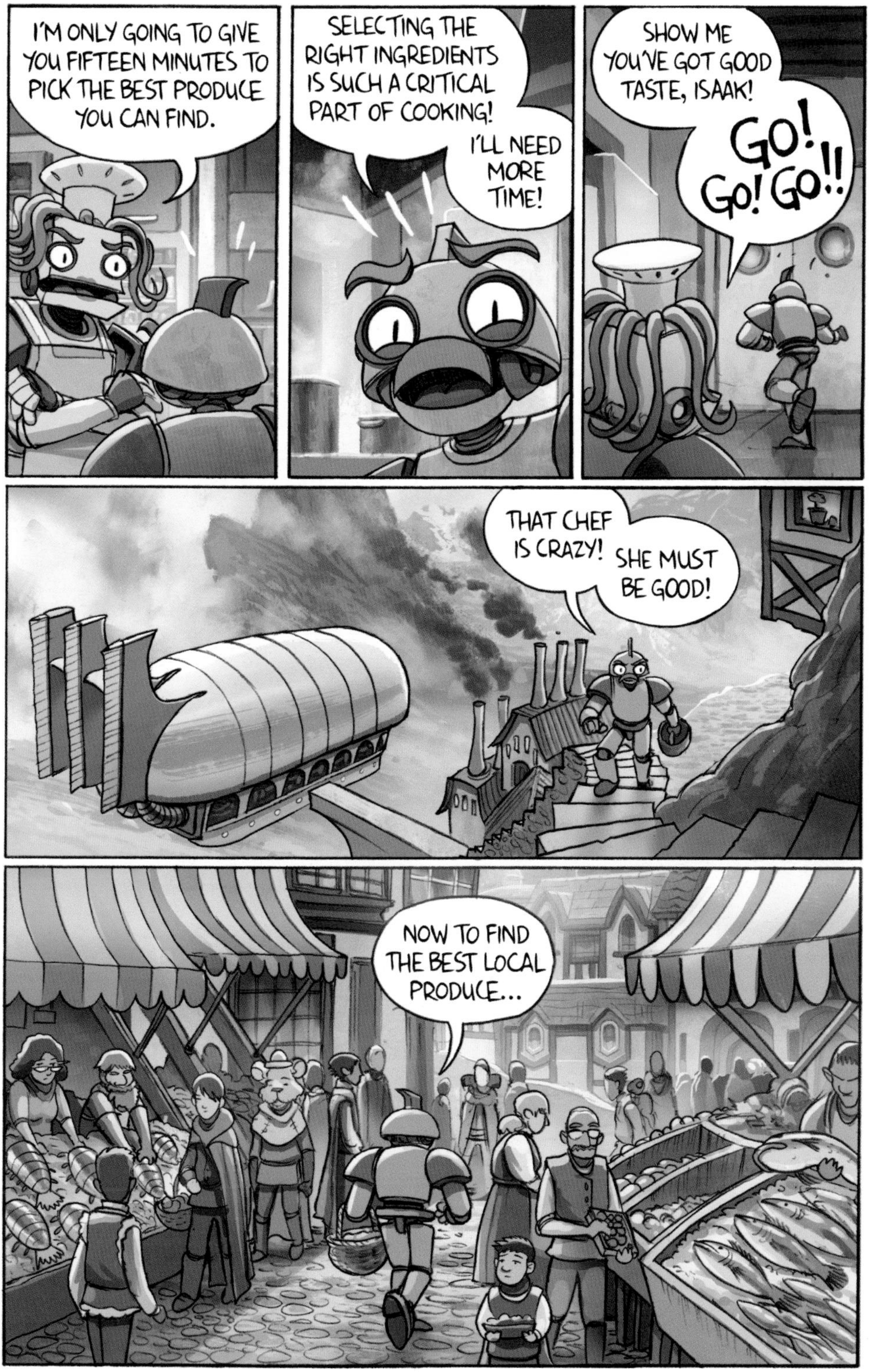
I'M ONLY GOING TO GIVE YOU FIFTEEN MINUTES TO PICK THE BEST PRODUCE YOU CAN FIND.
SELECTING THE RIGHT INGREDIENTS IS SUCH A CRITICAL PART OF COOKING!
I'LL NEED MORE TIME!
SHOW ME YOU'VE GOT GOOD TASTE, ISAAK!
GO! GO! GO!!
THAT CHEF IS CRAZY!
SHE MUST BE GOOD!
NOW TO FIND THE BEST LOCAL PRODUCE...

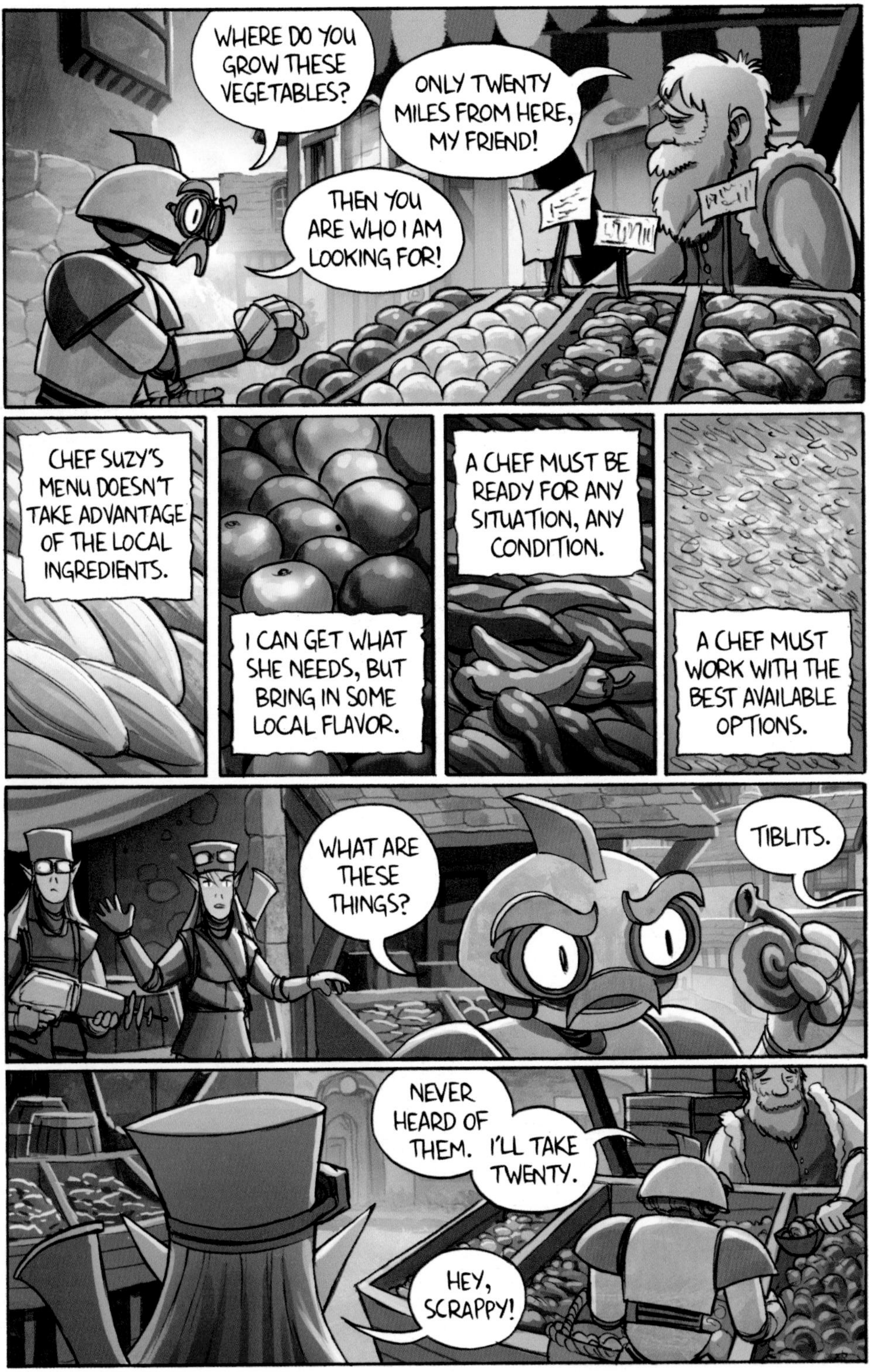
WHERE DO YOU GROW THESE VEGETABLES?
ONLY TWENTY MILES FROM HERE, MY FRIEND!
THEN YOU ARE WHO I AM LOOKING FOR!
CHEF SUZY'S MENU DOESN'T TAKE ADVANTAGE OF THE LOCAL INGREDIENTS.
I CAN GET WHAT SHE NEEDS, BUT BRING IN SOME LOCAL FLAVOR.
A CHEF MUST BE READY FOR ANY SITUATION, ANY CONDITION.
A CHEF MUST WORK WITH THE BEST AVAILABLE OPTIONS.
WHAT ARE THESE THINGS?
TIBLITS.
NEVER HEARD OF THEM.
I'LL TAKE TWENTY.
HEY, SCRAPPY!

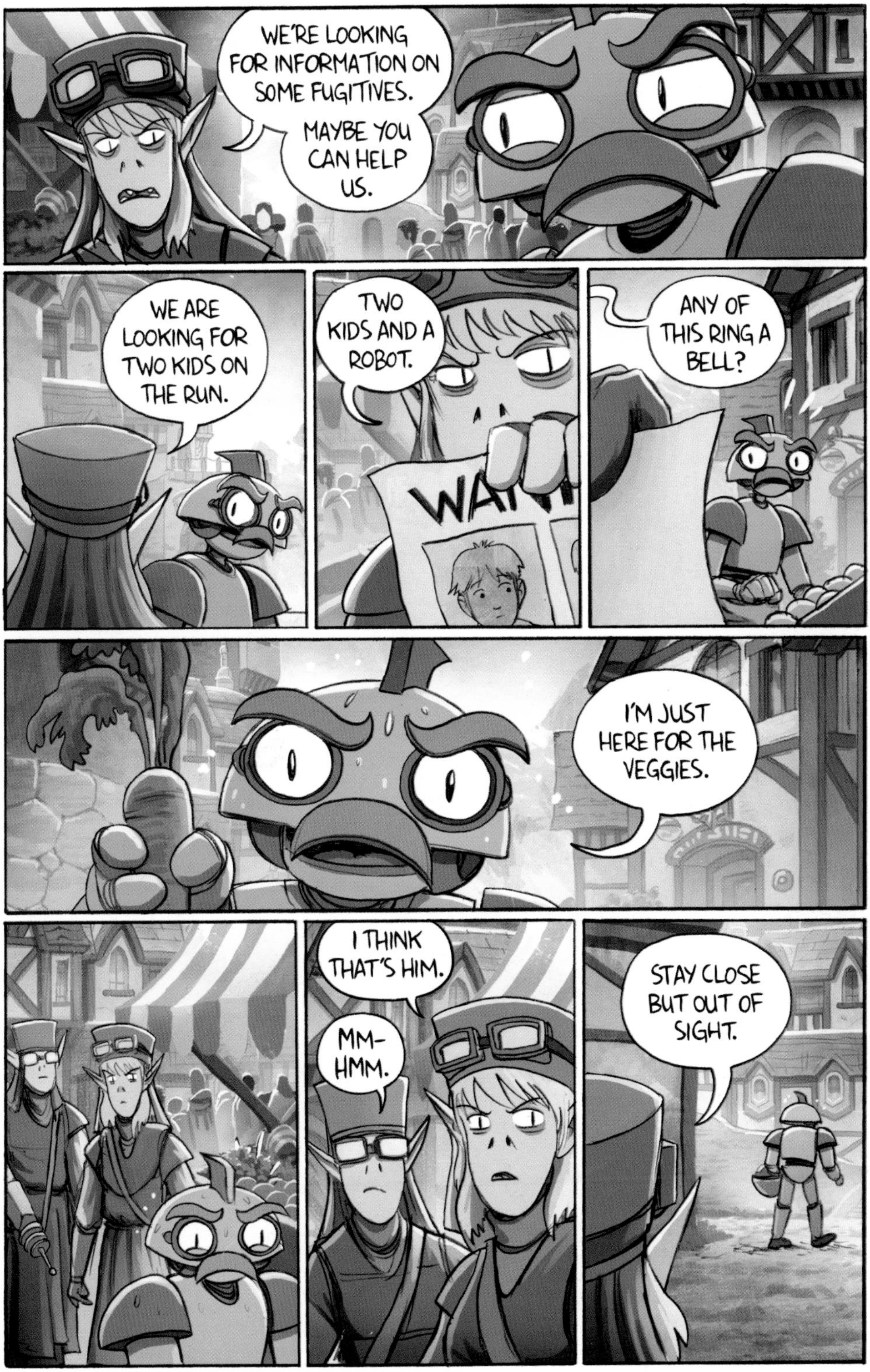
WE'RE LOOKING FOR INFORMATION ON SOME FUGITIVES.
MAYBE YOU CAN HELP US.
WE ARE LOOKING FOR TWO KIDS ON THE RUN.
TWO KIDS AND A ROBOT.
WAN
ANY OF THIS RING A BELL?
I'M JUST HERE FOR THE VEGGIES.
I THINK THAT'S HIM.
MM-HMM.
STAY CLOSE BUT OUT OF SIGHT.

ARE ALL THOSE PEOPLE LINING UP FOR DINNER?

YOU'RE NOT EVEN OPEN YET!

THAT'S RIGHT.

WE DON'T TAKE RESERVATIONS, SO THEY LINE UP EARLY IF THEY WANT A TABLE.

PEOPLE TRAVEL FROM ALL OVER THE WORLD FOR A MEAL HERE.

THAT'S AMAZING.

IT WASN'T ALWAYS LIKE THIS.

WE HAVE MANY CUSTOMERS NOW, BUT IT TOOK YEARS FOR THIS RESTAURANT TO GET TO A POINT WHERE I COULD SAY IT WAS WORKING OUT ALL RIGHT.

HOW LONG AGO DID YOU START WORKING AS A CHEF?

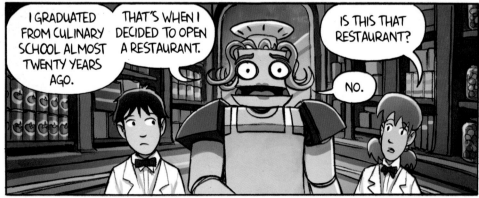

I GRADUATED FROM CULINARY SCHOOL ALMOST TWENTY YEARS AGO.

THAT'S WHEN I DECIDED TO OPEN A RESTAURANT.

IS THIS THAT RESTAURANT?

NO.

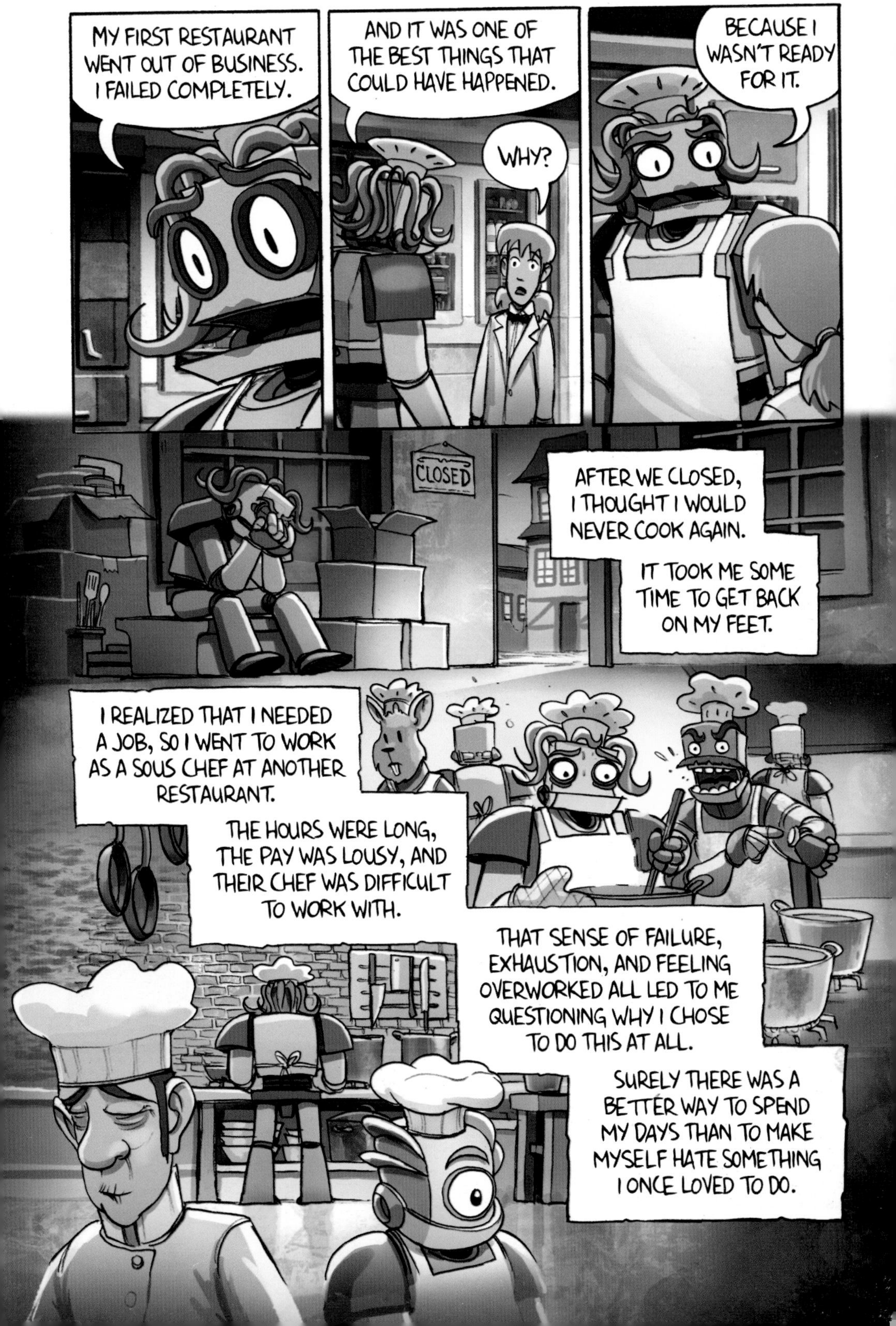
MY FIRST RESTAURANT WENT OUT OF BUSINESS. I FAILED COMPLETELY.
AND IT WAS ONE OF THE BEST THINGS THAT COULD HAVE HAPPENED.
WHY?
BECAUSE I WASN'T READY FOR IT.
CLOSED
AFTER WE CLOSED, I THOUGHT I WOULD NEVER COOK AGAIN.
IT TOOK ME SOME TIME TO GET BACK ON MY FEET.
I REALIZED THAT I NEEDED A JOB, SO I WENT TO WORK AS A SOUS CHEF AT ANOTHER RESTAURANT.
THE HOURS WERE LONG, THE PAY WAS LOUSY, AND THEIR CHEF WAS DIFFICULT TO WORK WITH.
THAT SENSE OF FAILURE, EXHAUSTION, AND FEELING OVERWORKED ALL LED TO ME QUESTIONING WHY I CHOSE TO DO THIS AT ALL.
SURELY THERE WAS A BETTER WAY TO SPEND MY DAYS THAN TO MAKE MYSELF HATE SOMETHING I ONCE LOVED TO DO.

WHILE I WORKED I SPENT A LOT OF TIME THINKING ABOUT WHY I DECIDED TO BE A CHEF.

WHY DID I DEDICATE SO MUCH OF MY LIFE TO THIS?

I USED TO THINK IT WAS FOR SUCCESS OR RECOGNITION, BUT I DIDN'T CARE ABOUT THOSE THINGS ANYMORE.

AND THEN ONE EVENING, WHILE PREPARING FOR A BUSY NIGHT AT WORK, I REALIZED WHAT IT WAS AND ALWAYS HAS BEEN.

IT'S FAMILY.

FAMILY?

THE REASON I'VE BEEN DOING THIS ALL ALONG.

TO NURTURE, TO CONNECT, TO FEED FAMILIES.

EVEN INSIDE THE KITCHEN.

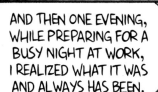

AS A CHILD, I BEGAN COOKING TO FEED MY BROTHERS AND SISTERS.

EVEN MY PARENTS AND GRANDPARENTS.

AND I'VE BEEN DOING IT EVER SINCE.

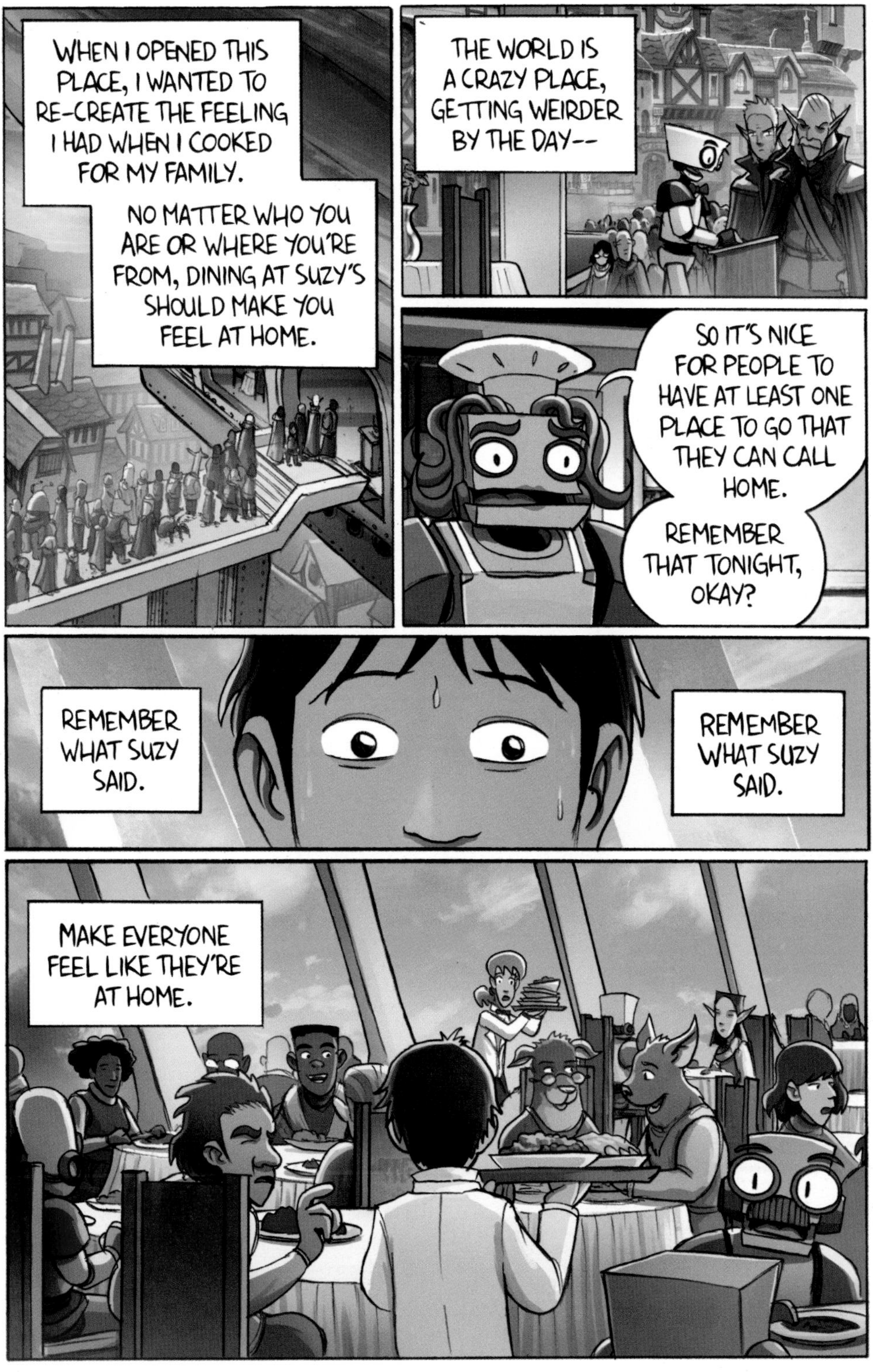
WHEN I OPENED THIS PLACE, I WANTED TO RE-CREATE THE FEELING I HAD WHEN I COOKED FOR MY FAMILY.
NO MATTER WHO YOU ARE OR WHERE YOU'RE FROM, DINING AT SUZY'S SHOULD MAKE YOU FEEL AT HOME.
THE WORLD IS A CRAZY PLACE, GETTING WEIRDER BY THE DAY--
SO IT'S NICE FOR PEOPLE TO HAVE AT LEAST ONE PLACE TO GO THAT THEY CAN CALL HOME.
REMEMBER THAT TONIGHT, OKAY?
REMEMBER WHAT SUZY SAID.
REMEMBER WHAT SUZY SAID.
MAKE EVERYONE FEEL LIKE THEY'RE AT HOME.

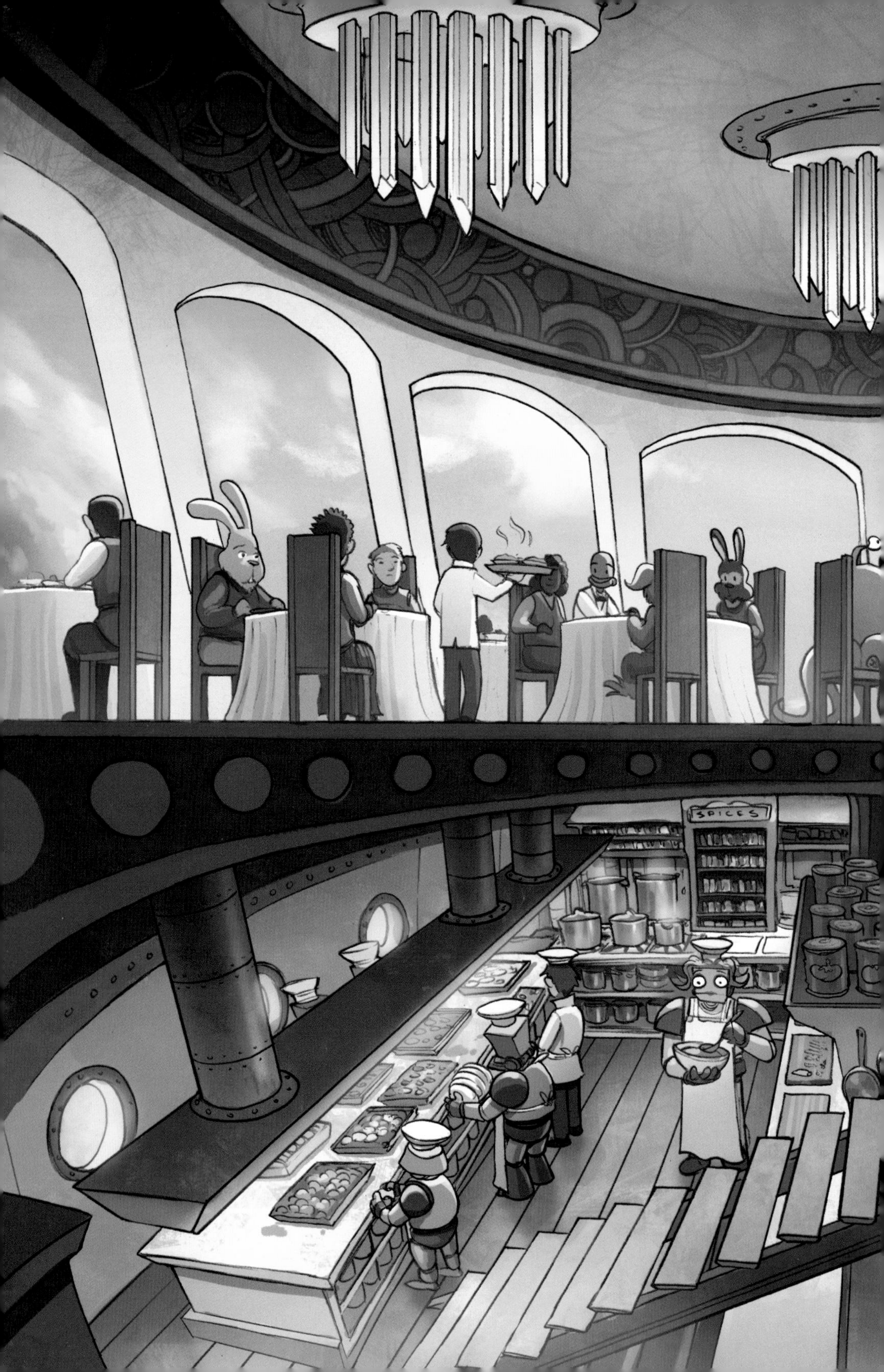
SPICES

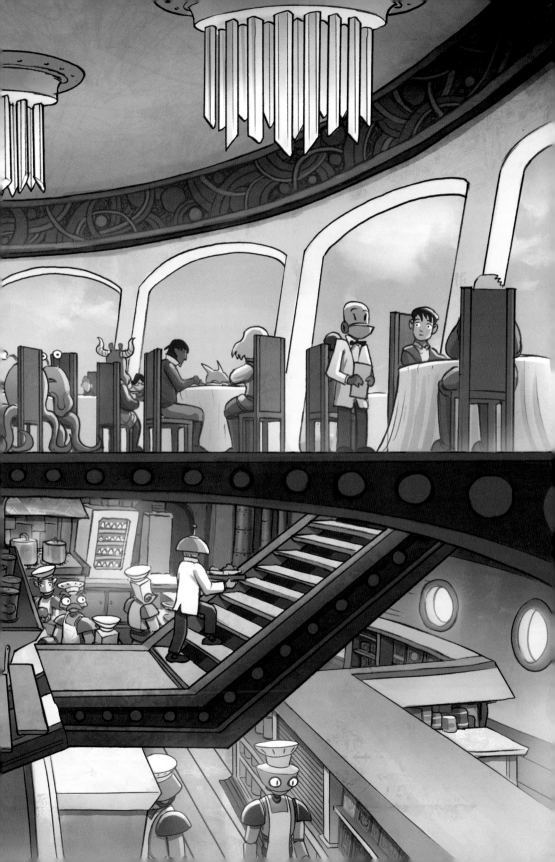

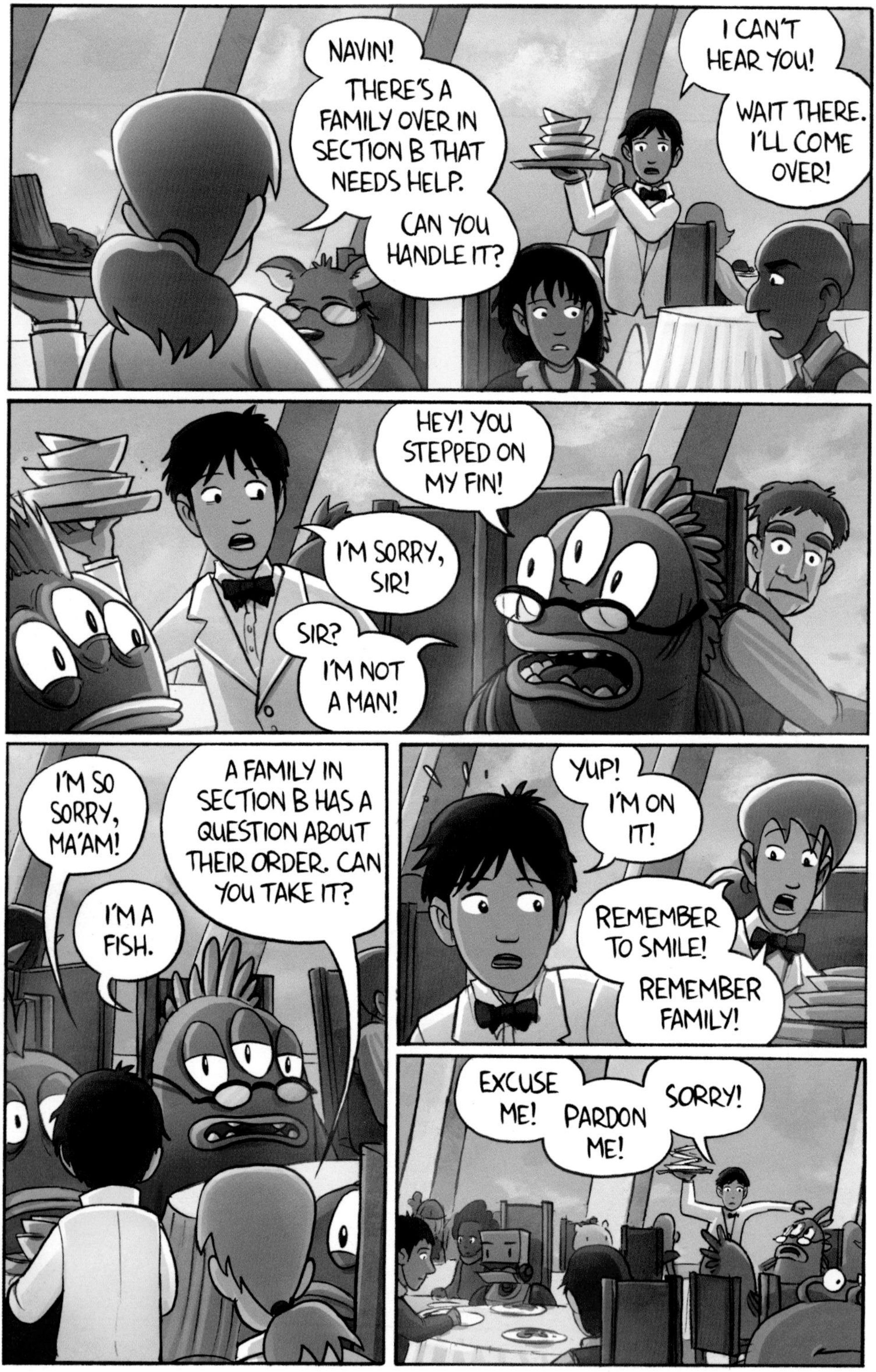
NAVIN!
THERE'S A FAMILY OVER IN SECTION B THAT NEEDS HELP.
CAN YOU HANDLE IT?
I CAN'T HEAR YOU!
WAIT THERE. I'LL COME OVER!
HEY! YOU STEPPED ON MY FIN!
I'M SORRY, SIR!
SIR?
I'M NOT A MAN!
I'M SO SORRY, MA'AM!
I'M A FISH.
A FAMILY IN SECTION B HAS A QUESTION ABOUT THEIR ORDER. CAN YOU TAKE IT?
YUP!
I'M ON IT!
REMEMBER TO SMILE!
REMEMBER FAMILY!
EXCUSE ME!
PARDON ME!
SORRY!

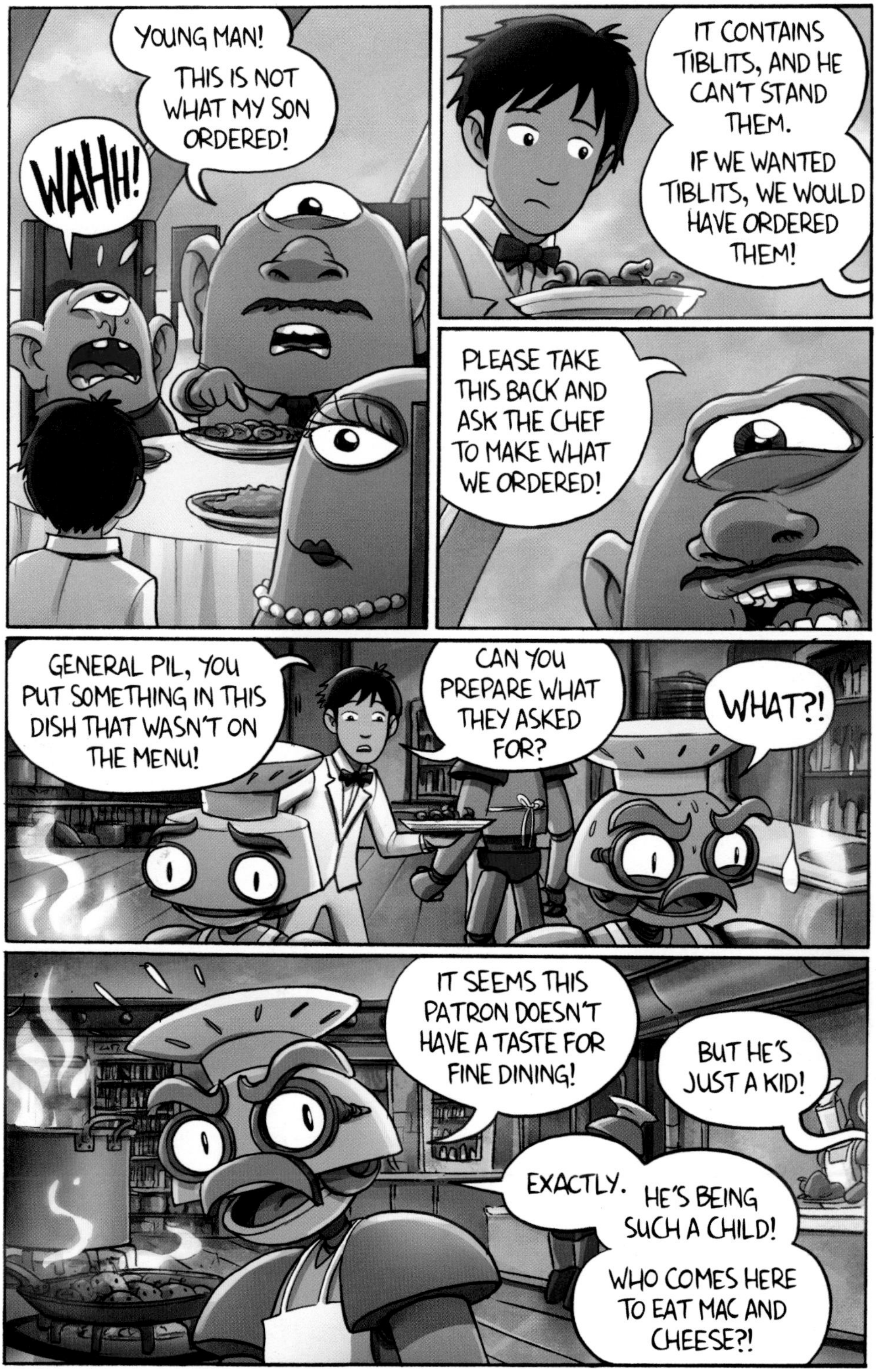
YOUNG MAN!
THIS IS NOT WHAT MY SON ORDERED!
WAHH!
IT CONTAINS TIBLITS, AND HE CAN'T STAND THEM.
IF WE WANTED TIBLITS, WE WOULD HAVE ORDERED THEM!
PLEASE TAKE THIS BACK AND ASK THE CHEF TO MAKE WHAT WE ORDERED!
GENERAL PIL, YOU PUT SOMETHING IN THIS DISH THAT WASN'T ON THE MENU!
CAN YOU PREPARE WHAT THEY ASKED FOR?
WHAT?!
IT SEEMS THIS PATRON DOESN'T HAVE A TASTE FOR FINE DINING!
BUT HE'S JUST A KID!
EXACTLY.
HE'S BEING SUCH A CHILD!
WHO COMES HERE TO EAT MAC AND CHEESE?!

HEY.

YOU ARE IN TERRIBLE DANGER HERE.

I DON'T KNOW WHO YOU THINK I AM, BUT--

CUT OUT THE BAD ACTING, COMMANDER.

I KNOW WHO YOU ARE.

AND I DON'T THINK I'M THE ONLY ONE HERE WHO DOES.

WANTED

WE NEED TO TALK.

MEET ME IN THE KITCHEN.

PSST! OVER HERE!

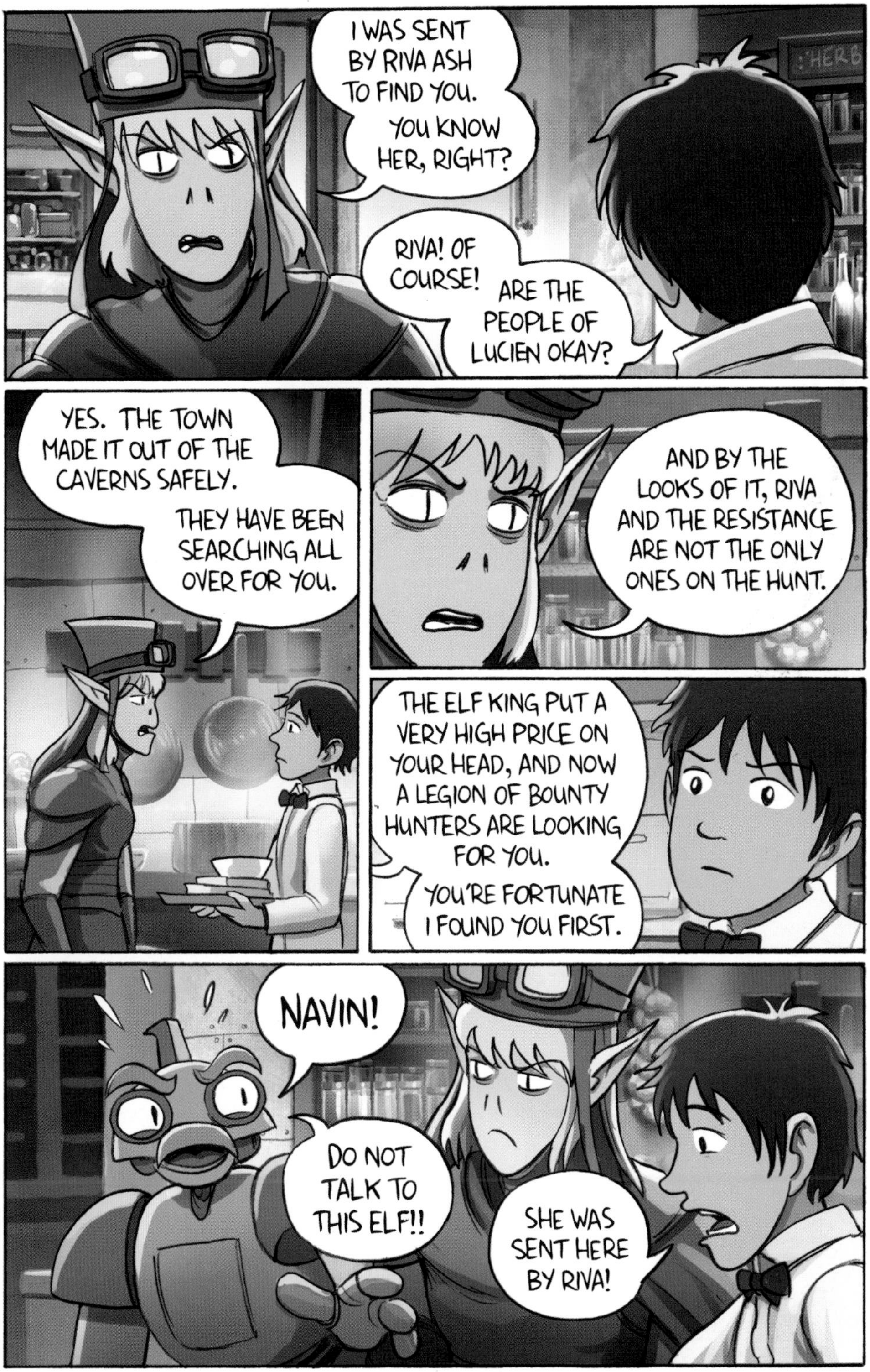

I WAS SENT BY RIVA ASH TO FIND YOU.
YOU KNOW HER, RIGHT?
RIVA! OF COURSE!
ARE THE PEOPLE OF LUCIEN OKAY?
YES. THE TOWN MADE IT OUT OF THE CAVERNS SAFELY.
THEY HAVE BEEN SEARCHING ALL OVER FOR YOU.
AND BY THE LOOKS OF IT, RIVA AND THE RESISTANCE ARE NOT THE ONLY ONES ON THE HUNT.
THE ELF KING PUT A VERY HIGH PRICE ON YOUR HEAD, AND NOW A LEGION OF BOUNTY HUNTERS ARE LOOKING FOR YOU.
YOU'RE FORTUNATE I FOUND YOU FIRST.
NAVIN!
DO NOT TALK TO THIS ELF!!
SHE WAS SENT HERE BY RIVA!

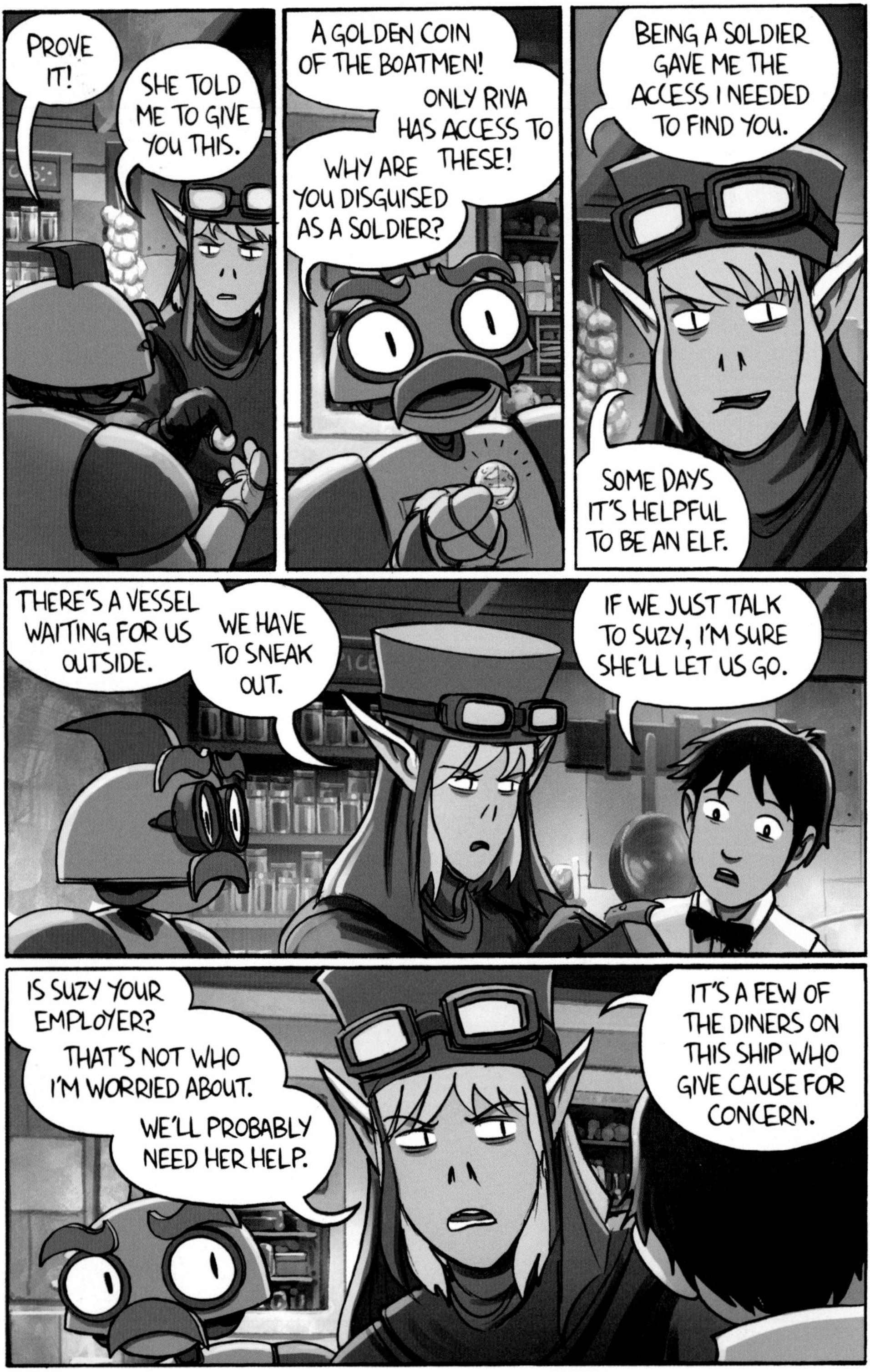

PROVE IT!
SHE TOLD ME TO GIVE YOU THIS.
A GOLDEN COIN OF THE BOATMEN!
ONLY RIVA HAS ACCESS TO THESE!
WHY ARE YOU DISGUISED AS A SOLDIER?
BEING A SOLDIER GAVE ME THE ACCESS I NEEDED TO FIND YOU.
SOME DAYS IT'S HELPFUL TO BE AN ELF.
THERE'S A VESSEL WAITING FOR US OUTSIDE.
WE HAVE TO SNEAK OUT.
IF WE JUST TALK TO SUZY, I'M SURE SHE'LL LET US GO.
IS SUZY YOUR EMPLOYER?
THAT'S NOT WHO I'M WORRIED ABOUT.
WE'LL PROBABLY NEED HER HELP.
IT'S A FEW OF THE DINERS ON THIS SHIP WHO GIVE CAUSE FOR CONCERN.

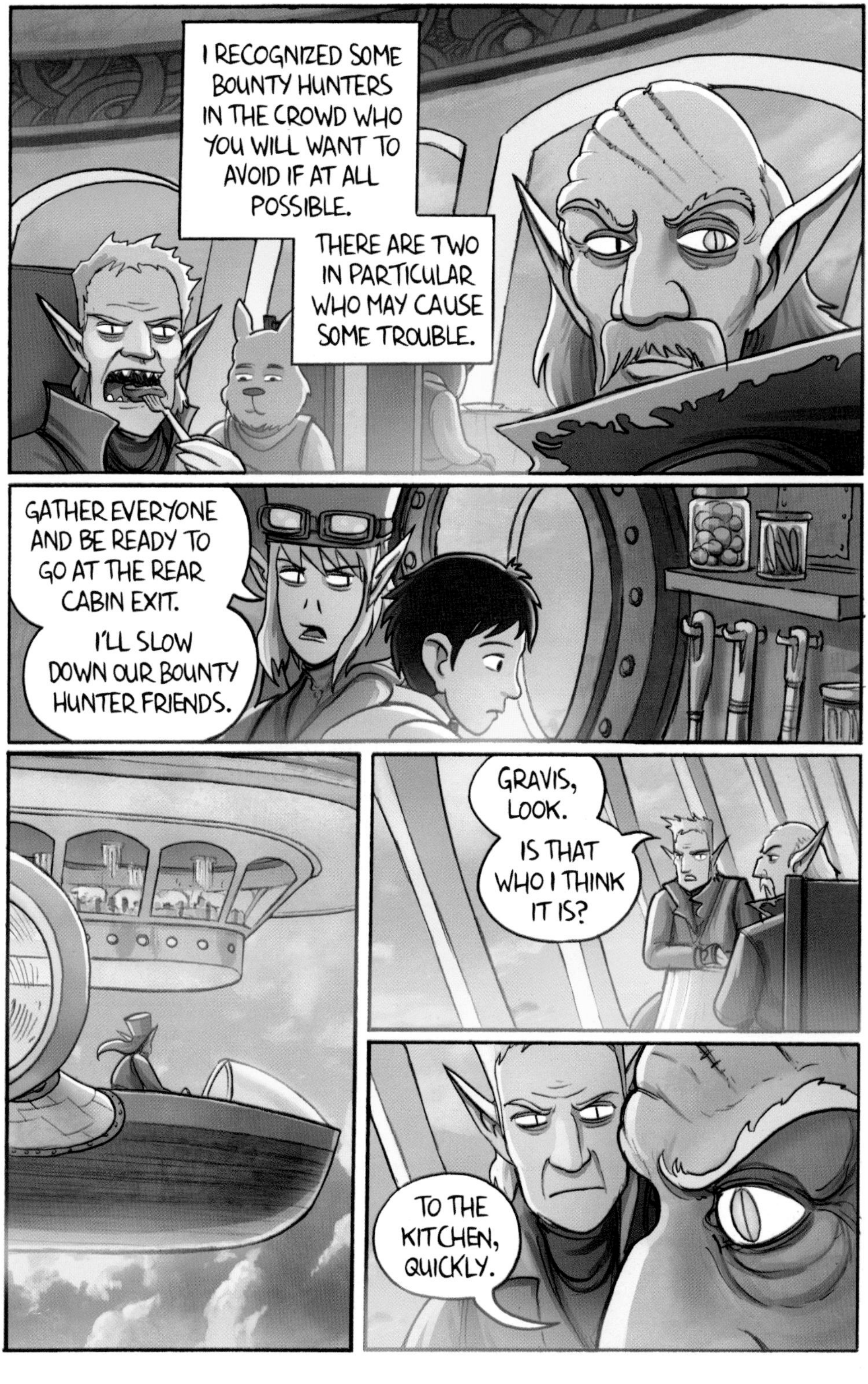
I RECOGNIZED SOME BOUNTY HUNTERS IN THE CROWD WHO YOU WILL WANT TO AVOID IF AT ALL POSSIBLE.
THERE ARE TWO IN PARTICULAR WHO MAY CAUSE SOME TROUBLE.
GATHER EVERYONE AND BE READY TO GO AT THE REAR CABIN EXIT.
I'LL SLOW DOWN OUR BOUNTY HUNTER FRIENDS.
GRAVIS, LOOK.
IS THAT WHO I THINK IT IS?
TO THE KITCHEN, QUICKLY.

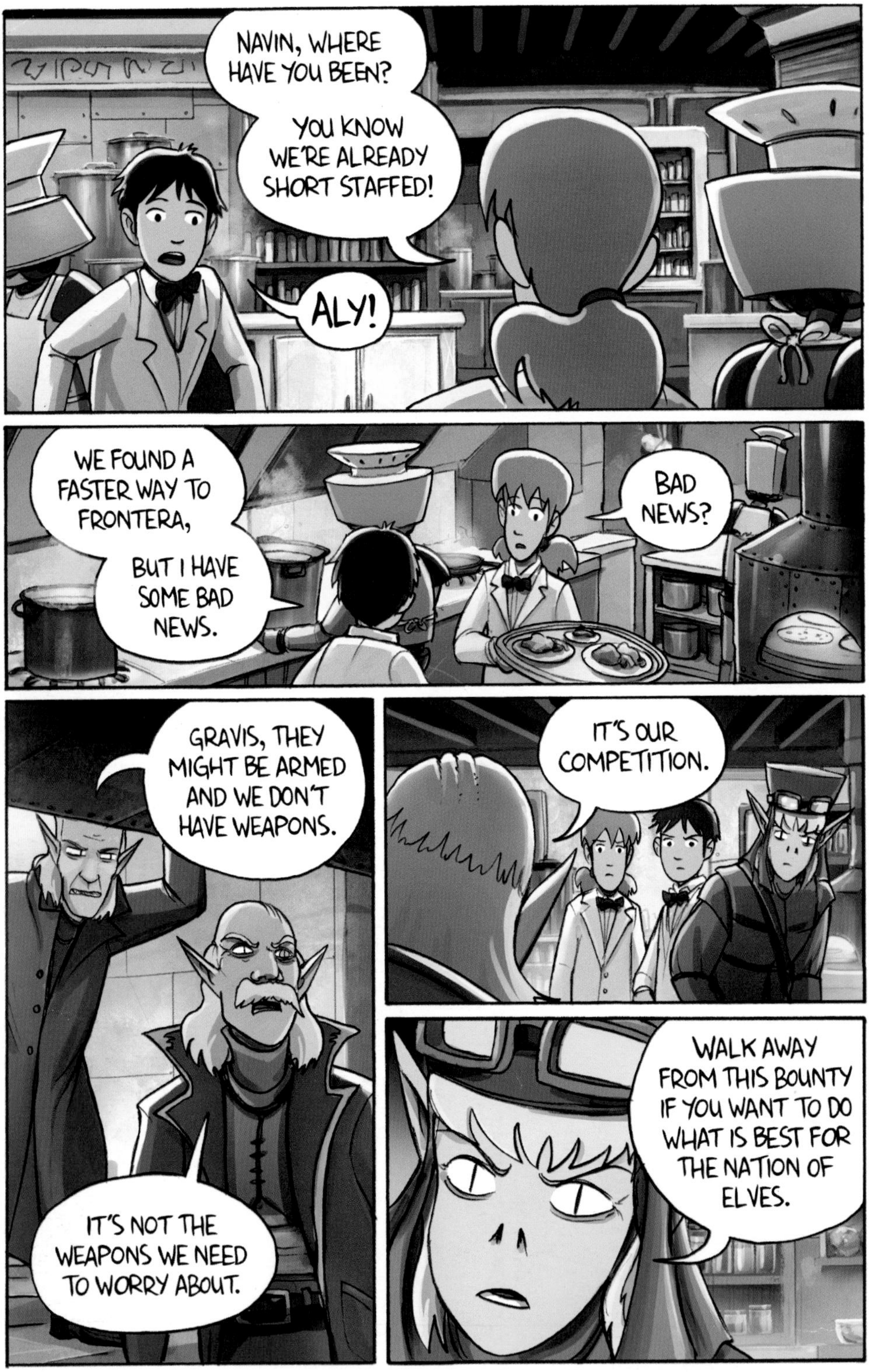
NAVIN, WHERE HAVE YOU BEEN?
YOU KNOW WE'RE ALREADY SHORT STAFFED!
ALY!
WE FOUND A FASTER WAY TO FRONTERA,
BUT I HAVE SOME BAD NEWS.
BAD NEWS?
GRAVIS, THEY MIGHT BE ARMED AND WE DON'T HAVE WEAPONS.
IT'S NOT THE WEAPONS WE NEED TO WORRY ABOUT.
IT'S OUR COMPETITION.
WALK AWAY FROM THIS BOUNTY IF YOU WANT TO DO WHAT IS BEST FOR THE NATION OF ELVES.

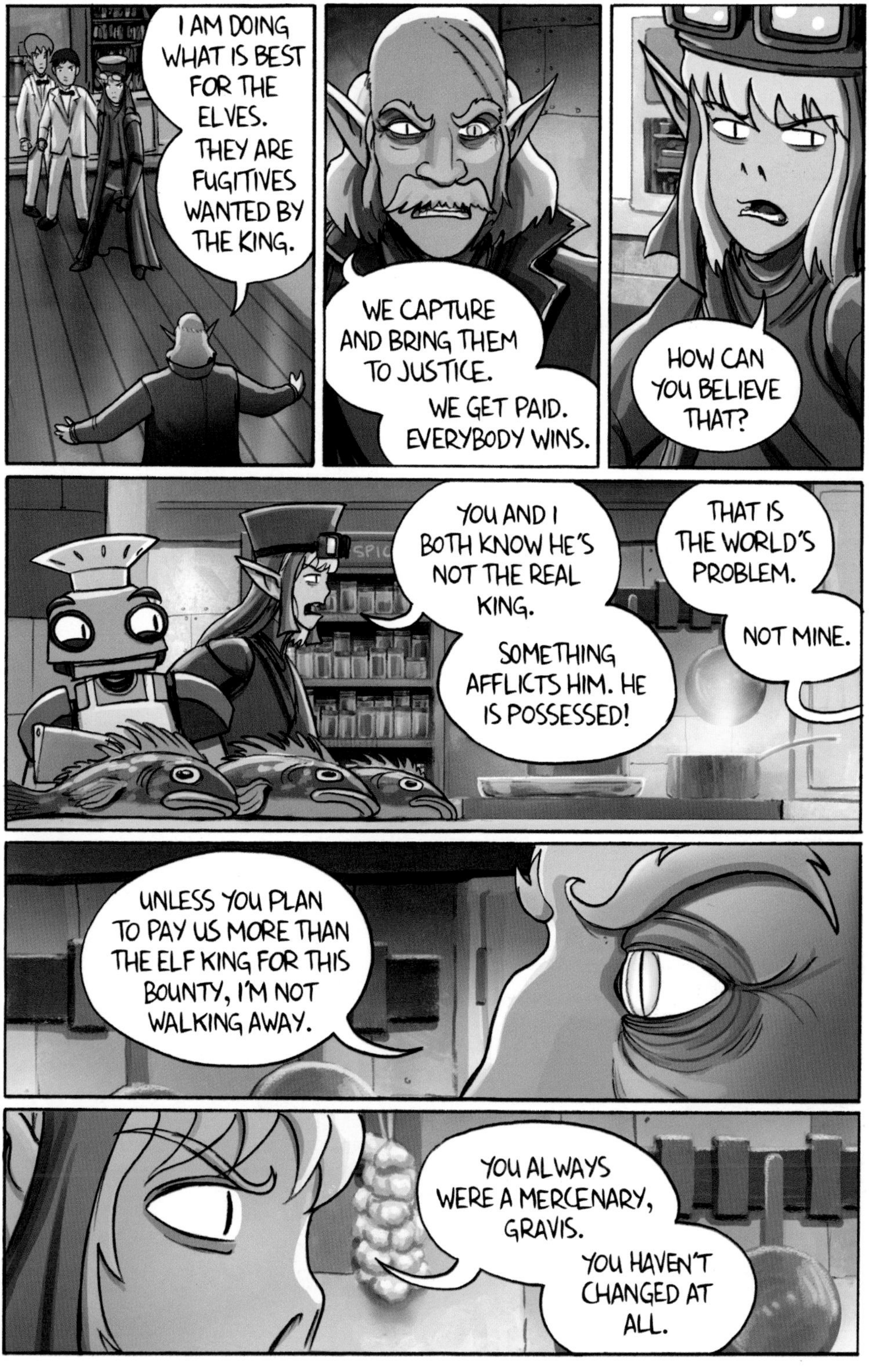
I AM DOING WHAT IS BEST FOR THE ELVES. THEY ARE FUGITIVES WANTED BY THE KING.
WE CAPTURE AND BRING THEM TO JUSTICE.
WE GET PAID. EVERYBODY WINS.
HOW CAN YOU BELIEVE THAT?
YOU AND I BOTH KNOW HE'S NOT THE REAL KING.
SOMETHING AFFLICTS HIM. HE IS POSSESSED!
THAT IS THE WORLD'S PROBLEM.
NOT MINE.
UNLESS YOU PLAN TO PAY US MORE THAN THE ELF KING FOR THIS BOUNTY, I'M NOT WALKING AWAY.
YOU ALWAYS WERE A MERCENARY, GRAVIS.
YOU HAVEN'T CHANGED AT ALL.

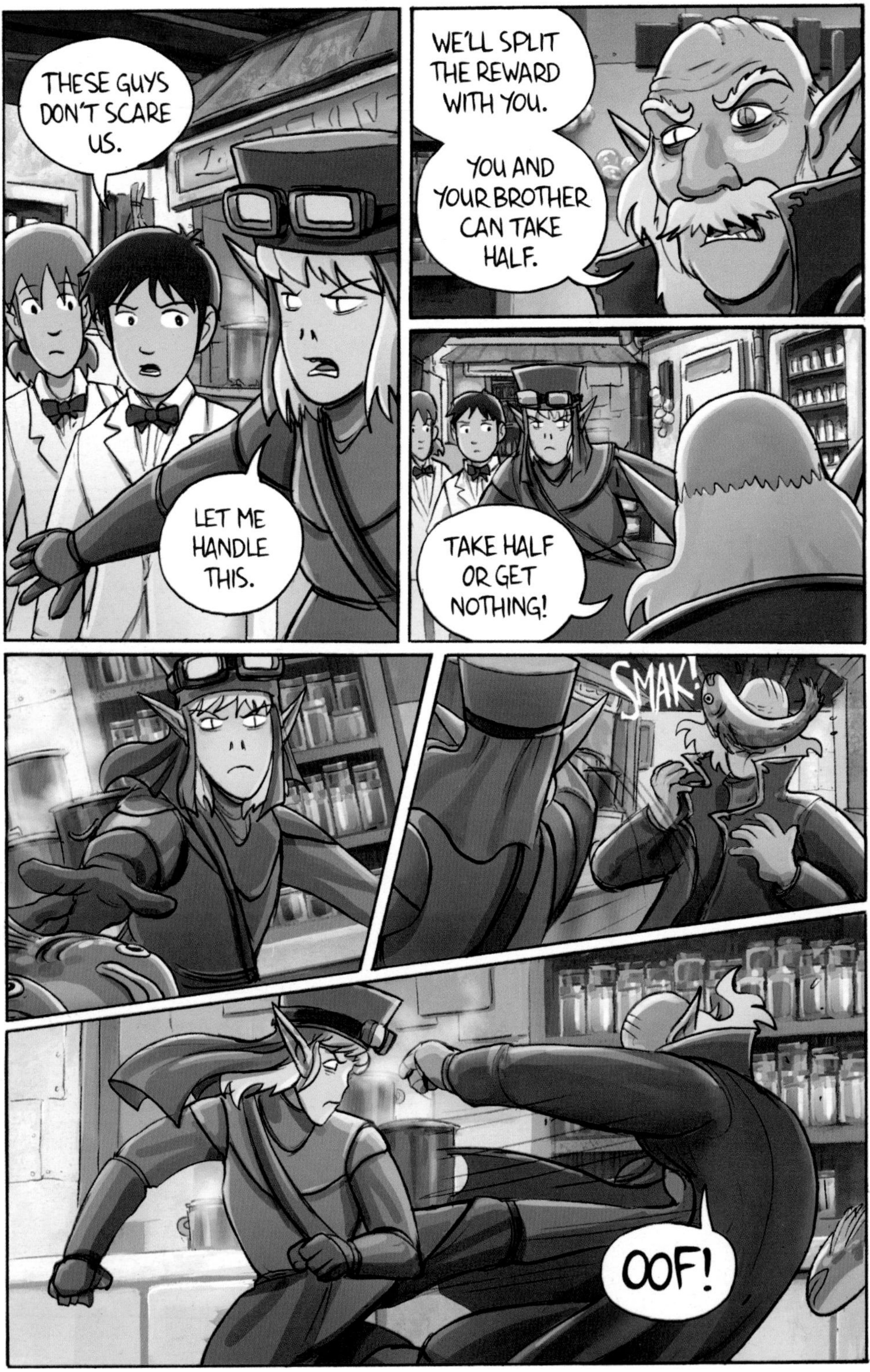
THESE GUYS DON'T SCARE US.
LET ME HANDLE THIS.
WE'LL SPLIT THE REWARD WITH YOU.
YOU AND YOUR BROTHER CAN TAKE HALF.
TAKE HALF OR GET NOTHING!
SMAK!
OOF!

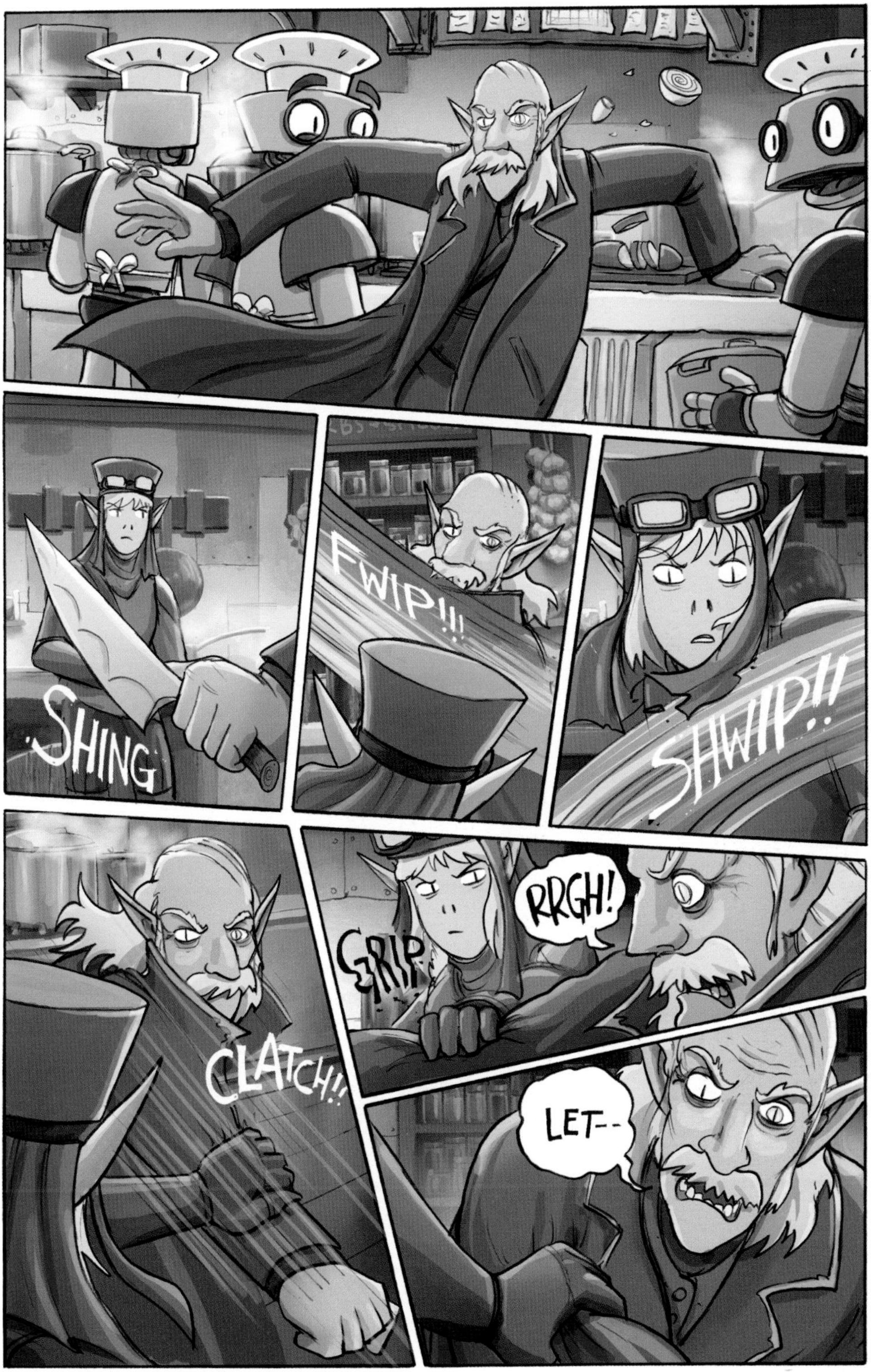
SHING
FWIP!!!
SHWIP!!
CLATCH!!
GRIP
RRGH!
LET--

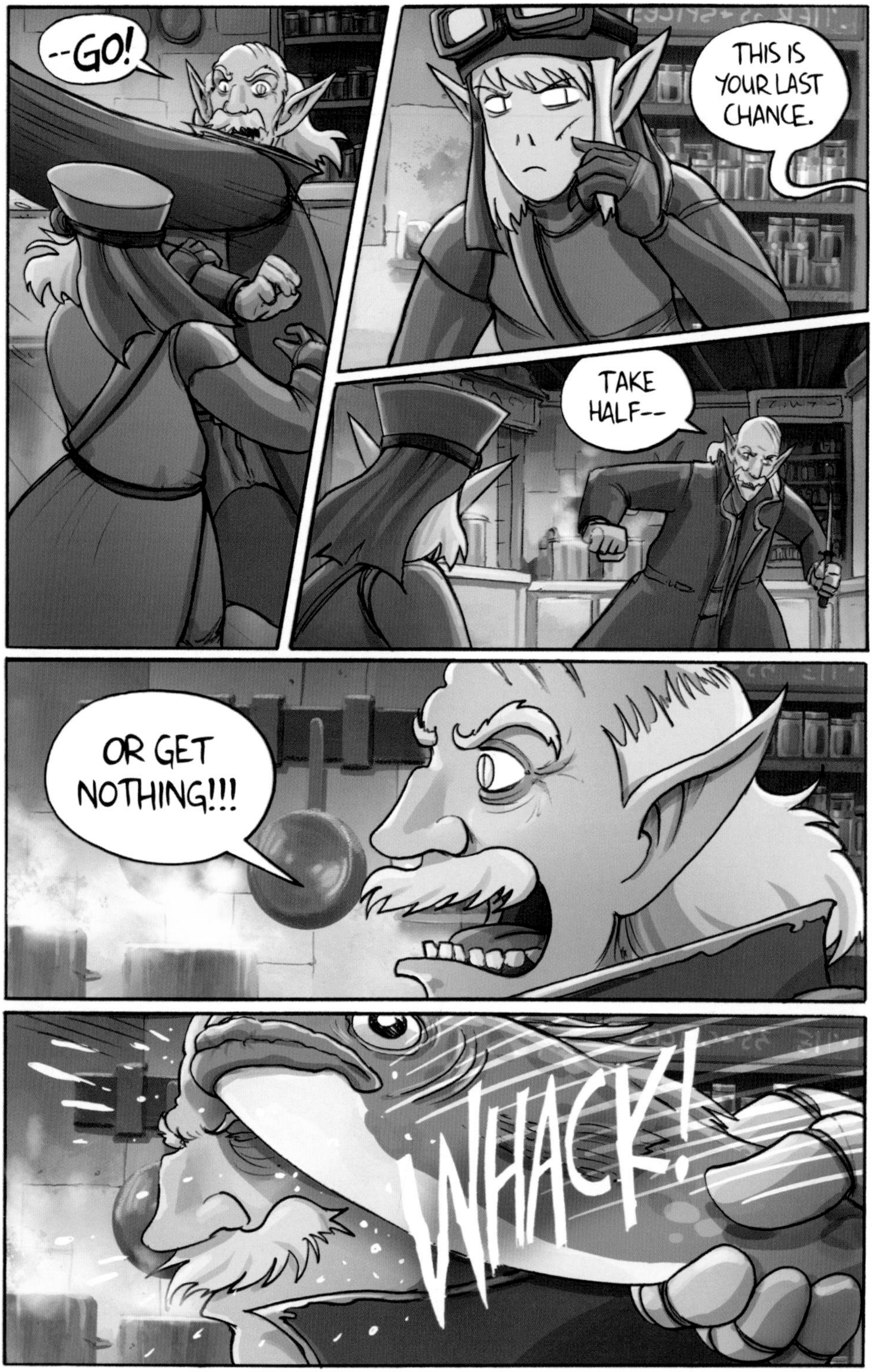
--GO!
THIS IS YOUR LAST CHANCE.
TAKE HALF--
OR GET NOTHING!!!
WHACK!

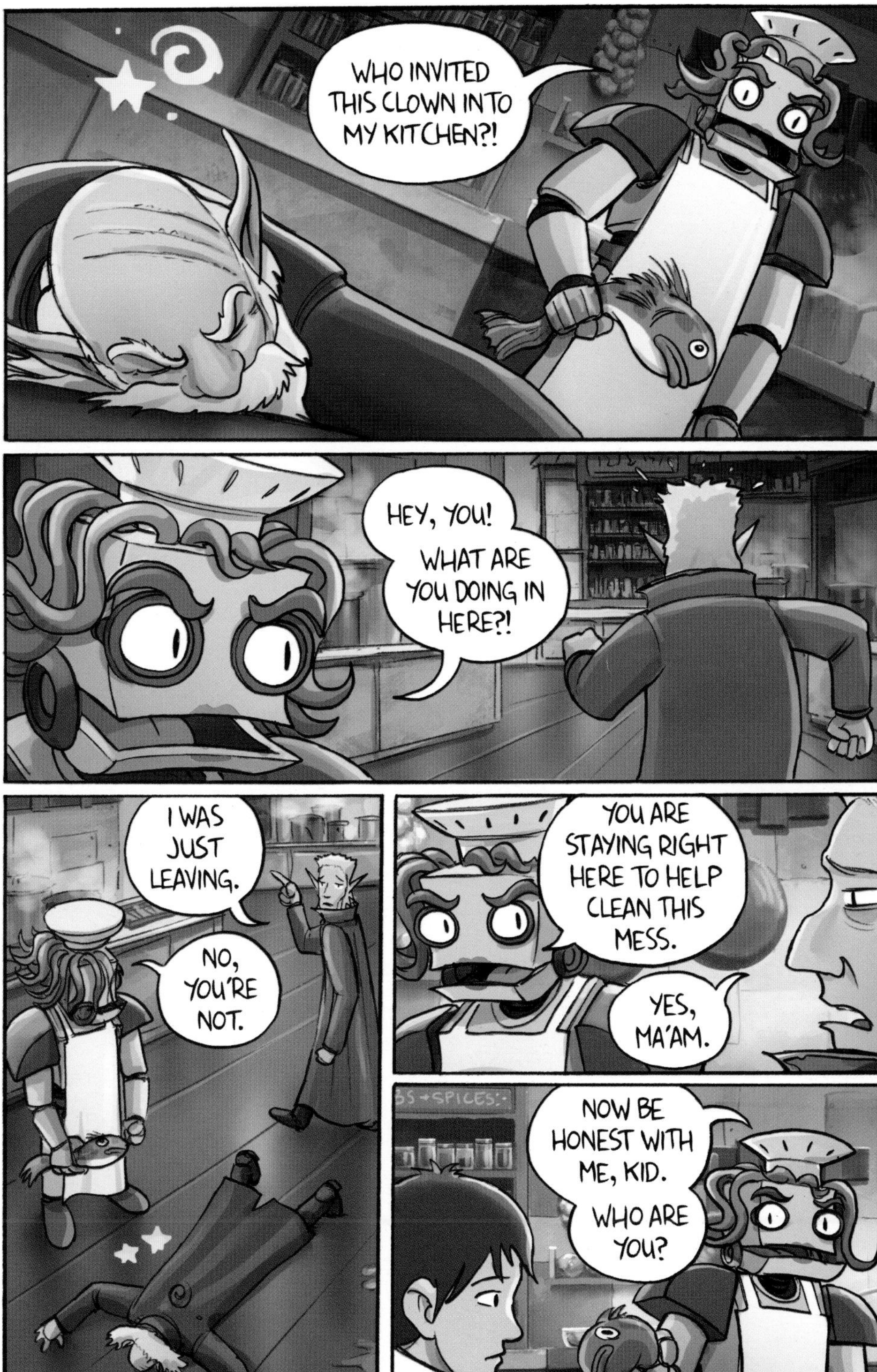
WHO INVITED THIS CLOWN INTO MY KITCHEN?!
HEY, YOU!
WHAT ARE YOU DOING IN HERE?!
I WAS JUST LEAVING.
NO, YOU'RE NOT.
YOU ARE STAYING RIGHT HERE TO HELP CLEAN THIS MESS.
YES, MA'AM.
NOW BE HONEST WITH ME, KID.
WHO ARE YOU?

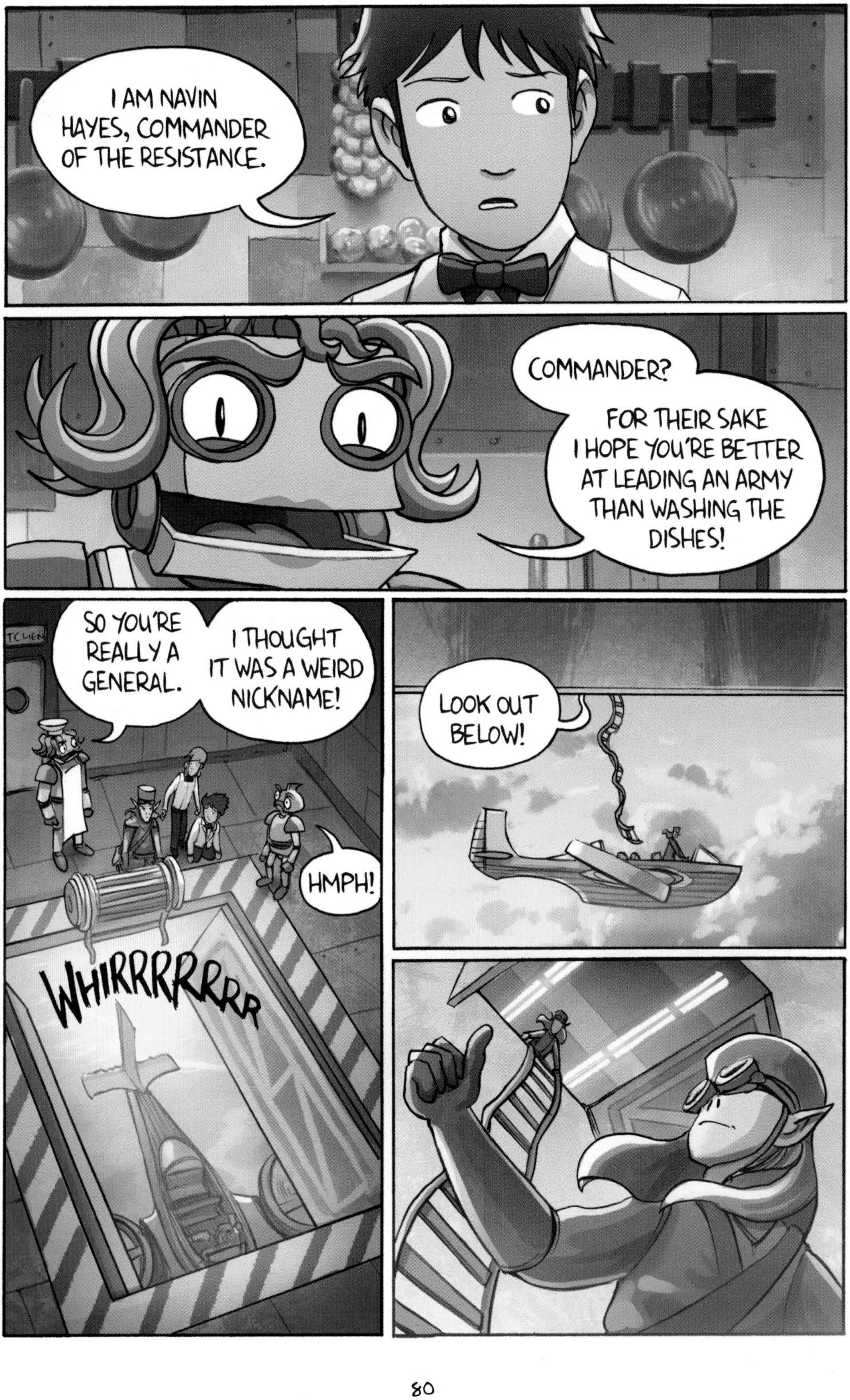
I AM NAVIN HAYES, COMMANDER OF THE RESISTANCE.
COMMANDER?
FOR THEIR SAKE I HOPE YOU'RE BETTER AT LEADING AN ARMY THAN WASHING THE DISHES!
SO YOU'RE REALLY A GENERAL.
I THOUGHT IT WAS A WEIRD NICKNAME!
HMPH!
WHIRRRRRRR
LOOK OUT BELOW!

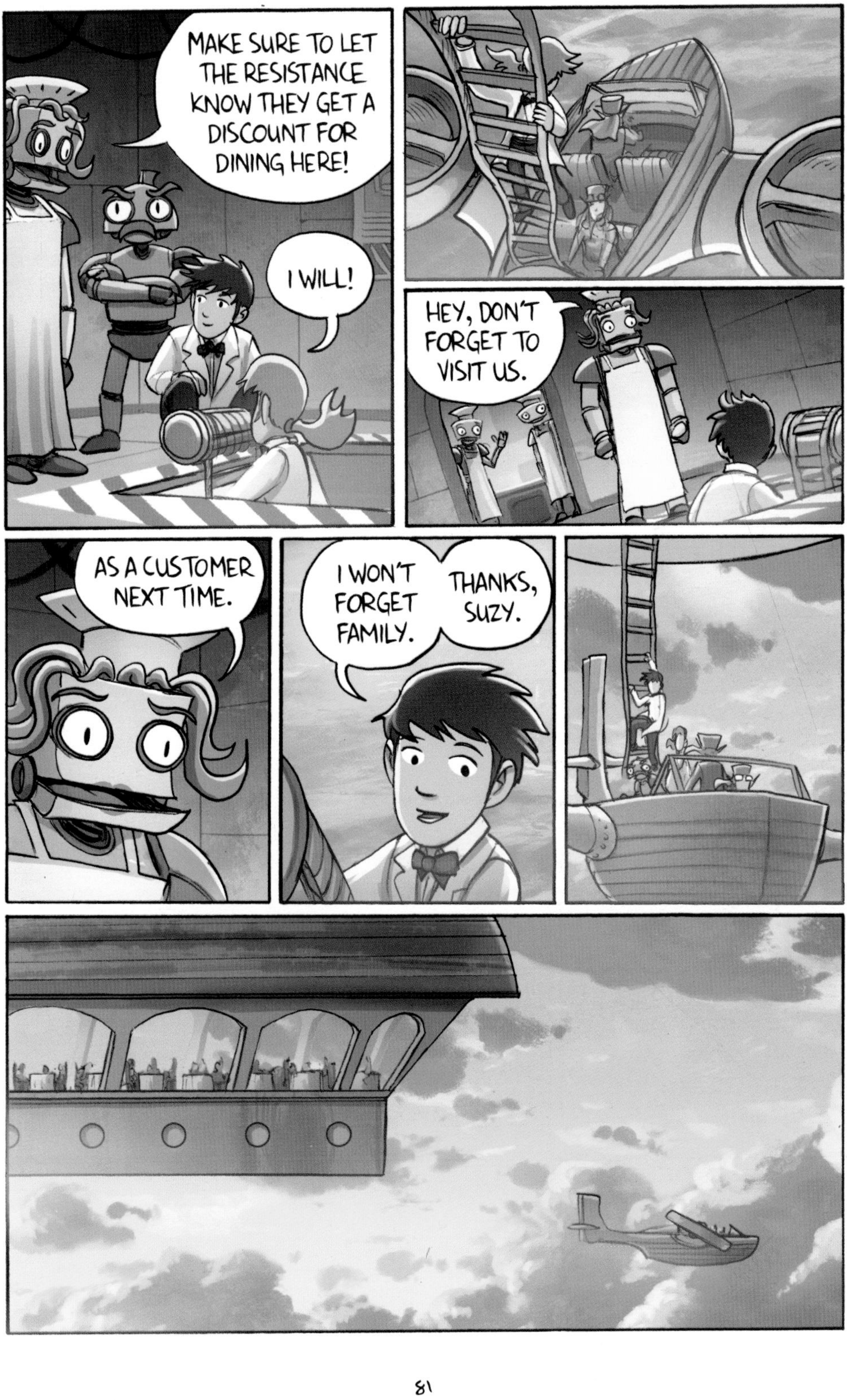
MAKE SURE TO LET THE RESISTANCE KNOW THEY GET A DISCOUNT FOR DINING HERE!
I WILL!
HEY, DON'T FORGET TO VISIT US.
AS A CUSTOMER NEXT TIME.
I WON'T FORGET FAMILY.
THANKS, SUZY.

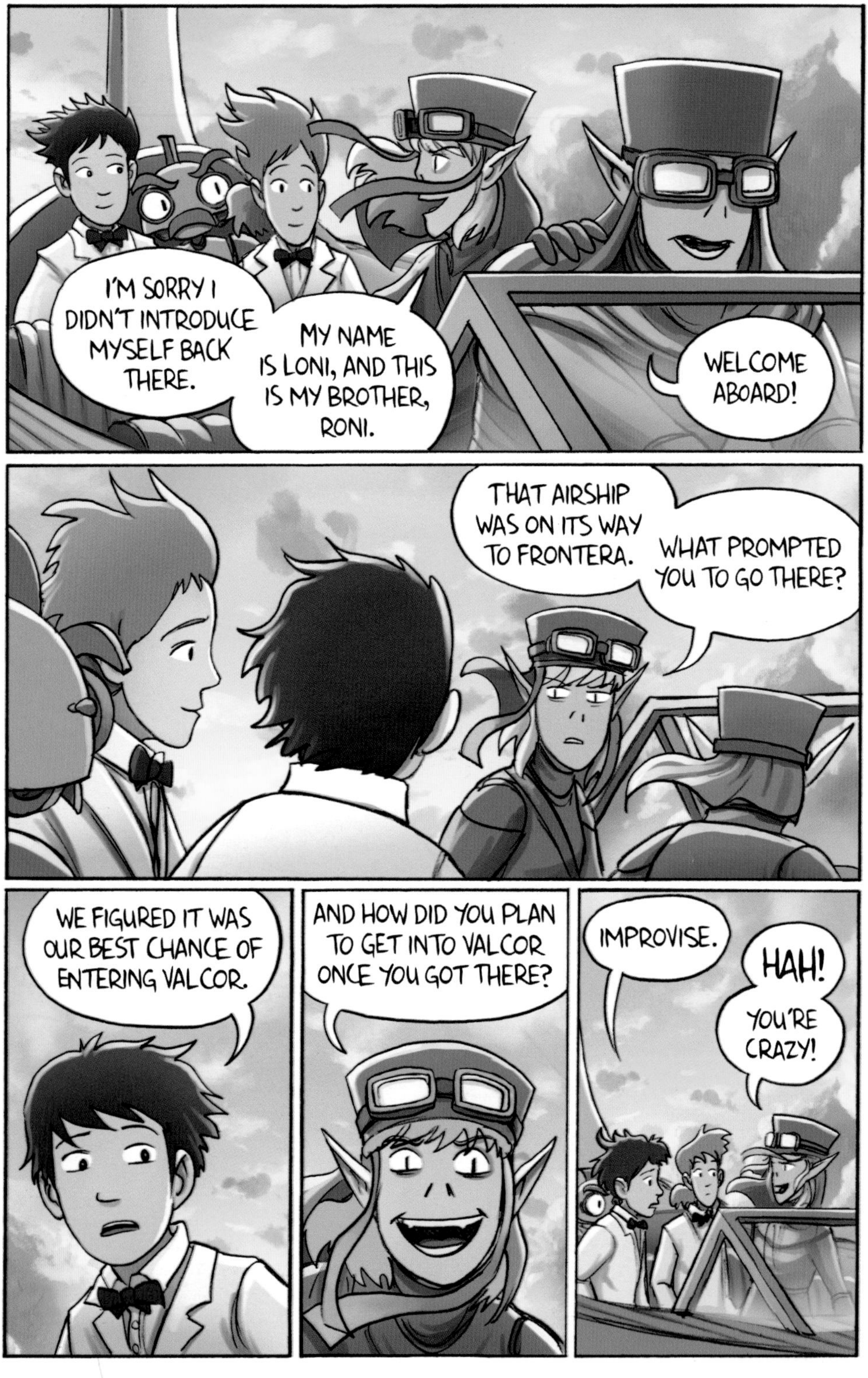
I'M SORRY I DIDN'T INTRODUCE MYSELF BACK THERE.
MY NAME IS LONI, AND THIS IS MY BROTHER, RONI.
WELCOME ABOARD!
THAT AIRSHIP WAS ON ITS WAY TO FRONTERA.
WHAT PROMPTED YOU TO GO THERE?
WE FIGURED IT WAS OUR BEST CHANCE OF ENTERING VALCOR.
AND HOW DID YOU PLAN TO GET INTO VALCOR ONCE YOU GOT THERE?
IMPROVISE.
HAH!
YOU'RE CRAZY!

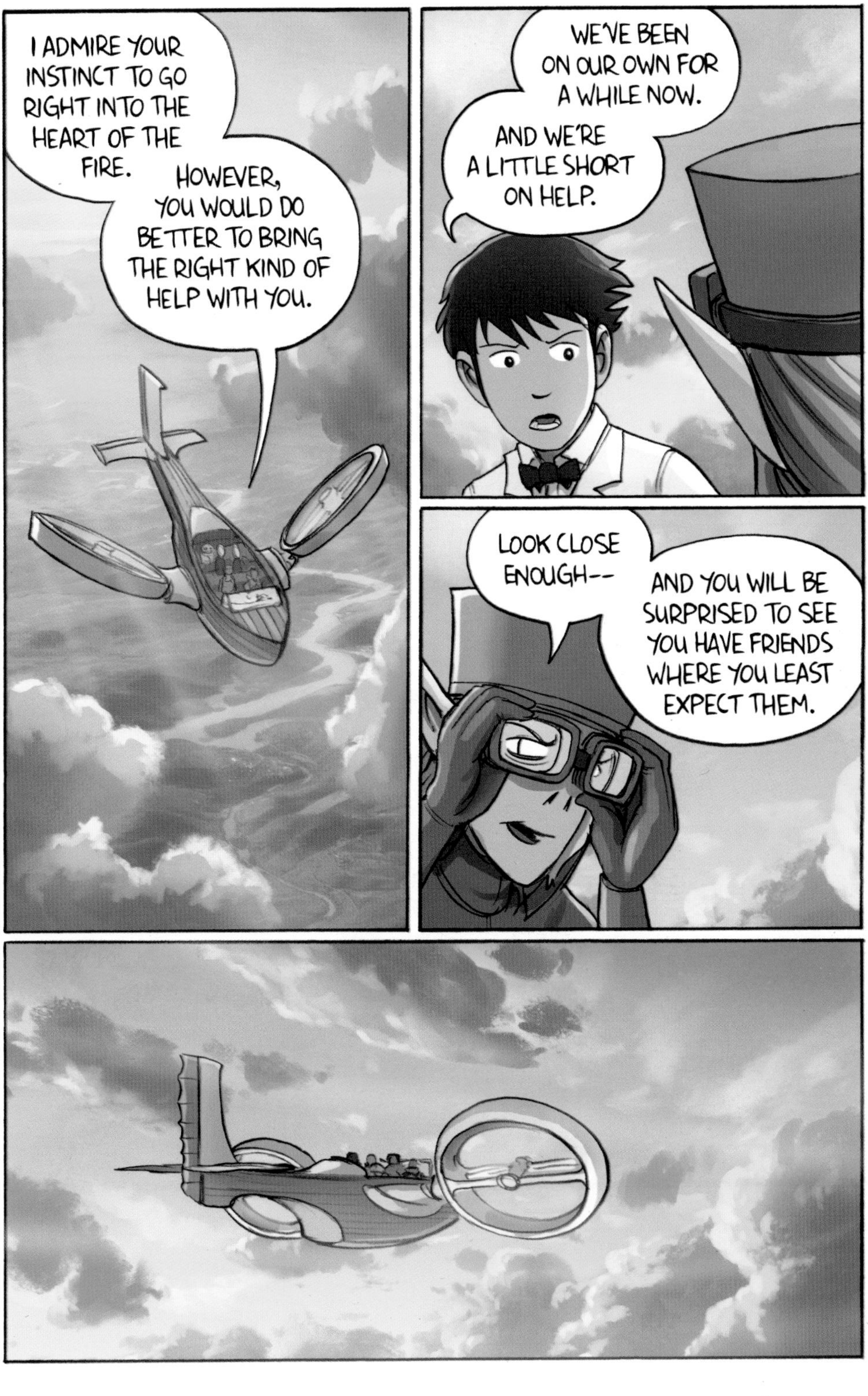
I ADMIRE YOUR INSTINCT TO GO RIGHT INTO THE HEART OF THE FIRE.
HOWEVER, YOU WOULD DO BETTER TO BRING THE RIGHT KIND OF HELP WITH YOU.
WE'VE BEEN ON OUR OWN FOR A WHILE NOW.
AND WE'RE A LITTLE SHORT ON HELP.
LOOK CLOSE ENOUGH--
AND YOU WILL BE SURPRISED TO SEE YOU HAVE FRIENDS WHERE YOU LEAST EXPECT THEM.

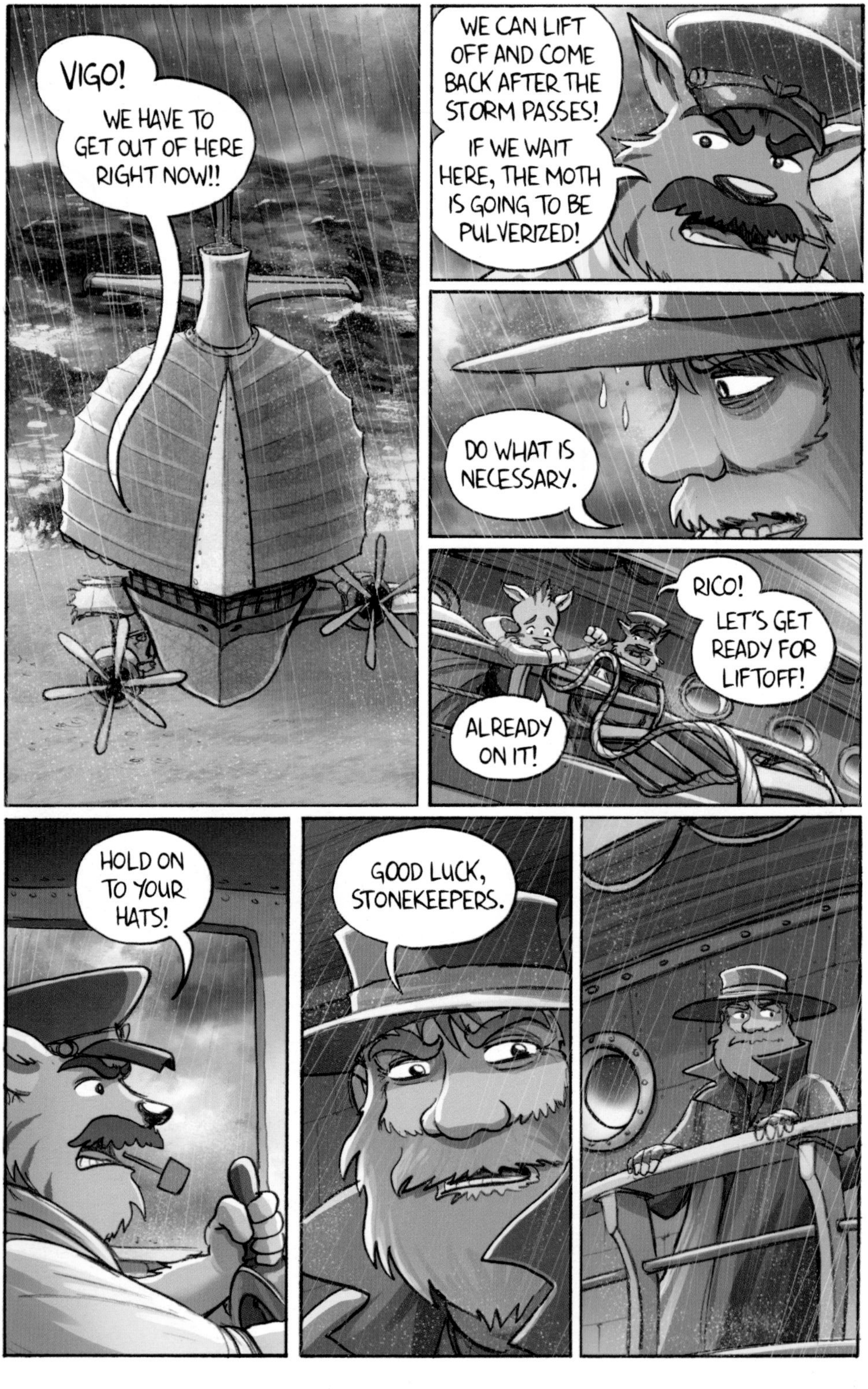
VIGO!
WE HAVE TO GET OUT OF HERE RIGHT NOW!!
WE CAN LIFT OFF AND COME BACK AFTER THE STORM PASSES!
IF WE WAIT HERE, THE MOTH IS GOING TO BE PULVERIZED!
DO WHAT IS NECESSARY.
RICO!
LET'S GET READY FOR LIFTOFF!
ALREADY ON IT!
HOLD ON TO YOUR HATS!
GOOD LUCK, STONEKEEPERS.

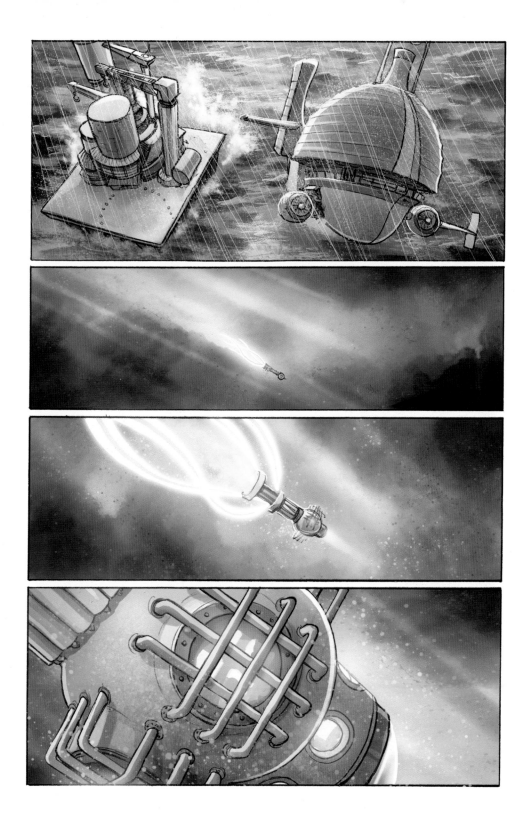

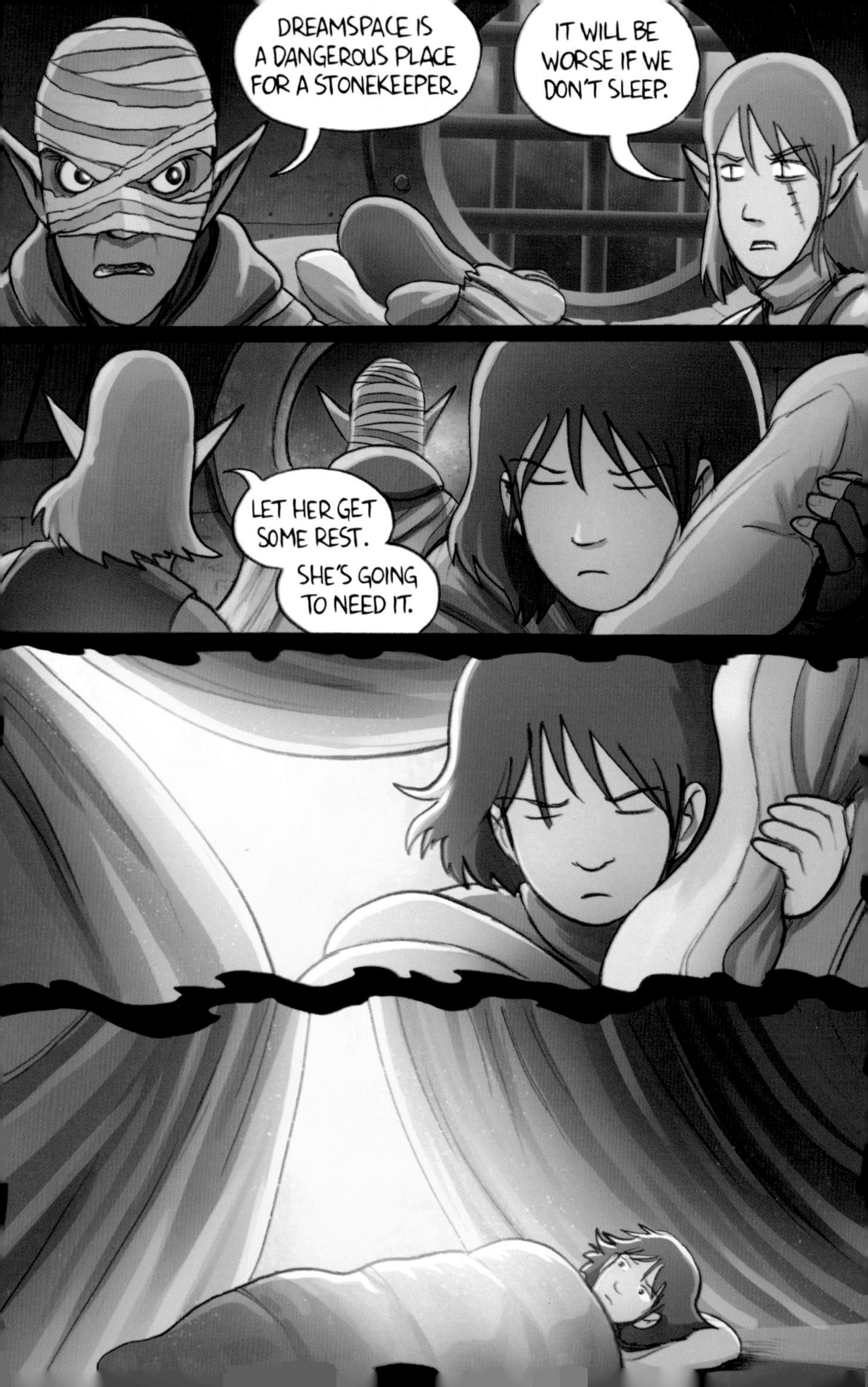
DREAMSPACE IS A DANGEROUS PLACE FOR A STONEKEEPER.
IT WILL BE WORSE IF WE DON'T SLEEP.
LET HER GET SOME REST.
SHE'S GOING TO NEED IT.

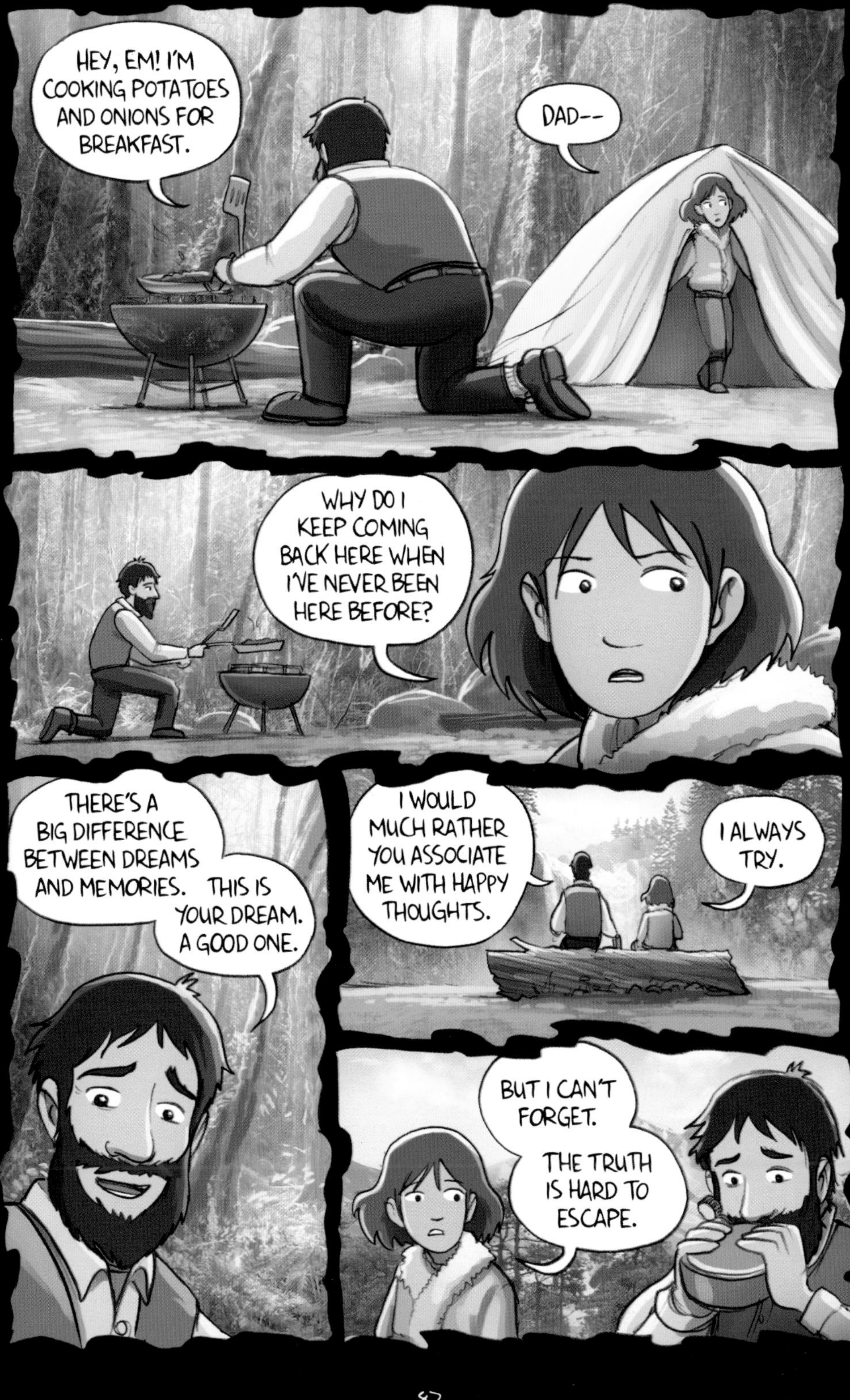
HEY, EM! I'M COOKING POTATOES AND ONIONS FOR BREAKFAST.
DAD--
WHY DO I KEEP COMING BACK HERE WHEN I'VE NEVER BEEN HERE BEFORE?
THERE'S A BIG DIFFERENCE BETWEEN DREAMS AND MEMORIES.
THIS IS YOUR DREAM. A GOOD ONE.
I WOULD MUCH RATHER YOU ASSOCIATE ME WITH HAPPY THOUGHTS.
I ALWAYS TRY.
BUT I CAN'T FORGET.
THE TRUTH IS HARD TO ESCAPE.

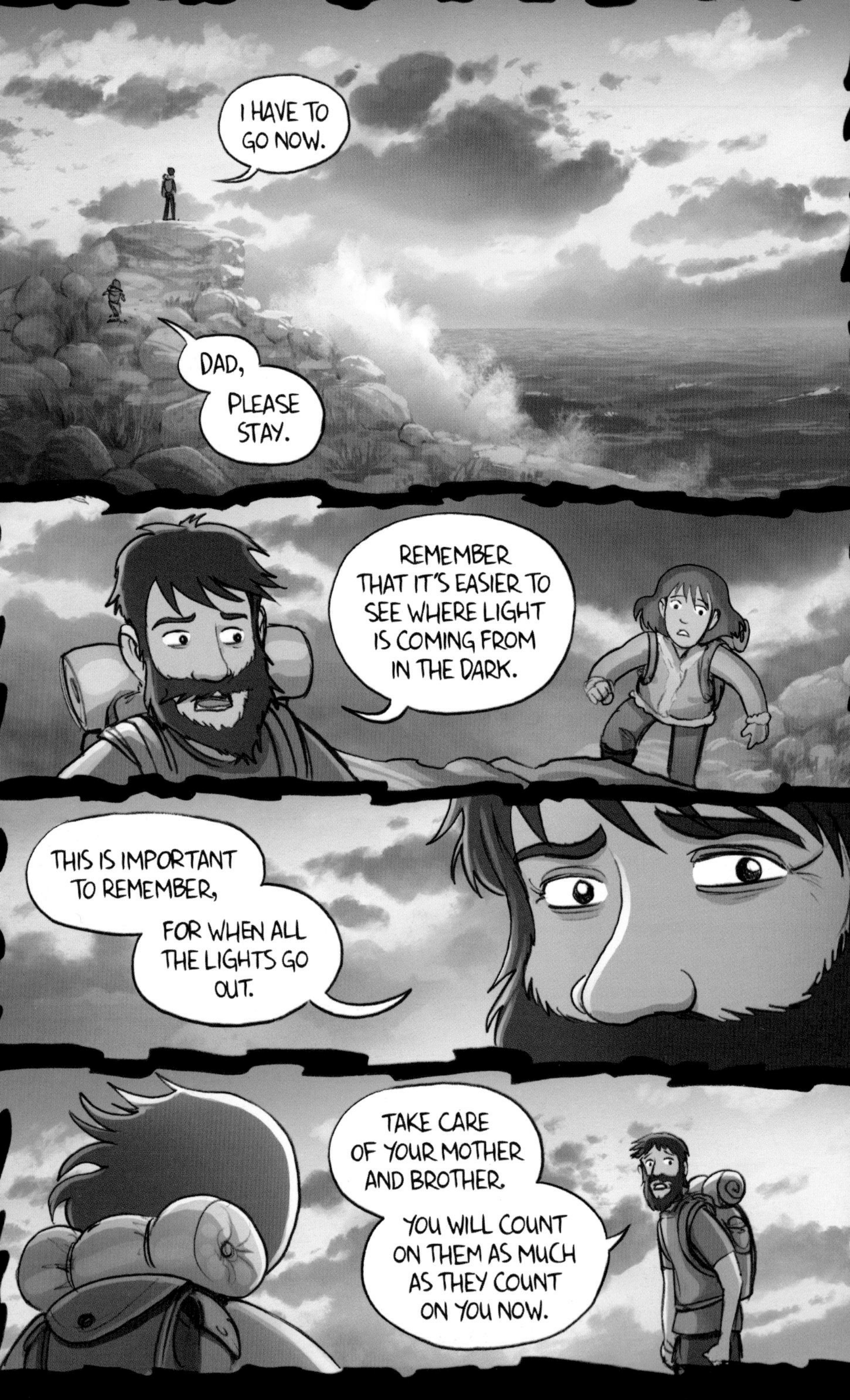
I HAVE TO GO NOW.
DAD,
PLEASE STAY.
REMEMBER THAT IT'S EASIER TO SEE WHERE LIGHT IS COMING FROM IN THE DARK.
THIS IS IMPORTANT TO REMEMBER,
FOR WHEN ALL THE LIGHTS GO OUT.
TAKE CARE OF YOUR MOTHER AND BROTHER.
YOU WILL COUNT ON THEM AS MUCH AS THEY COUNT ON YOU NOW.

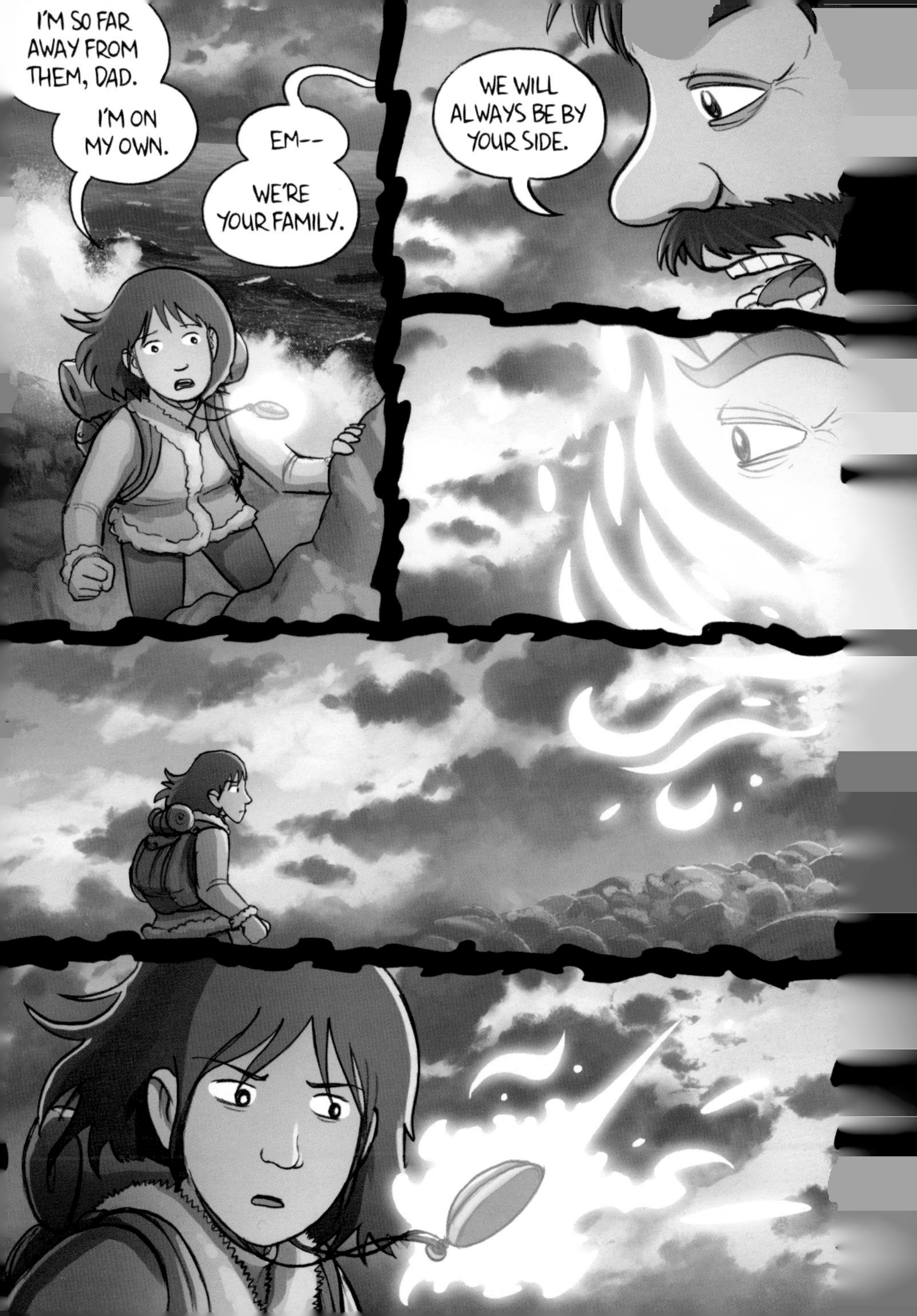
I'M SO FAR AWAY FROM THEM, DAD.
I'M ON MY OWN.
EM--
WE'RE YOUR FAMILY.
WE WILL ALWAYS BE BY YOUR SIDE.

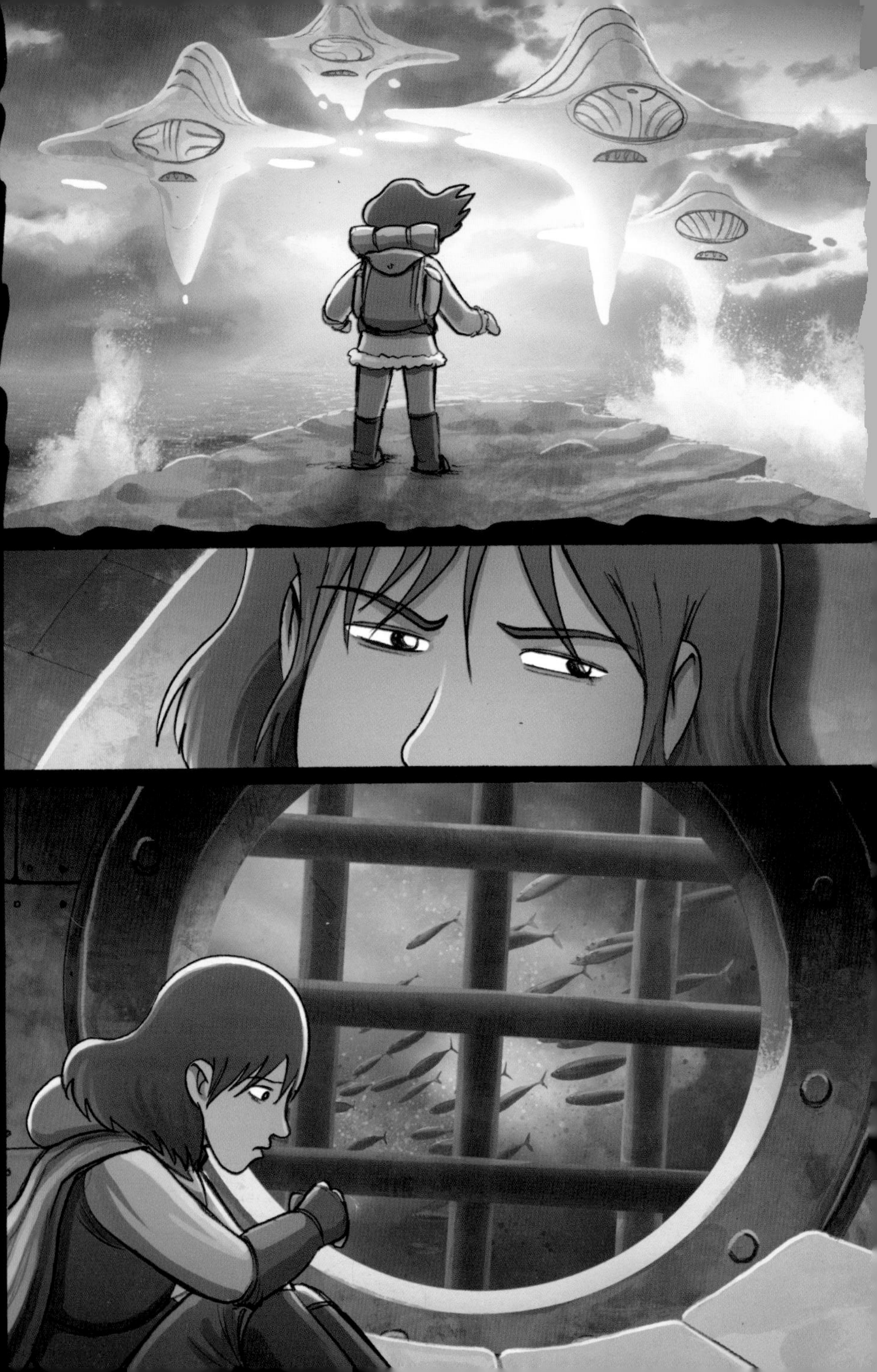

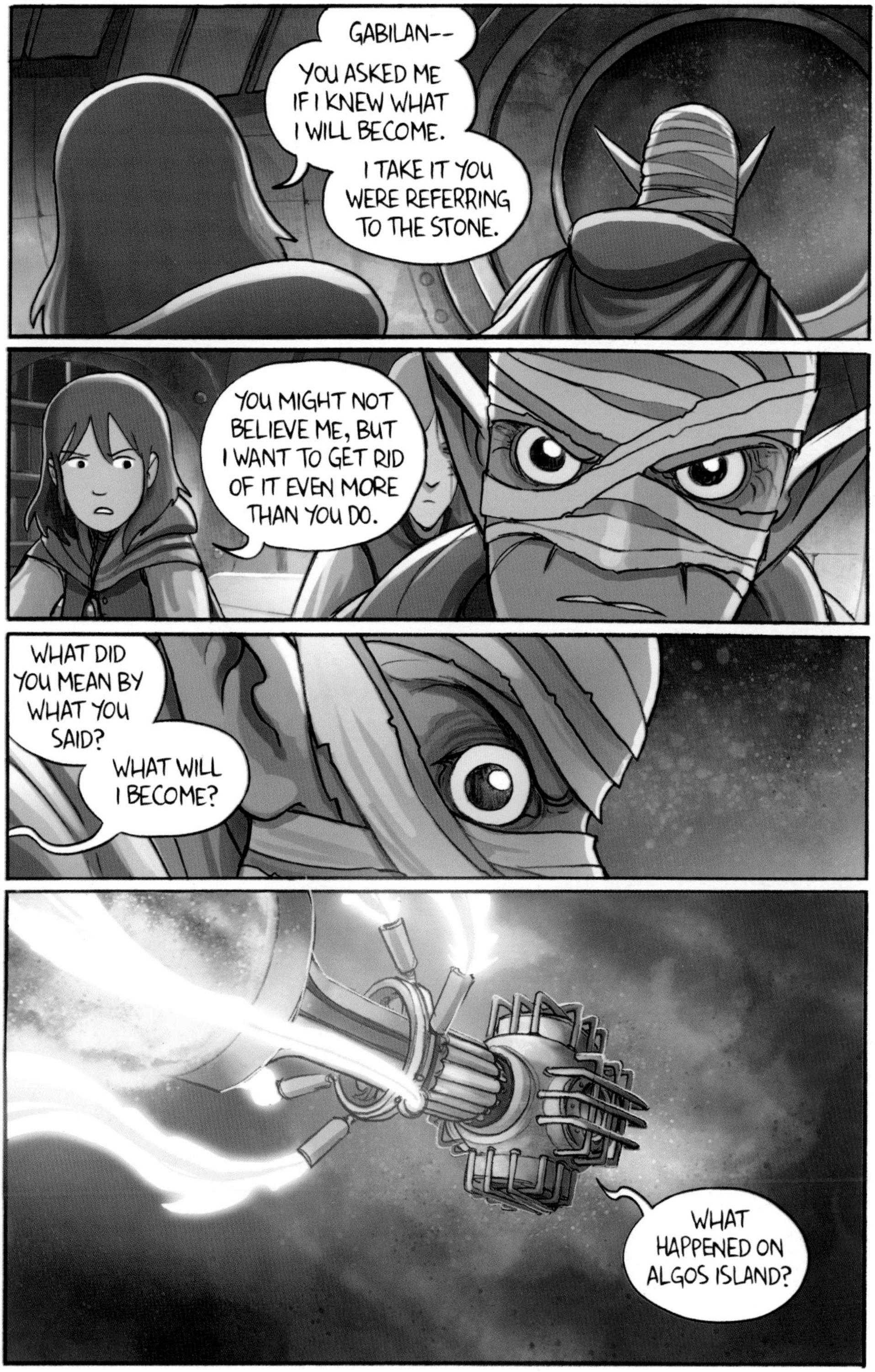
GABILAN--
YOU ASKED ME IF I KNEW WHAT I WILL BECOME.
I TAKE IT YOU WERE REFERRING TO THE STONE.
YOU MIGHT NOT BELIEVE ME, BUT I WANT TO GET RID OF IT EVEN MORE THAN YOU DO.
WHAT DID YOU MEAN BY WHAT YOU SAID?
WHAT WILL I BECOME?
WHAT HAPPENED ON ALGOS ISLAND?

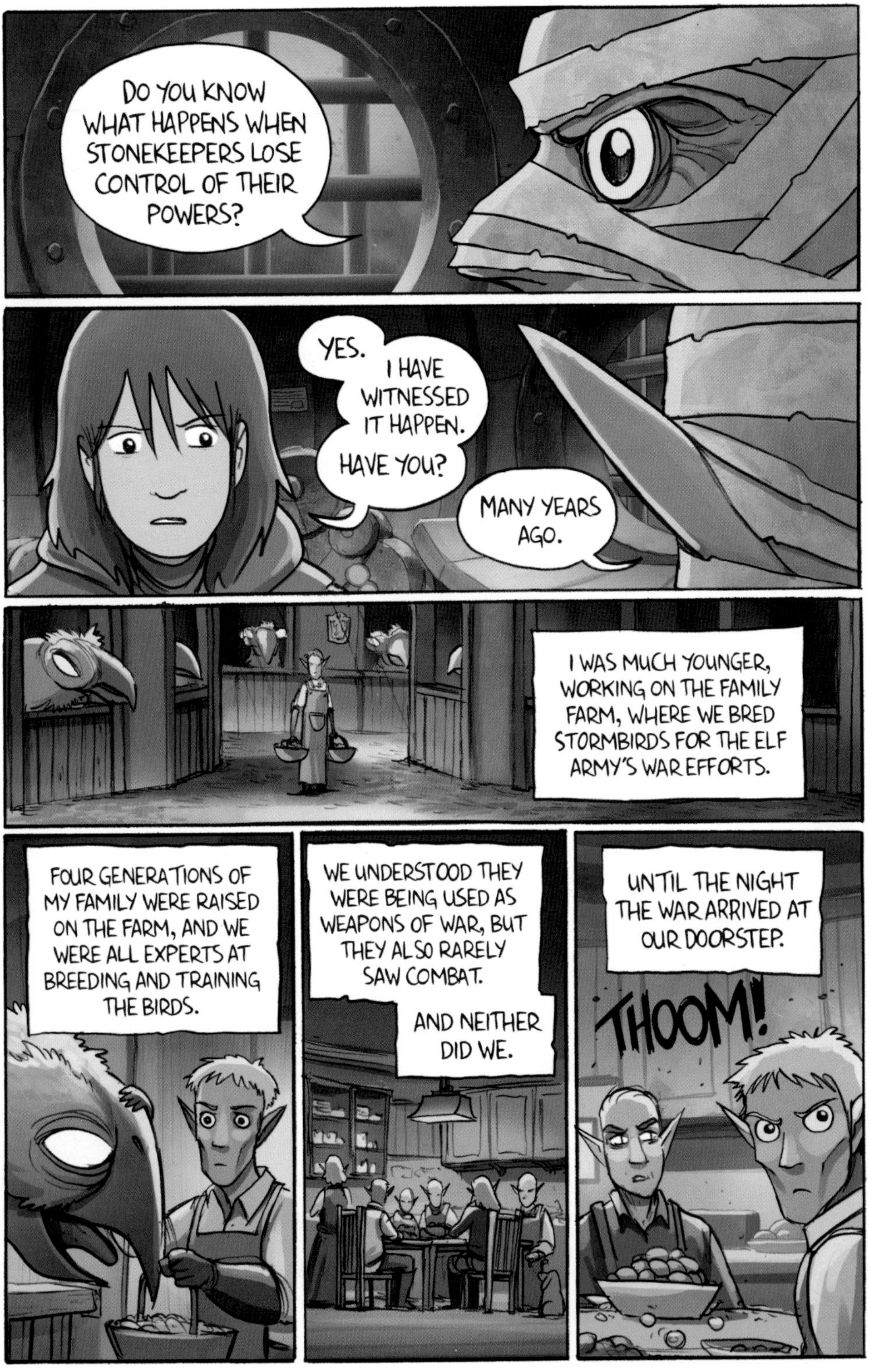
DO YOU KNOW WHAT HAPPENS WHEN STONEKEEPERS LOSE CONTROL OF THEIR POWERS?
YES.
I HAVE WITNESSED IT HAPPEN.
HAVE YOU?
MANY YEARS AGO.
I WAS MUCH YOUNGER, WORKING ON THE FAMILY FARM, WHERE WE BRED STORMBIRDS FOR THE ELF ARMY'S WAR EFFORTS.
FOUR GENERATIONS OF MY FAMILY WERE RAISED ON THE FARM, AND WE WERE ALL EXPERTS AT BREEDING AND TRAINING THE BIRDS.
WE UNDERSTOOD THEY WERE BEING USED AS WEAPONS OF WAR, BUT THEY ALSO RARELY SAW COMBAT.
AND NEITHER DID WE.
UNTIL THE NIGHT THE WAR ARRIVED AT OUR DOORSTEP.
THOOM!

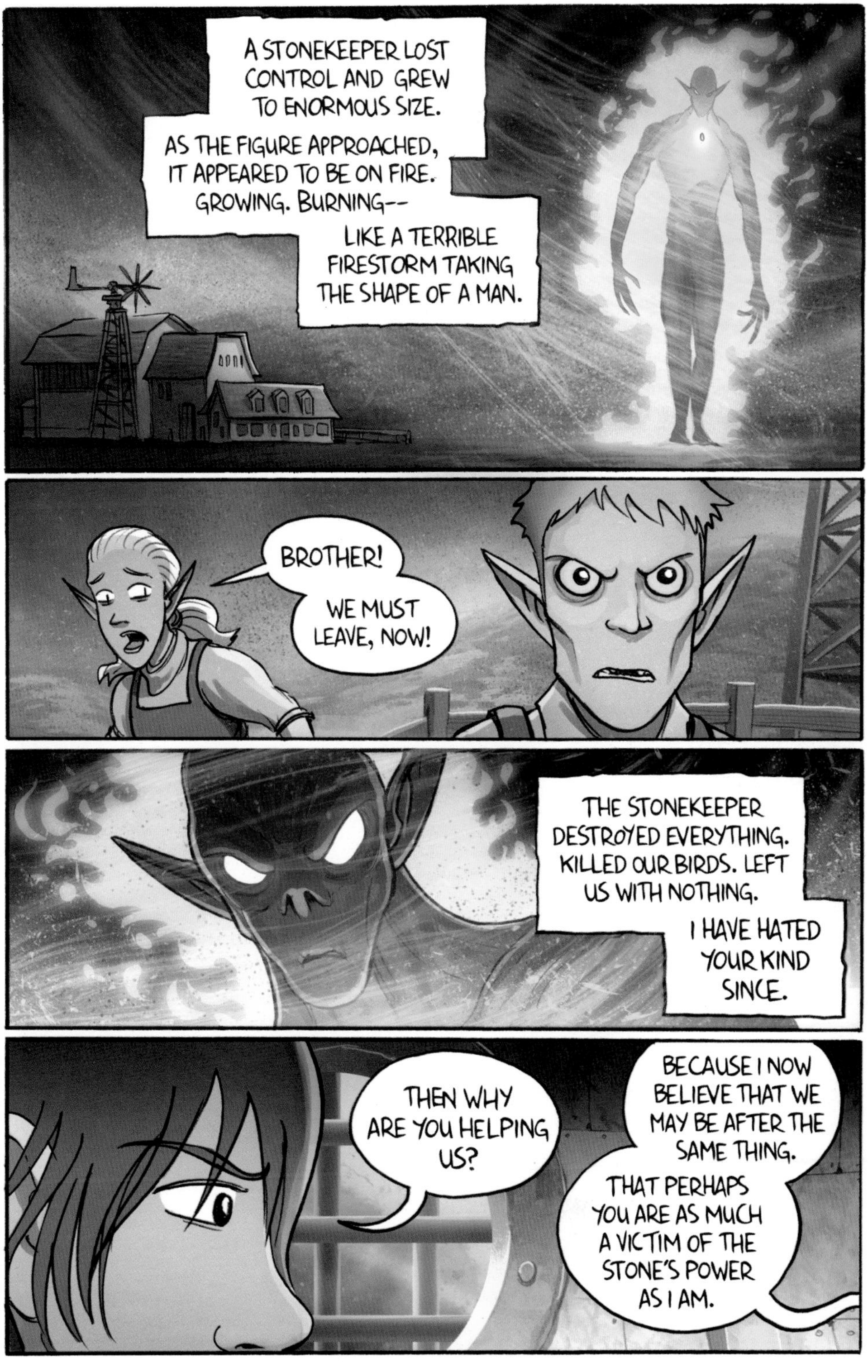
A STONEKEEPER LOST CONTROL AND GREW TO ENORMOUS SIZE.
AS THE FIGURE APPROACHED, IT APPEARED TO BE ON FIRE. GROWING. BURNING--
LIKE A TERRIBLE FIRESTORM TAKING THE SHAPE OF A MAN.
BROTHER!
WE MUST LEAVE, NOW!
THE STONEKEEPER DESTROYED EVERYTHING. KILLED OUR BIRDS. LEFT US WITH NOTHING.
I HAVE HATED YOUR KIND SINCE.
THEN WHY ARE YOU HELPING US?
BECAUSE I NOW BELIEVE THAT WE MAY BE AFTER THE SAME THING.
THAT PERHAPS YOU ARE AS MUCH A VICTIM OF THE STONE'S POWER AS I AM.

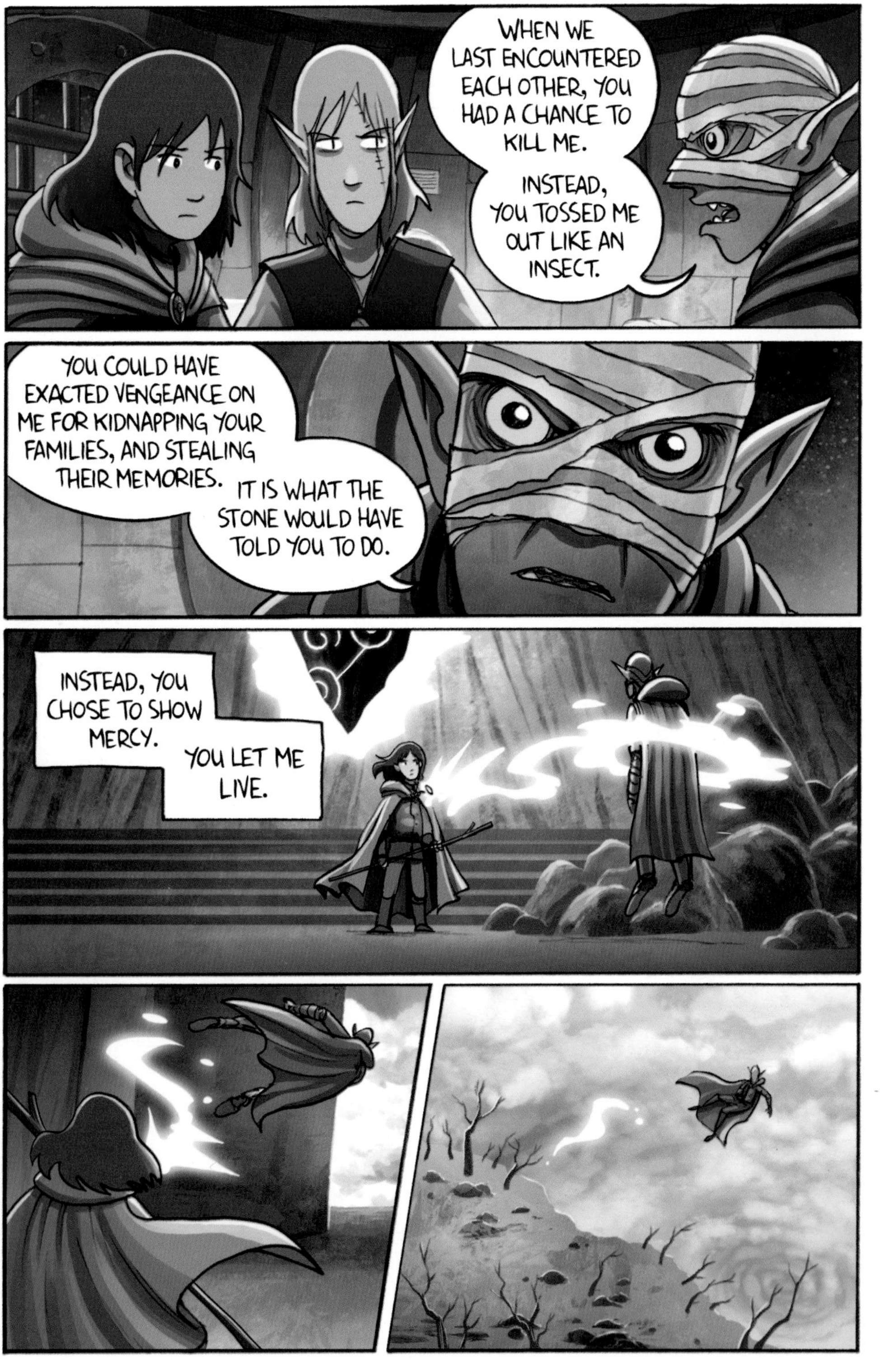

WHEN WE LAST ENCOUNTERED EACH OTHER, YOU HAD A CHANCE TO KILL ME.
INSTEAD, YOU TOSSED ME OUT LIKE AN INSECT.
YOU COULD HAVE EXACTED VENGEANCE ON ME FOR KIDNAPPING YOUR FAMILIES, AND STEALING THEIR MEMORIES.
IT IS WHAT THE STONE WOULD HAVE TOLD YOU TO DO.
INSTEAD, YOU CHOSE TO SHOW MERCY.
YOU LET ME LIVE.

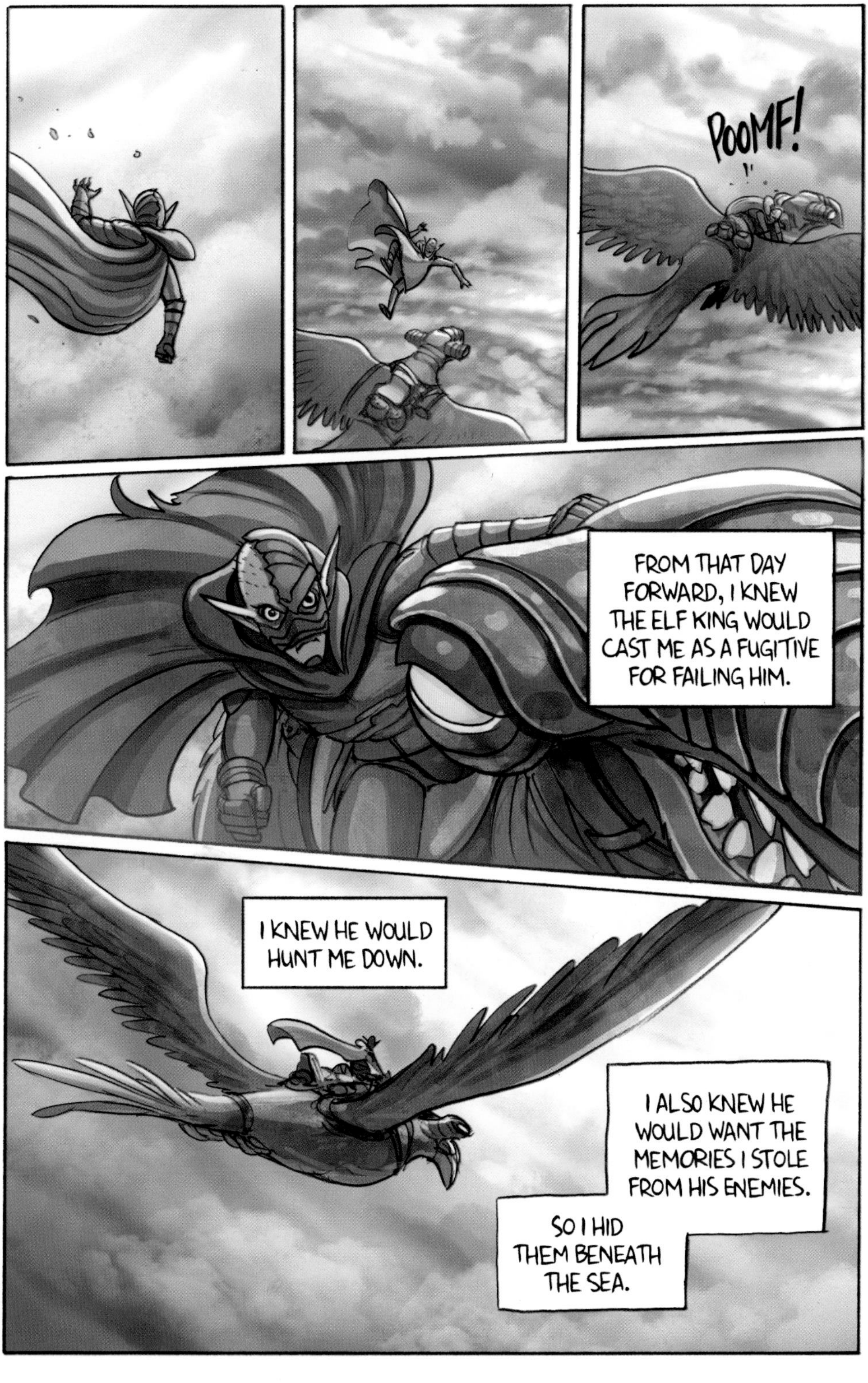
POOMF!
FROM THAT DAY FORWARD, I KNEW THE ELF KING WOULD CAST ME AS A FUGITIVE FOR FAILING HIM.
I KNEW HE WOULD HUNT ME DOWN.
I ALSO KNEW HE WOULD WANT THE MEMORIES I STOLE FROM HIS ENEMIES.
SO I HID THEM BENEATH THE SEA.

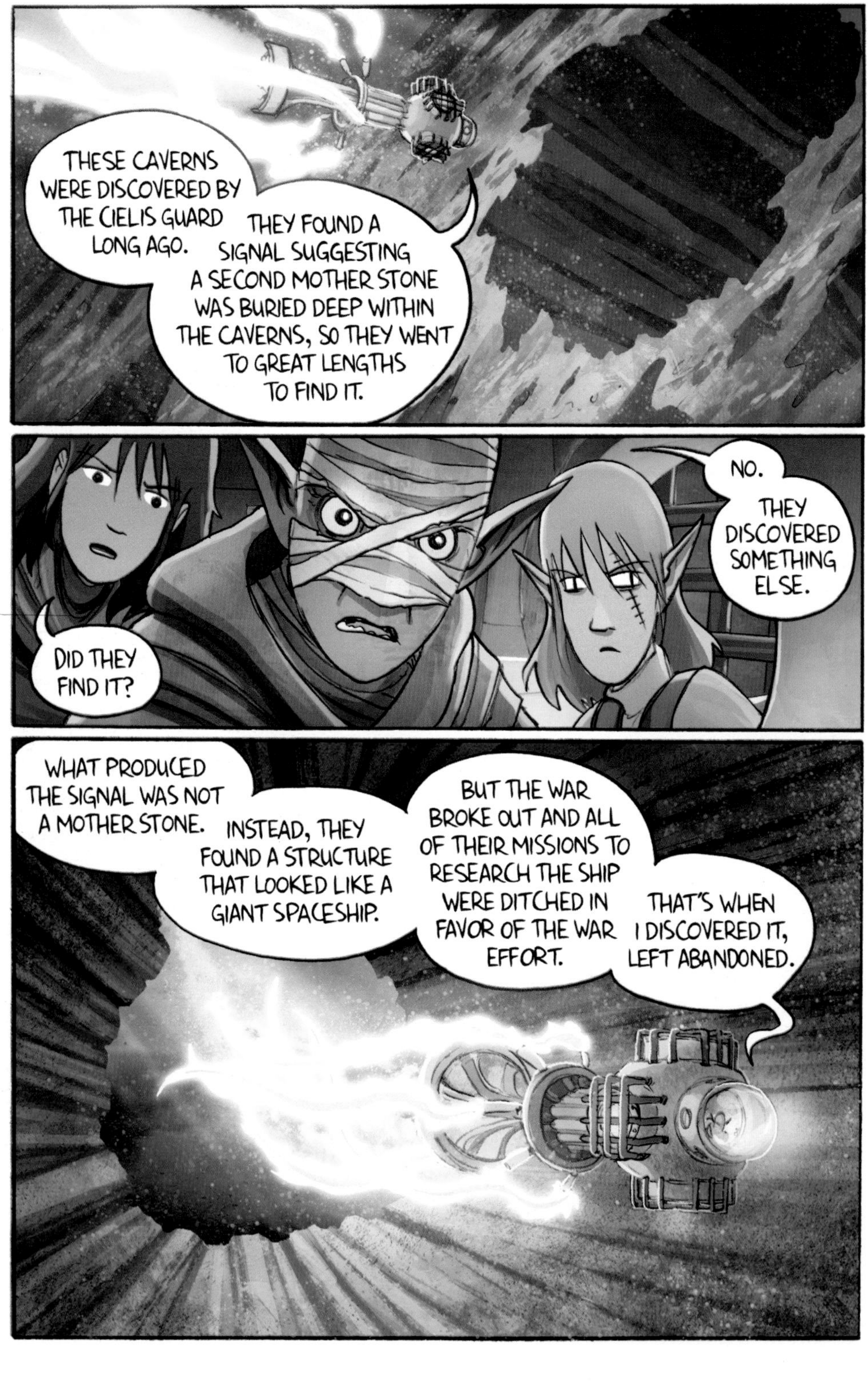
THESE CAVERNS WERE DISCOVERED BY THE CIELIS GUARD LONG AGO.
THEY FOUND A SIGNAL SUGGESTING A SECOND MOTHER STONE WAS BURIED DEEP WITHIN THE CAVERNS, SO THEY WENT TO GREAT LENGTHS TO FIND IT.
DID THEY FIND IT?
NO.
THEY DISCOVERED SOMETHING ELSE.
WHAT PRODUCED THE SIGNAL WAS NOT A MOTHER STONE.
INSTEAD, THEY FOUND A STRUCTURE THAT LOOKED LIKE A GIANT SPACESHIP.
BUT THE WAR BROKE OUT AND ALL OF THEIR MISSIONS TO RESEARCH THE SHIP WERE DITCHED IN FAVOR OF THE WAR EFFORT.
THAT'S WHEN I DISCOVERED IT, LEFT ABANDONED.

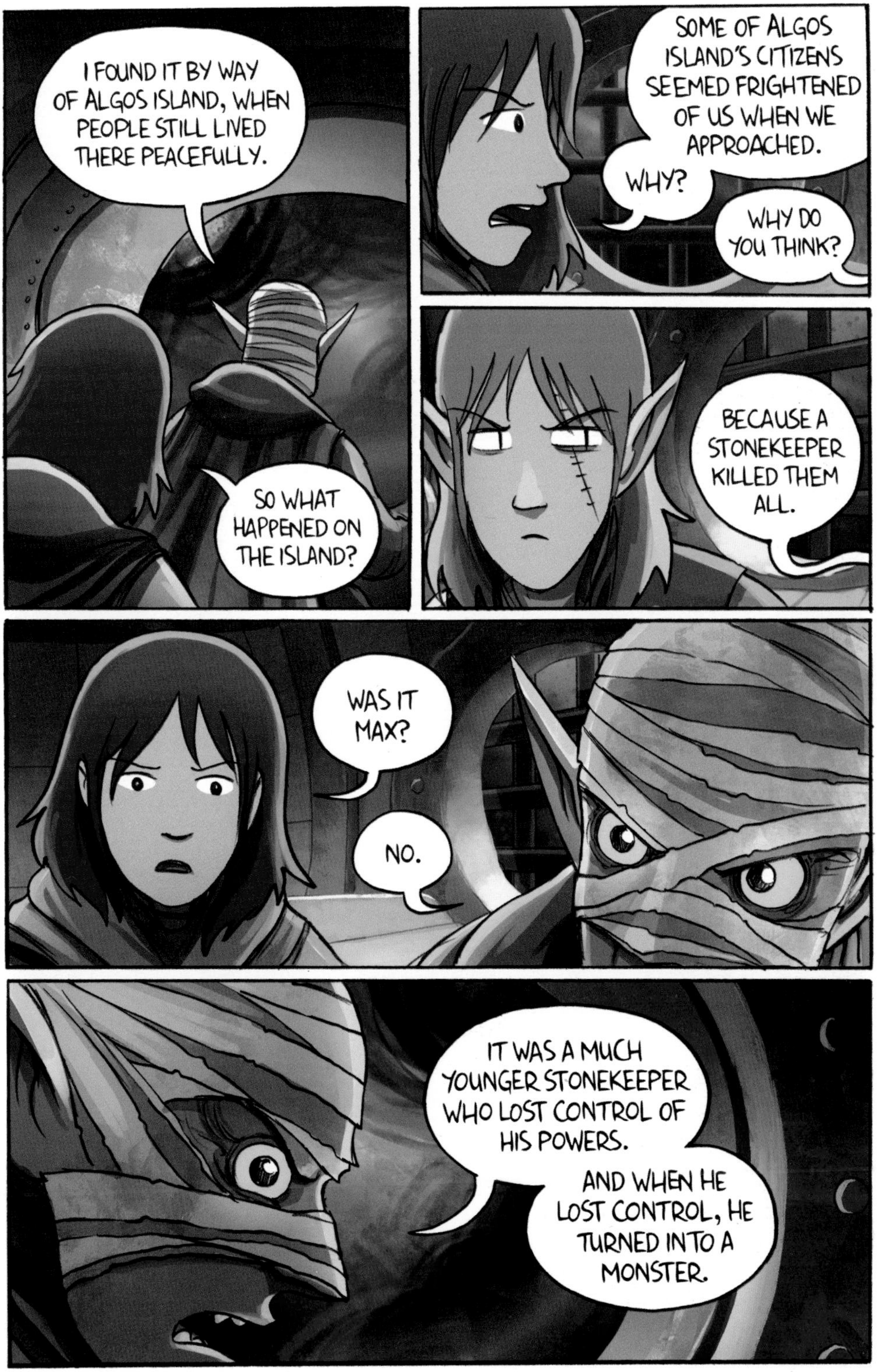
I FOUND IT BY WAY OF ALGOS ISLAND, WHEN PEOPLE STILL LIVED THERE PEACEFULLY.
SO WHAT HAPPENED ON THE ISLAND?
SOME OF ALGOS ISLAND'S CITIZENS SEEMED FRIGHTENED OF US WHEN WE APPROACHED.
WHY?
WHY DO YOU THINK?
BECAUSE A STONEKEEPER KILLED THEM ALL.
WAS IT MAX?
NO.
IT WAS A MUCH YOUNGER STONEKEEPER WHO LOST CONTROL OF HIS POWERS.
AND WHEN HE LOST CONTROL, HE TURNED INTO A MONSTER.

HE WAS THE STONEKEEPER WHO ATTACKED YOUR FAMILY.

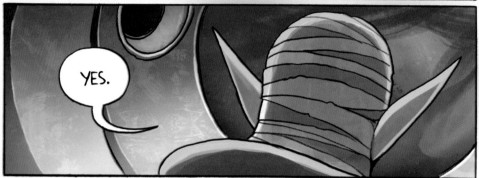

YES.

I SPENT YEARS STUDYING HIS LIFE, TRYING TO FIGURE OUT WHY IT HAPPENED.

I WANTED TO KNOW HOW SUCH MONSTERS WERE CREATED.

I WANTED TO KNOW, SO I COULD STOP THEM.

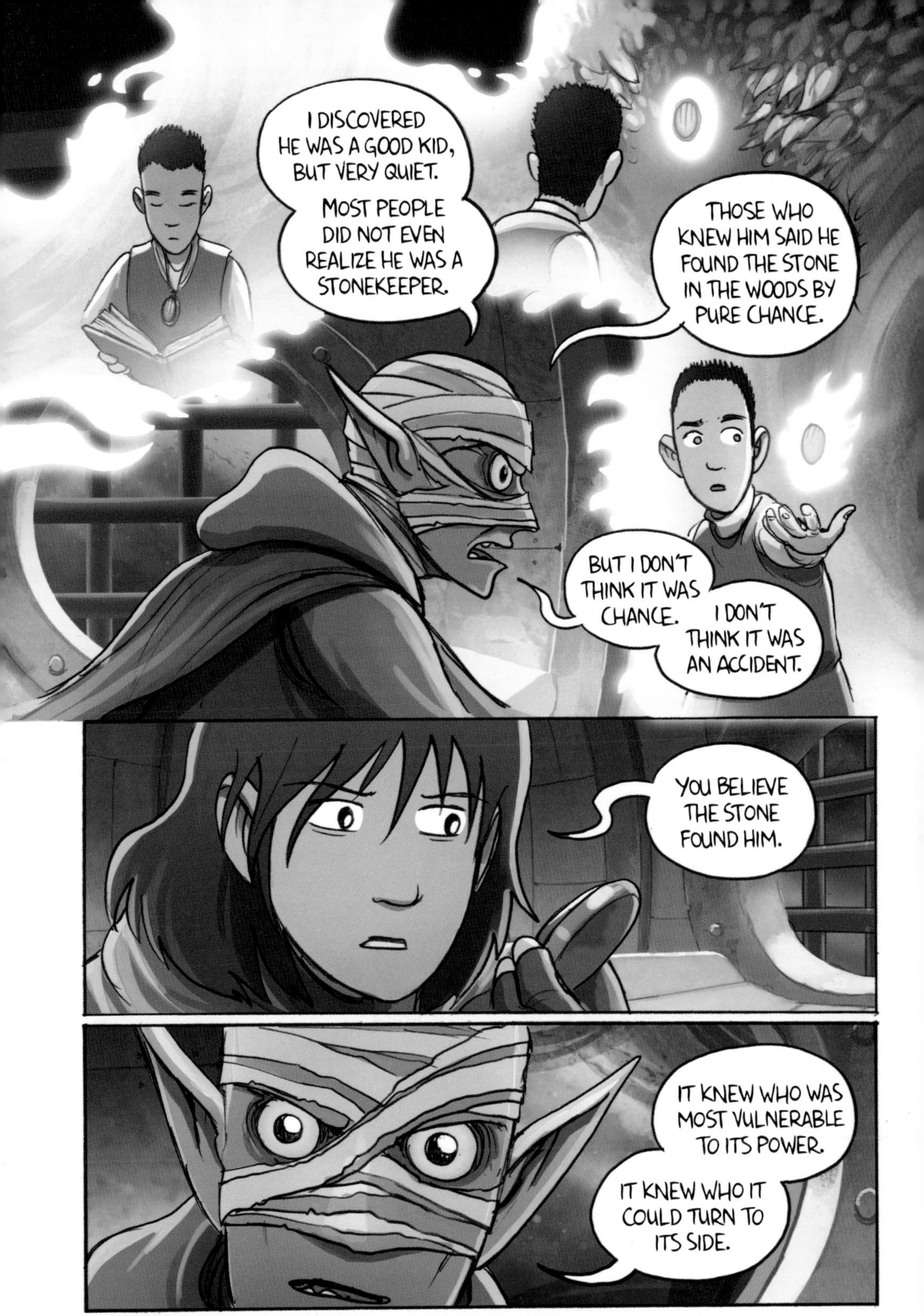
I DISCOVERED HE WAS A GOOD KID, BUT VERY QUIET.
MOST PEOPLE DID NOT EVEN REALIZE HE WAS A STONEKEEPER.
THOSE WHO KNEW HIM SAID HE FOUND THE STONE IN THE WOODS BY PURE CHANCE.
BUT I DON'T THINK IT WAS CHANCE.
I DON'T THINK IT WAS AN ACCIDENT.
YOU BELIEVE THE STONE FOUND HIM.
IT KNEW WHO WAS MOST VULNERABLE TO ITS POWER.
IT KNEW WHO IT COULD TURN TO ITS SIDE.

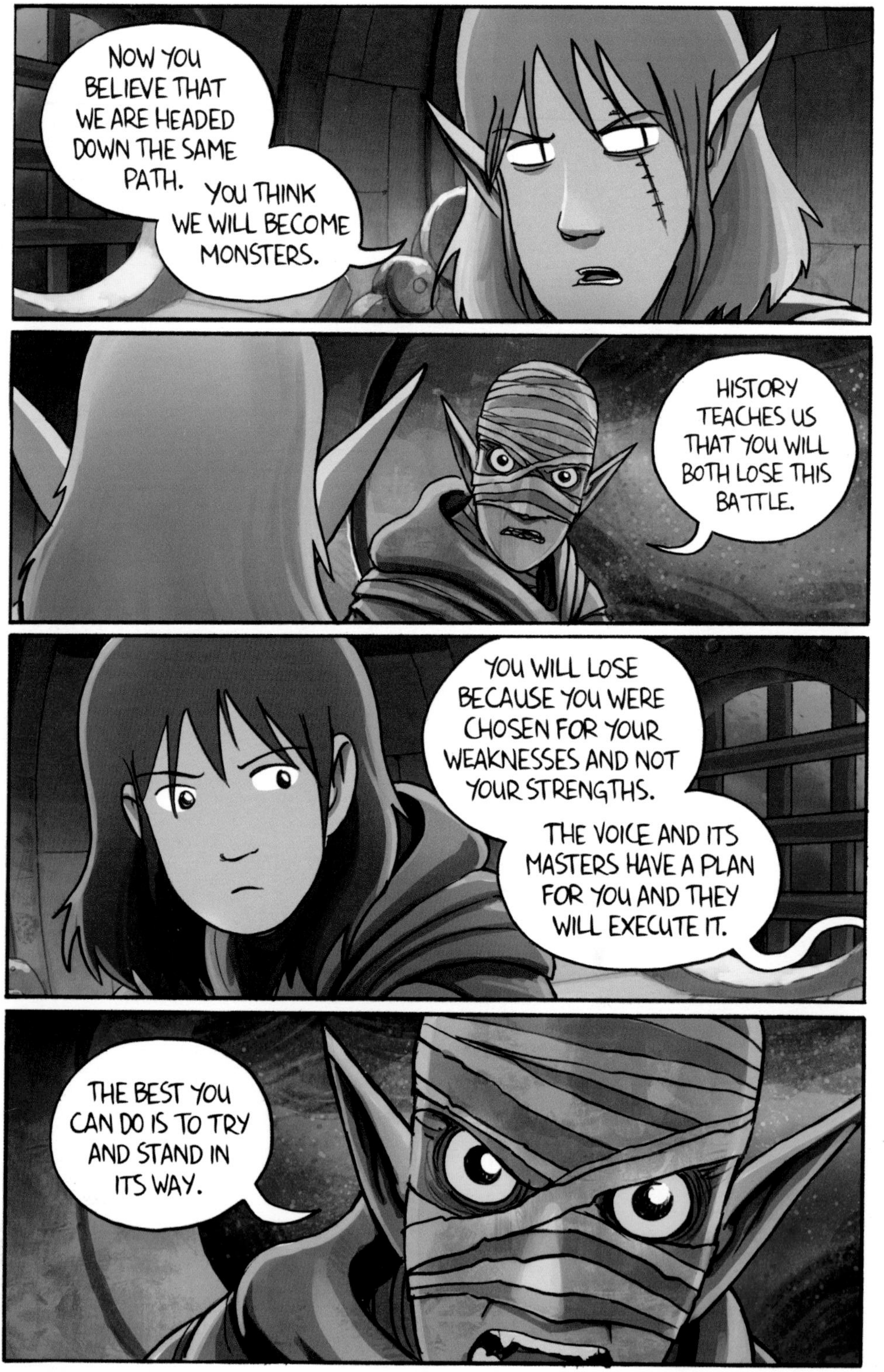
NOW YOU BELIEVE THAT WE ARE HEADED DOWN THE SAME PATH.
YOU THINK WE WILL BECOME MONSTERS.
HISTORY TEACHES US THAT YOU WILL BOTH LOSE THIS BATTLE.
YOU WILL LOSE BECAUSE YOU WERE CHOSEN FOR YOUR WEAKNESSES AND NOT YOUR STRENGTHS.
THE VOICE AND ITS MASTERS HAVE A PLAN FOR YOU AND THEY WILL EXECUTE IT.
THE BEST YOU CAN DO IS TO TRY AND STAND IN ITS WAY.

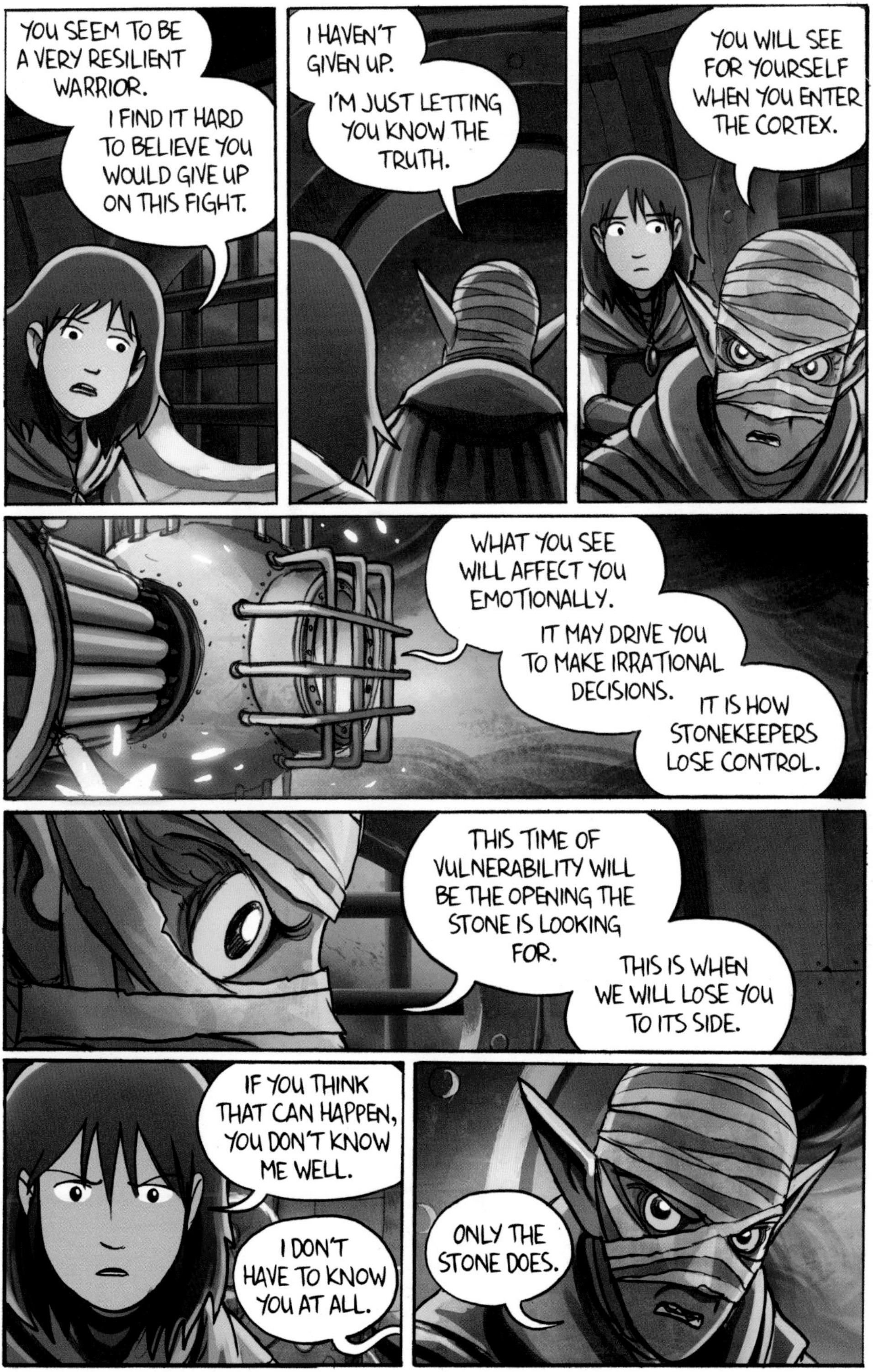
YOU SEEM TO BE A VERY RESILIENT WARRIOR.
I FIND IT HARD TO BELIEVE YOU WOULD GIVE UP ON THIS FIGHT.
I HAVEN'T GIVEN UP.
I'M JUST LETTING YOU KNOW THE TRUTH.
YOU WILL SEE FOR YOURSELF WHEN YOU ENTER THE CORTEX.
WHAT YOU SEE WILL AFFECT YOU EMOTIONALLY.
IT MAY DRIVE YOU TO MAKE IRRATIONAL DECISIONS.
IT IS HOW STONEKEEPERS LOSE CONTROL.
THIS TIME OF VULNERABILITY WILL BE THE OPENING THE STONE IS LOOKING FOR.
THIS IS WHEN WE WILL LOSE YOU TO ITS SIDE.
IF YOU THINK THAT CAN HAPPEN, YOU DON'T KNOW ME WELL.
I DON'T HAVE TO KNOW YOU AT ALL.
ONLY THE STONE DOES.

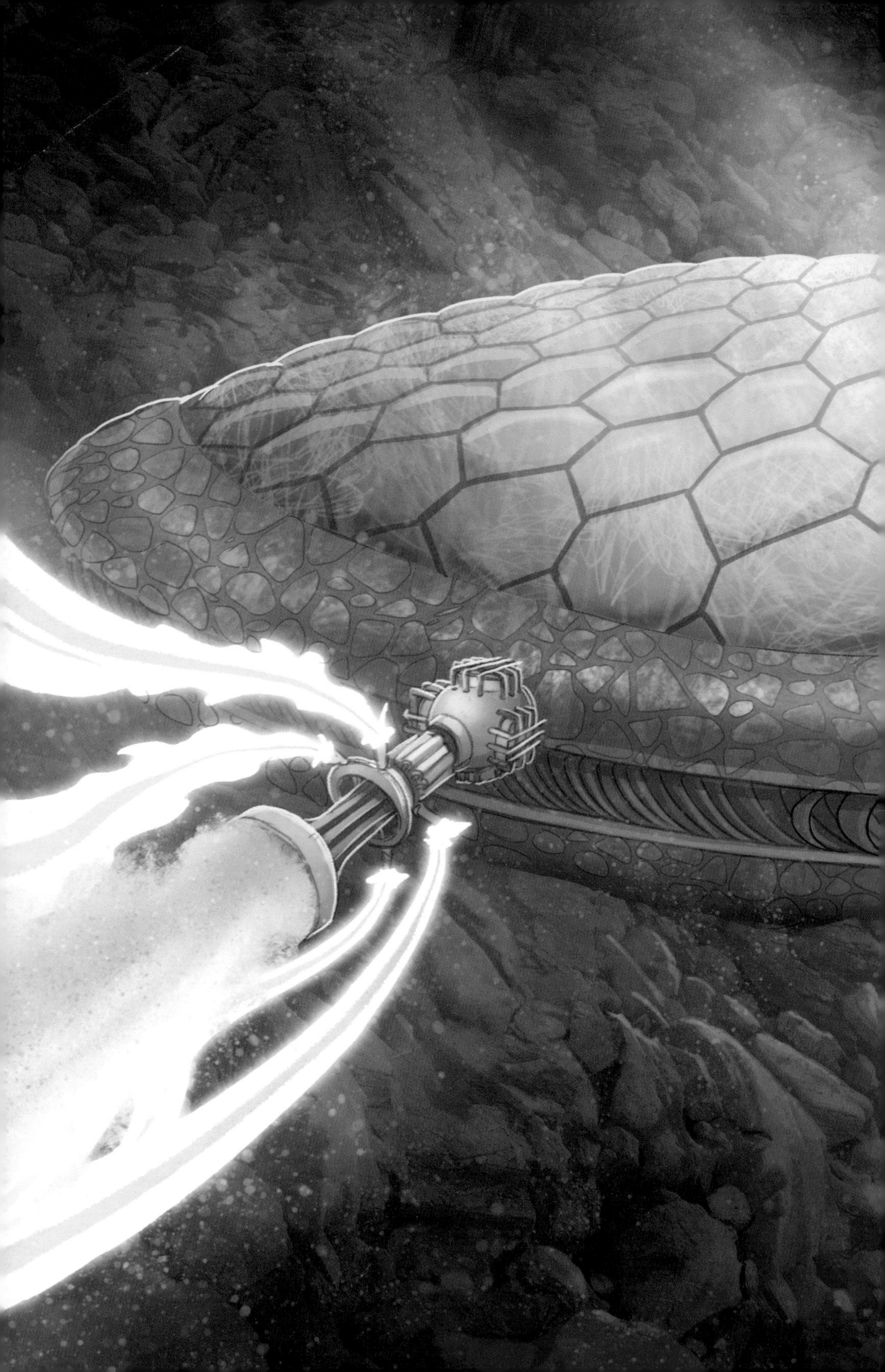

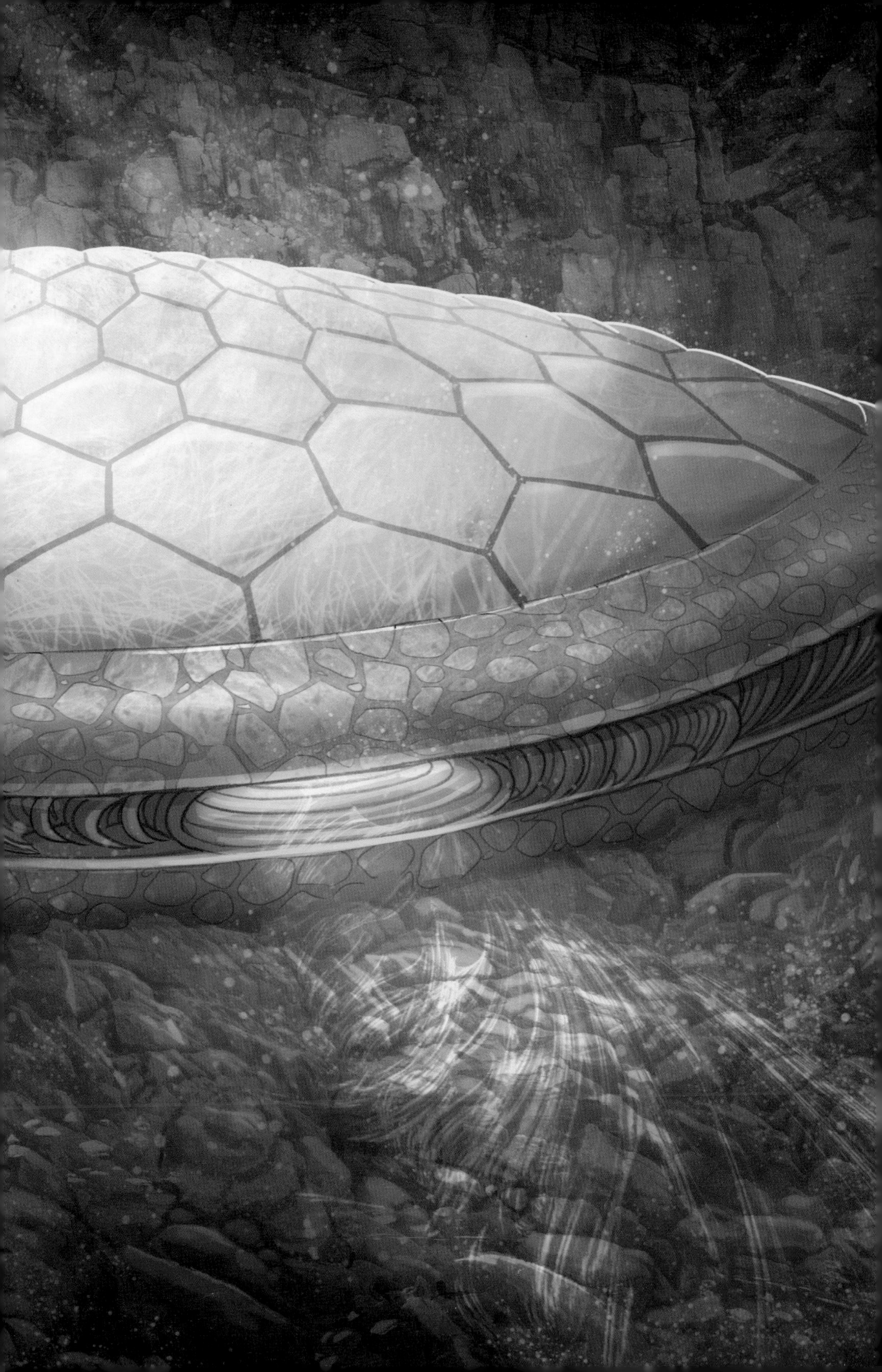

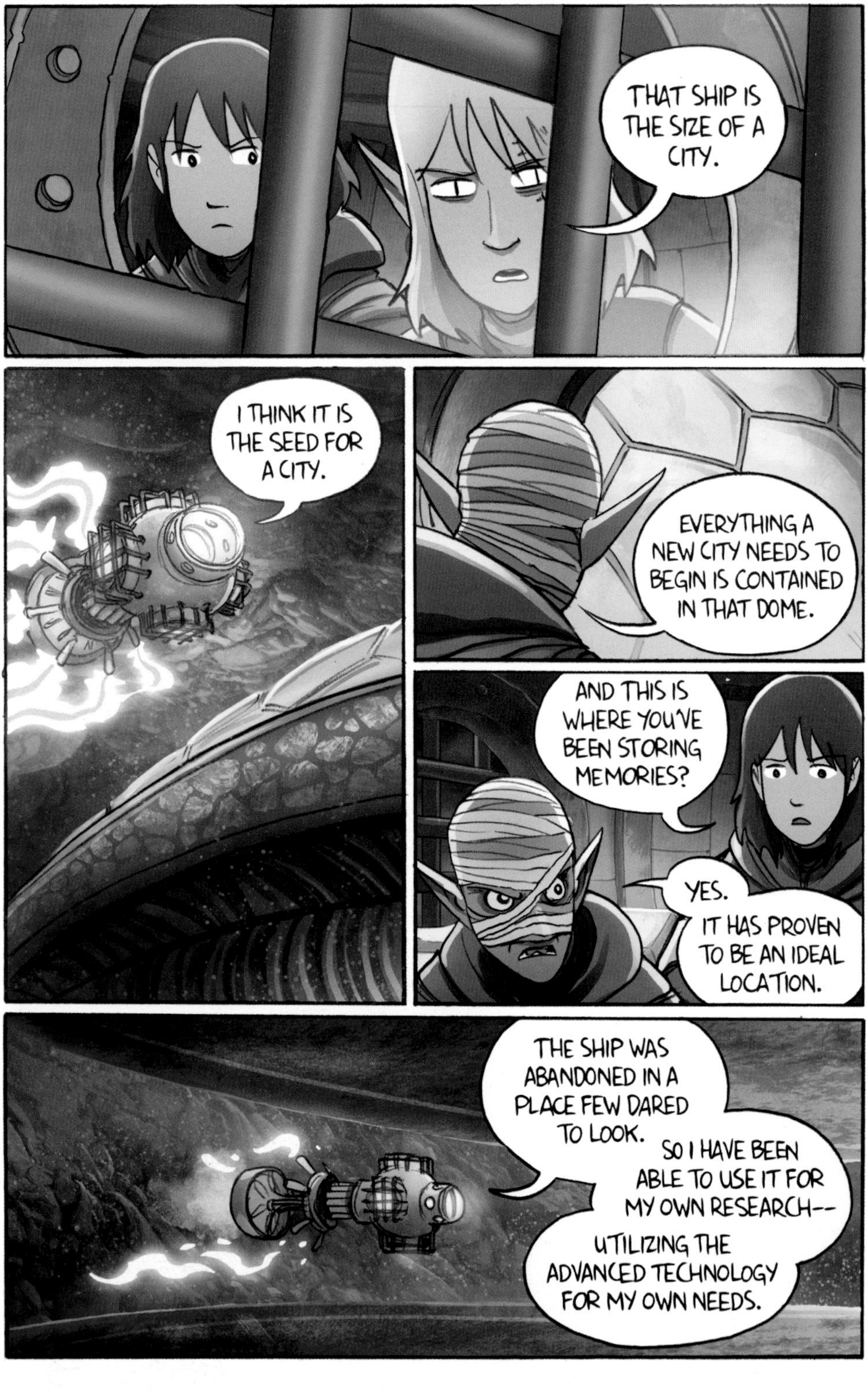
THAT SHIP IS THE SIZE OF A CITY.
I THINK IT IS THE SEED FOR A CITY.
EVERYTHING A NEW CITY NEEDS TO BEGIN IS CONTAINED IN THAT DOME.
AND THIS IS WHERE YOU'VE BEEN STORING MEMORIES?
YES.
IT HAS PROVEN TO BE AN IDEAL LOCATION.
THE SHIP WAS ABANDONED IN A PLACE FEW DARED TO LOOK.
SO I HAVE BEEN ABLE TO USE IT FOR MY OWN RESEARCH--
UTILIZING THE ADVANCED TECHNOLOGY FOR MY OWN NEEDS.

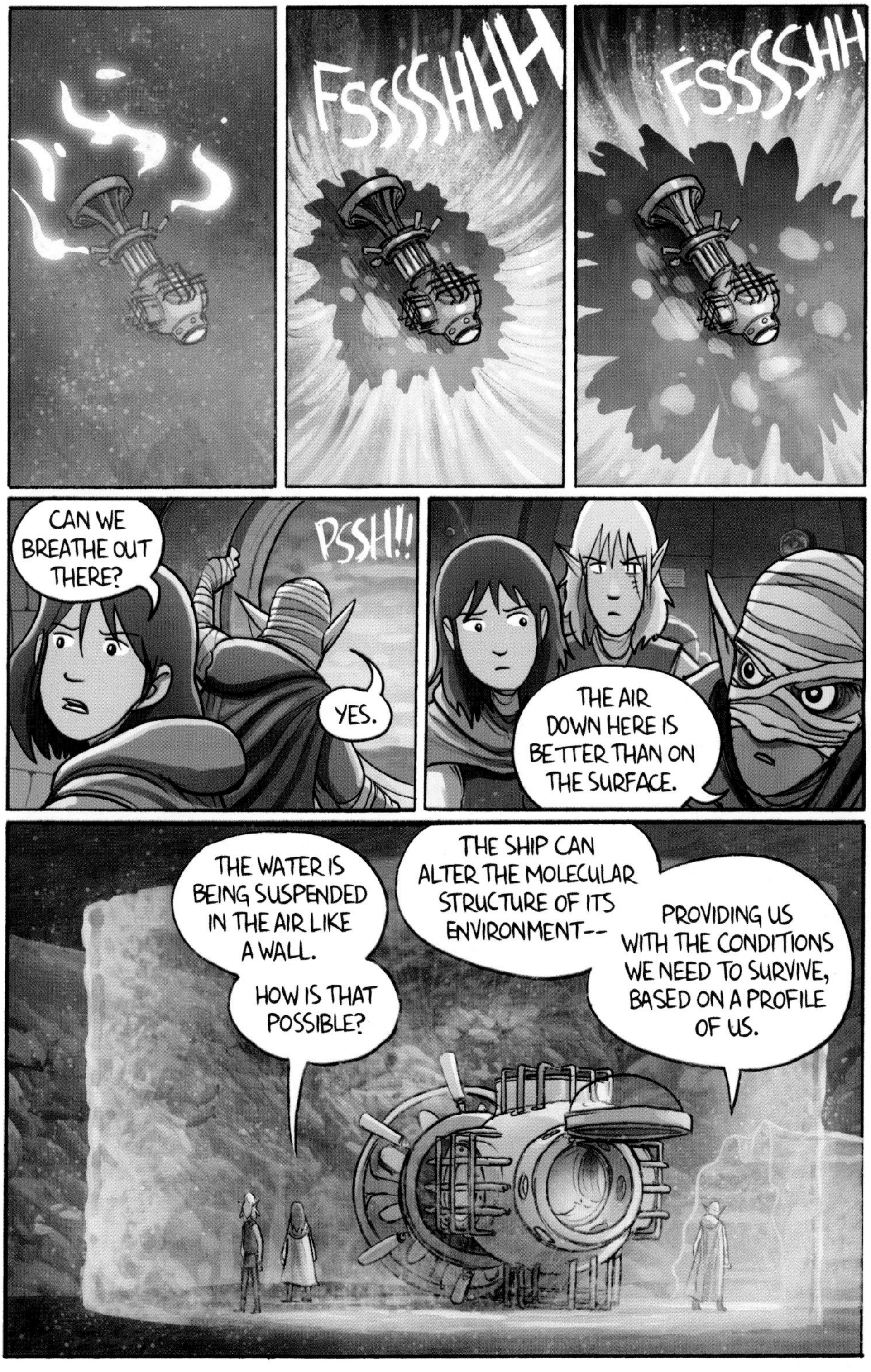
FSSSSHHH
FSSSSHH
CAN WE BREATHE OUT THERE?
PSSH!!
YES.
THE AIR DOWN HERE IS BETTER THAN ON THE SURFACE.
THE WATER IS BEING SUSPENDED IN THE AIR LIKE A WALL.
HOW IS THAT POSSIBLE?
THE SHIP CAN ALTER THE MOLECULAR STRUCTURE OF ITS ENVIRONMENT--
PROVIDING US WITH THE CONDITIONS WE NEED TO SURVIVE, BASED ON A PROFILE OF US.

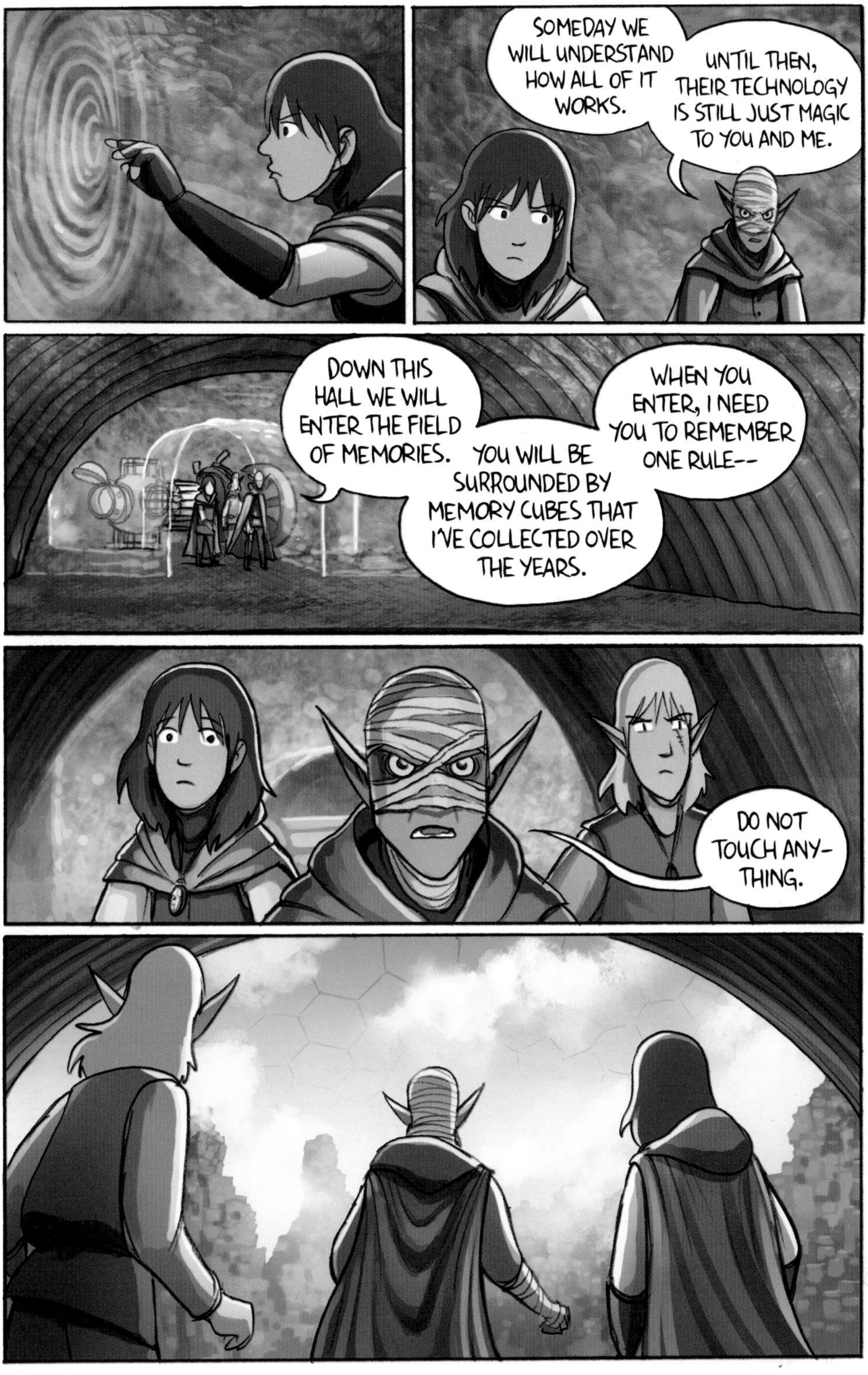
SOMEDAY WE WILL UNDERSTAND HOW ALL OF IT WORKS.
UNTIL THEN, THEIR TECHNOLOGY IS STILL JUST MAGIC TO YOU AND ME.
DOWN THIS HALL WE WILL ENTER THE FIELD OF MEMORIES.
YOU WILL BE SURROUNDED BY MEMORY CUBES THAT I'VE COLLECTED OVER THE YEARS.
WHEN YOU ENTER, I NEED YOU TO REMEMBER ONE RULE--
DO NOT TOUCH ANY-THING.

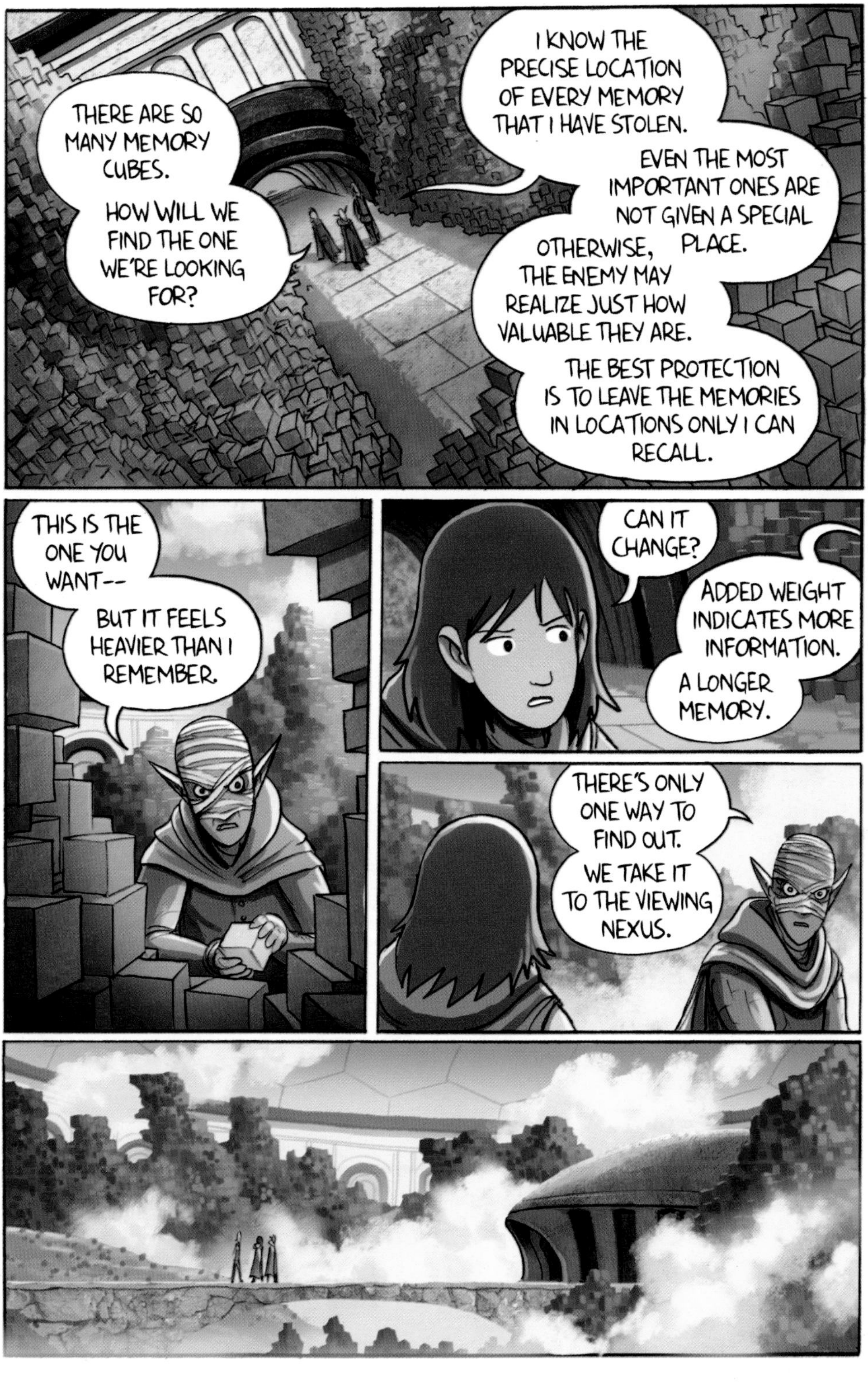
THERE ARE SO MANY MEMORY CUBES.
HOW WILL WE FIND THE ONE WE'RE LOOKING FOR?
I KNOW THE PRECISE LOCATION OF EVERY MEMORY THAT I HAVE STOLEN.
EVEN THE MOST IMPORTANT ONES ARE NOT GIVEN A SPECIAL PLACE.
OTHERWISE, THE ENEMY MAY REALIZE JUST HOW VALUABLE THEY ARE.
THE BEST PROTECTION IS TO LEAVE THE MEMORIES IN LOCATIONS ONLY I CAN RECALL.
THIS IS THE ONE YOU WANT--
BUT IT FEELS HEAVIER THAN I REMEMBER.
CAN IT CHANGE?
ADDED WEIGHT INDICATES MORE INFORMATION.
A LONGER MEMORY.
THERE'S ONLY ONE WAY TO FIND OUT.
WE TAKE IT TO THE VIEWING NEXUS.

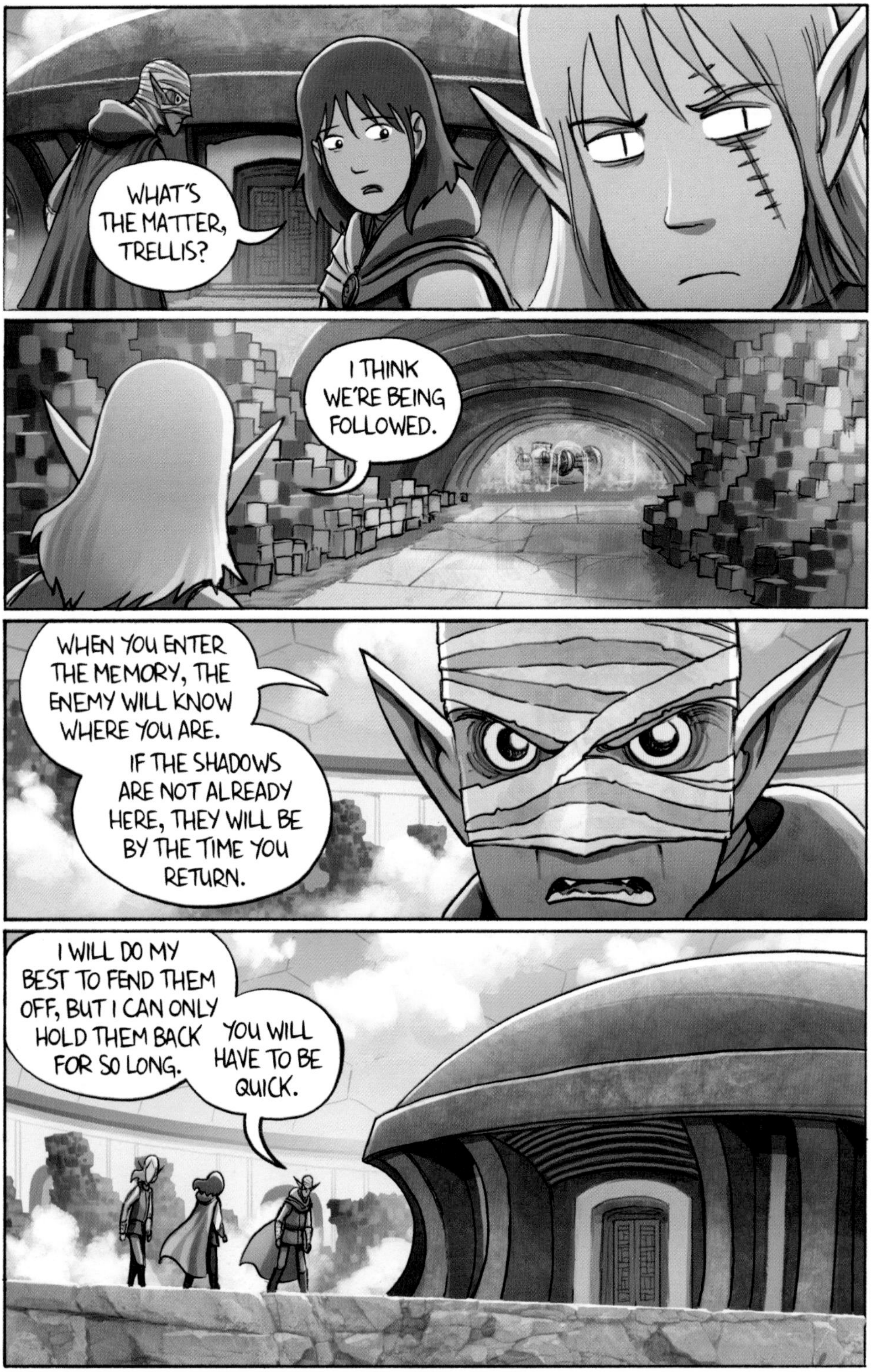
WHAT'S THE MATTER, TRELLIS?
I THINK WE'RE BEING FOLLOWED.
WHEN YOU ENTER THE MEMORY, THE ENEMY WILL KNOW WHERE YOU ARE.
IF THE SHADOWS ARE NOT ALREADY HERE, THEY WILL BE BY THE TIME YOU RETURN.
I WILL DO MY BEST TO FEND THEM OFF, BUT I CAN ONLY HOLD THEM BACK FOR SO LONG.
YOU WILL HAVE TO BE QUICK.

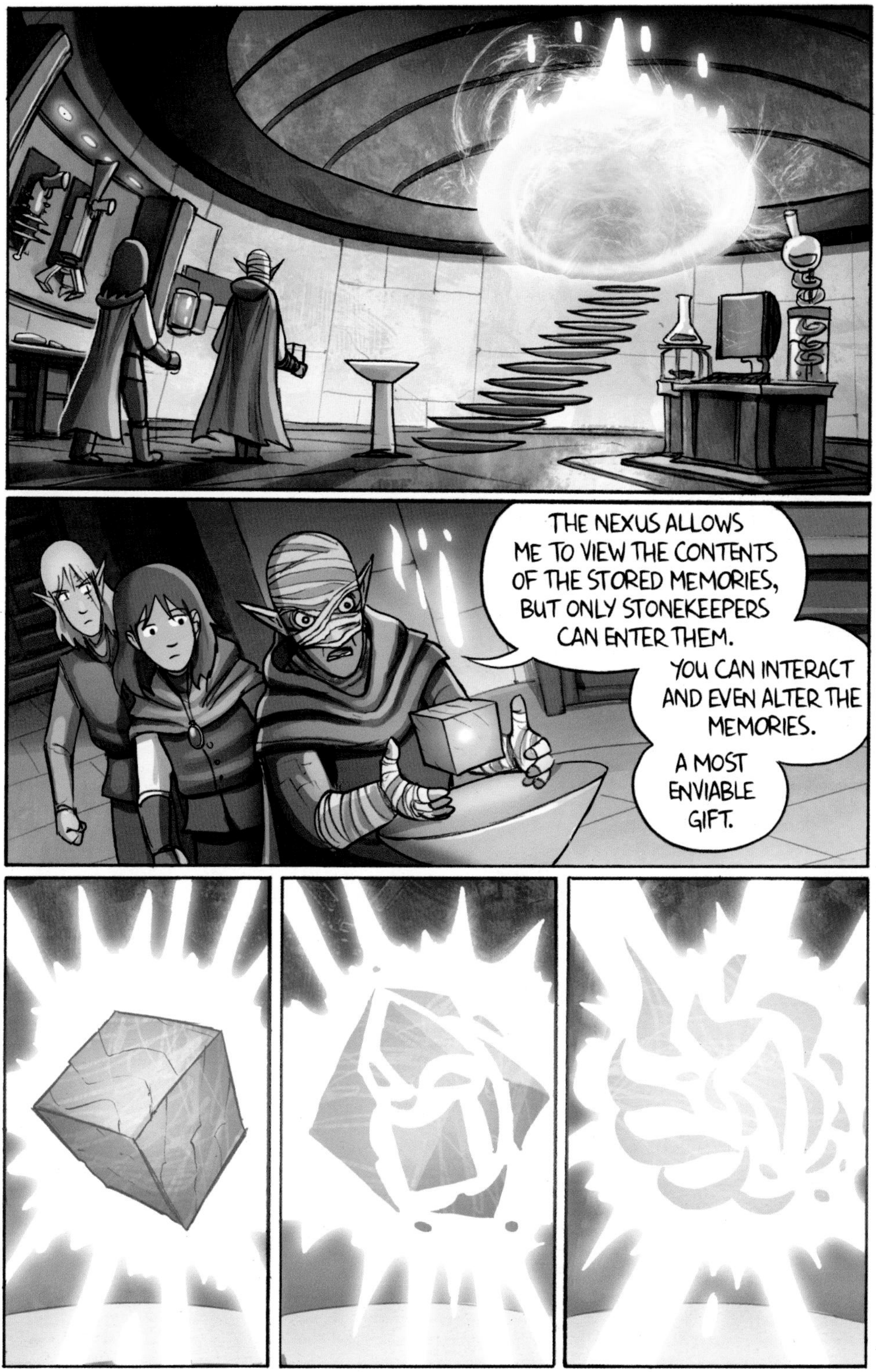
THE NEXUS ALLOWS ME TO VIEW THE CONTENTS OF THE STORED MEMORIES, BUT ONLY STONEKEEPERS CAN ENTER THEM.
YOU CAN INTERACT AND EVEN ALTER THE MEMORIES.
A MOST ENVIABLE GIFT.

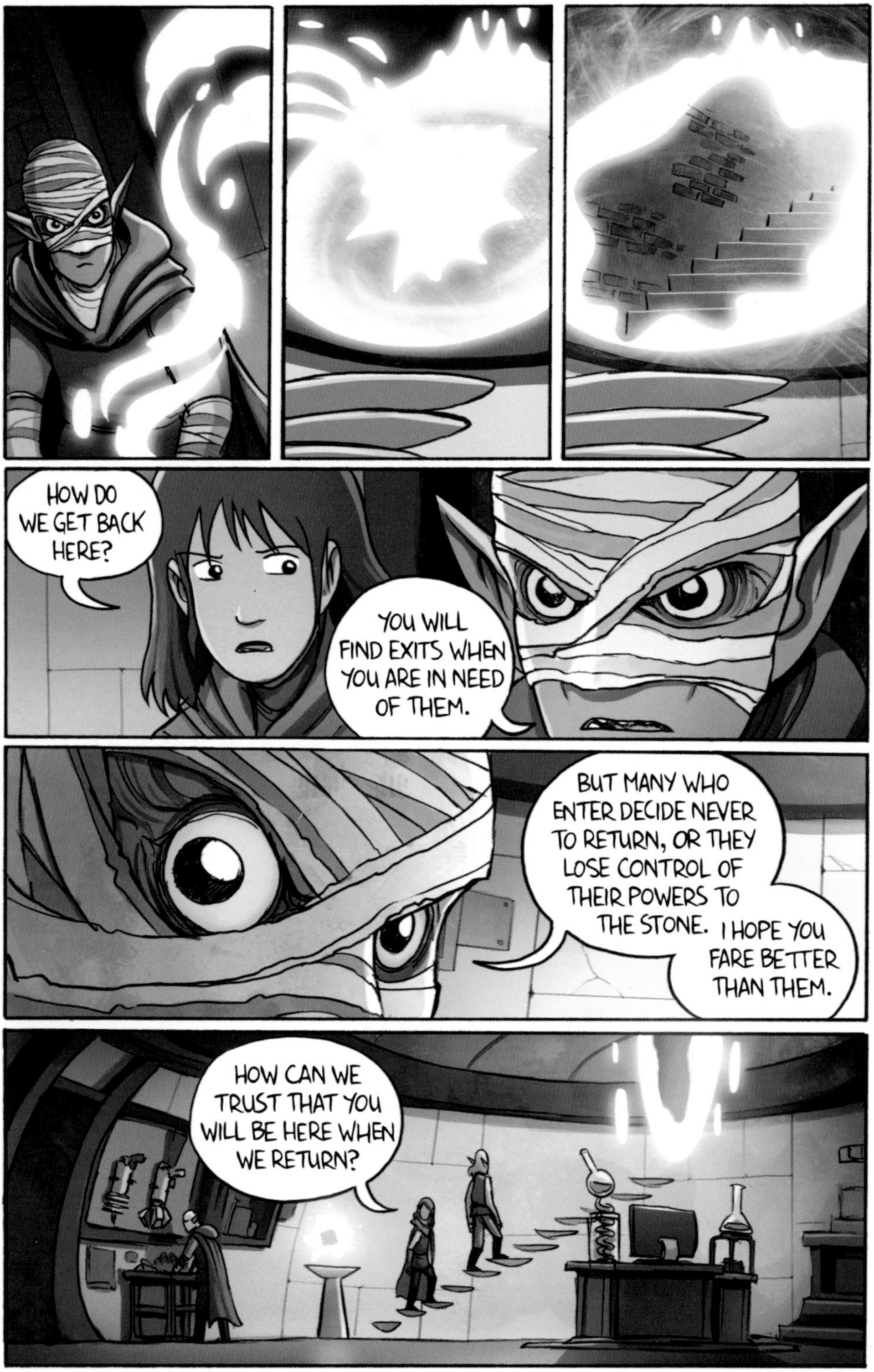
HOW DO WE GET BACK HERE?
YOU WILL FIND EXITS WHEN YOU ARE IN NEED OF THEM.
BUT MANY WHO ENTER DECIDE NEVER TO RETURN, OR THEY LOSE CONTROL OF THEIR POWERS TO THE STONE.
I HOPE YOU FARE BETTER THAN THEM.
HOW CAN WE TRUST THAT YOU WILL BE HERE WHEN WE RETURN?

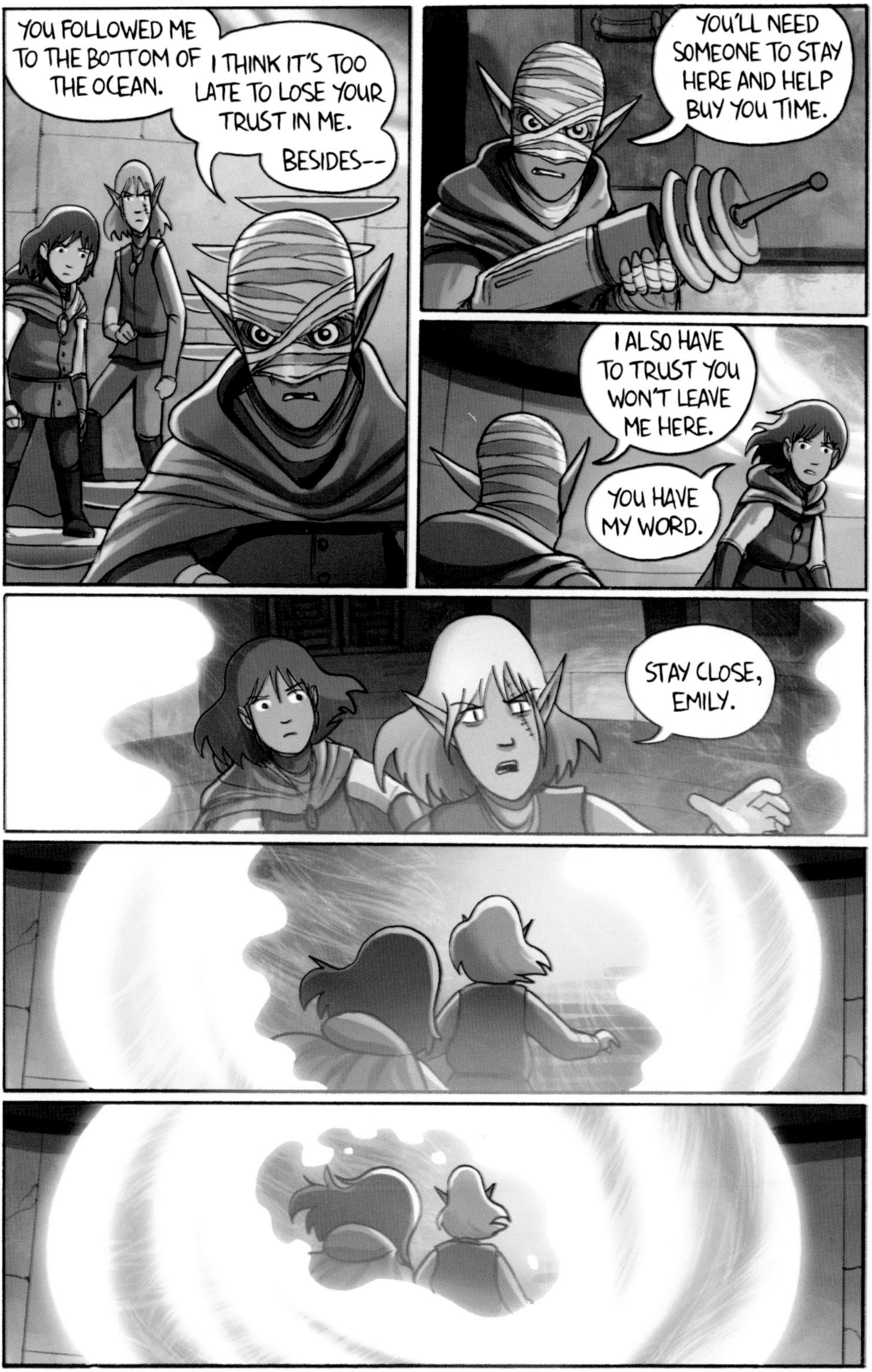
YOU FOLLOWED ME TO THE BOTTOM OF THE OCEAN.
I THINK IT'S TOO LATE TO LOSE YOUR TRUST IN ME.
BESIDES--
YOU'LL NEED SOMEONE TO STAY HERE AND HELP BUY YOU TIME.
I ALSO HAVE TO TRUST YOU WON'T LEAVE ME HERE.
YOU HAVE MY WORD.
STAY CLOSE, EMILY.

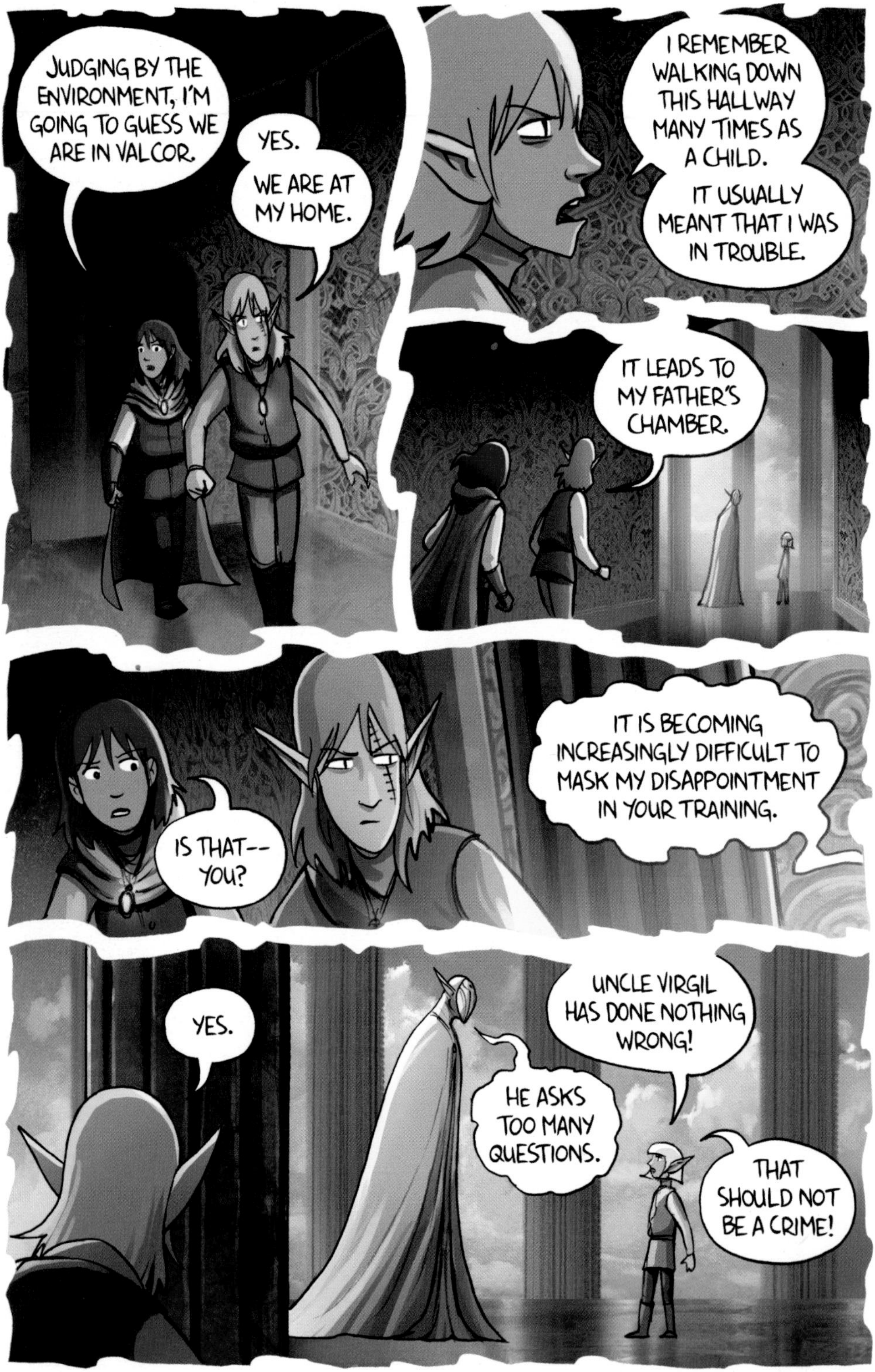
JUDGING BY THE ENVIRONMENT, I'M GOING TO GUESS WE ARE IN VALCOR.
YES.
WE ARE AT MY HOME.
I REMEMBER WALKING DOWN THIS HALLWAY MANY TIMES AS A CHILD.
IT USUALLY MEANT THAT I WAS IN TROUBLE.
IT LEADS TO MY FATHER'S CHAMBER.
IT IS BECOMING INCREASINGLY DIFFICULT TO MASK MY DISAPPOINTMENT IN YOUR TRAINING.
IS THAT--YOU?
YES.
UNCLE VIRGIL HAS DONE NOTHING WRONG!
HE ASKS TOO MANY QUESTIONS.
THAT SHOULD NOT BE A CRIME!

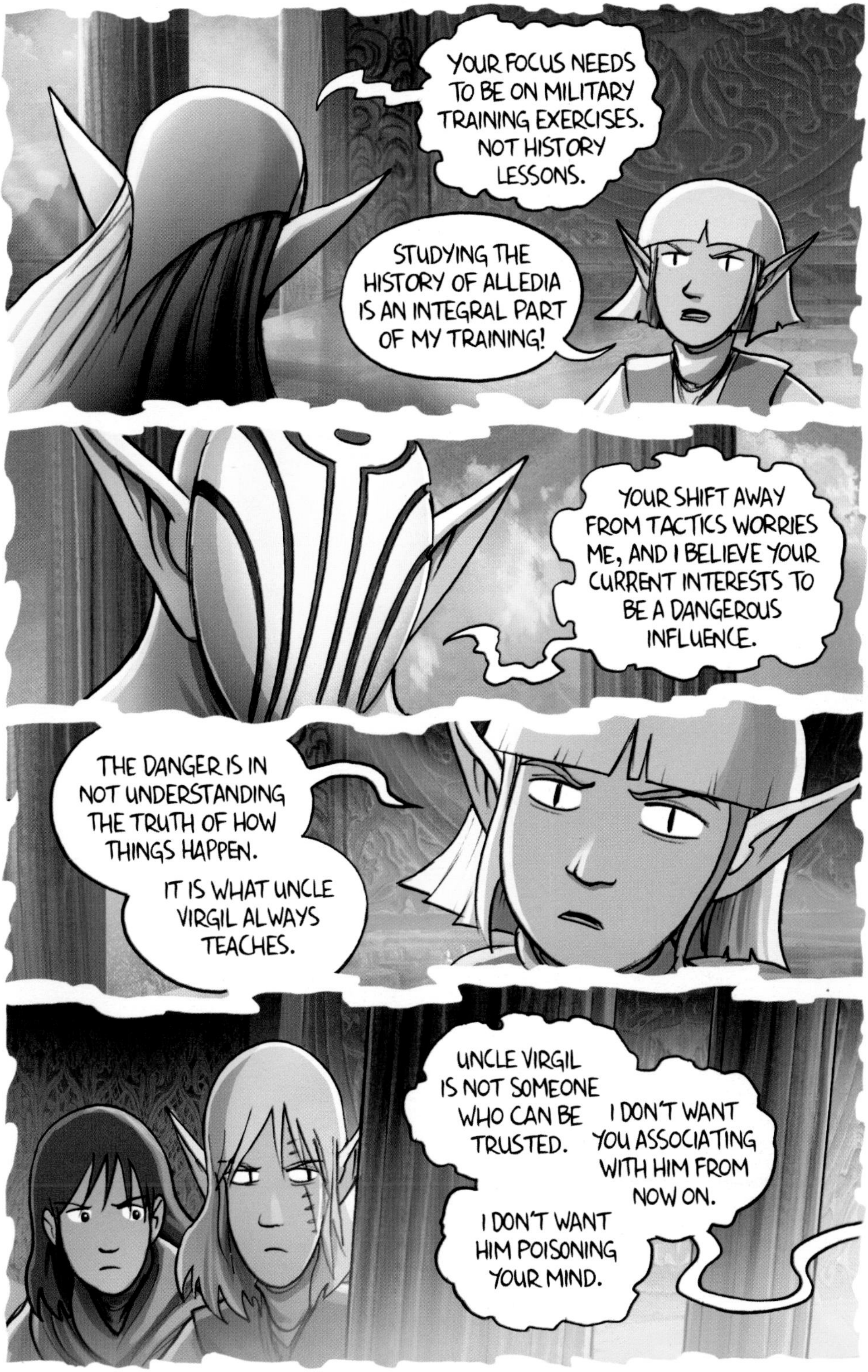
YOUR FOCUS NEEDS TO BE ON MILITARY TRAINING EXERCISES. NOT HISTORY LESSONS.
STUDYING THE HISTORY OF ALLEDIA IS AN INTEGRAL PART OF MY TRAINING!
YOUR SHIFT AWAY FROM TACTICS WORRIES ME, AND I BELIEVE YOUR CURRENT INTERESTS TO BE A DANGEROUS INFLUENCE.
THE DANGER IS IN NOT UNDERSTANDING THE TRUTH OF HOW THINGS HAPPEN.
IT IS WHAT UNCLE VIRGIL ALWAYS TEACHES.
UNCLE VIRGIL IS NOT SOMEONE WHO CAN BE TRUSTED.
I DON'T WANT YOU ASSOCIATING WITH HIM FROM NOW ON.
I DON'T WANT HIM POISONING YOUR MIND.

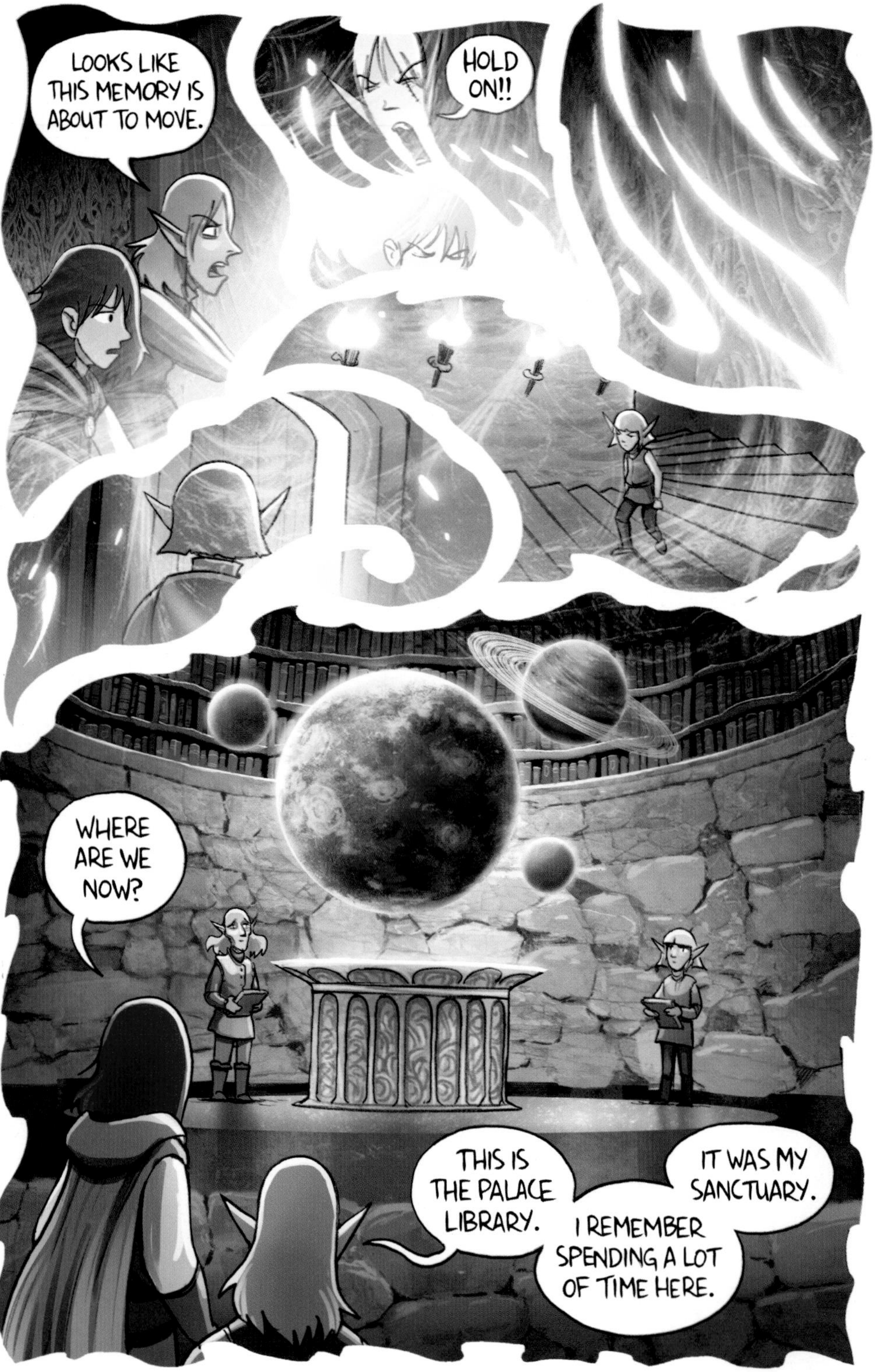
LOOKS LIKE THIS MEMORY IS ABOUT TO MOVE.
HOLD ON!!
WHERE ARE WE NOW?
THIS IS THE PALACE LIBRARY.
IT WAS MY SANCTUARY.
I REMEMBER SPENDING A LOT OF TIME HERE.

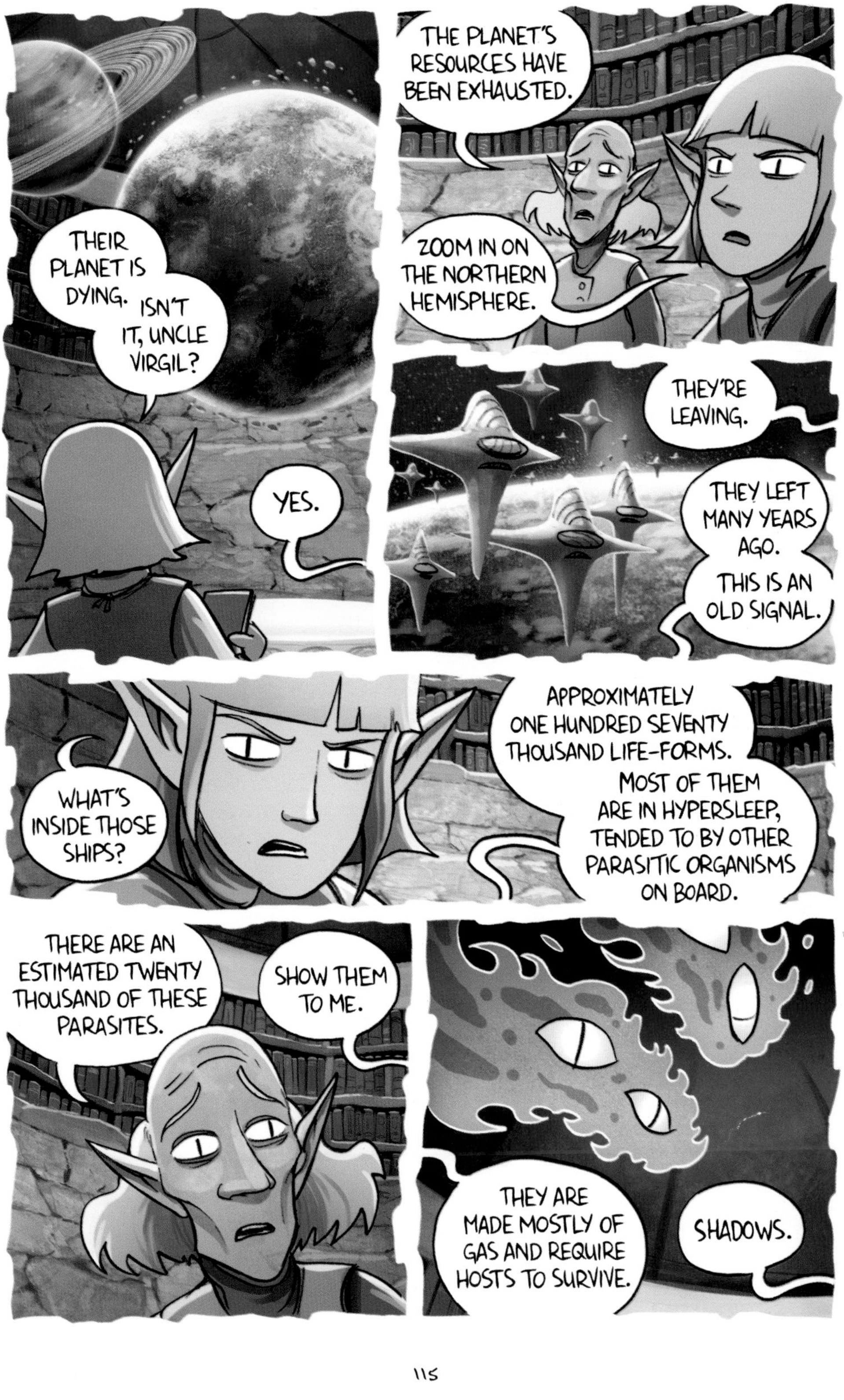
THEIR PLANET IS DYING.
ISN'T IT, UNCLE VIRGIL?
YES.
THE PLANET'S RESOURCES HAVE BEEN EXHAUSTED.
ZOOM IN ON THE NORTHERN HEMISPHERE.
THEY'RE LEAVING.
THEY LEFT MANY YEARS AGO.
THIS IS AN OLD SIGNAL.
WHAT'S INSIDE THOSE SHIPS?
APPROXIMATELY ONE HUNDRED SEVENTY THOUSAND LIFE-FORMS.
MOST OF THEM ARE IN HYPERSLEEP, TENDED TO BY OTHER PARASITIC ORGANISMS ON BOARD.
THERE ARE AN ESTIMATED TWENTY THOUSAND OF THESE PARASITES.
SHOW THEM TO ME.
THEY ARE MADE MOSTLY OF GAS AND REQUIRE HOSTS TO SURVIVE.
SHADOWS.

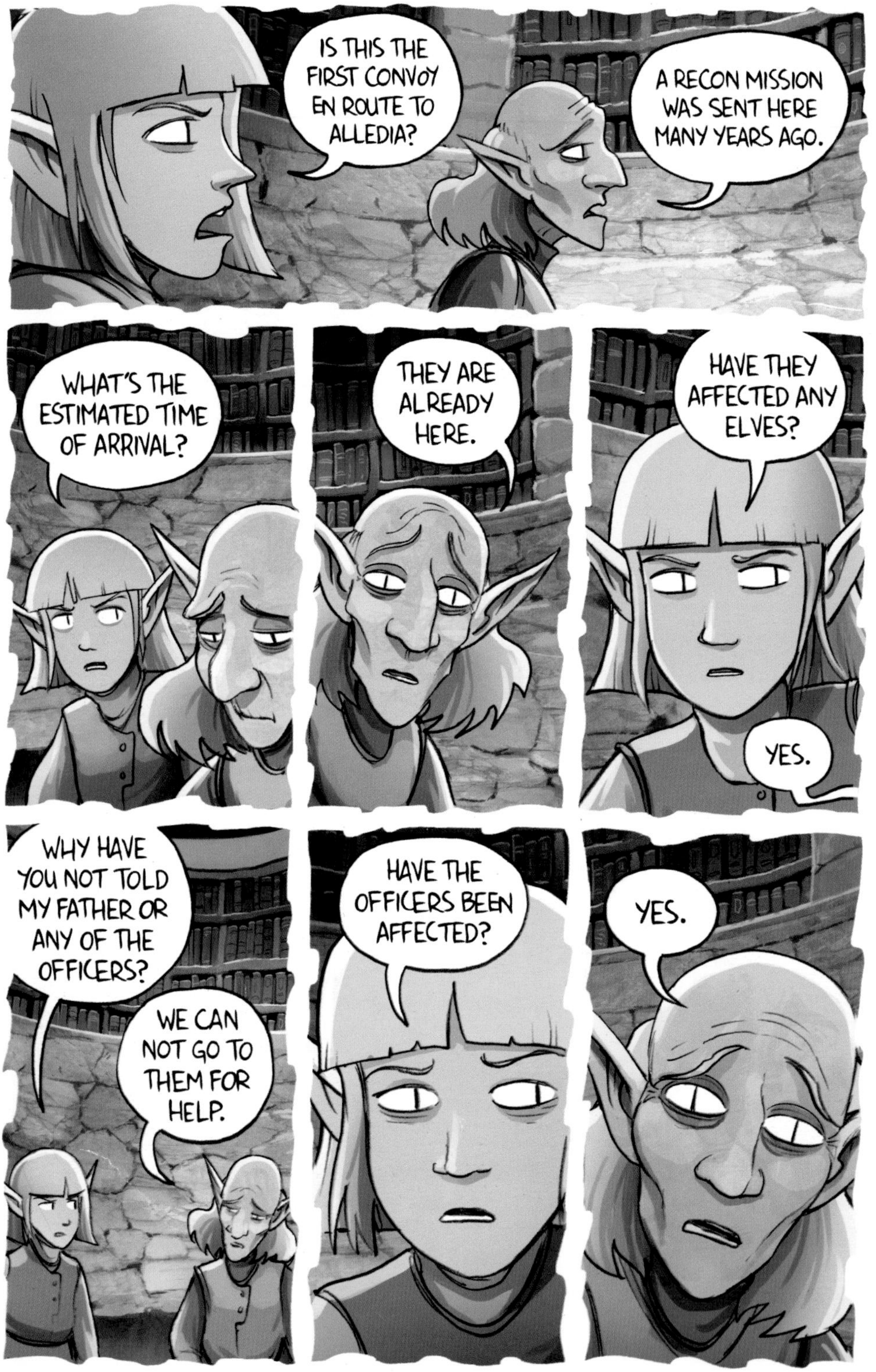
IS THIS THE FIRST CONVOY EN ROUTE TO ALLEDIA?
A RECON MISSION WAS SENT HERE MANY YEARS AGO.
WHAT'S THE ESTIMATED TIME OF ARRIVAL?
THEY ARE ALREADY HERE.
HAVE THEY AFFECTED ANY ELVES?
YES.
WHY HAVE YOU NOT TOLD MY FATHER OR ANY OF THE OFFICERS?
WE CAN NOT GO TO THEM FOR HELP.
HAVE THE OFFICERS BEEN AFFECTED?
YES.

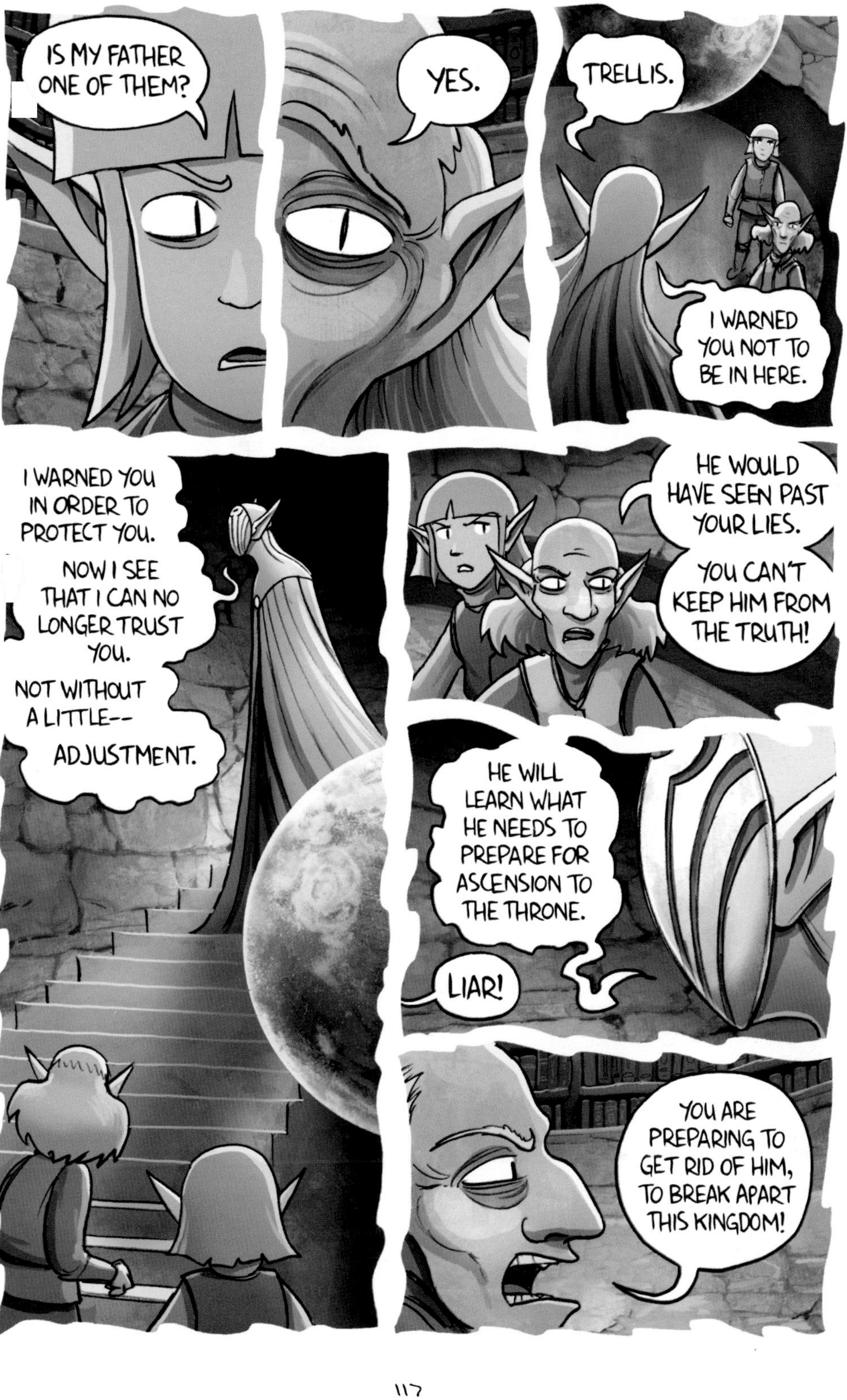
IS MY FATHER ONE OF THEM?
YES.
TRELLIS.
I WARNED YOU NOT TO BE IN HERE.
I WARNED YOU IN ORDER TO PROTECT YOU.
NOW I SEE THAT I CAN NO LONGER TRUST YOU.
NOT WITHOUT A LITTLE--
ADJUSTMENT.
HE WOULD HAVE SEEN PAST YOUR LIES.
YOU CAN'T KEEP HIM FROM THE TRUTH!
HE WILL LEARN WHAT HE NEEDS TO PREPARE FOR ASCENSION TO THE THRONE.
LIAR!
YOU ARE PREPARING TO GET RID OF HIM, TO BREAK APART THIS KINGDOM!

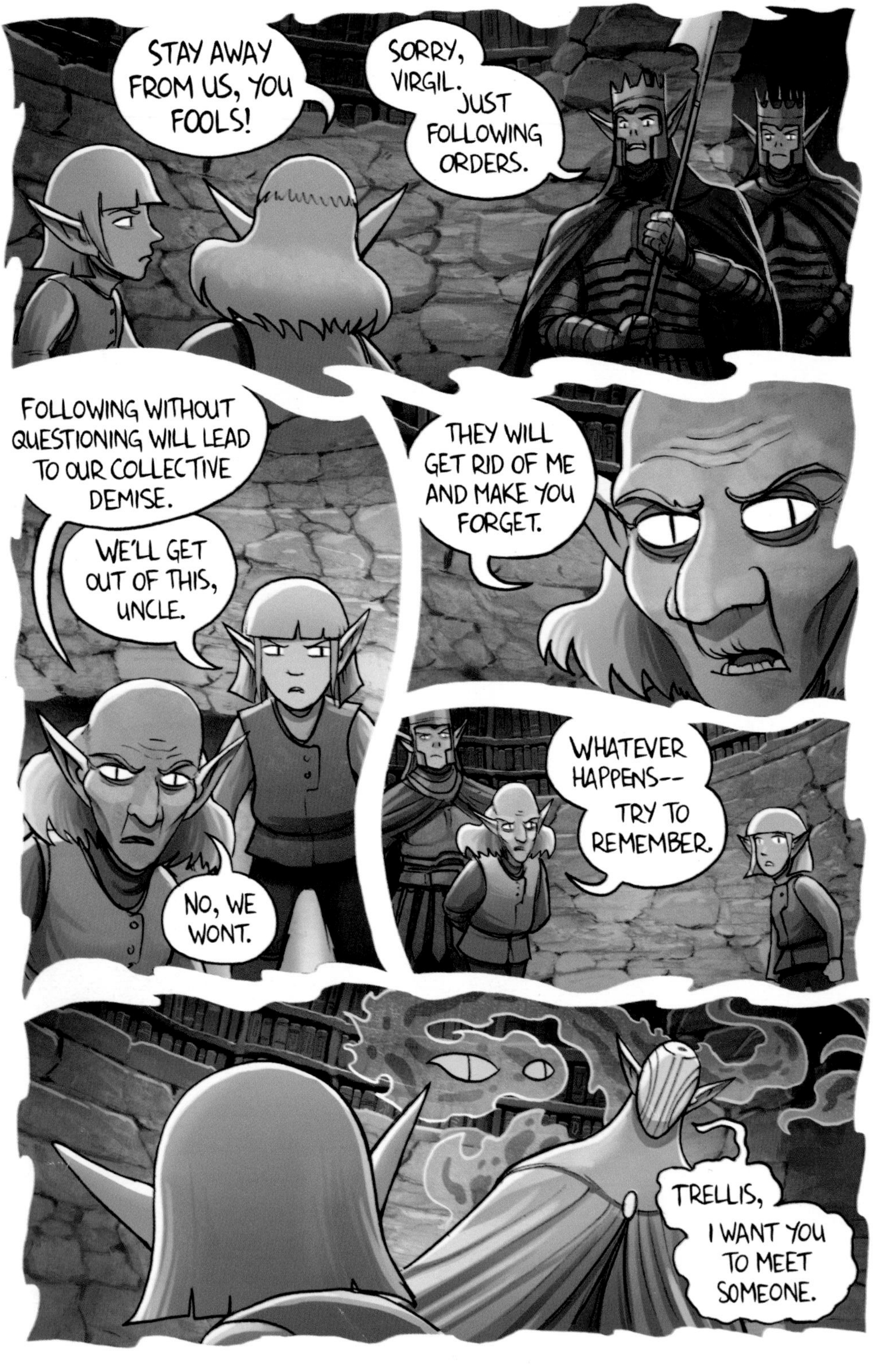
STAY AWAY FROM US, YOU FOOLS!
SORRY, VIRGIL.
JUST FOLLOWING ORDERS.
FOLLOWING WITHOUT QUESTIONING WILL LEAD TO OUR COLLECTIVE DEMISE.
WE'LL GET OUT OF THIS, UNCLE.
NO, WE WONT.
THEY WILL GET RID OF ME AND MAKE YOU FORGET.
WHATEVER HAPPENS--
TRY TO REMEMBER.
TRELLIS,
I WANT YOU TO MEET SOMEONE.

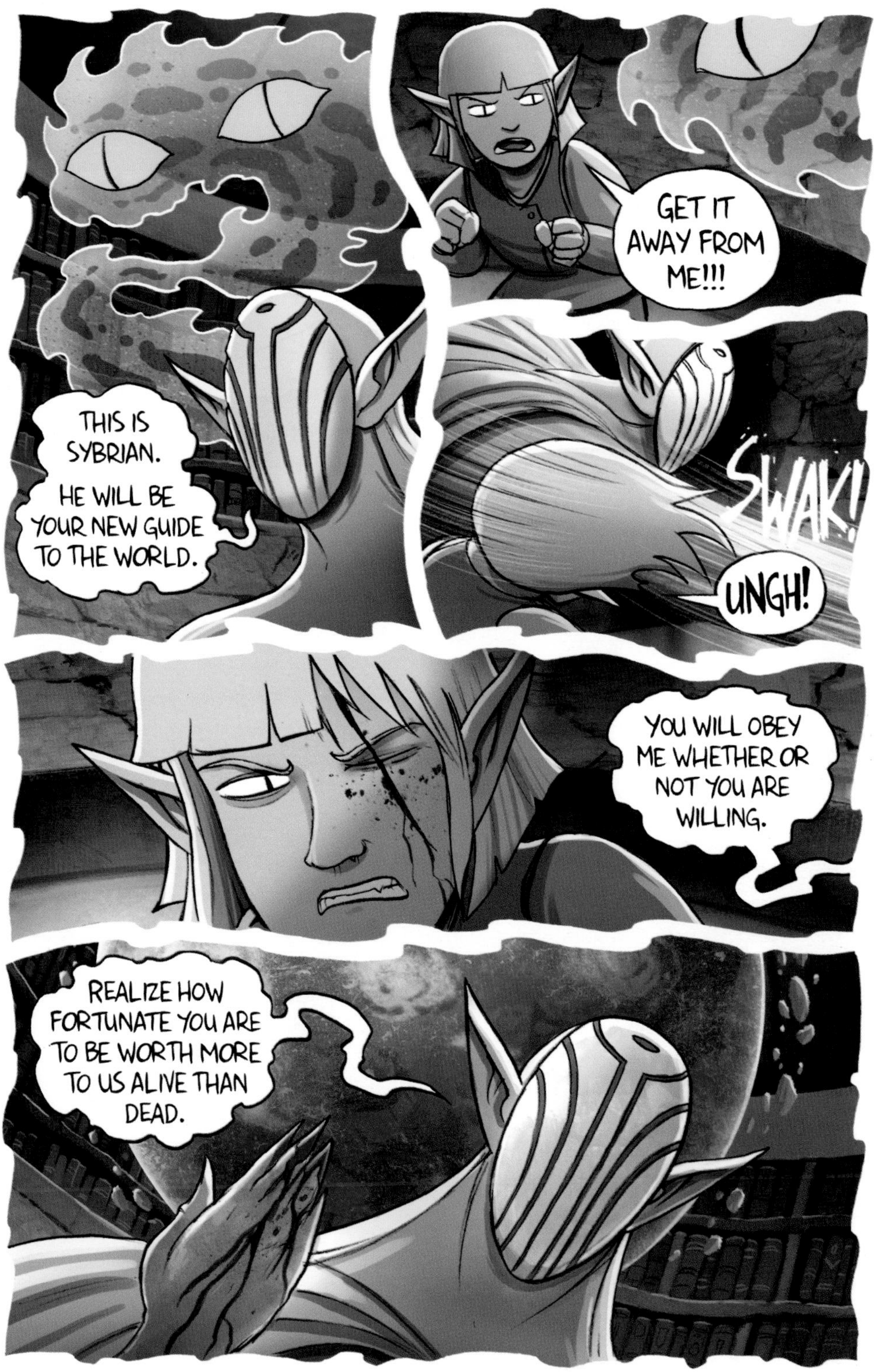
GET IT AWAY FROM ME!!!
THIS IS SYBRIAN.
HE WILL BE YOUR NEW GUIDE TO THE WORLD.
SWAK!
UNGH!
YOU WILL OBEY ME WHETHER OR NOT YOU ARE WILLING.
REALIZE HOW FORTUNATE YOU ARE TO BE WORTH MORE TO US ALIVE THAN DEAD.

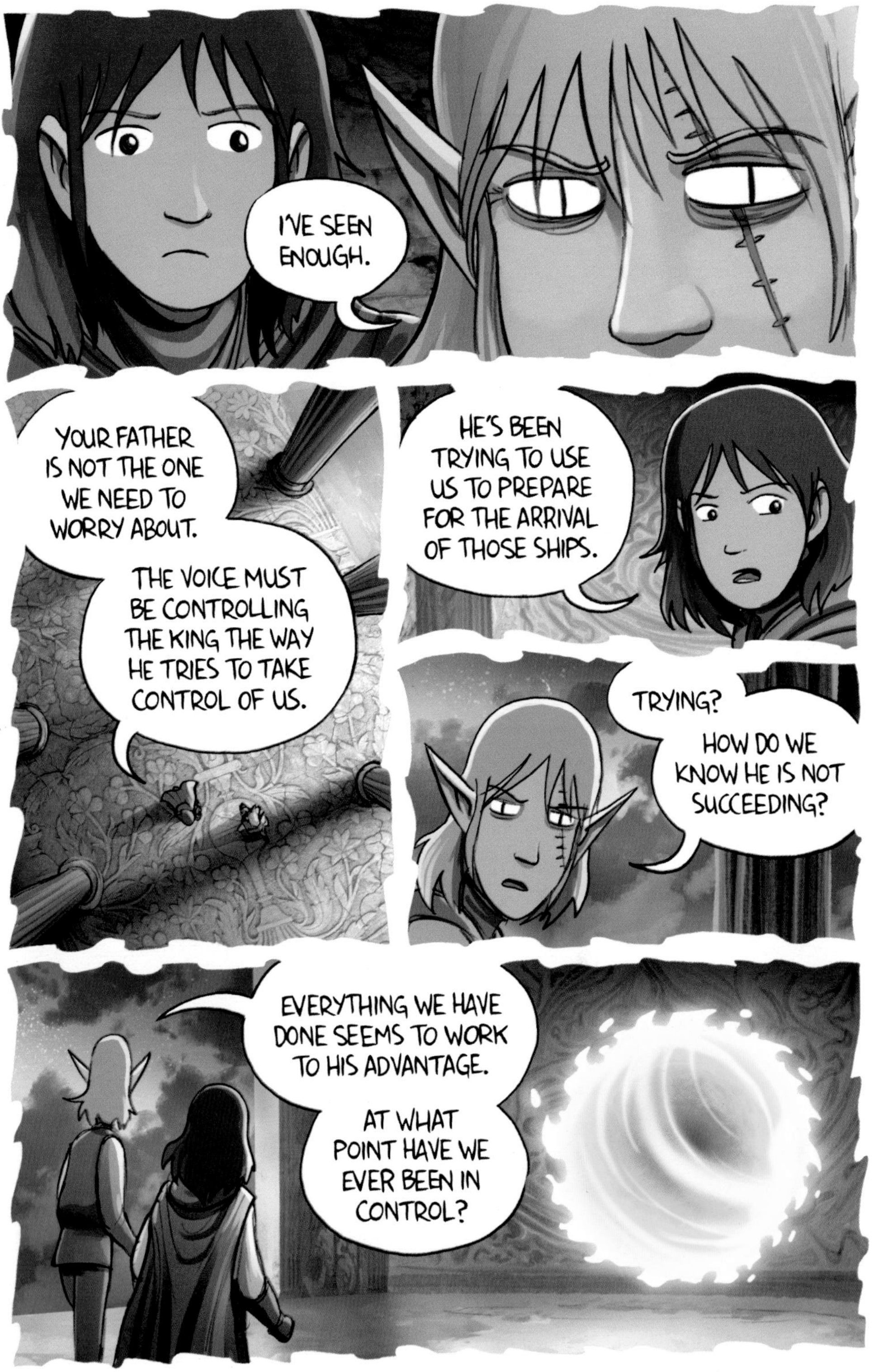
I'VE SEEN ENOUGH.
YOUR FATHER IS NOT THE ONE WE NEED TO WORRY ABOUT.
THE VOICE MUST BE CONTROLLING THE KING THE WAY HE TRIES TO TAKE CONTROL OF US.
HE'S BEEN TRYING TO USE US TO PREPARE FOR THE ARRIVAL OF THOSE SHIPS.
TRYING?
HOW DO WE KNOW HE IS NOT SUCCEEDING?
EVERYTHING WE HAVE DONE SEEMS TO WORK TO HIS ADVANTAGE.
AT WHAT POINT HAVE WE EVER BEEN IN CONTROL?

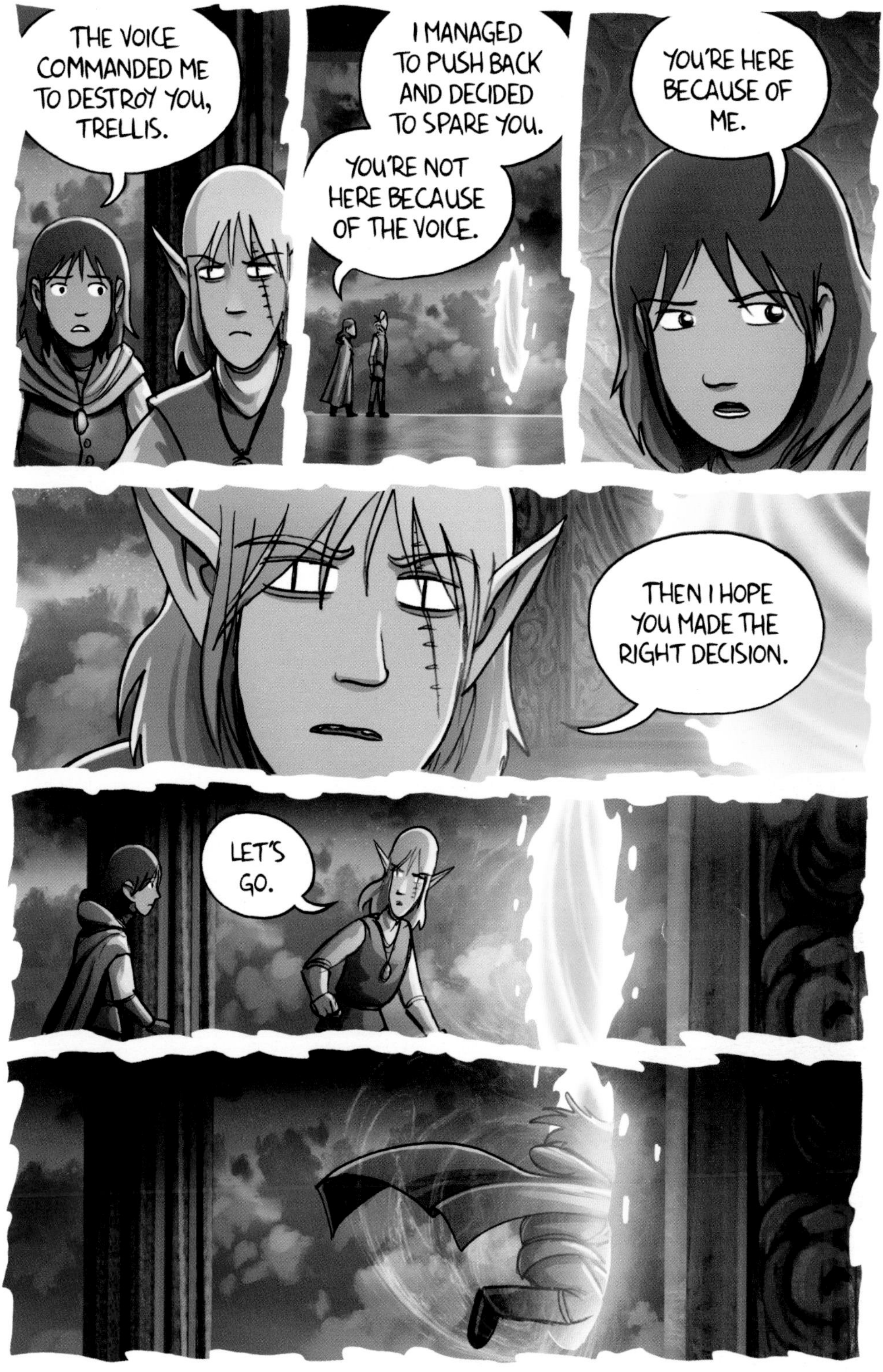
THE VOICE COMMANDED ME TO DESTROY YOU, TRELLIS.
I MANAGED TO PUSH BACK AND DECIDED TO SPARE YOU.
YOU'RE NOT HERE BECAUSE OF THE VOICE.
YOU'RE HERE BECAUSE OF ME.
THEN I HOPE YOU MADE THE RIGHT DECISION.
LET'S GO.

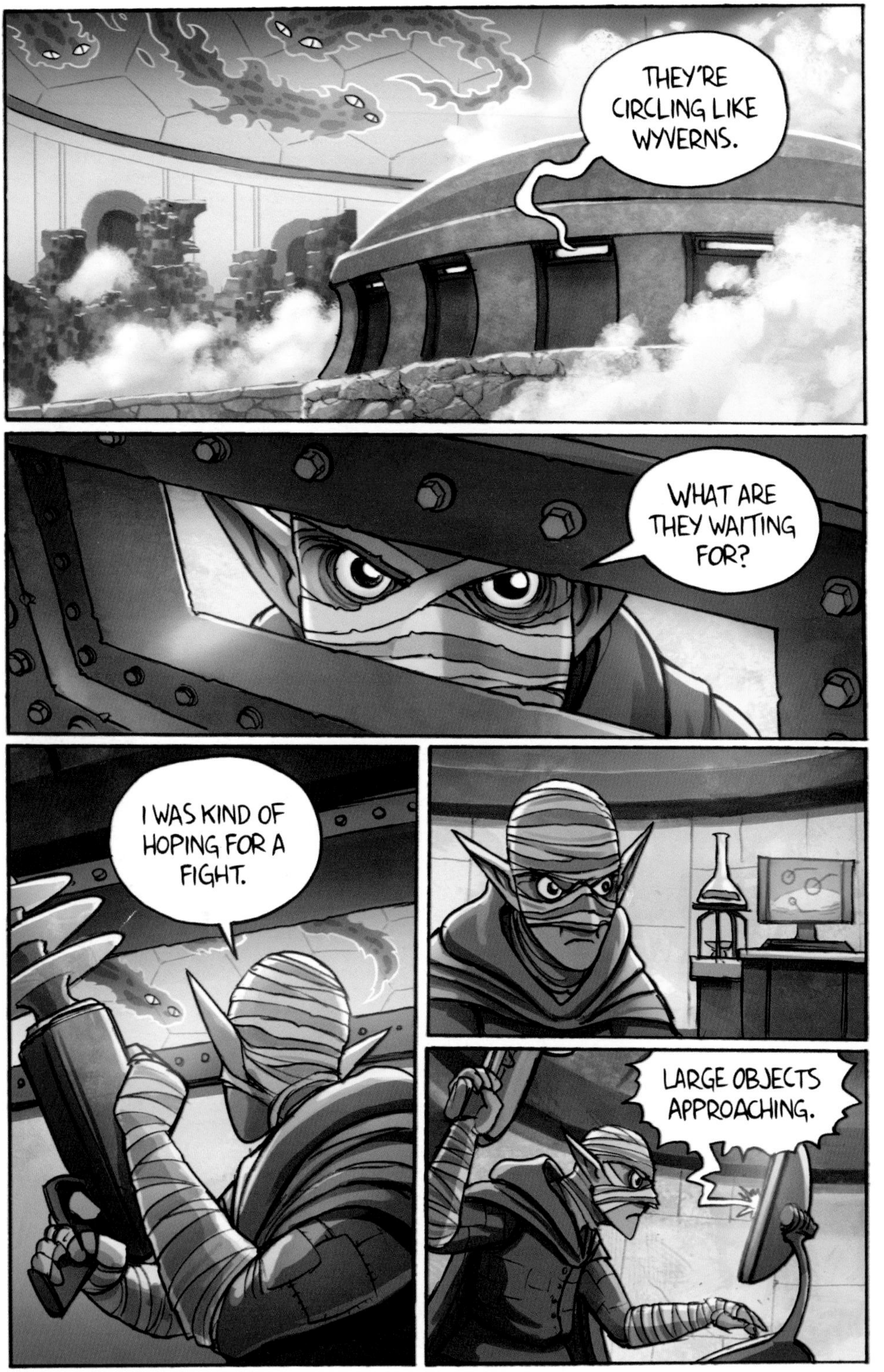
THEY'RE CIRCLING LIKE WYVERNS.
WHAT ARE THEY WAITING FOR?
I WAS KIND OF HOPING FOR A FIGHT.
LARGE OBJECTS APPROACHING.

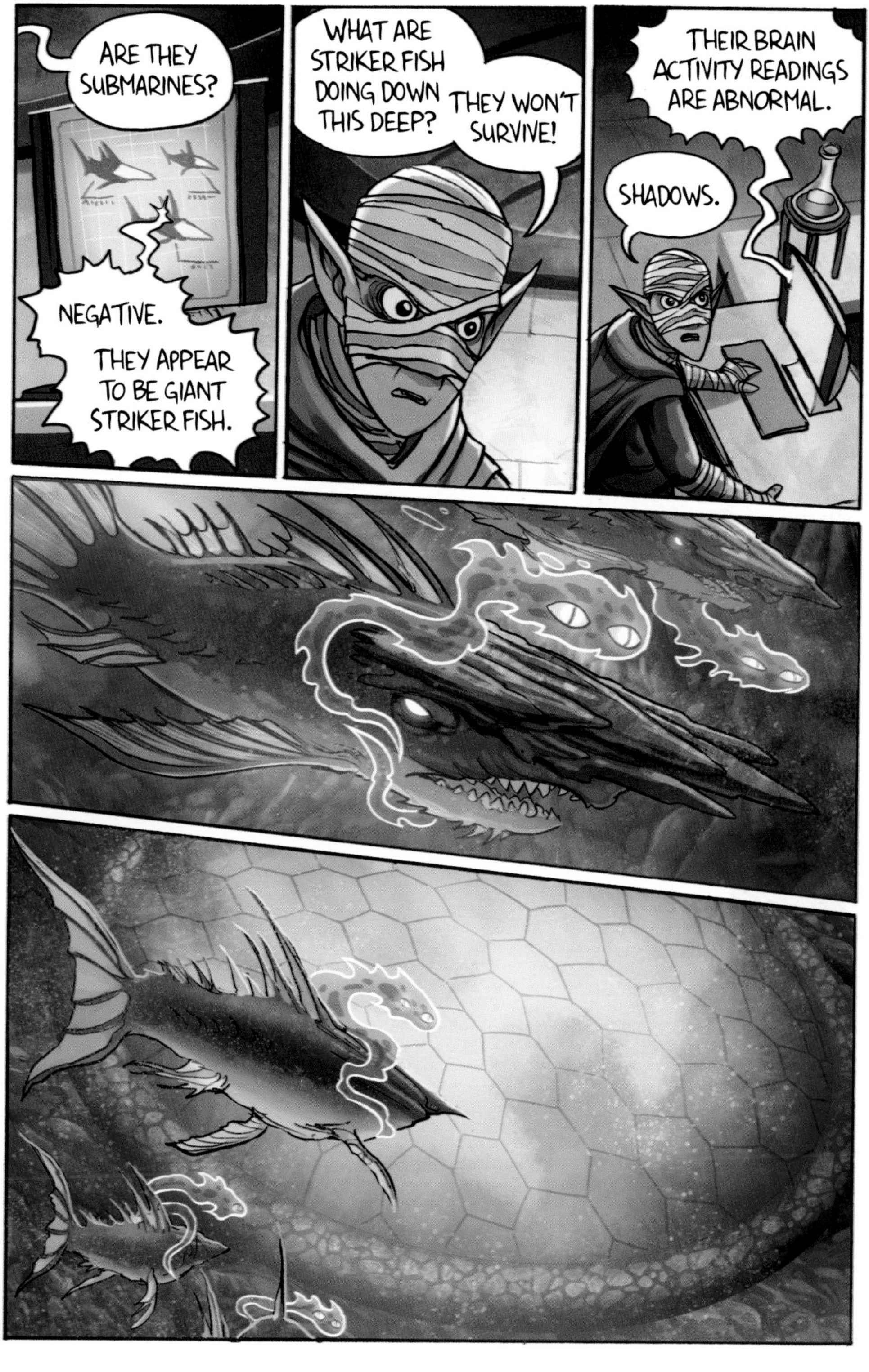
ARE THEY SUBMARINES?
NEGATIVE.
THEY APPEAR TO BE GIANT STRIKER FISH.
WHAT ARE STRIKER FISH DOING DOWN THIS DEEP?
THEY WON'T SURVIVE!
THEIR BRAIN ACTIVITY READINGS ARE ABNORMAL.
SHADOWS.

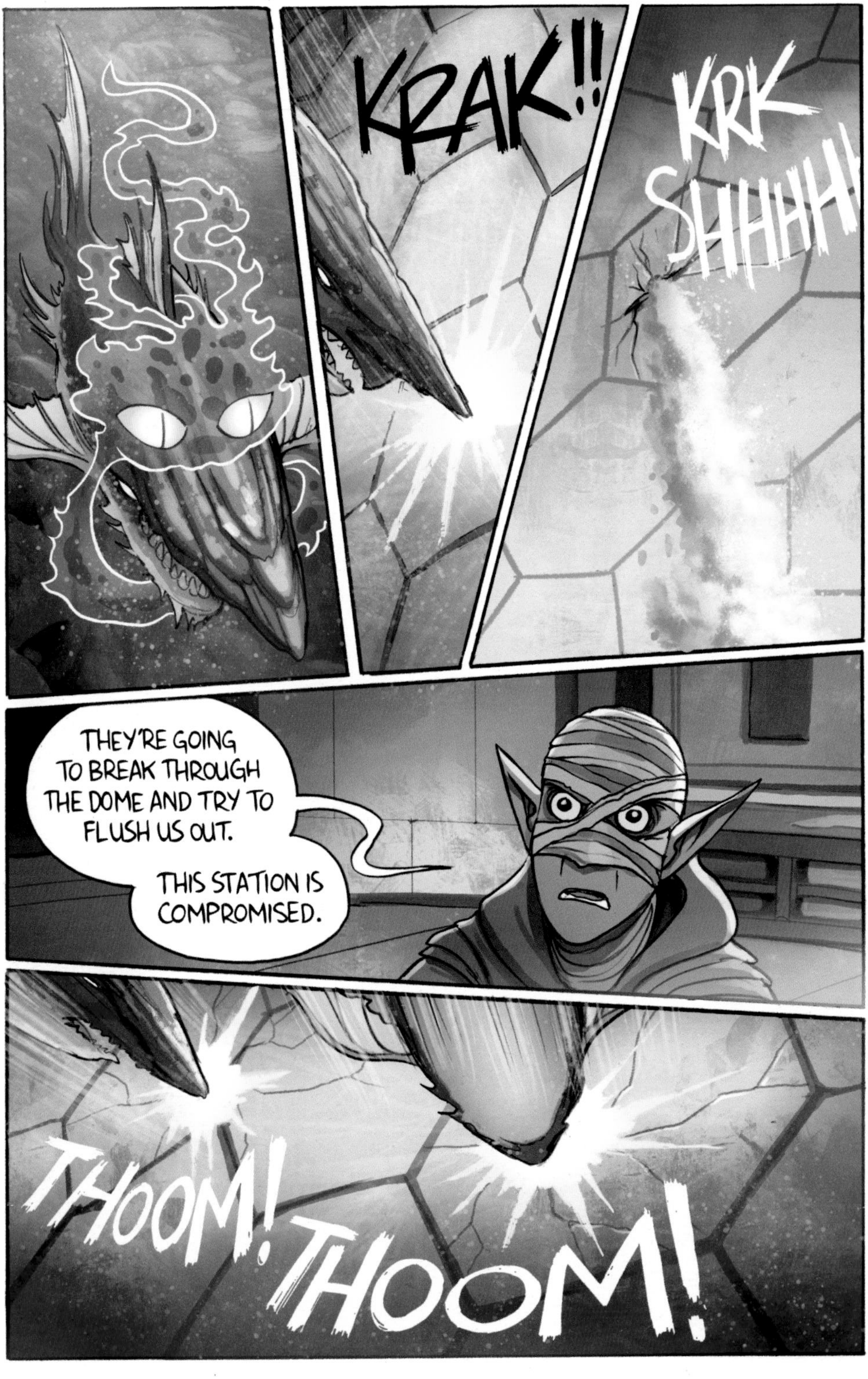
KRAK!!
KRK
SHHHH
THEY'RE GOING TO BREAK THROUGH THE DOME AND TRY TO FLUSH US OUT.
THIS STATION IS COMPROMISED.
THOOM! THOOM!

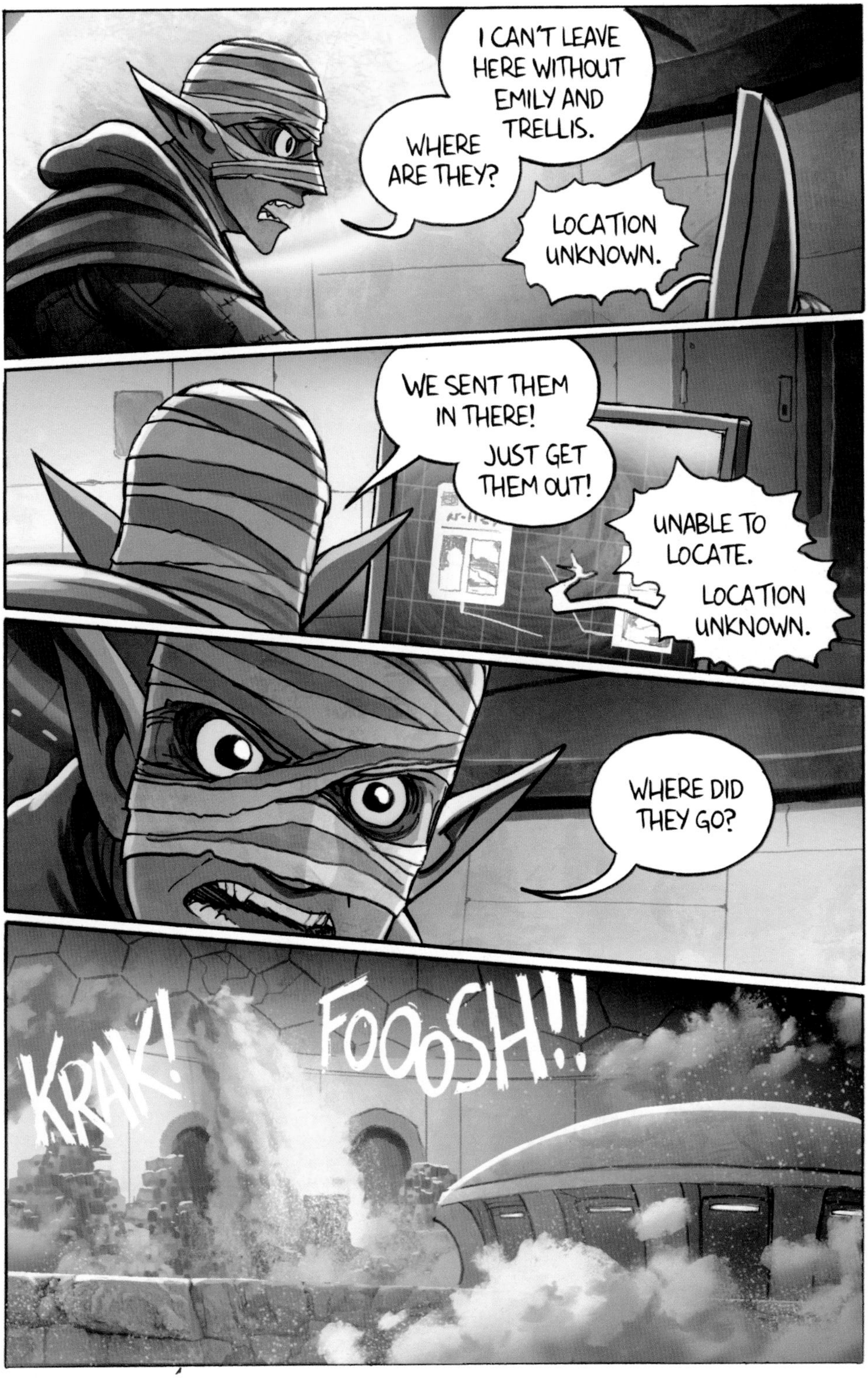
I CAN'T LEAVE HERE WITHOUT EMILY AND TRELLIS.
WHERE ARE THEY?
LOCATION UNKNOWN.
WE SENT THEM IN THERE!
JUST GET THEM OUT!
UNABLE TO LOCATE.
LOCATION UNKNOWN.
WHERE DID THEY GO?
KRAK!
FOOOSH!!

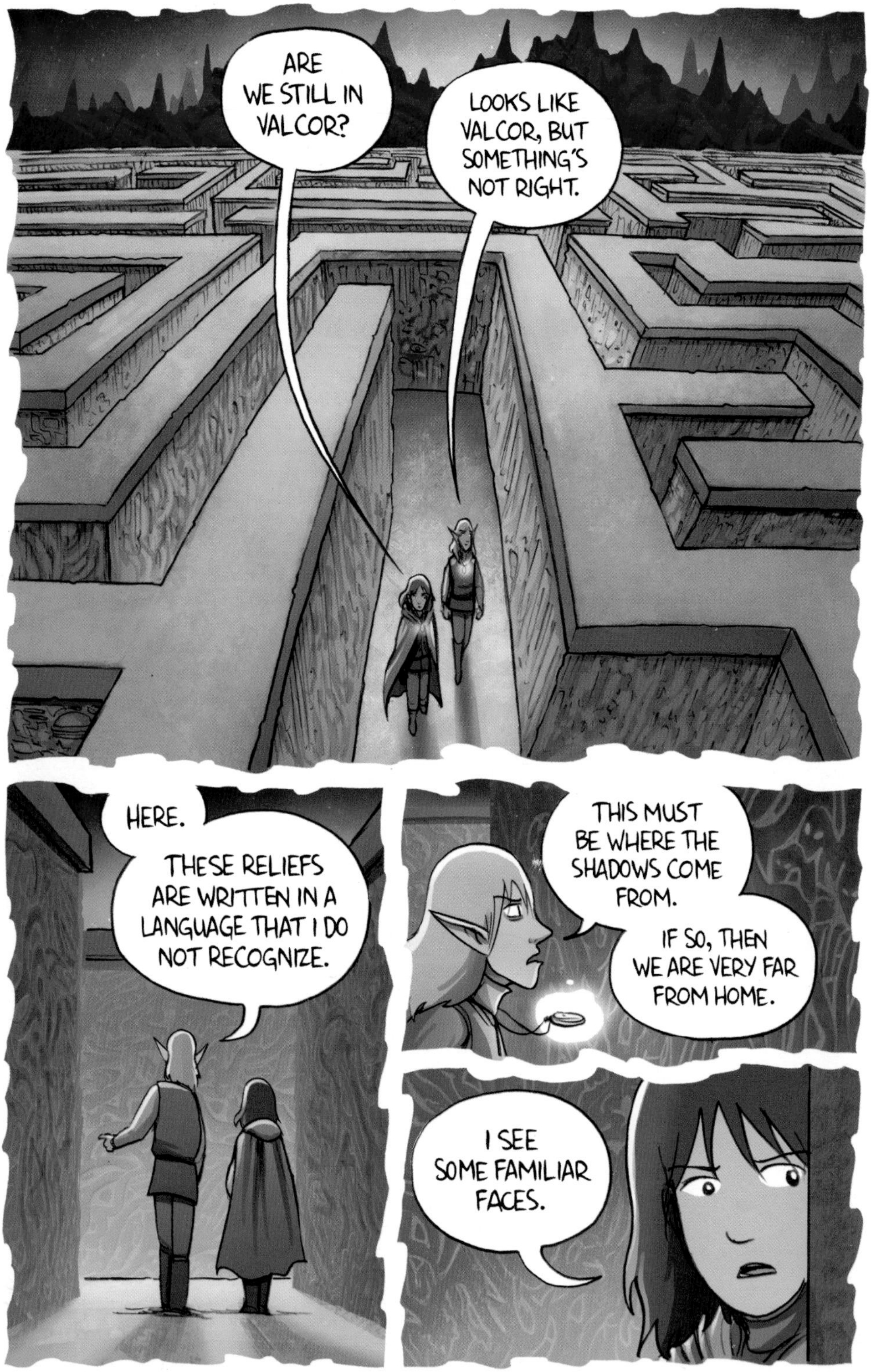
ARE WE STILL IN VALCOR?
LOOKS LIKE VALCOR, BUT SOMETHING'S NOT RIGHT.
HERE.
THESE RELIEFS ARE WRITTEN IN A LANGUAGE THAT I DO NOT RECOGNIZE.
THIS MUST BE WHERE THE SHADOWS COME FROM.
IF SO, THEN WE ARE VERY FAR FROM HOME.
I SEE SOME FAMILIAR FACES.

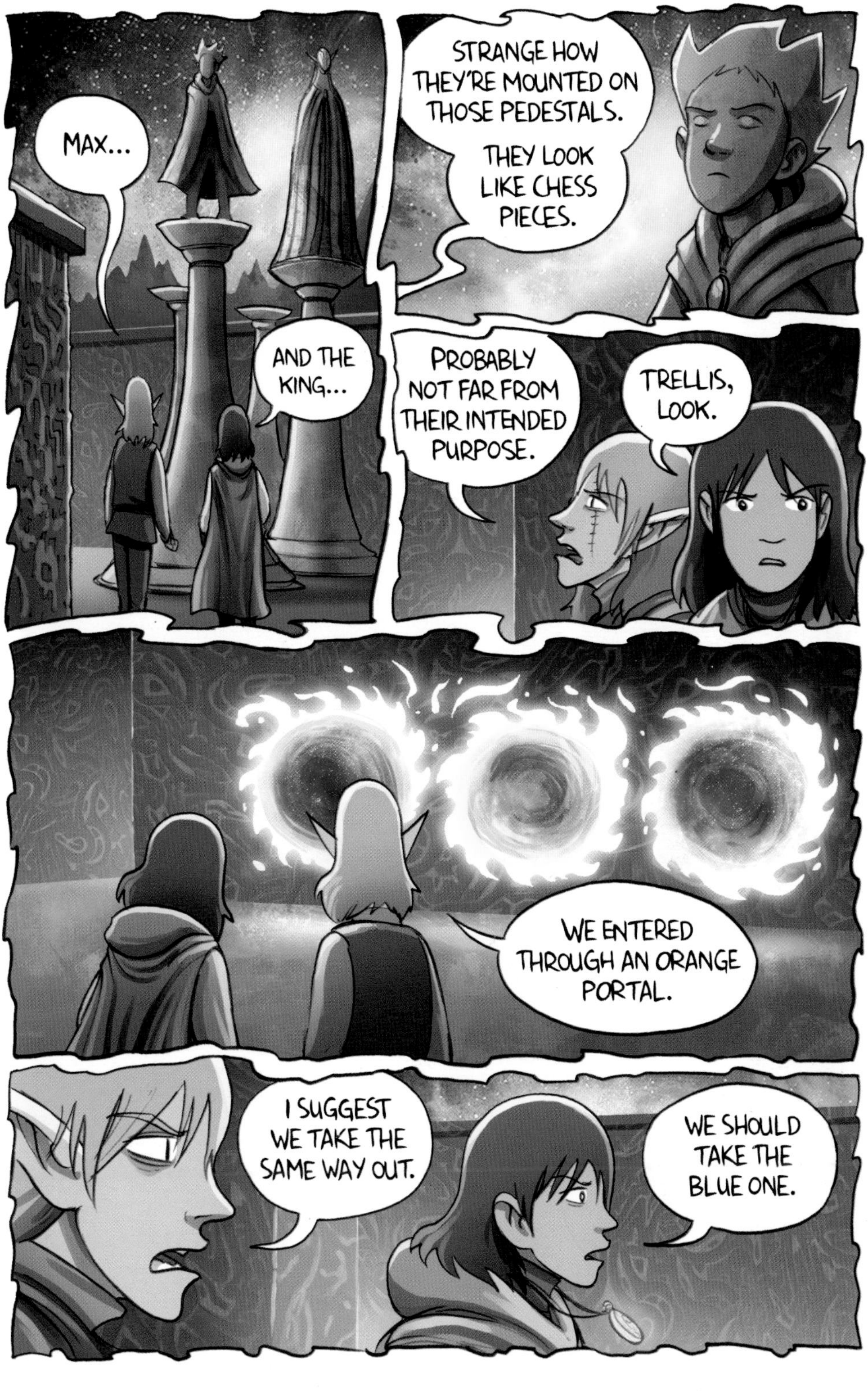
MAX...
STRANGE HOW THEY'RE MOUNTED ON THOSE PEDESTALS.
THEY LOOK LIKE CHESS PIECES.
AND THE KING...
PROBABLY NOT FAR FROM THEIR INTENDED PURPOSE.
TRELLIS, LOOK.
WE ENTERED THROUGH AN ORANGE PORTAL.
I SUGGEST WE TAKE THE SAME WAY OUT.
WE SHOULD TAKE THE BLUE ONE.

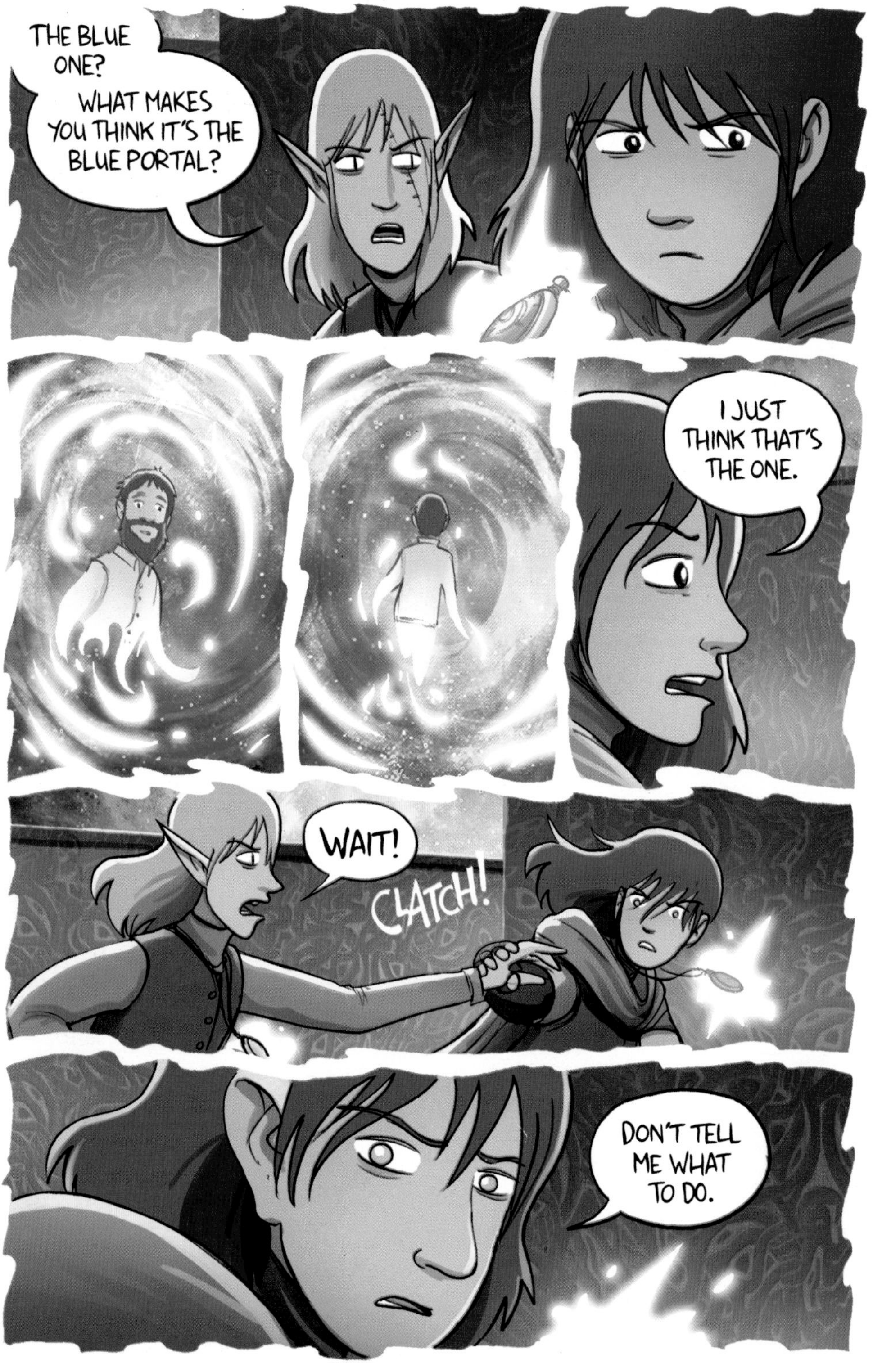
THE BLUE ONE?
WHAT MAKES YOU THINK IT'S THE BLUE PORTAL?
I JUST THINK THAT'S THE ONE.
WAIT!
CLATCH!
DON'T TELL ME WHAT TO DO.

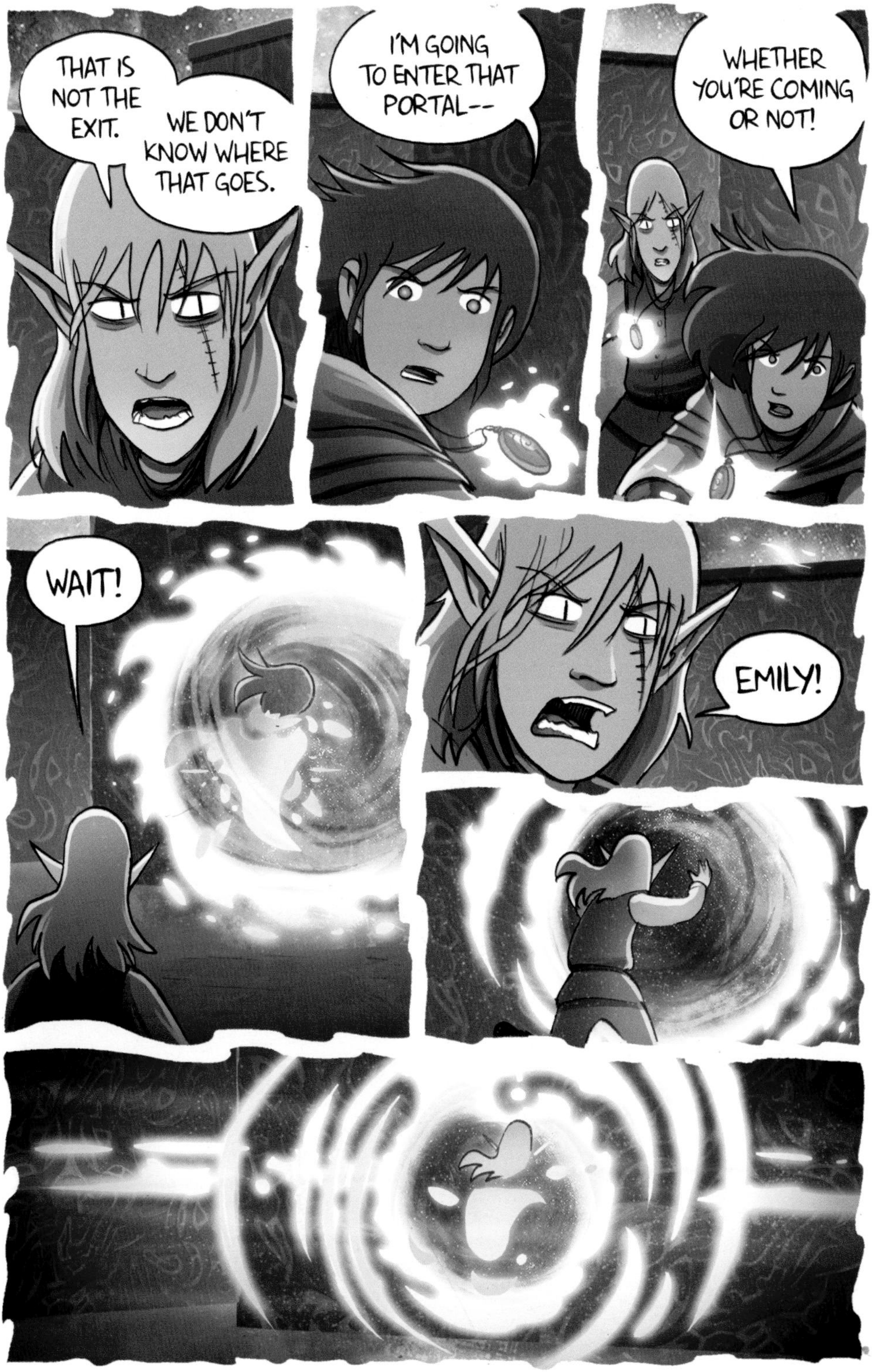
THAT IS NOT THE EXIT.
WE DON'T KNOW WHERE THAT GOES.
I'M GOING TO ENTER THAT PORTAL--
WHETHER YOU'RE COMING OR NOT!
WAIT!
EMILY!

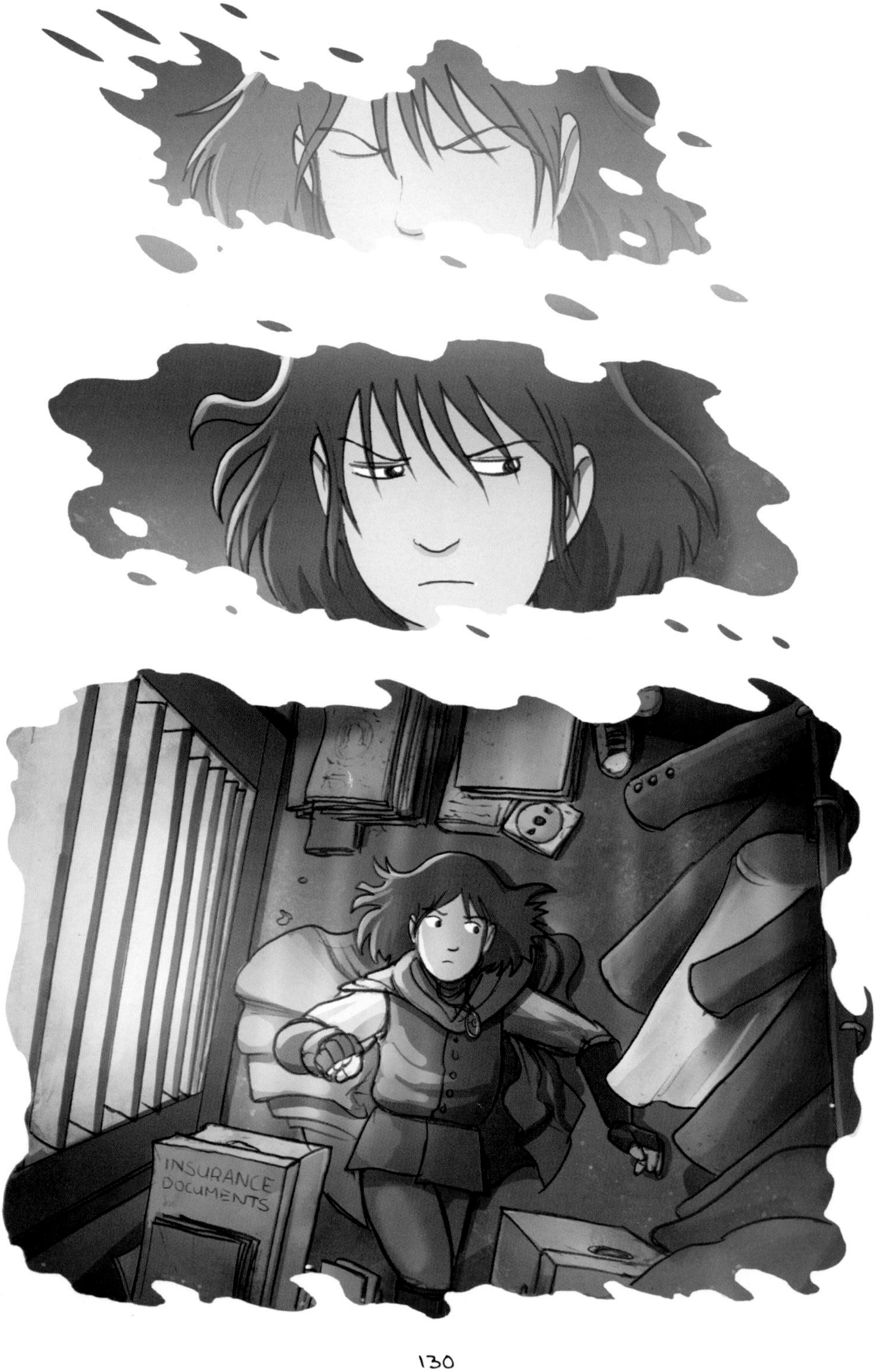
INSURANCE DOCUMENTS

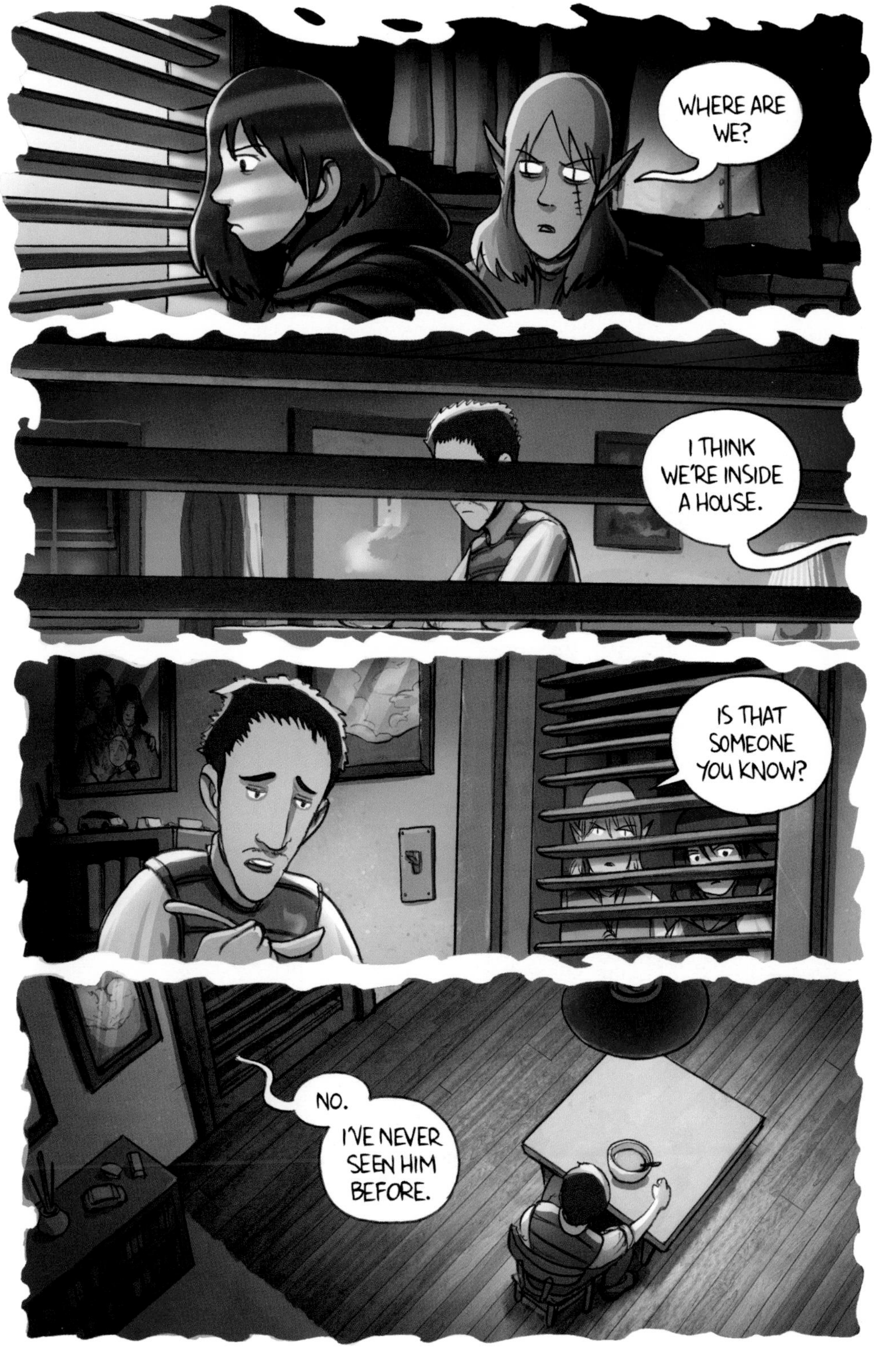
WHERE ARE WE?
I THINK WE'RE INSIDE A HOUSE.
IS THAT SOMEONE YOU KNOW?
NO.
I'VE NEVER SEEN HIM BEFORE.

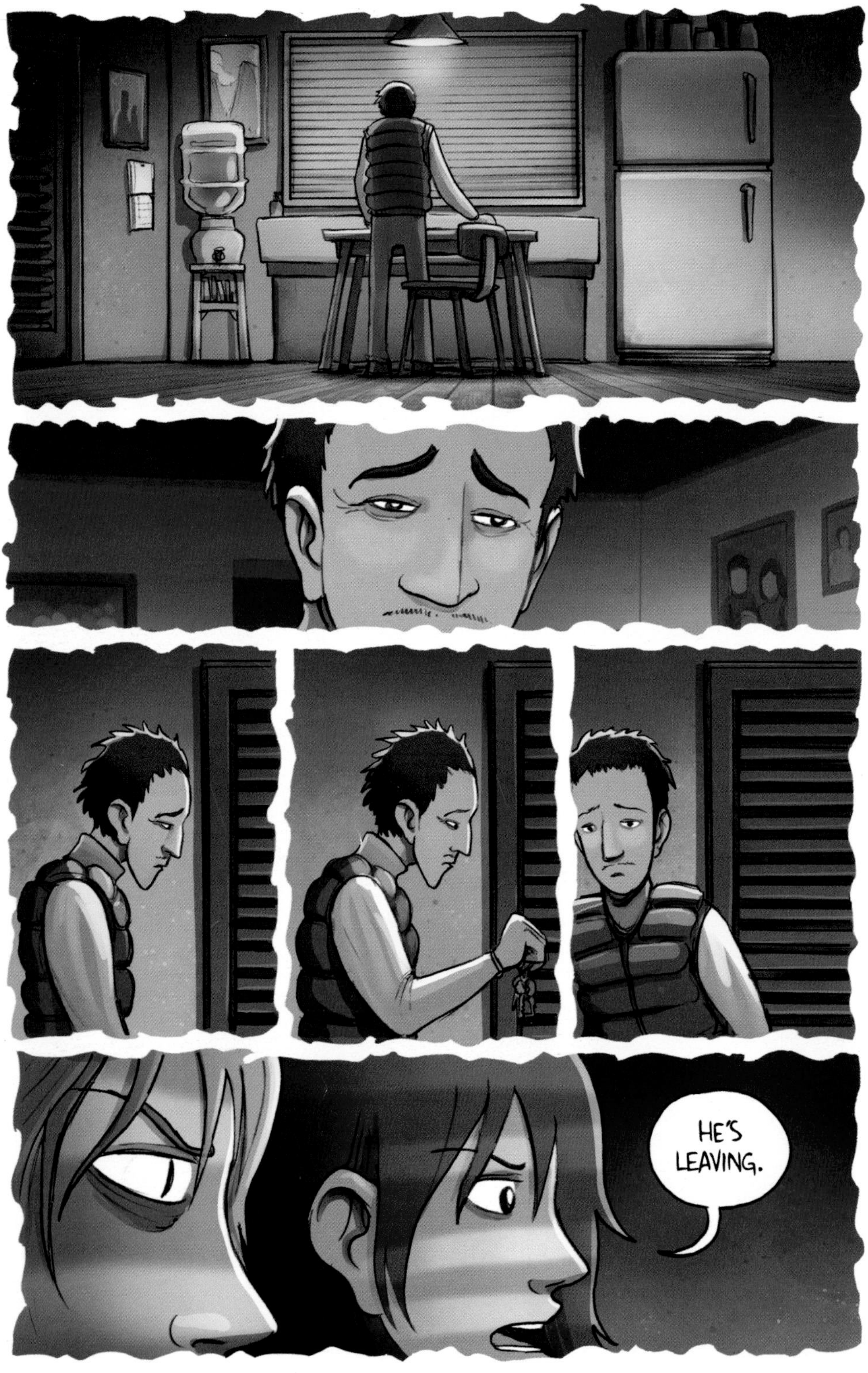
HE'S
LEAVING.

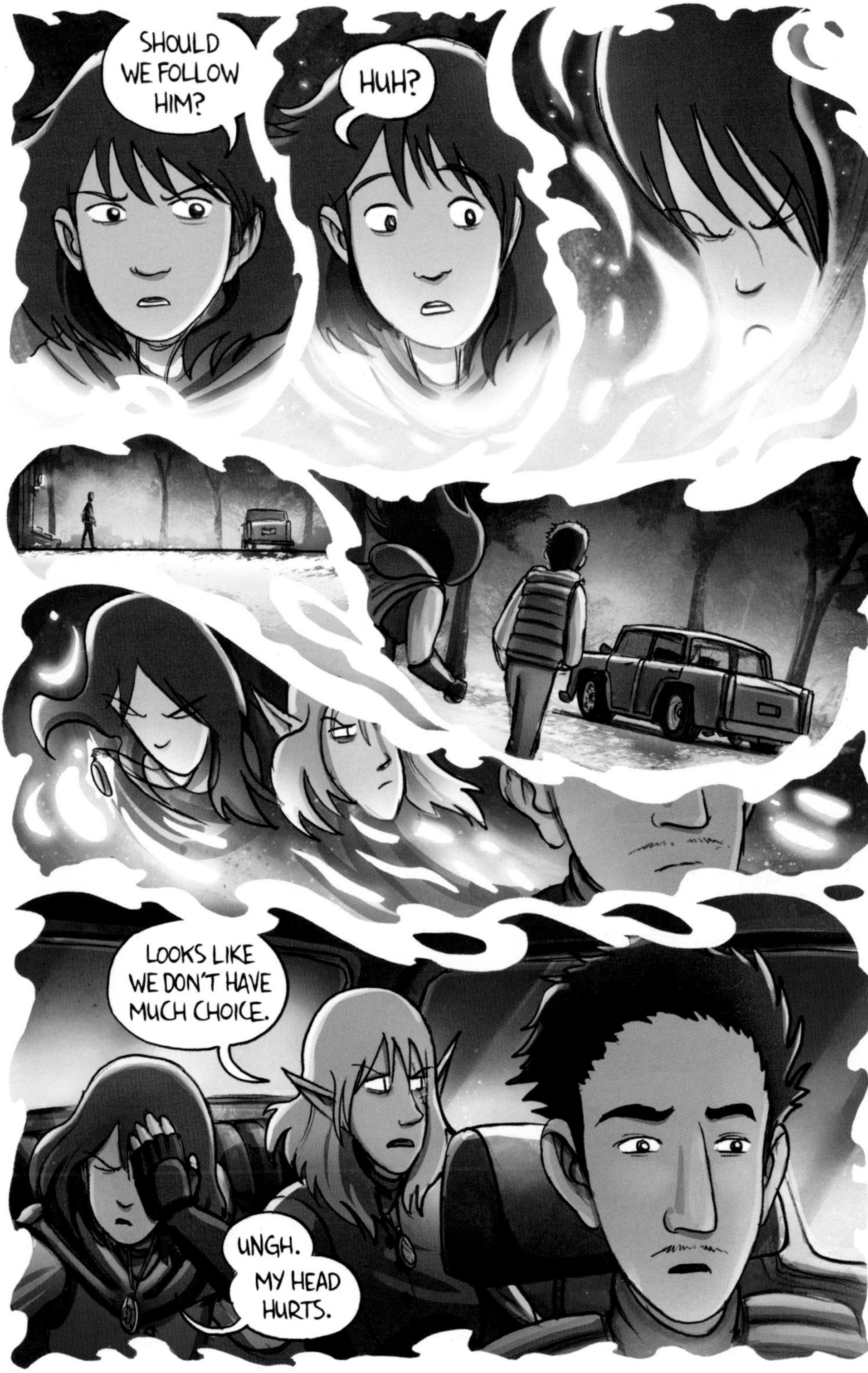
SHOULD WE FOLLOW HIM?
HUH?
LOOKS LIKE WE DON'T HAVE MUCH CHOICE.
UNGH.
MY HEAD HURTS.

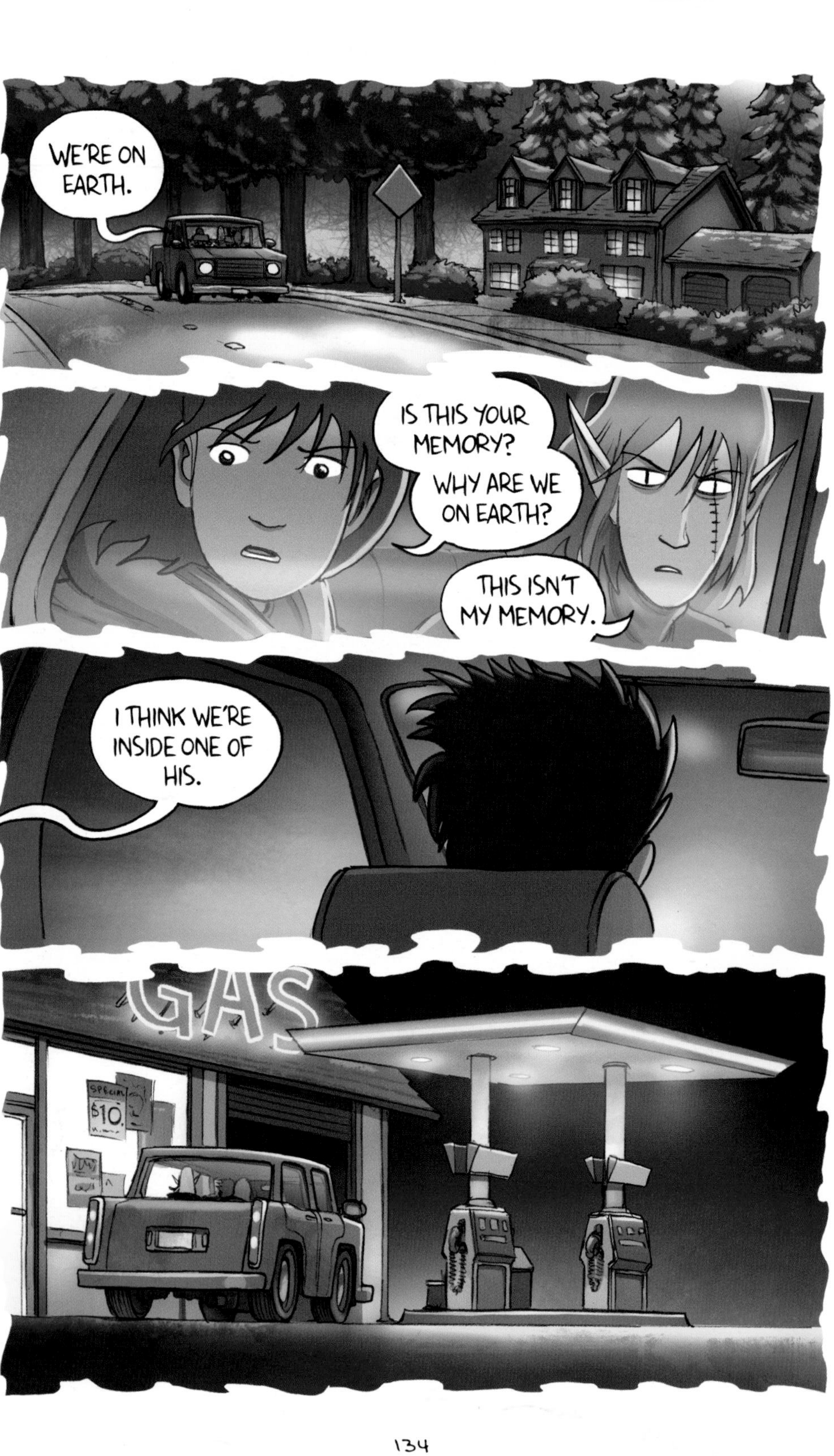
WE'RE ON EARTH.
IS THIS YOUR MEMORY?
WHY ARE WE ON EARTH?
THIS ISN'T MY MEMORY.
I THINK WE'RE INSIDE ONE OF HIS.
GAS
$10.

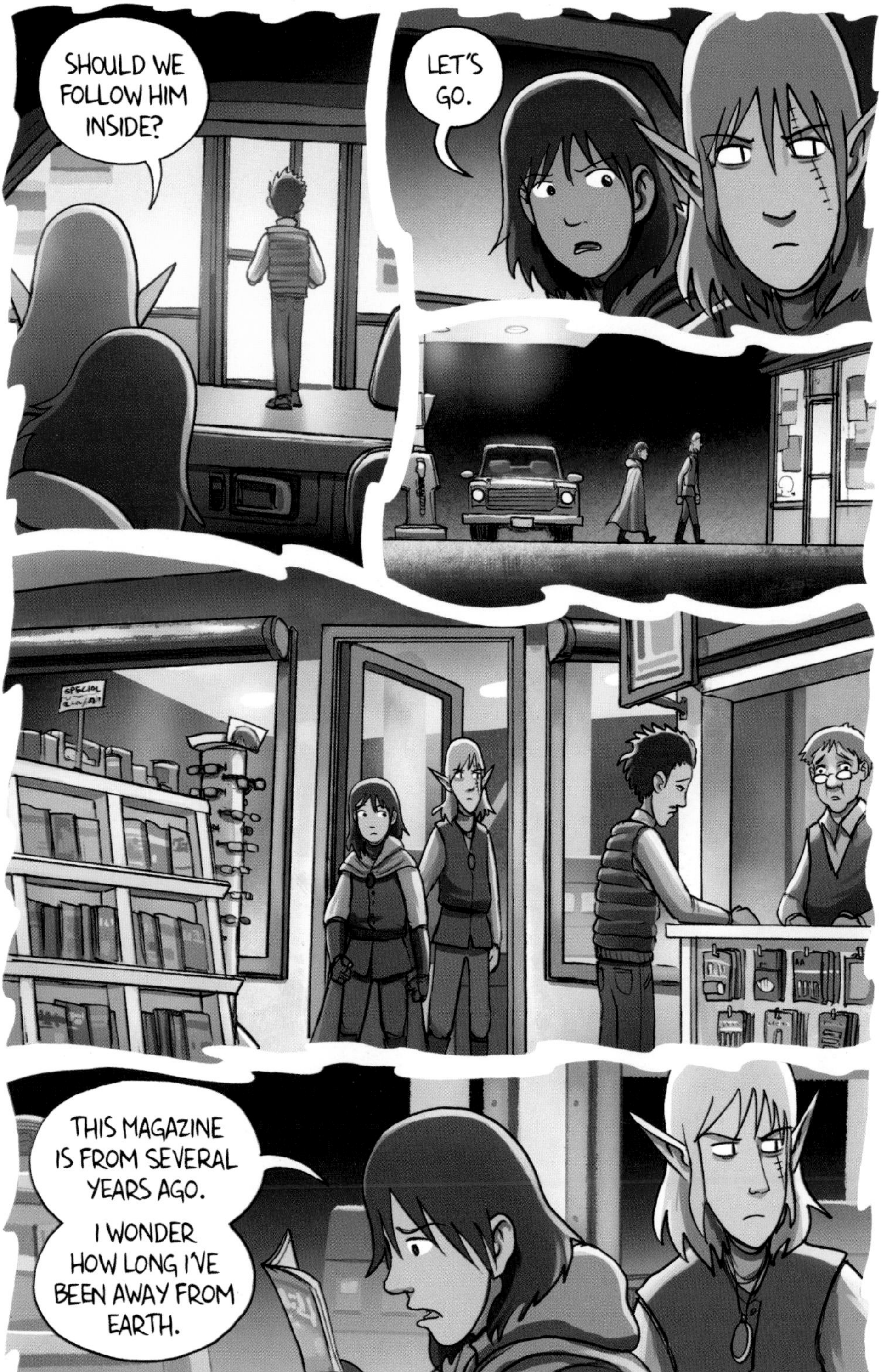
SHOULD WE FOLLOW HIM INSIDE?
LET'S GO.
THIS MAGAZINE IS FROM SEVERAL YEARS AGO.
I WONDER HOW LONG I'VE BEEN AWAY FROM EARTH.

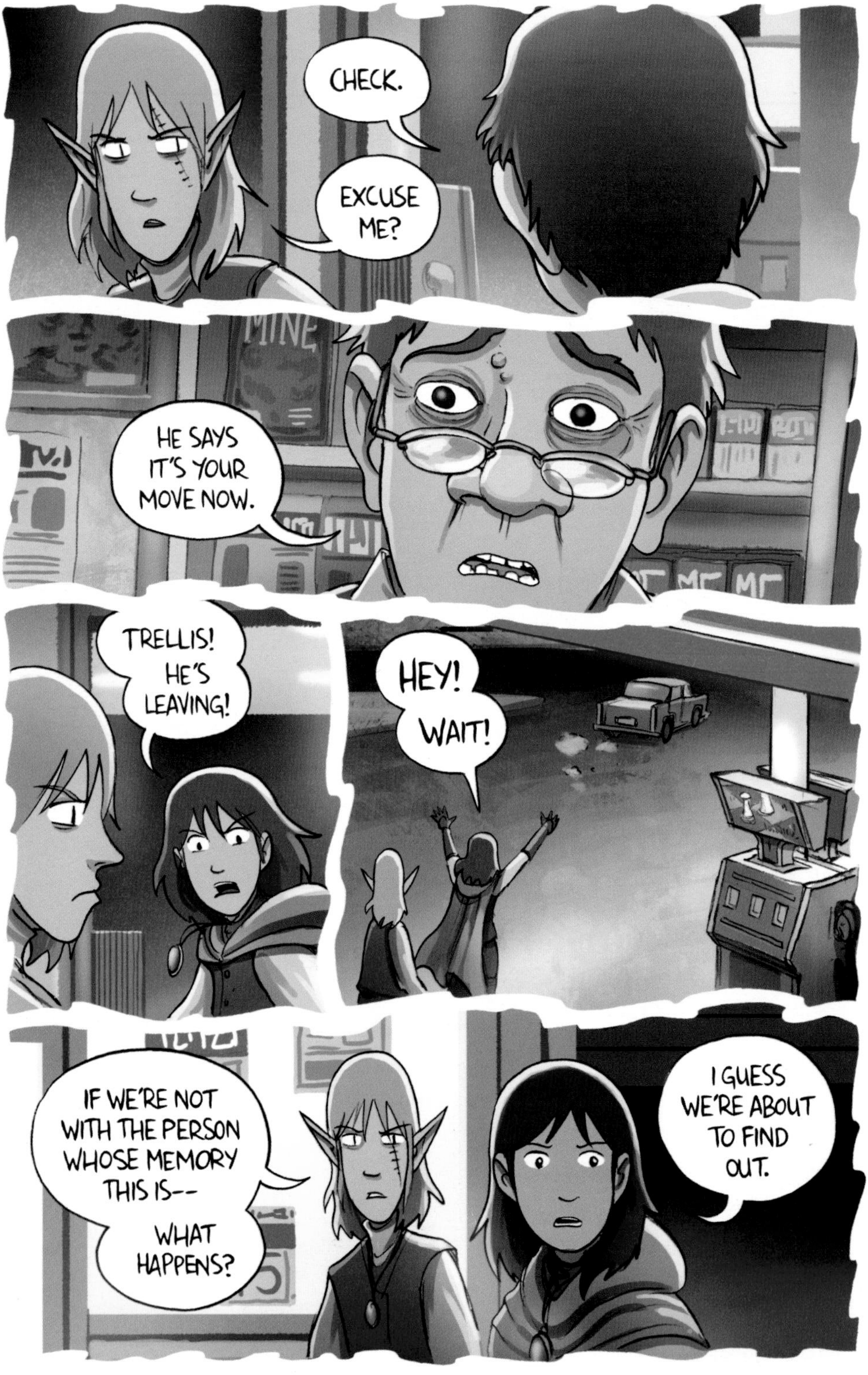
CHECK.
EXCUSE ME?
HE SAYS IT'S YOUR MOVE NOW.
TRELLIS! HE'S LEAVING!
HEY! WAIT!
IF WE'RE NOT WITH THE PERSON WHOSE MEMORY THIS IS--
WHAT HAPPENS?
I GUESS WE'RE ABOUT TO FIND OUT.

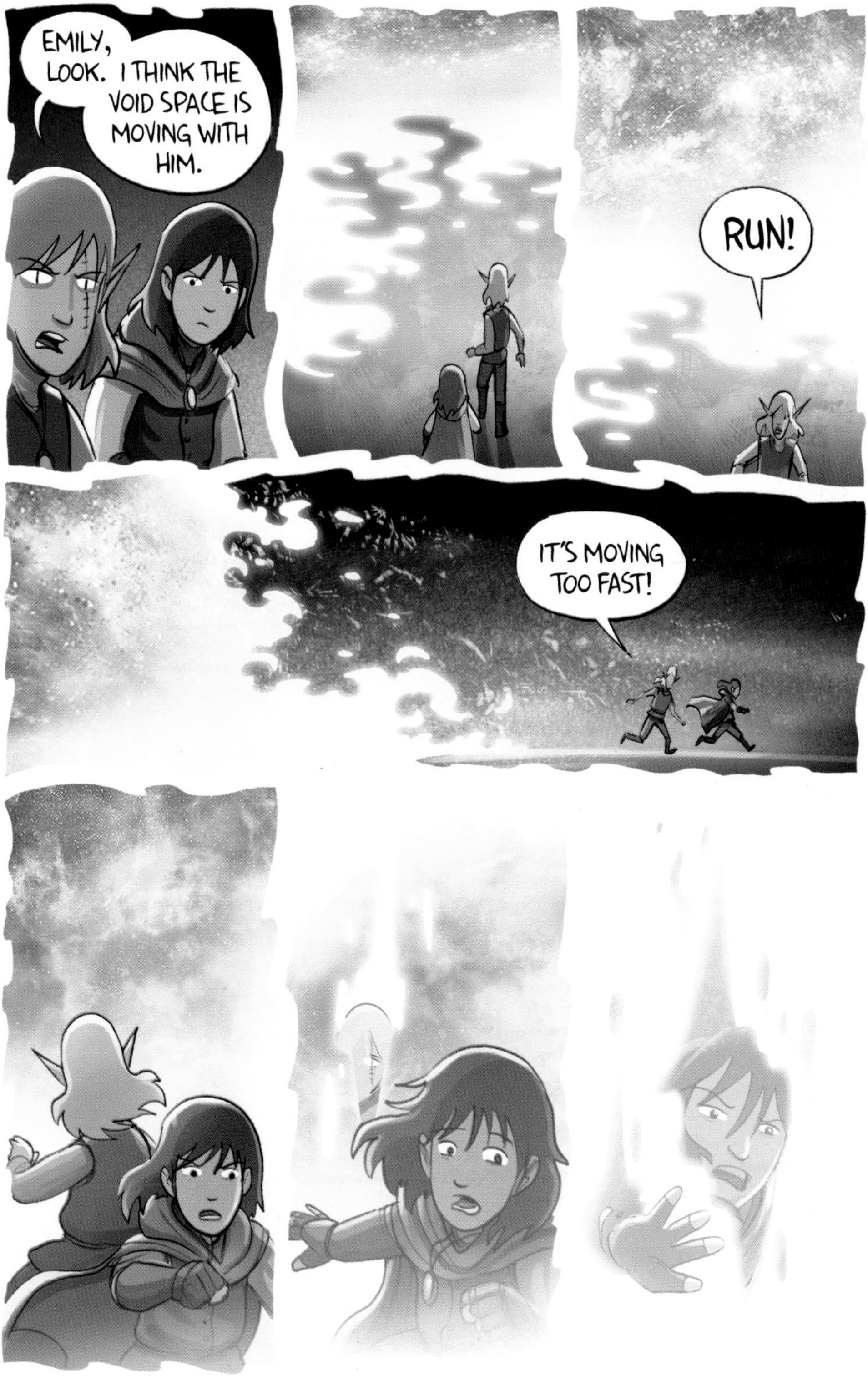
EMILY, LOOK. I THINK THE VOID SPACE IS MOVING WITH HIM.
RUN!
IT'S MOVING TOO FAST!

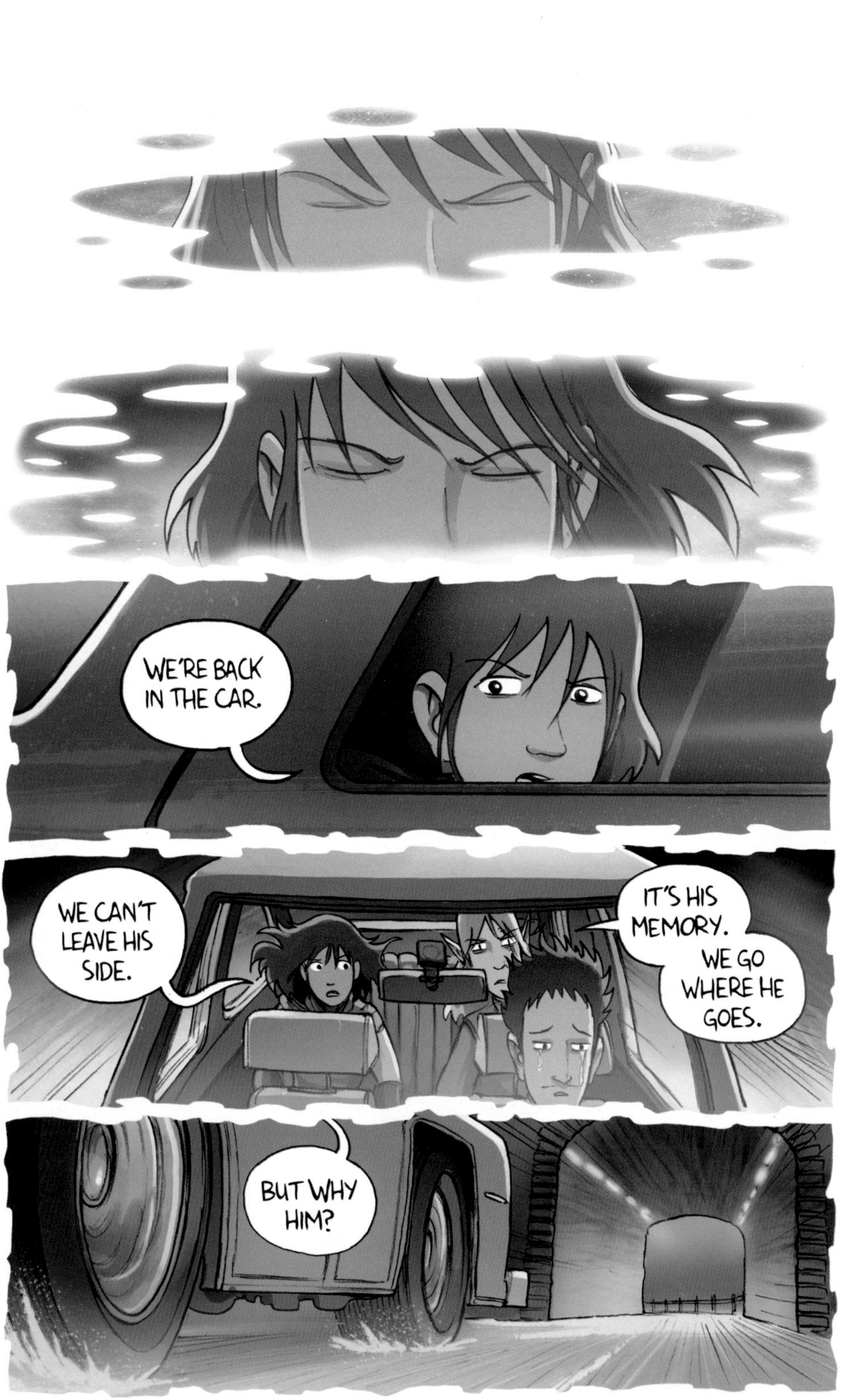
WE'RE BACK IN THE CAR.
WE CAN'T LEAVE HIS SIDE.
IT'S HIS MEMORY.
WE GO WHERE HE GOES.
BUT WHY HIM?

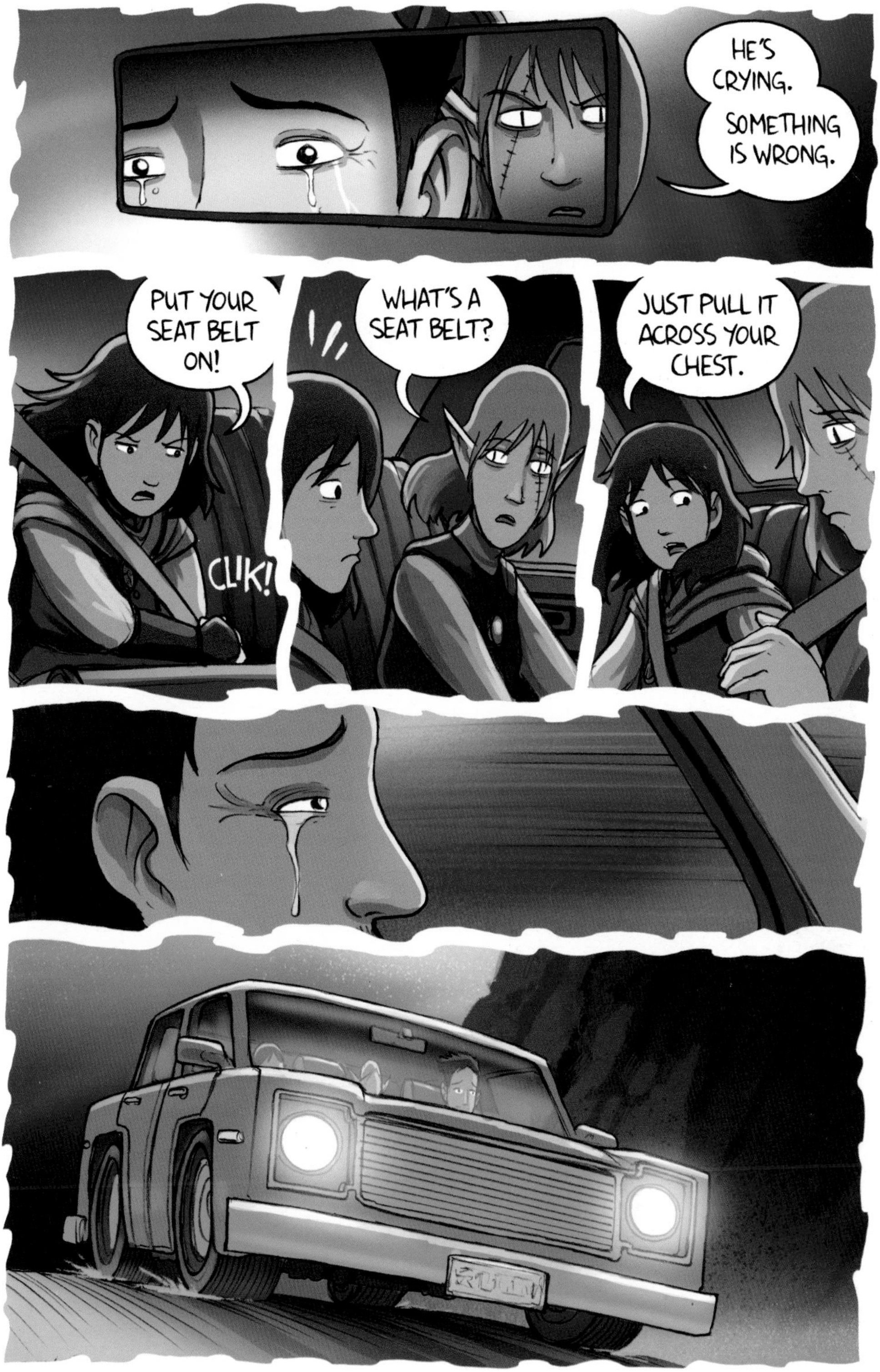
HE'S CRYING.
SOMETHING IS WRONG.
PUT YOUR SEAT BELT ON!
CLIK!
WHAT'S A SEAT BELT?
JUST PULL IT ACROSS YOUR CHEST.

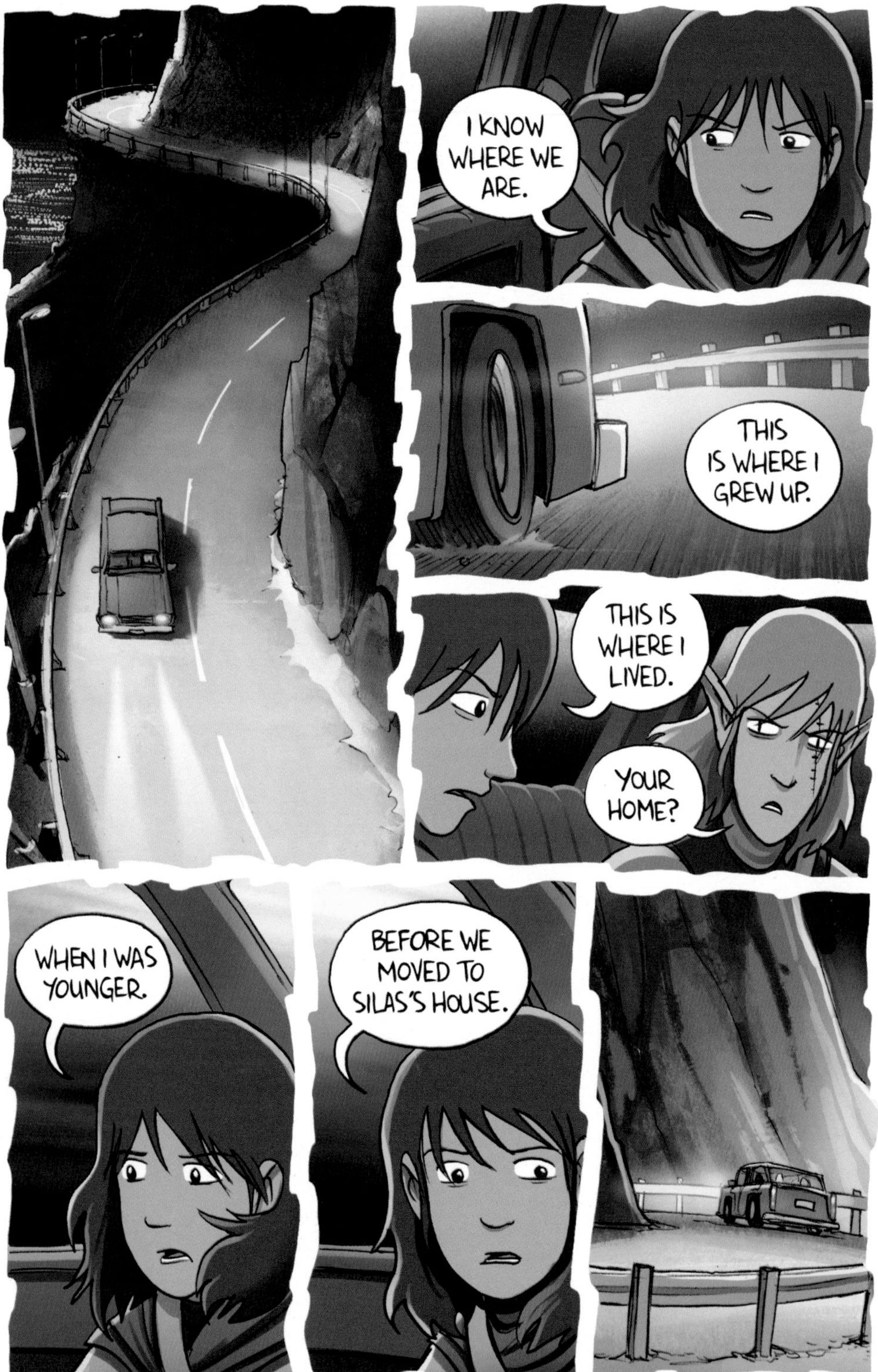
I KNOW WHERE WE ARE.
THIS IS WHERE I GREW UP.
THIS IS WHERE I LIVED.
YOUR HOME?
WHEN I WAS YOUNGER.
BEFORE WE MOVED TO SILAS'S HOUSE.

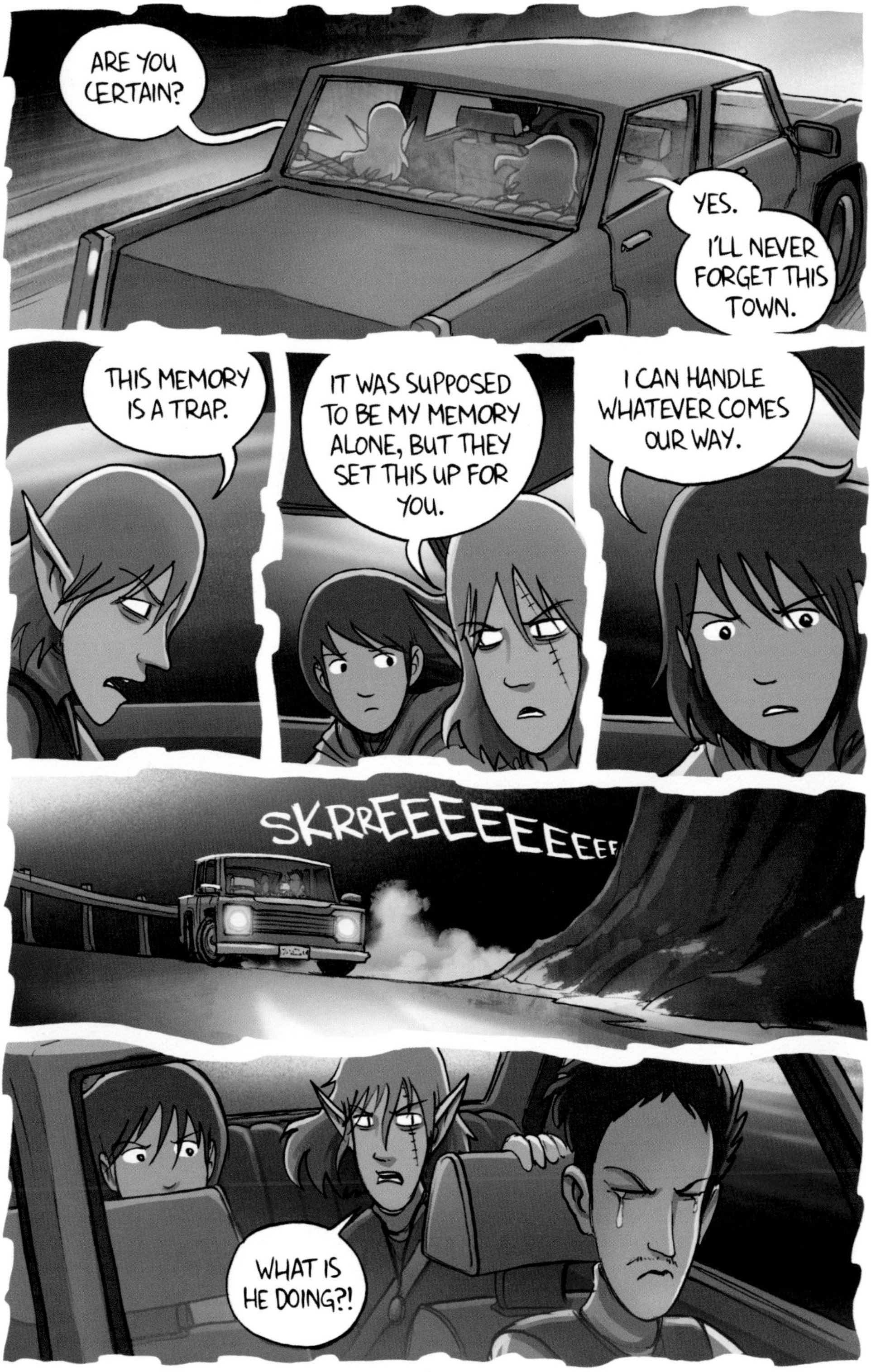
ARE YOU CERTAIN?
YES.
I'LL NEVER FORGET THIS TOWN.
THIS MEMORY IS A TRAP.
IT WAS SUPPOSED TO BE MY MEMORY ALONE, BUT THEY SET THIS UP FOR YOU.
I CAN HANDLE WHATEVER COMES OUR WAY.
SKRREEEEEEEEE
WHAT IS HE DOING?!

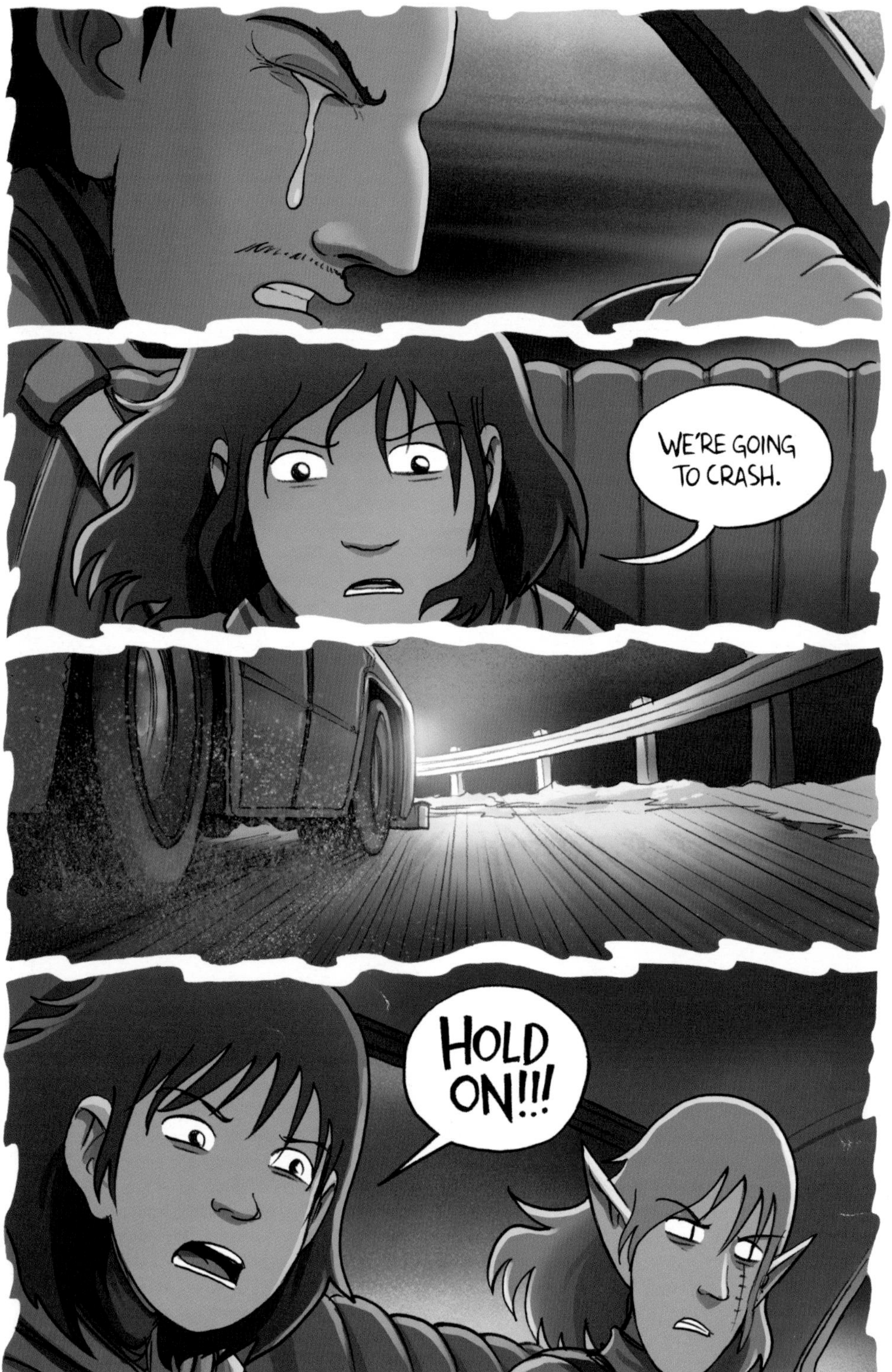
WE'RE GOING TO CRASH.
HOLD ON!!!

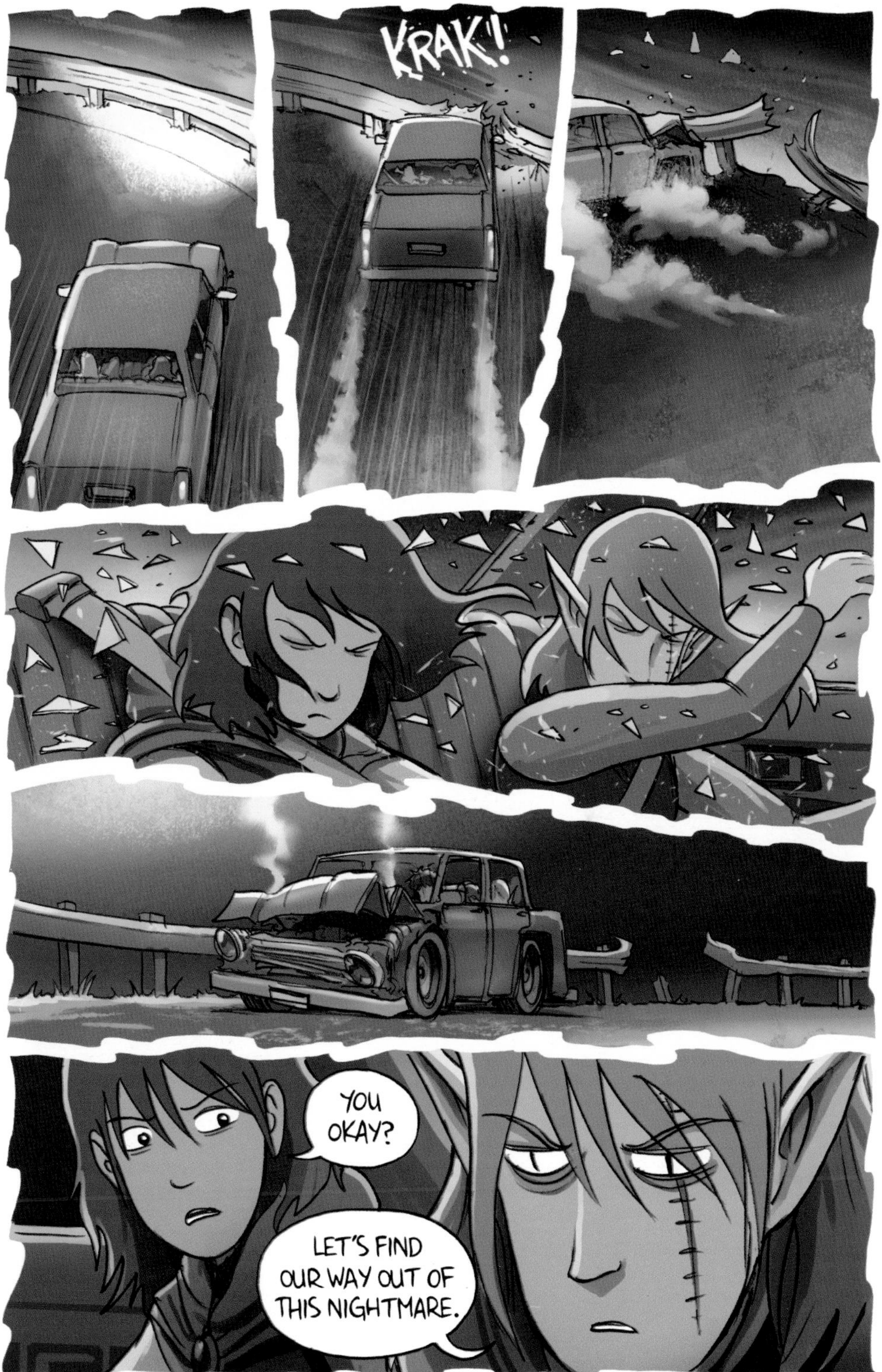
KRAK!
YOU OKAY?
LET'S FIND OUR WAY OUT OF THIS NIGHTMARE.

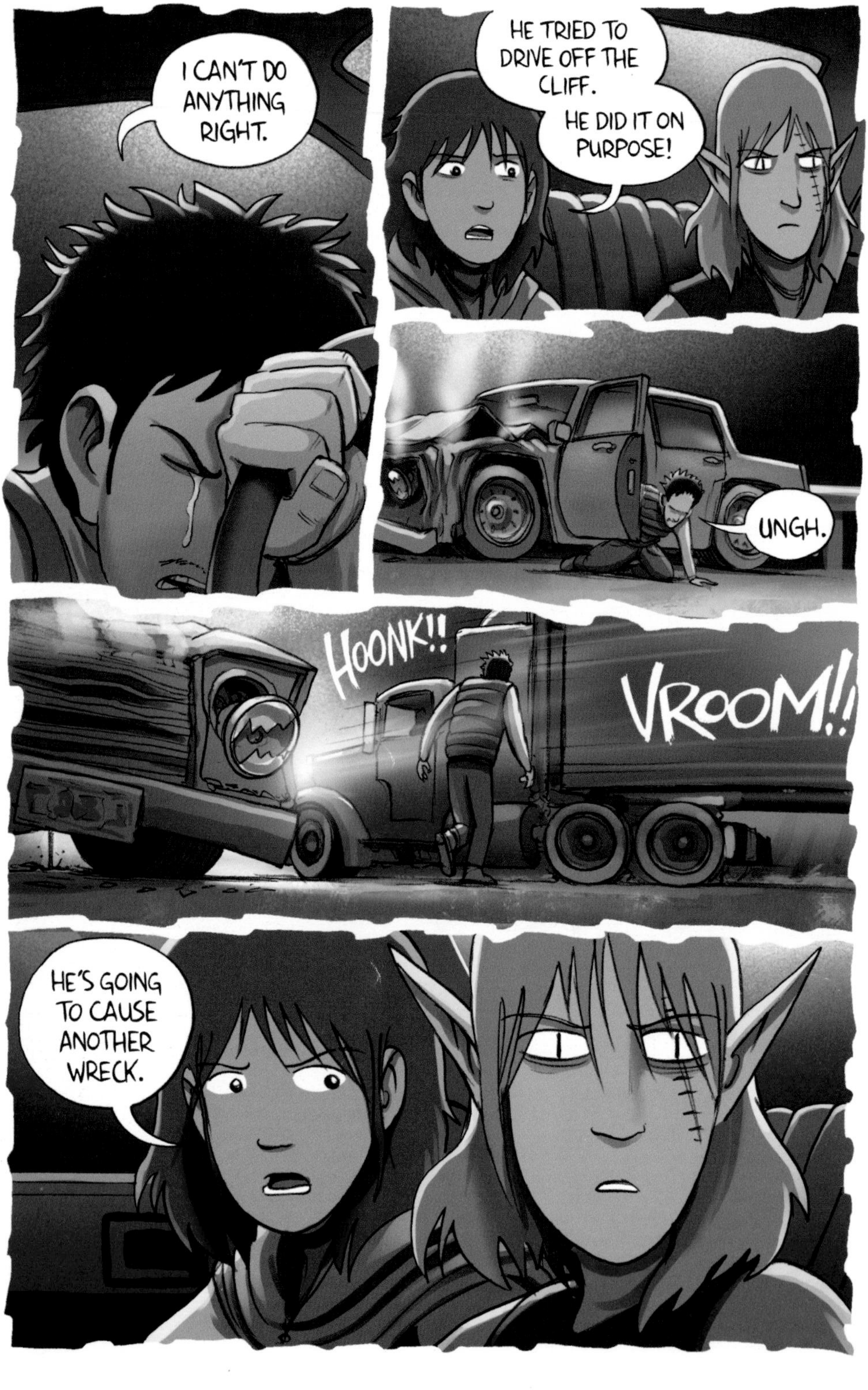
I CAN'T DO ANYTHING RIGHT.
HE TRIED TO DRIVE OFF THE CLIFF.
HE DID IT ON PURPOSE!
UNGH.
HOONK!!
VROOM!!
HE'S GOING TO CAUSE ANOTHER WRECK.

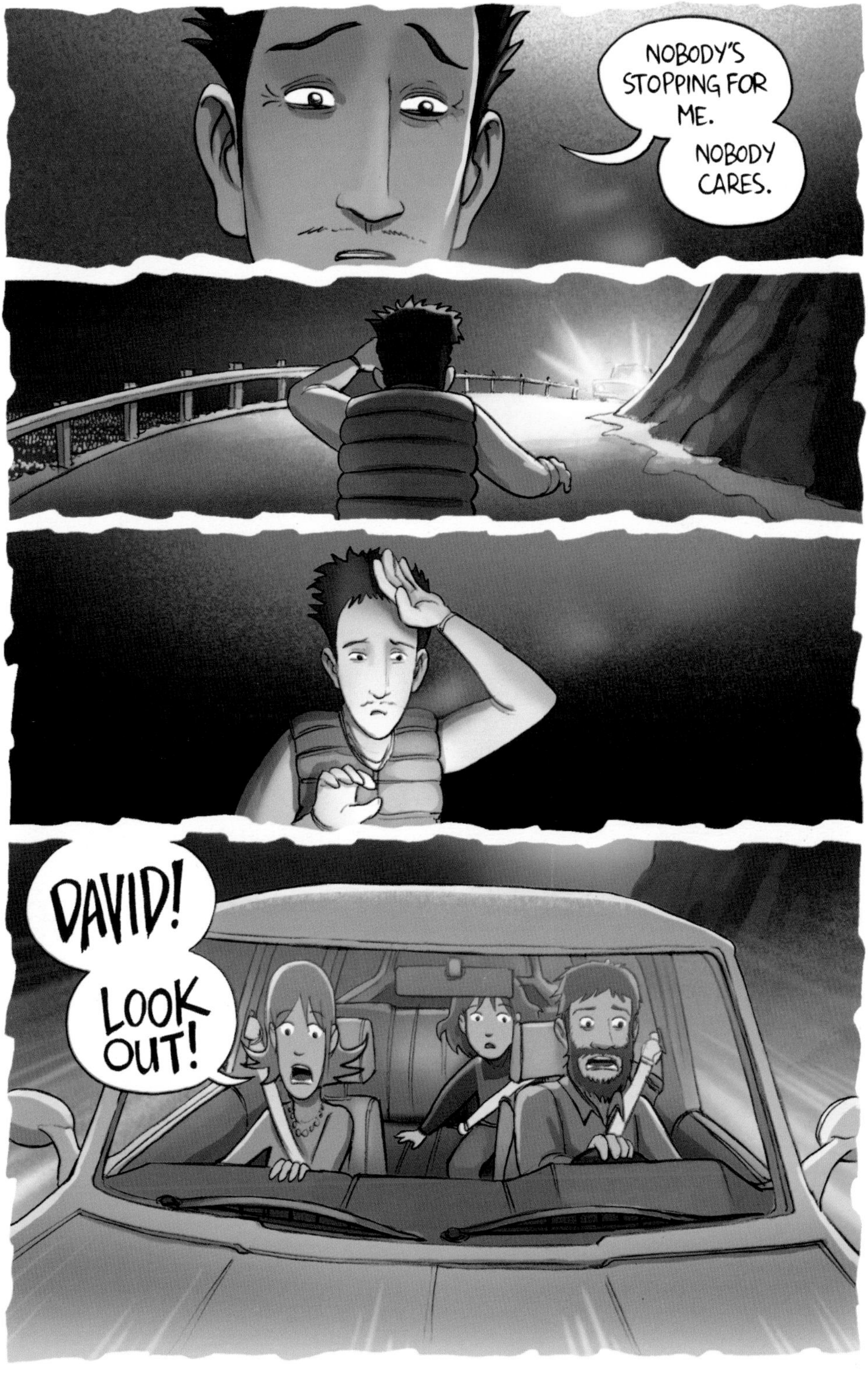
NOBODY'S STOPPING FOR ME.
NOBODY CARES.
DAVID!
LOOK OUT!

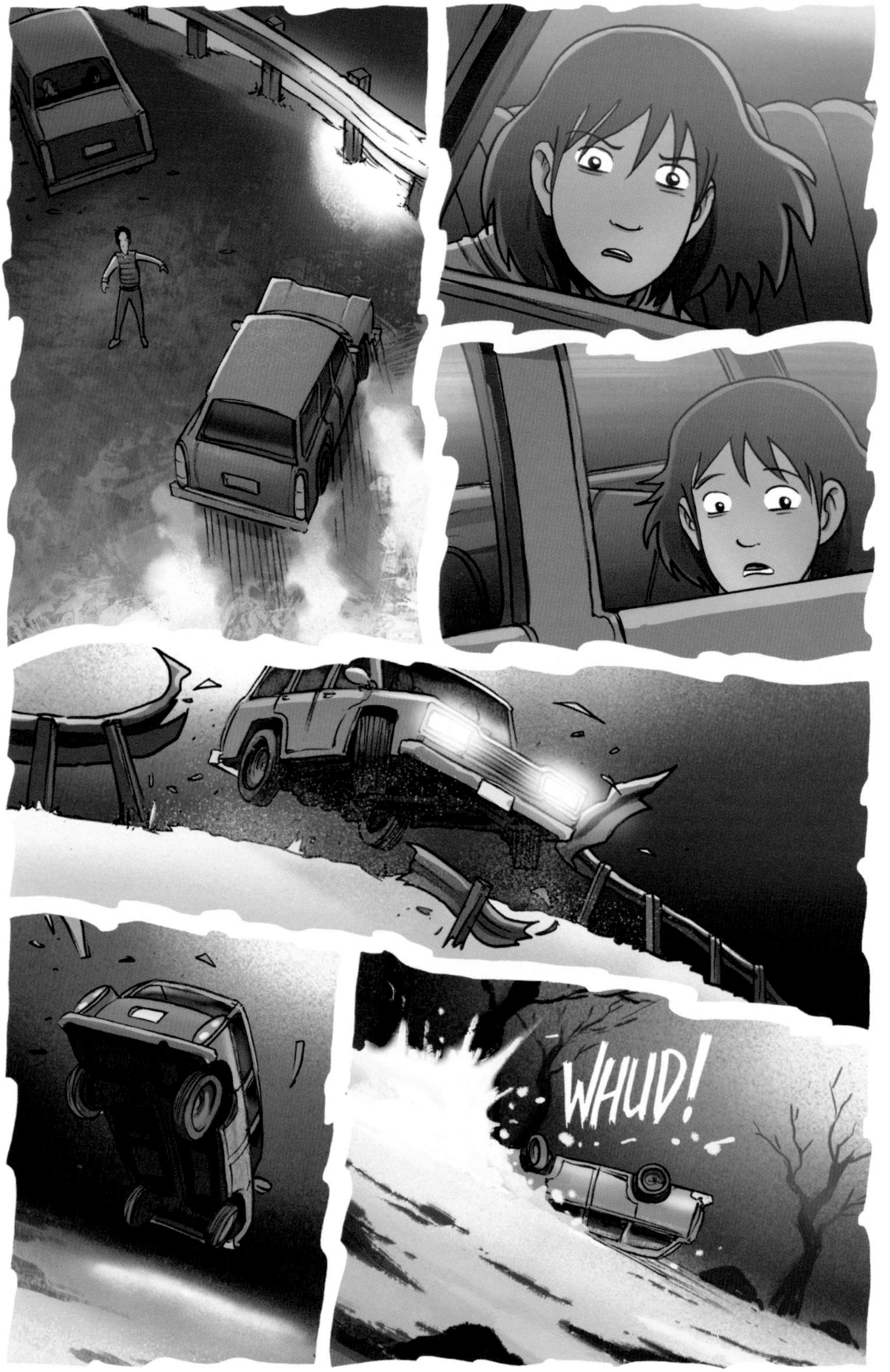
WHUD!

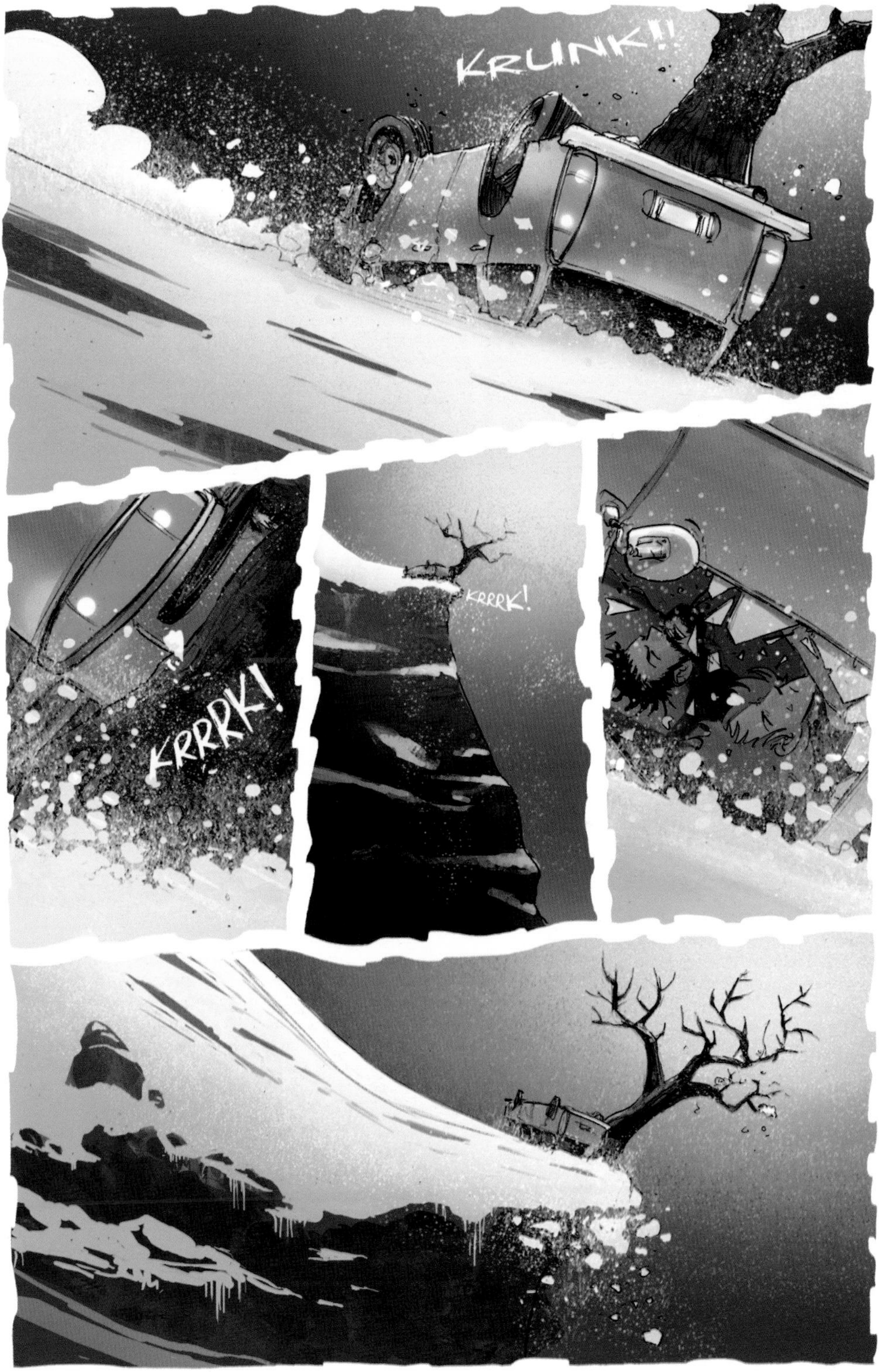
KRUNK!!
KRRRK!
KRRRK!

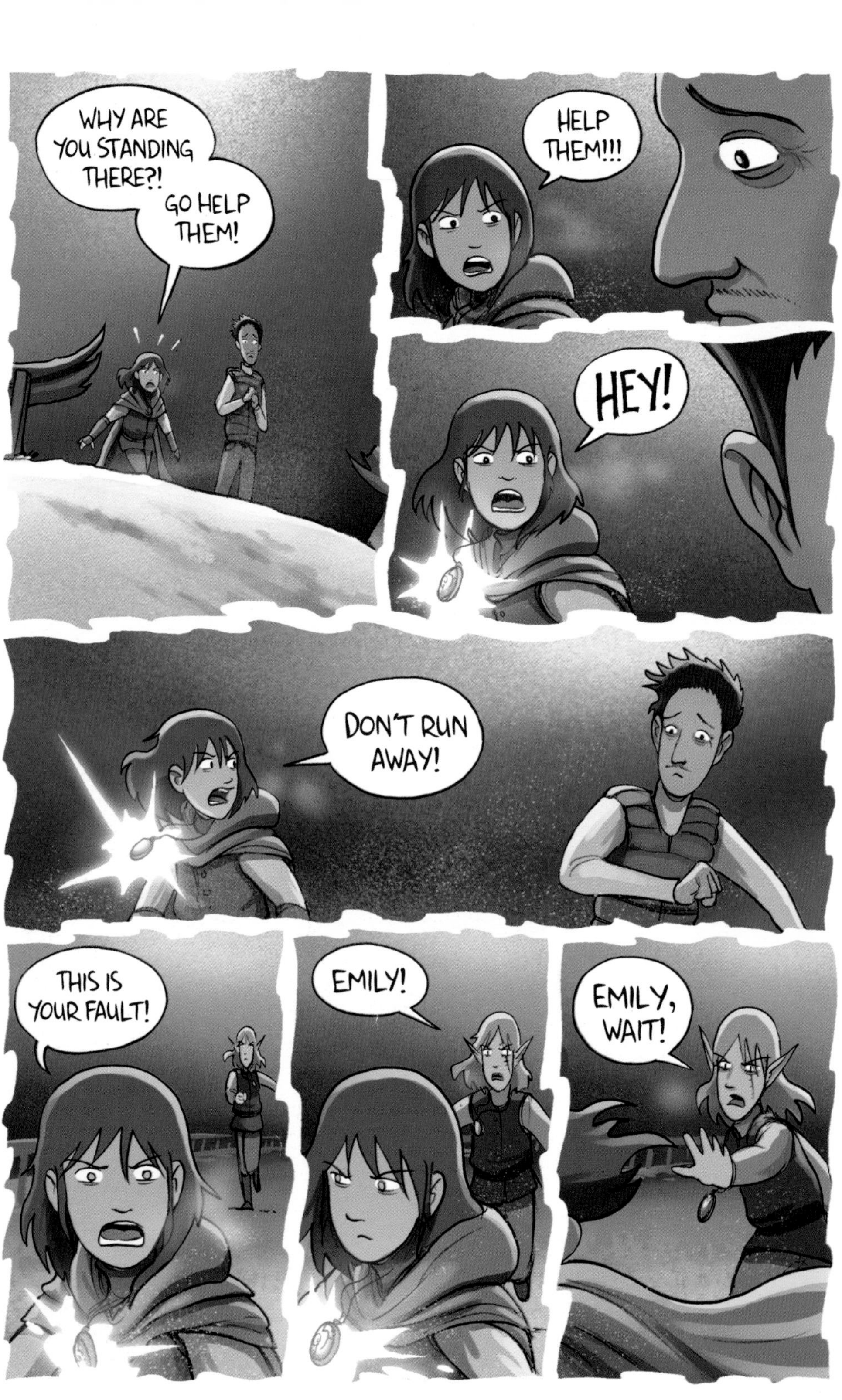
WHY ARE YOU STANDING THERE?!
GO HELP THEM!
HELP THEM!!!
HEY!
DON'T RUN AWAY!
THIS IS YOUR FAULT!
EMILY!
EMILY, WAIT!

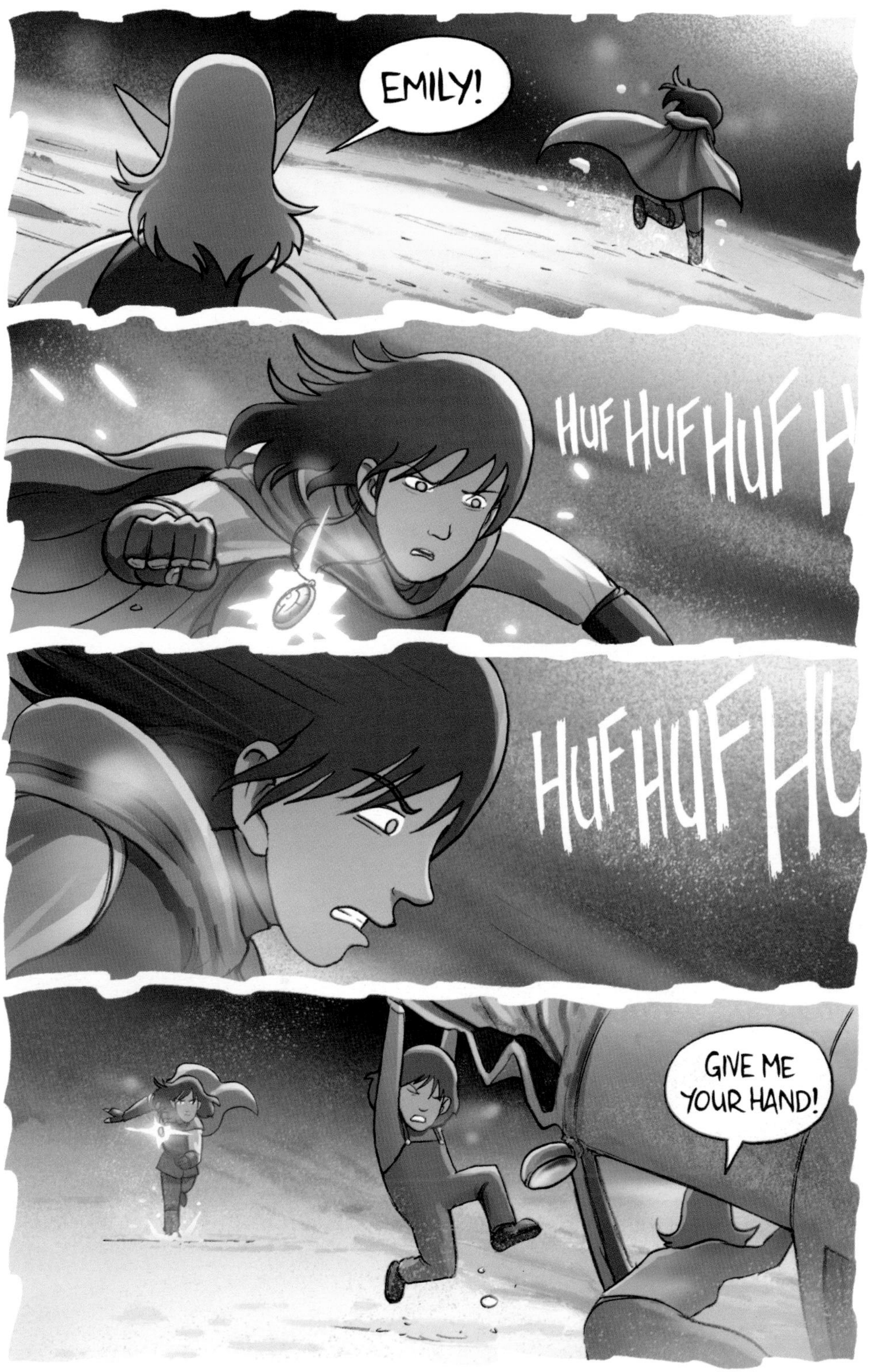
EMILY!
HUF HUF HUF H
HUF HUF HU
GIVE ME YOUR HAND!

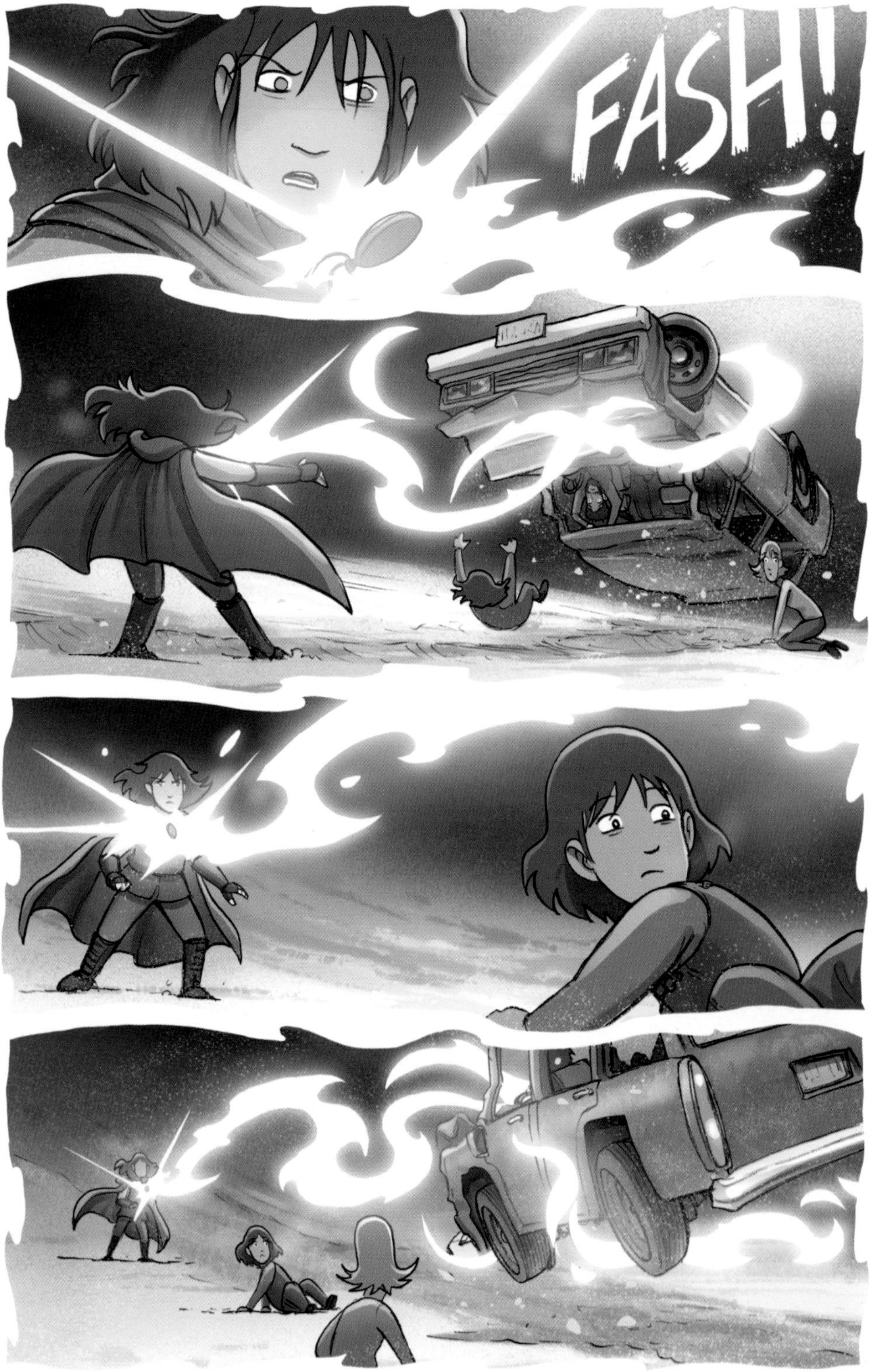
FASH!

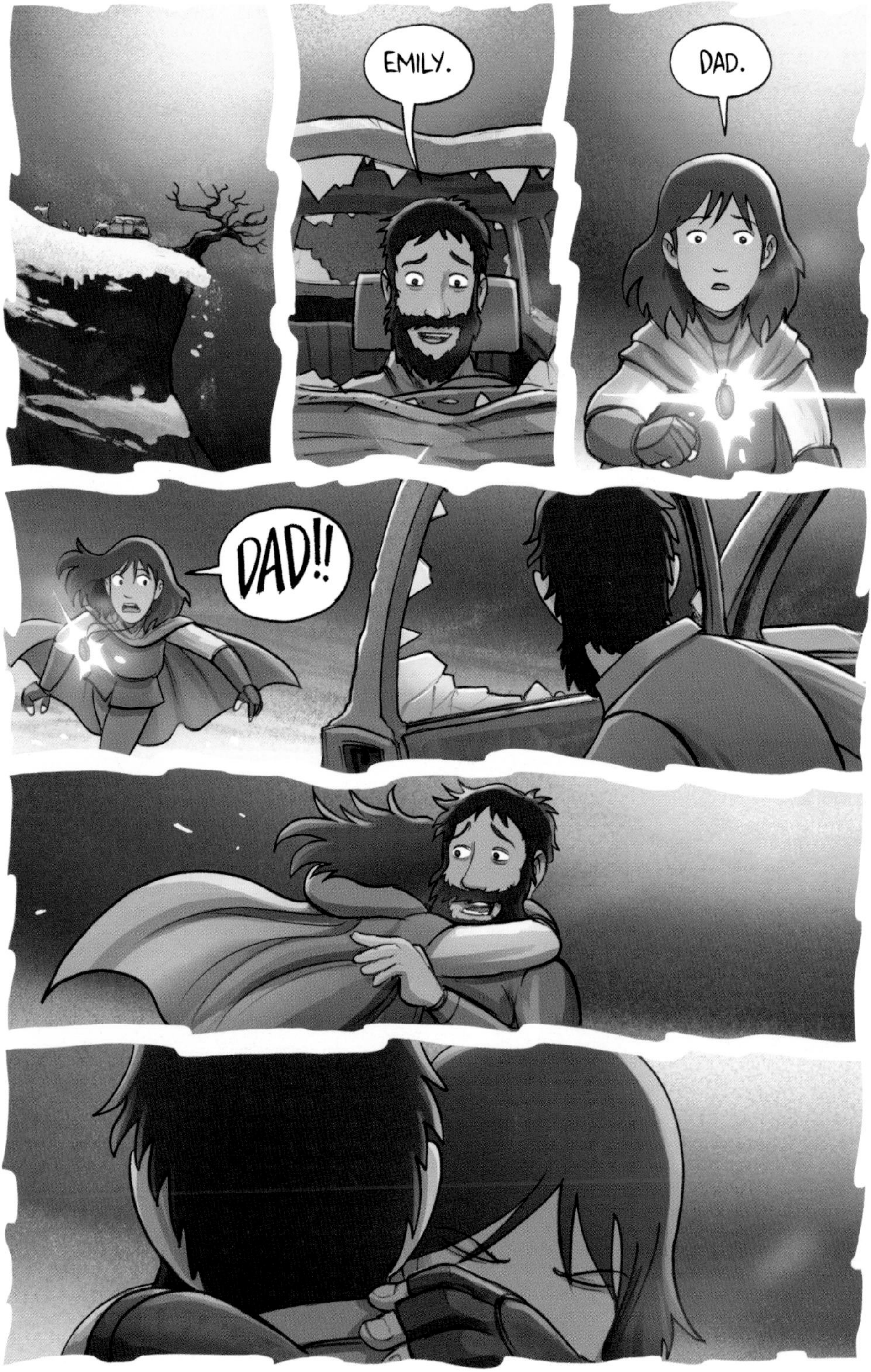
EMILY.
DAD.
DAD!!

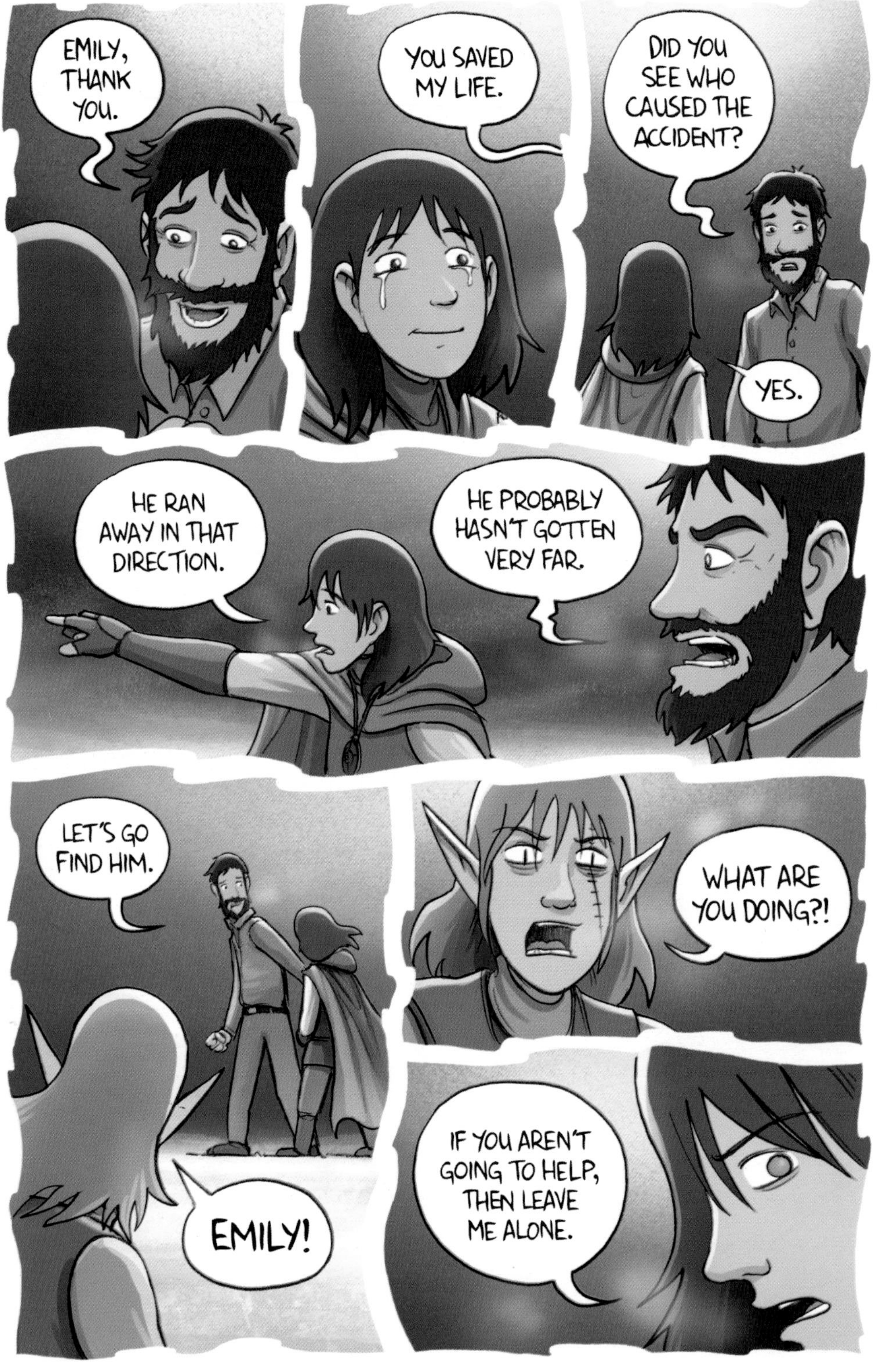
EMILY, THANK YOU.
YOU SAVED MY LIFE.
DID YOU SEE WHO CAUSED THE ACCIDENT?
YES.
HE RAN AWAY IN THAT DIRECTION.
HE PROBABLY HASN'T GOTTEN VERY FAR.
LET'S GO FIND HIM.
EMILY!
WHAT ARE YOU DOING?!
IF YOU AREN'T GOING TO HELP, THEN LEAVE ME ALONE.

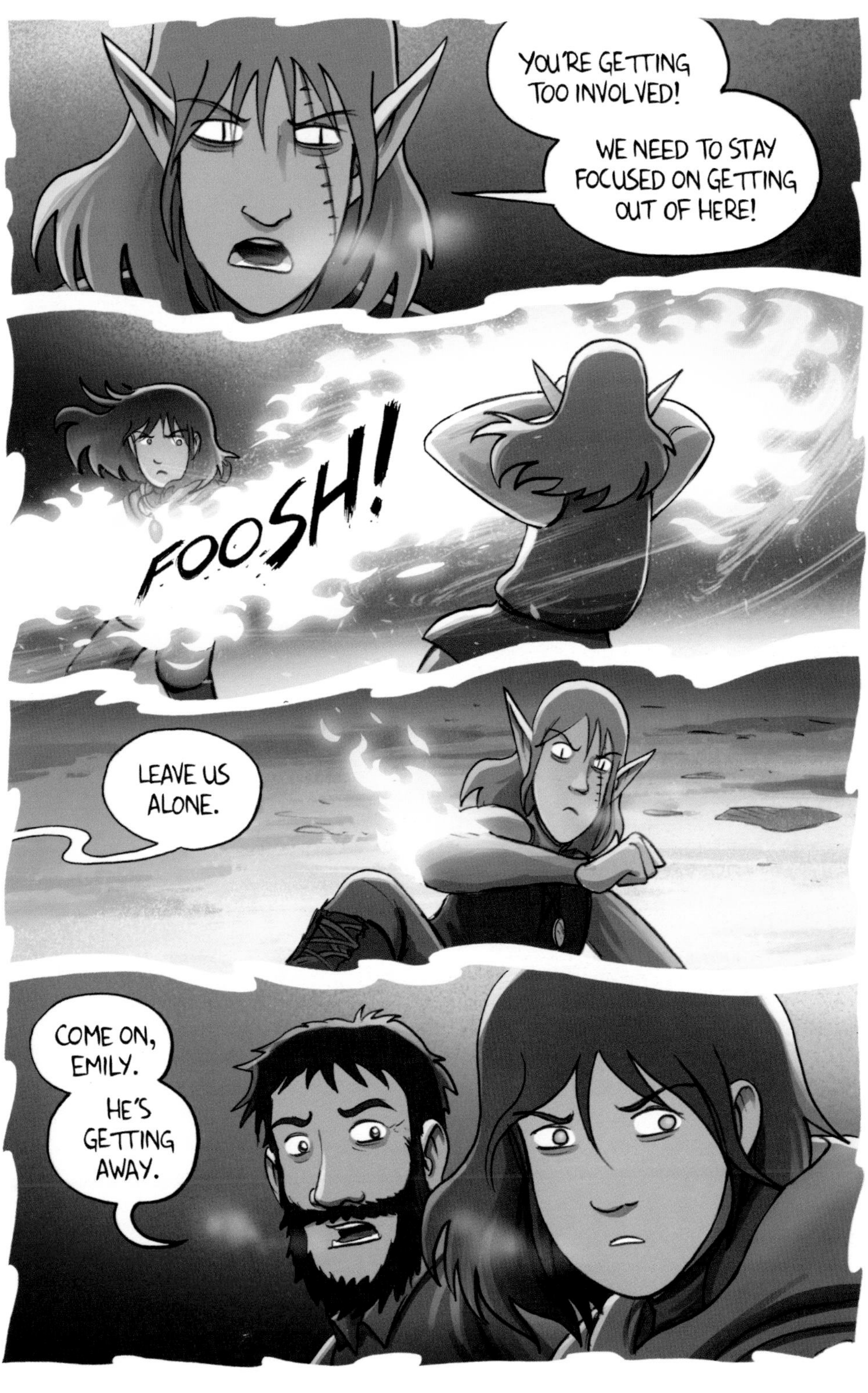
YOU'RE GETTING TOO INVOLVED!
WE NEED TO STAY FOCUSED ON GETTING OUT OF HERE!
FOOSH!
LEAVE US ALONE.
COME ON, EMILY.
HE'S GETTING AWAY.

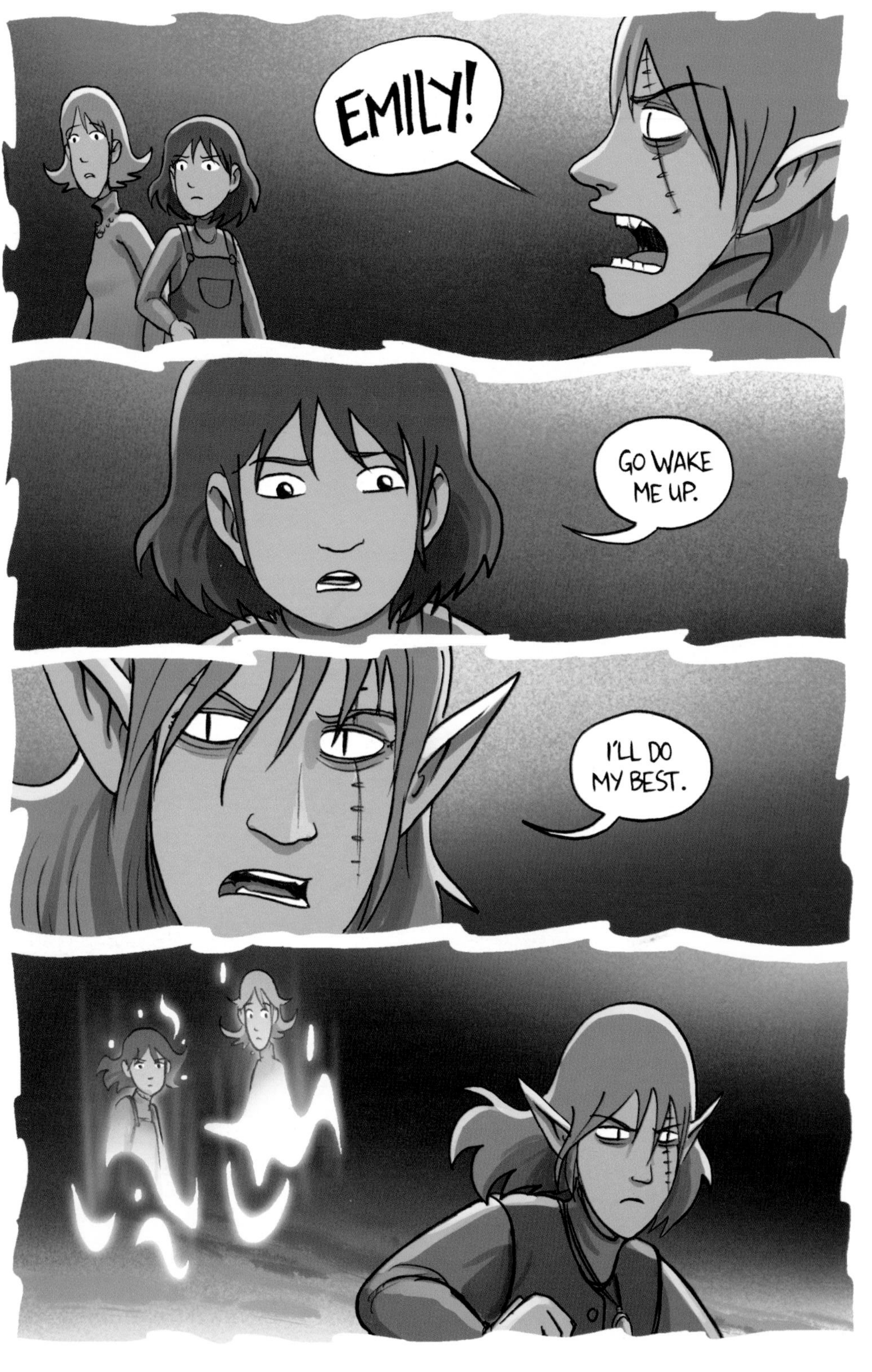
EMILY!
GO WAKE ME UP.
I'LL DO MY BEST.

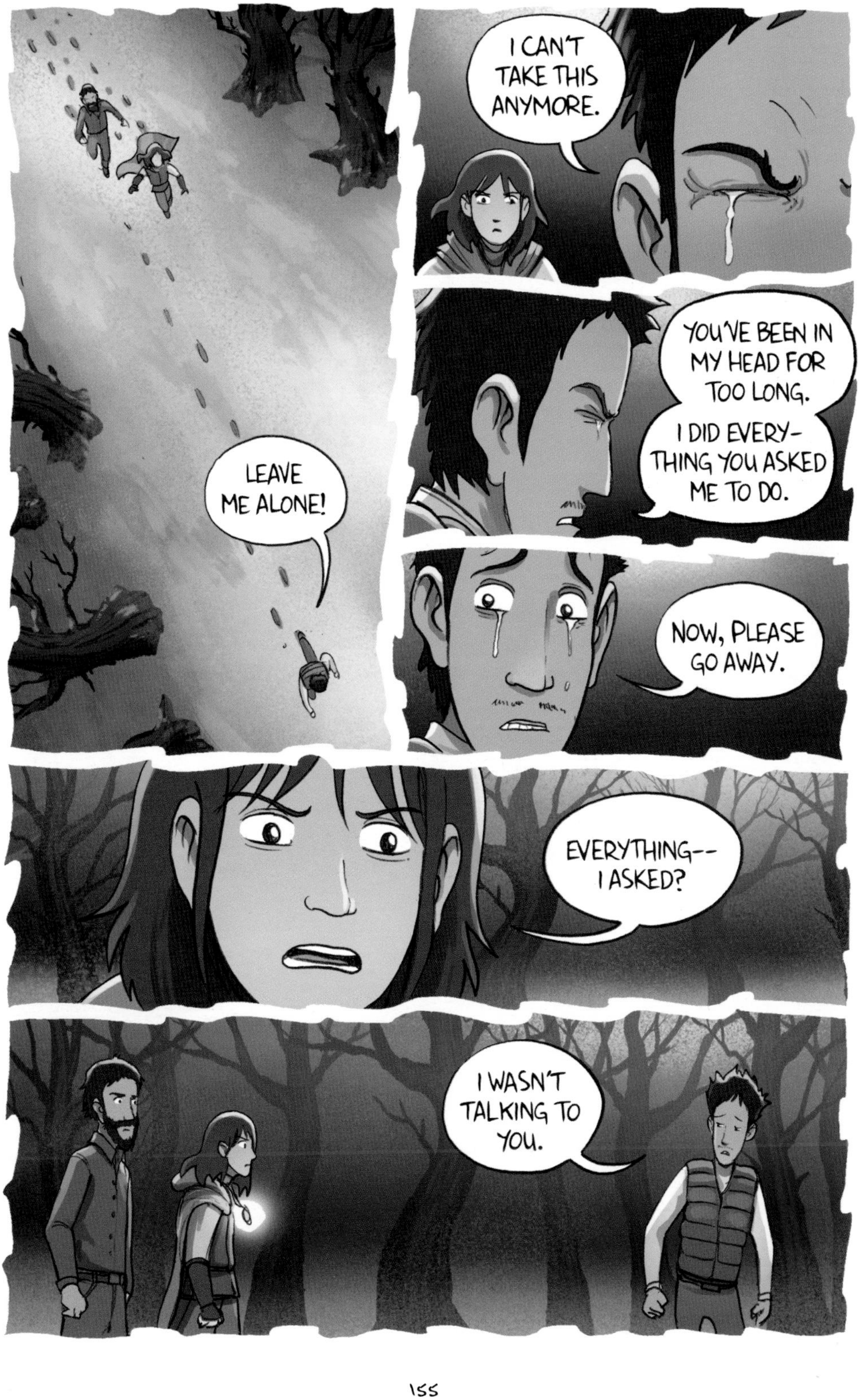
LEAVE ME ALONE!
I CAN'T TAKE THIS ANYMORE.
YOU'VE BEEN IN MY HEAD FOR TOO LONG.
I DID EVERY-THING YOU ASKED ME TO DO.
NOW, PLEASE GO AWAY.
EVERYTHING-- I ASKED?
I WASN'T TALKING TO YOU.

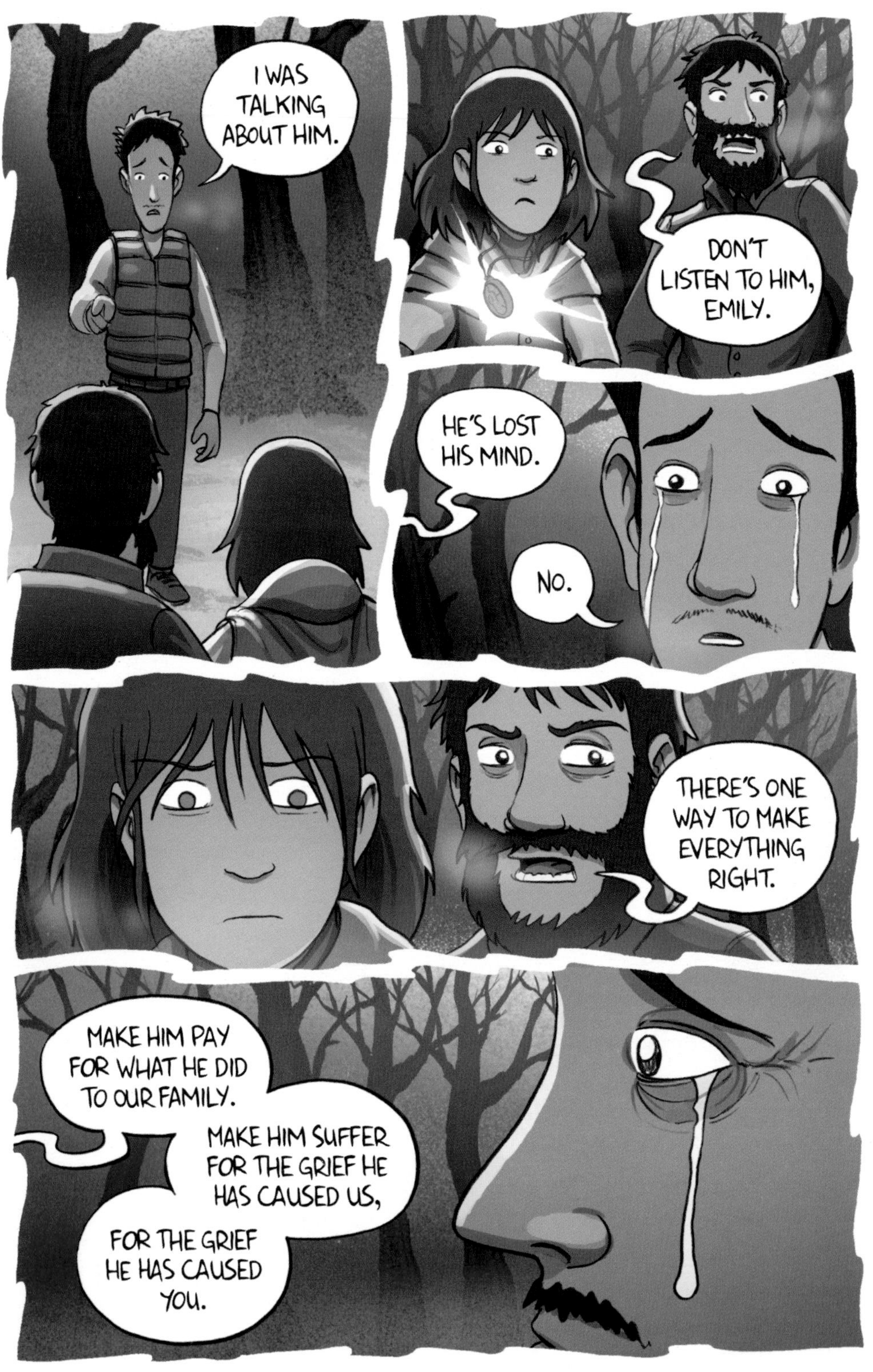
I WAS TALKING ABOUT HIM.
DON'T LISTEN TO HIM, EMILY.
HE'S LOST HIS MIND.
NO.
THERE'S ONE WAY TO MAKE EVERYTHING RIGHT.
MAKE HIM PAY FOR WHAT HE DID TO OUR FAMILY.
MAKE HIM SUFFER FOR THE GRIEF HE HAS CAUSED US,
FOR THE GRIEF HE HAS CAUSED YOU.

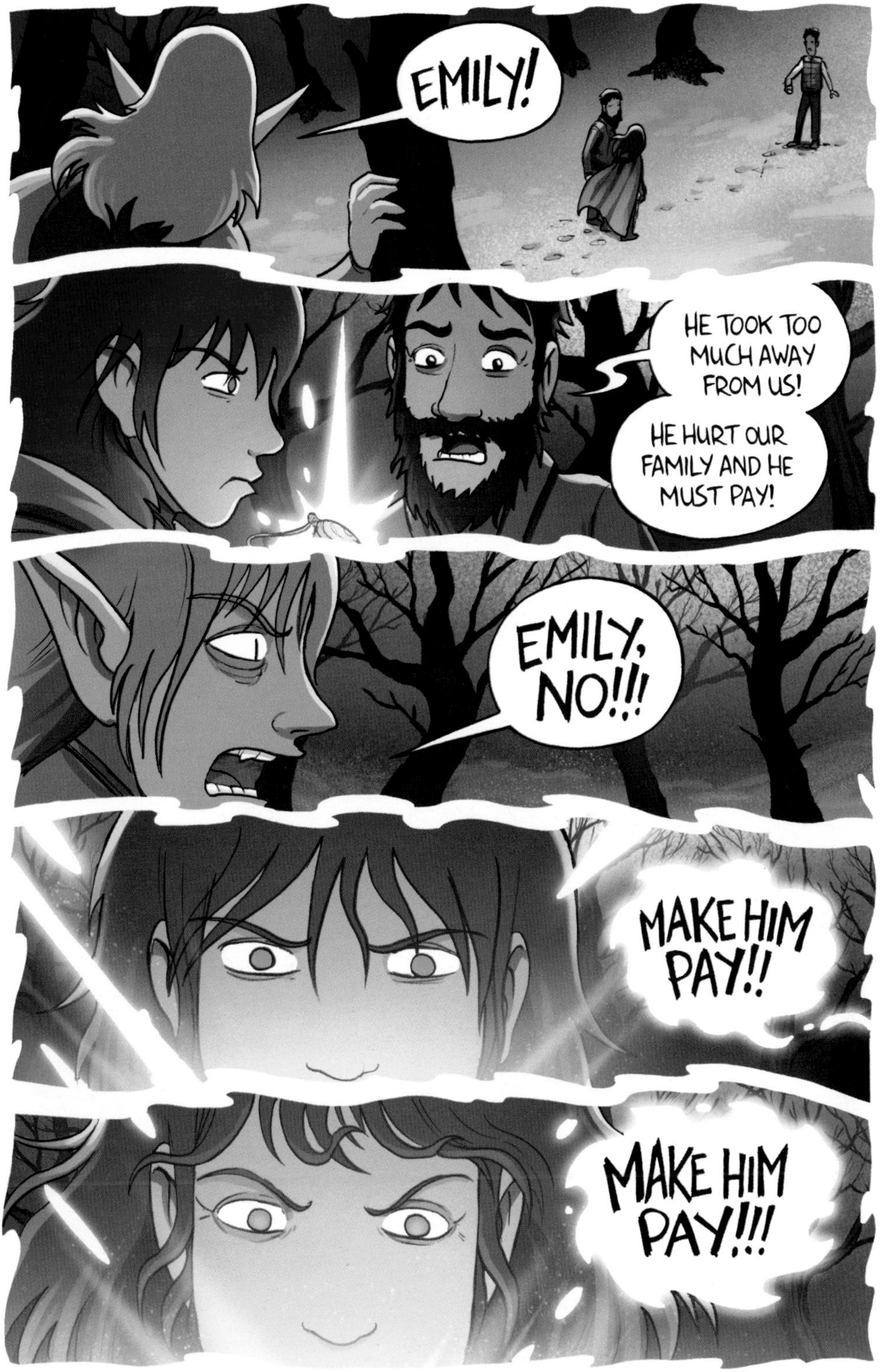
EMILY!
HE TOOK TOO MUCH AWAY FROM US!
HE HURT OUR FAMILY AND HE MUST PAY!
EMILY, NO!!!
MAKE HIM PAY!!
MAKE HIM PAY!!!

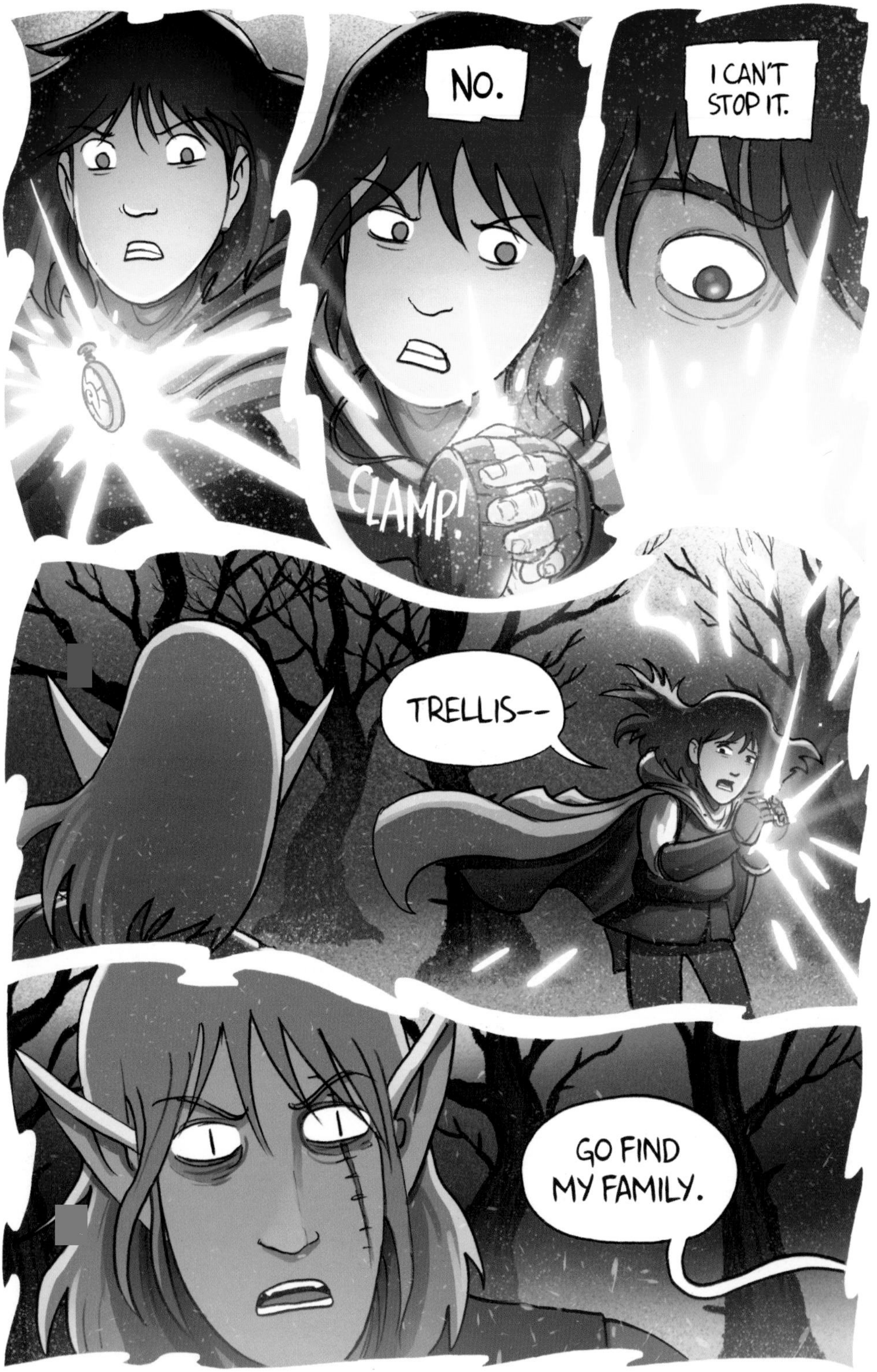
NO.
I CAN'T STOP IT.
CLAMP!
TRELLIS--
GO FIND MY FAMILY.

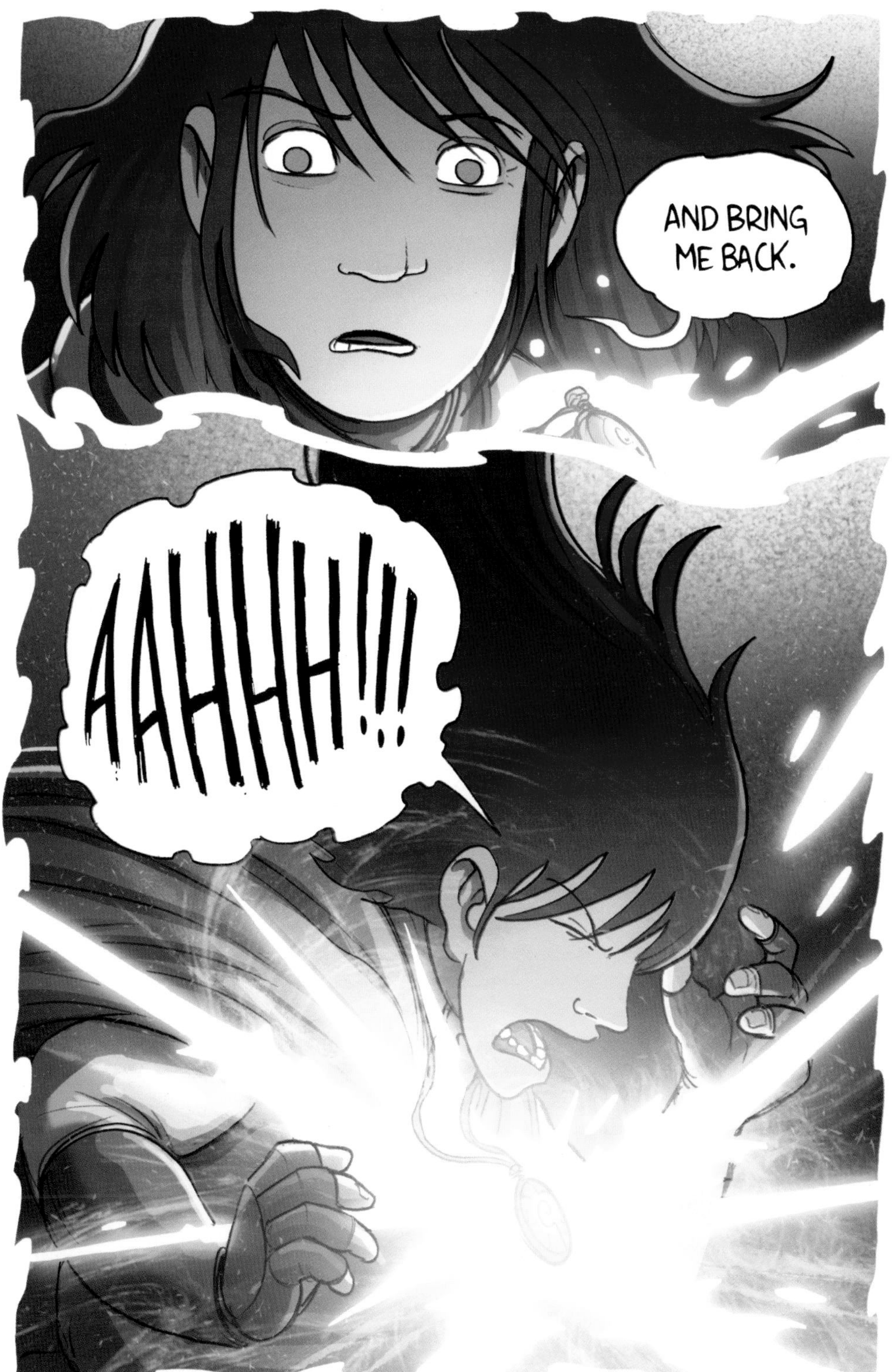
AND BRING ME BACK.
AAHHHH!!!

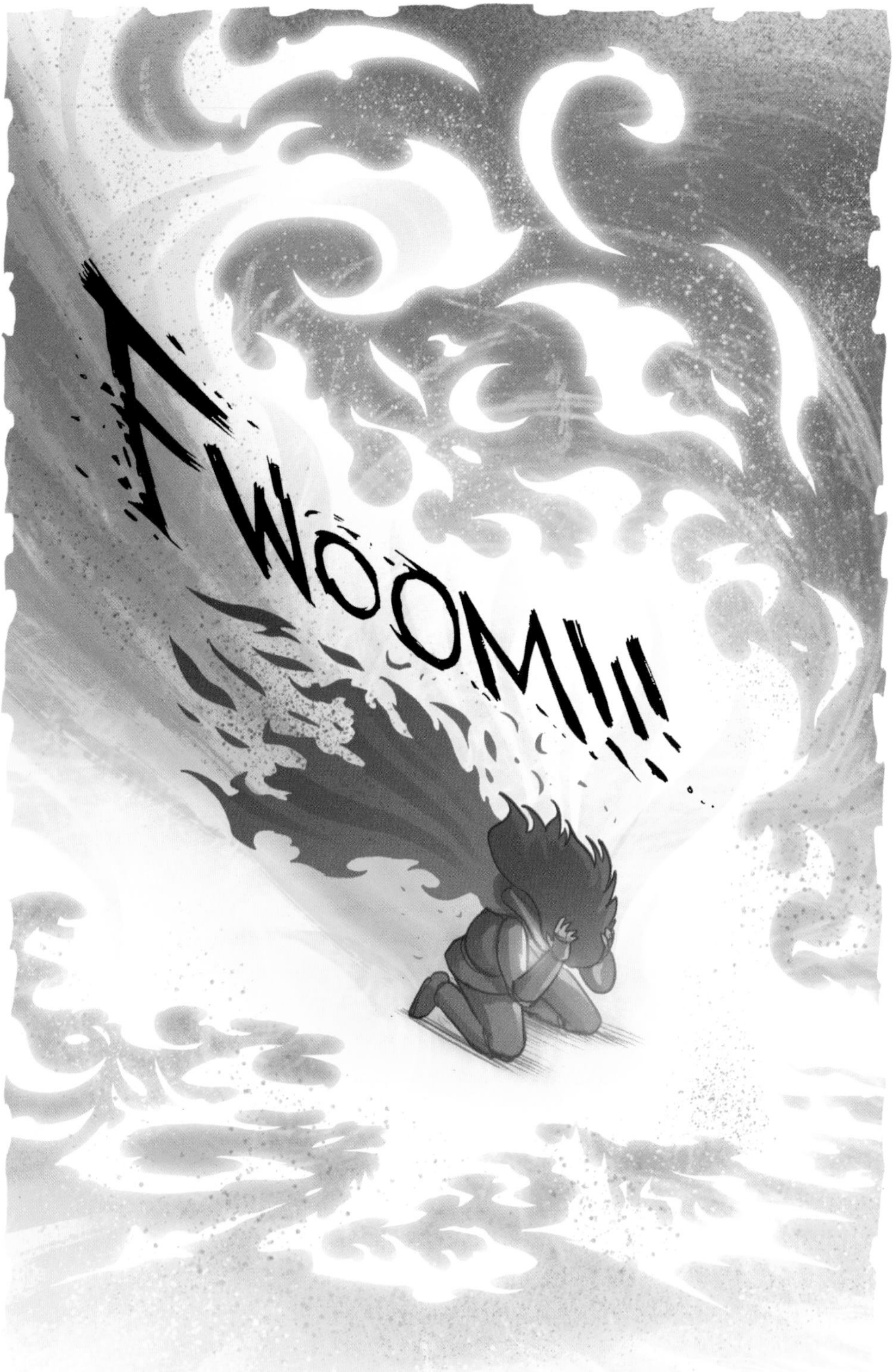
ZWOOM!!!

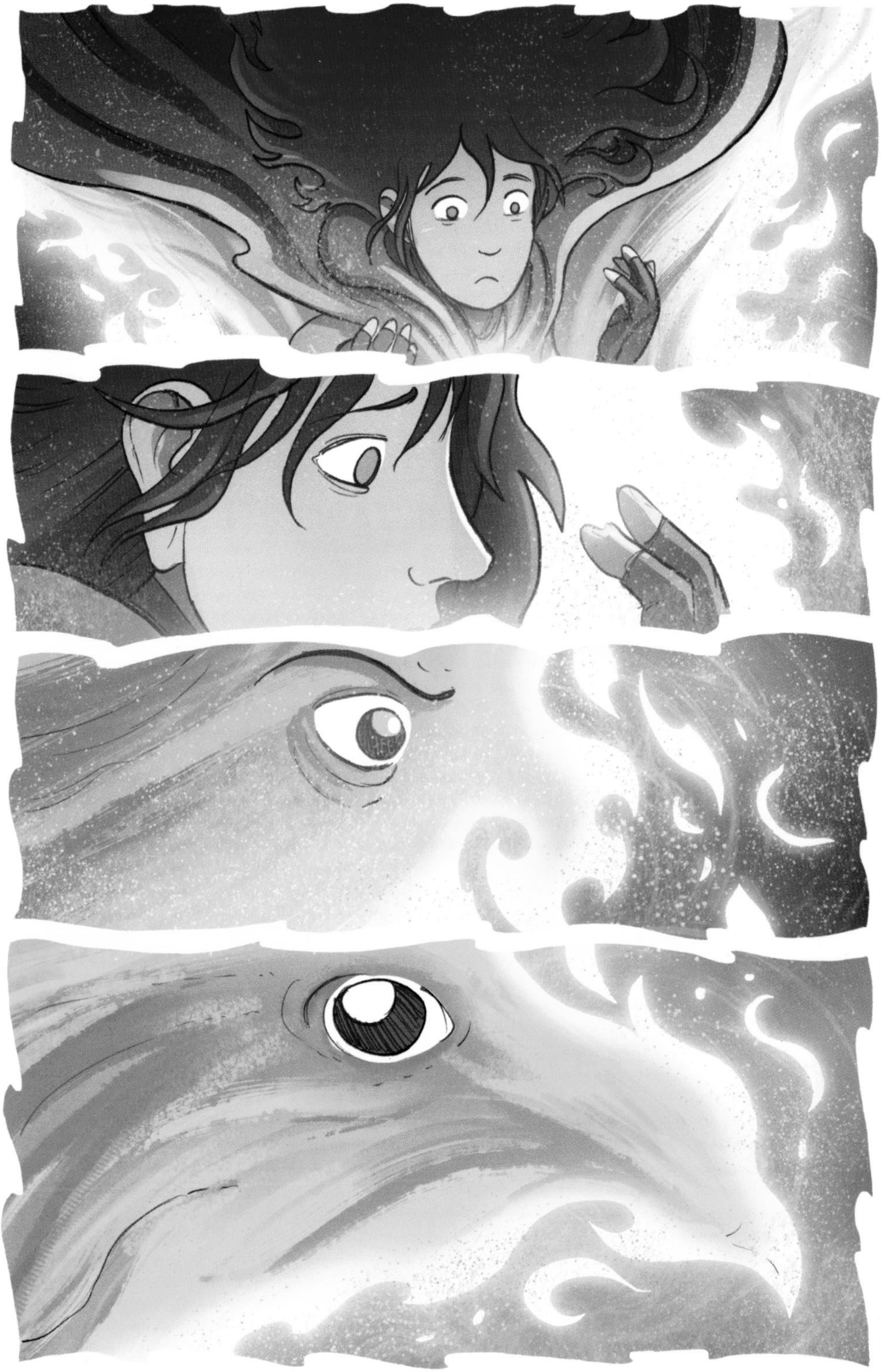

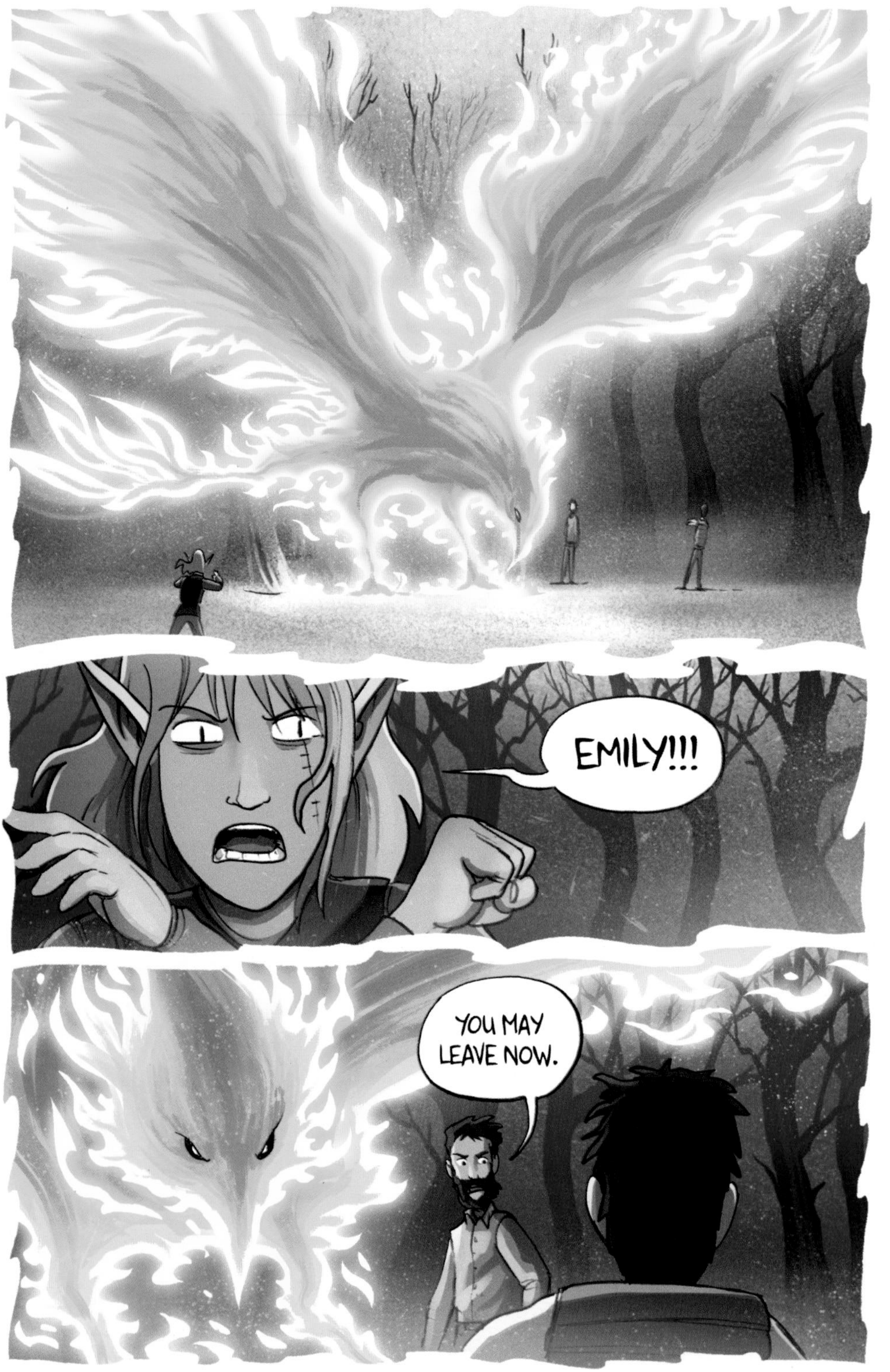
EMILY!!!
YOU MAY LEAVE NOW.

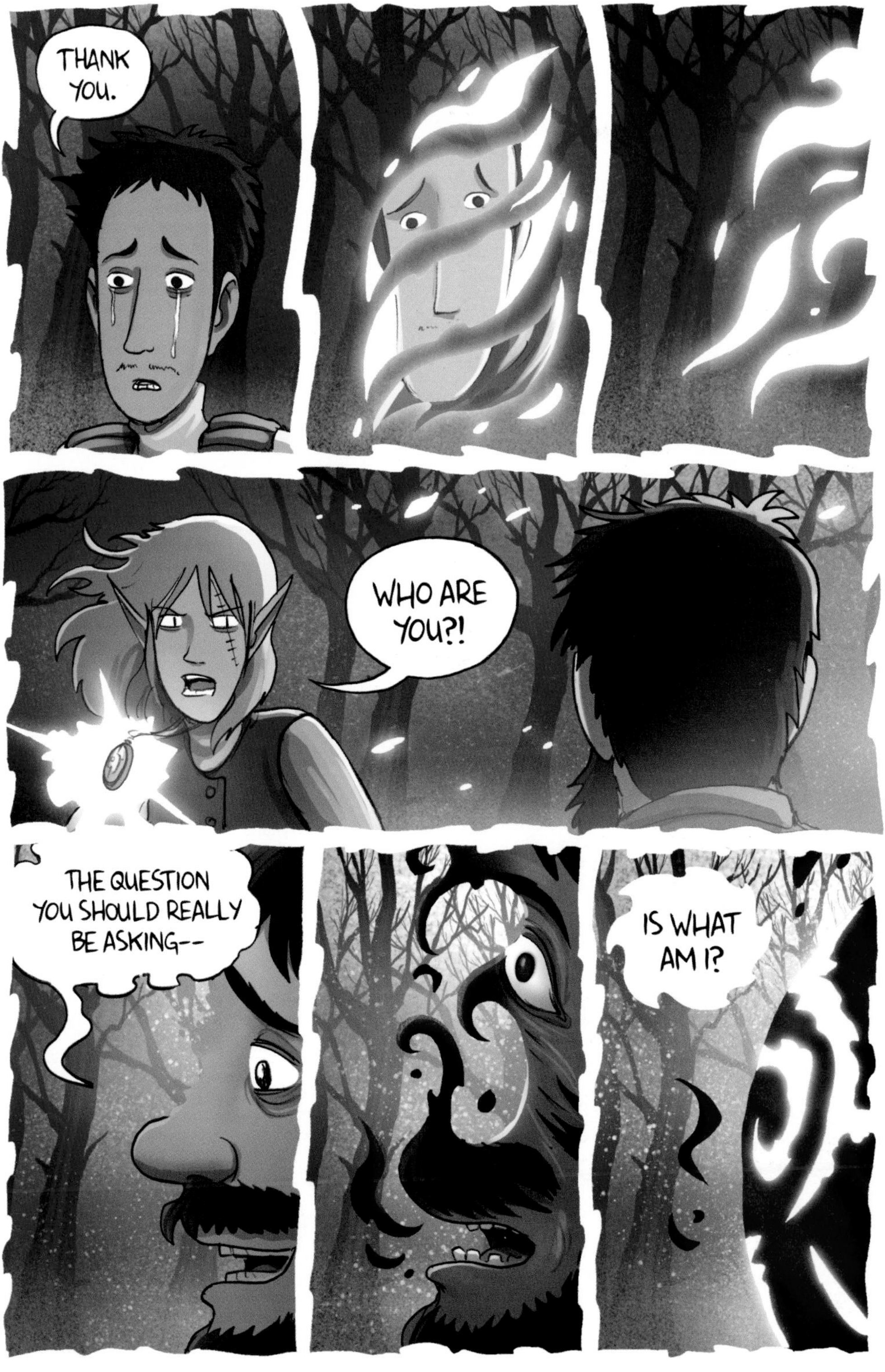
THANK YOU.
WHO ARE YOU?!
THE QUESTION YOU SHOULD REALLY BE ASKING--
IS WHAT AM I?

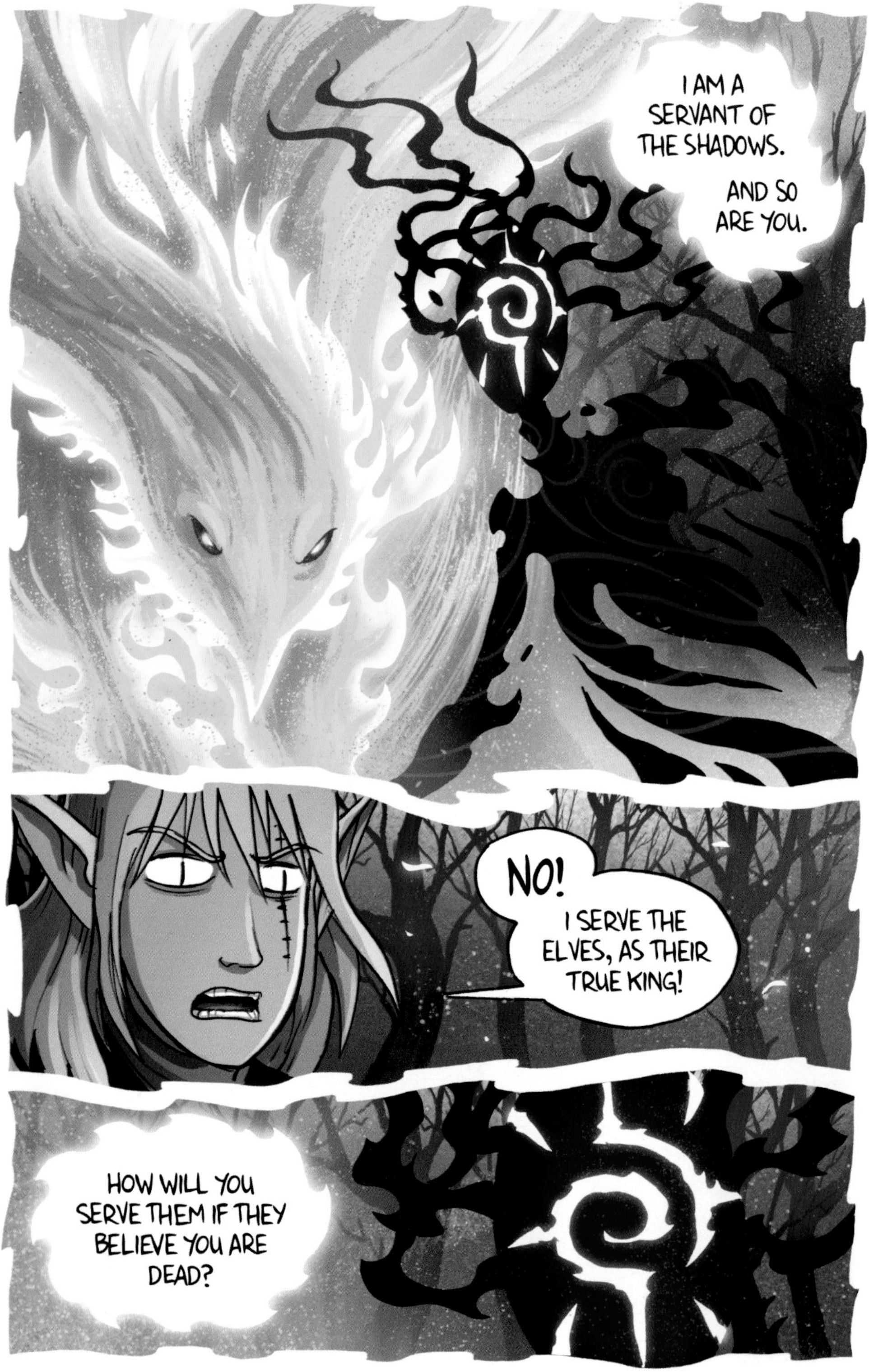
I AM A SERVANT OF THE SHADOWS.
AND SO ARE YOU.
NO!
I SERVE THE ELVES, AS THEIR TRUE KING!
HOW WILL YOU SERVE THEM IF THEY BELIEVE YOU ARE DEAD?

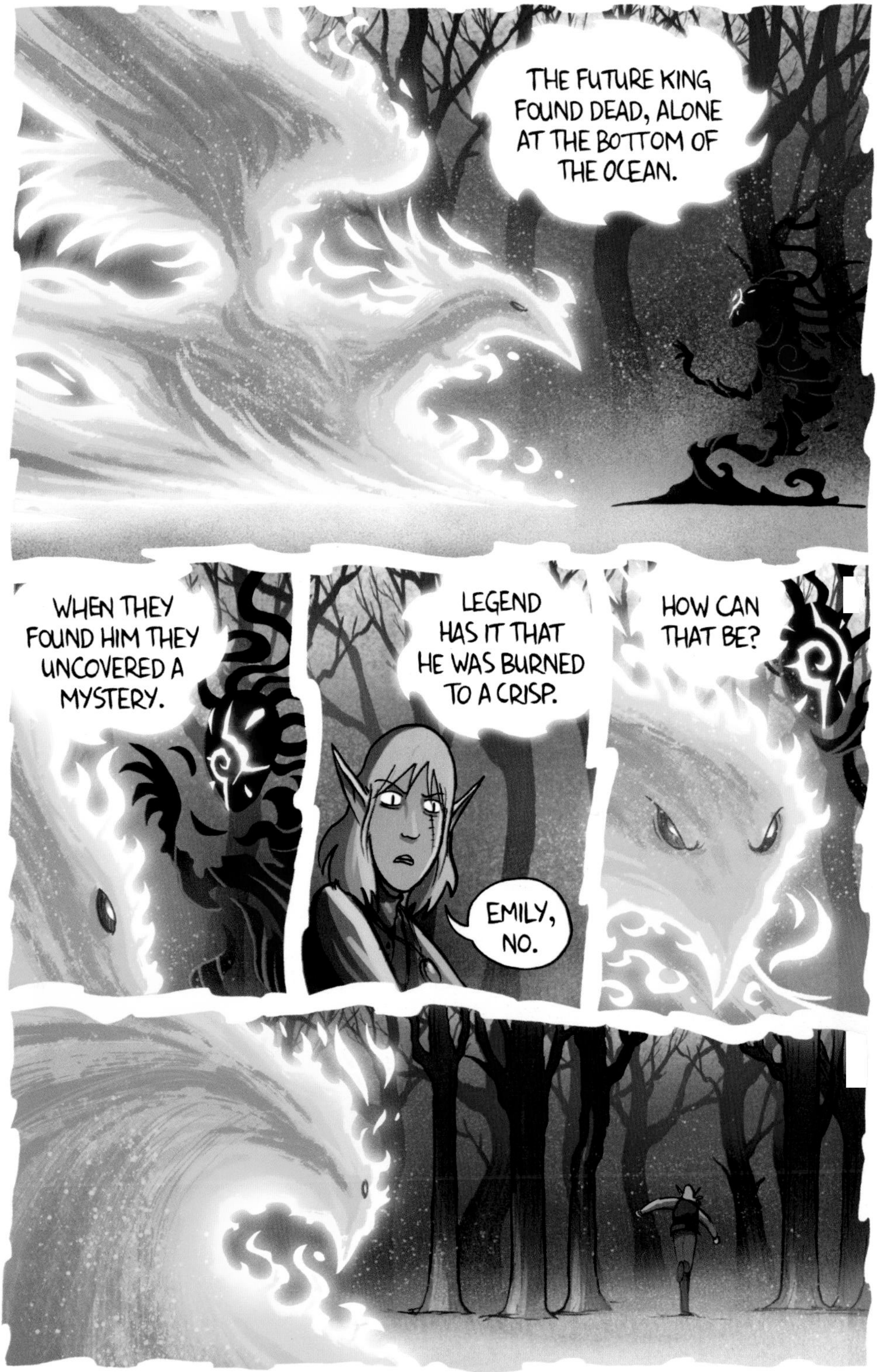
THE FUTURE KING FOUND DEAD, ALONE AT THE BOTTOM OF THE OCEAN.
WHEN THEY FOUND HIM THEY UNCOVERED A MYSTERY.
LEGEND HAS IT THAT HE WAS BURNED TO A CRISP.
EMILY, NO.
HOW CAN THAT BE?

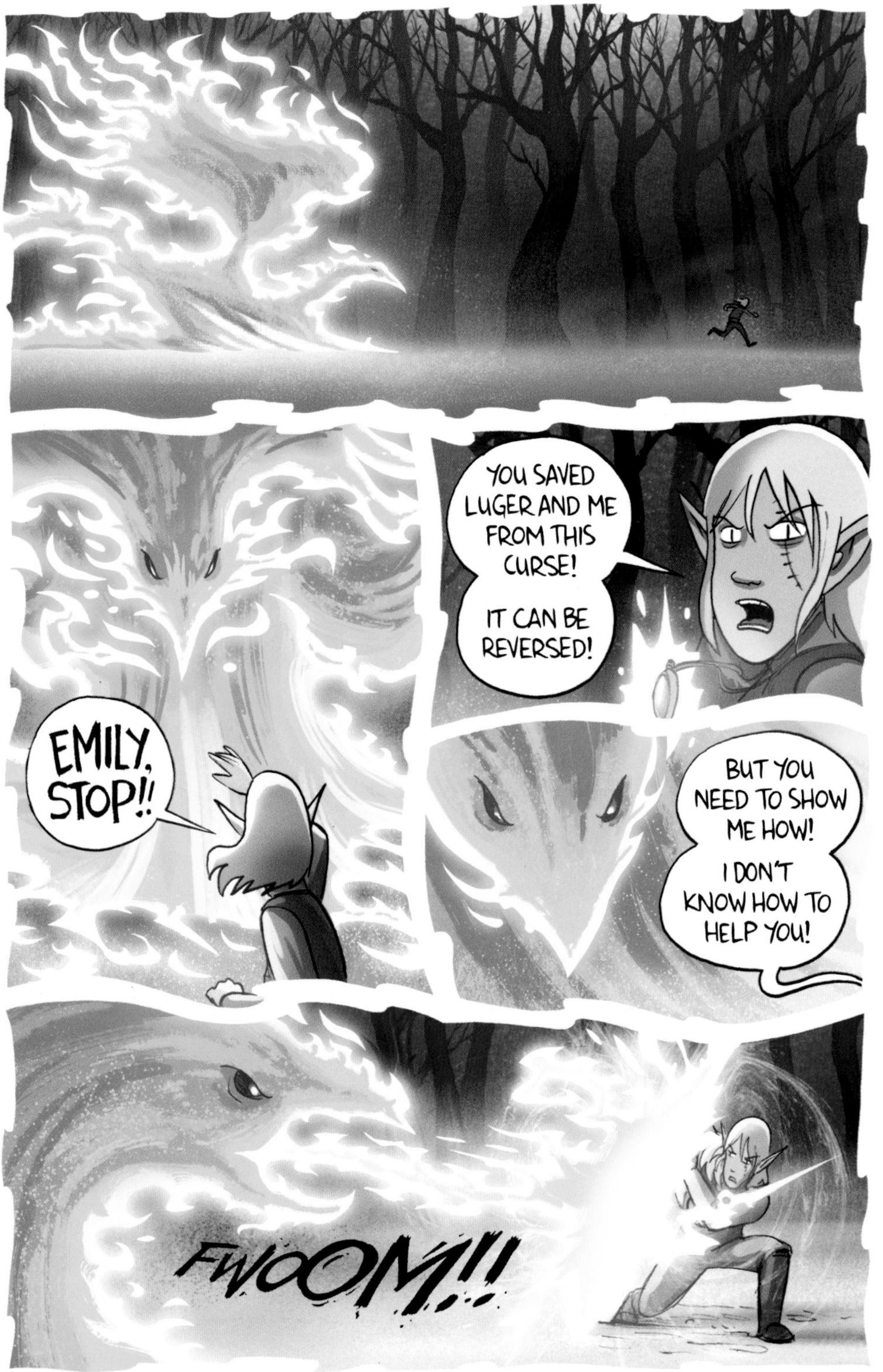
YOU SAVED LUGER AND ME FROM THIS CURSE!
IT CAN BE REVERSED!
EMILY, STOP!!
BUT YOU NEED TO SHOW ME HOW!
I DON'T KNOW HOW TO HELP YOU!
FWOOM!!

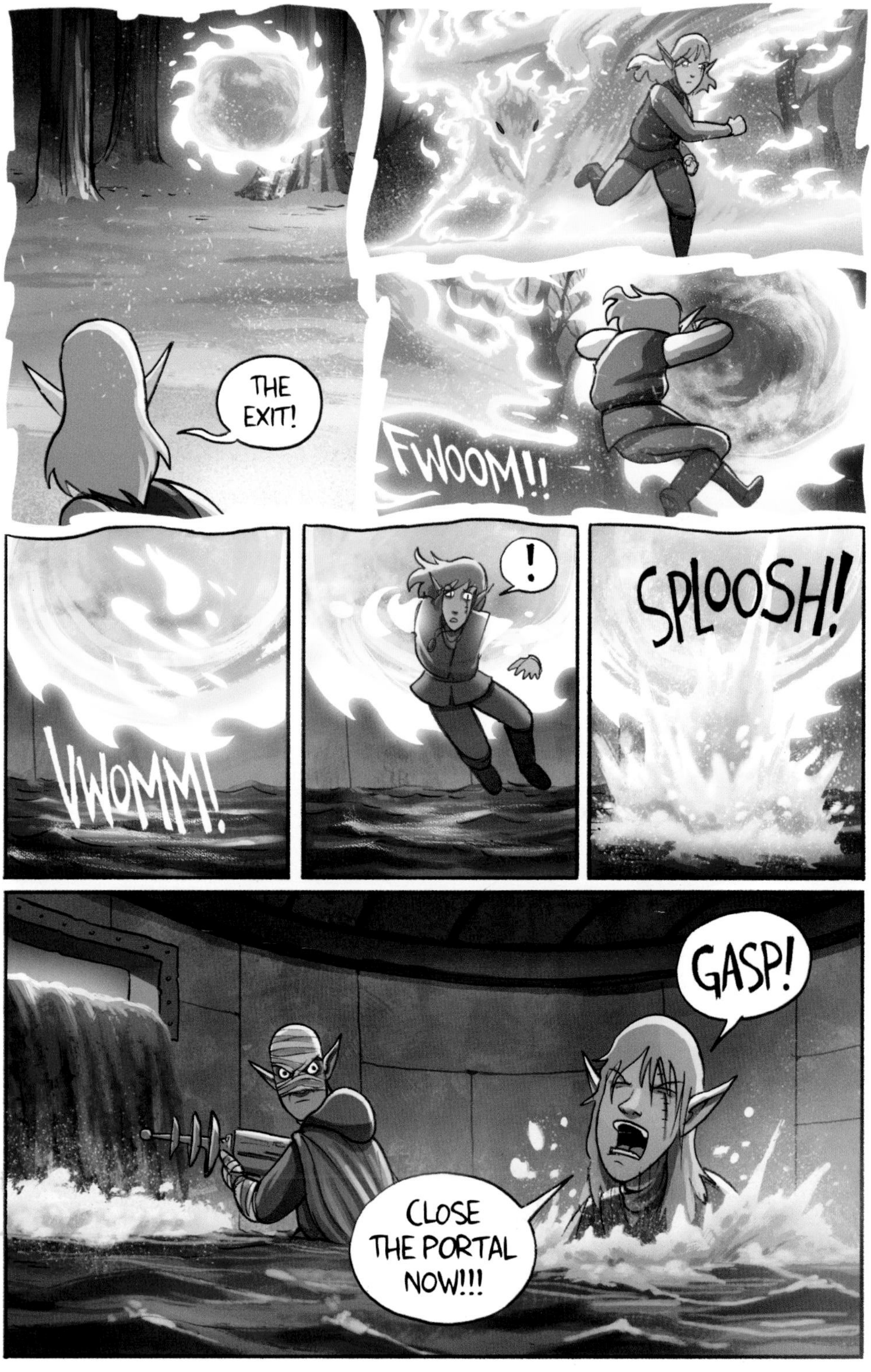
THE EXIT!
FWOOM!!
VWOMM!
!
SPLOOSH!
GASP!
CLOSE THE PORTAL NOW!!!

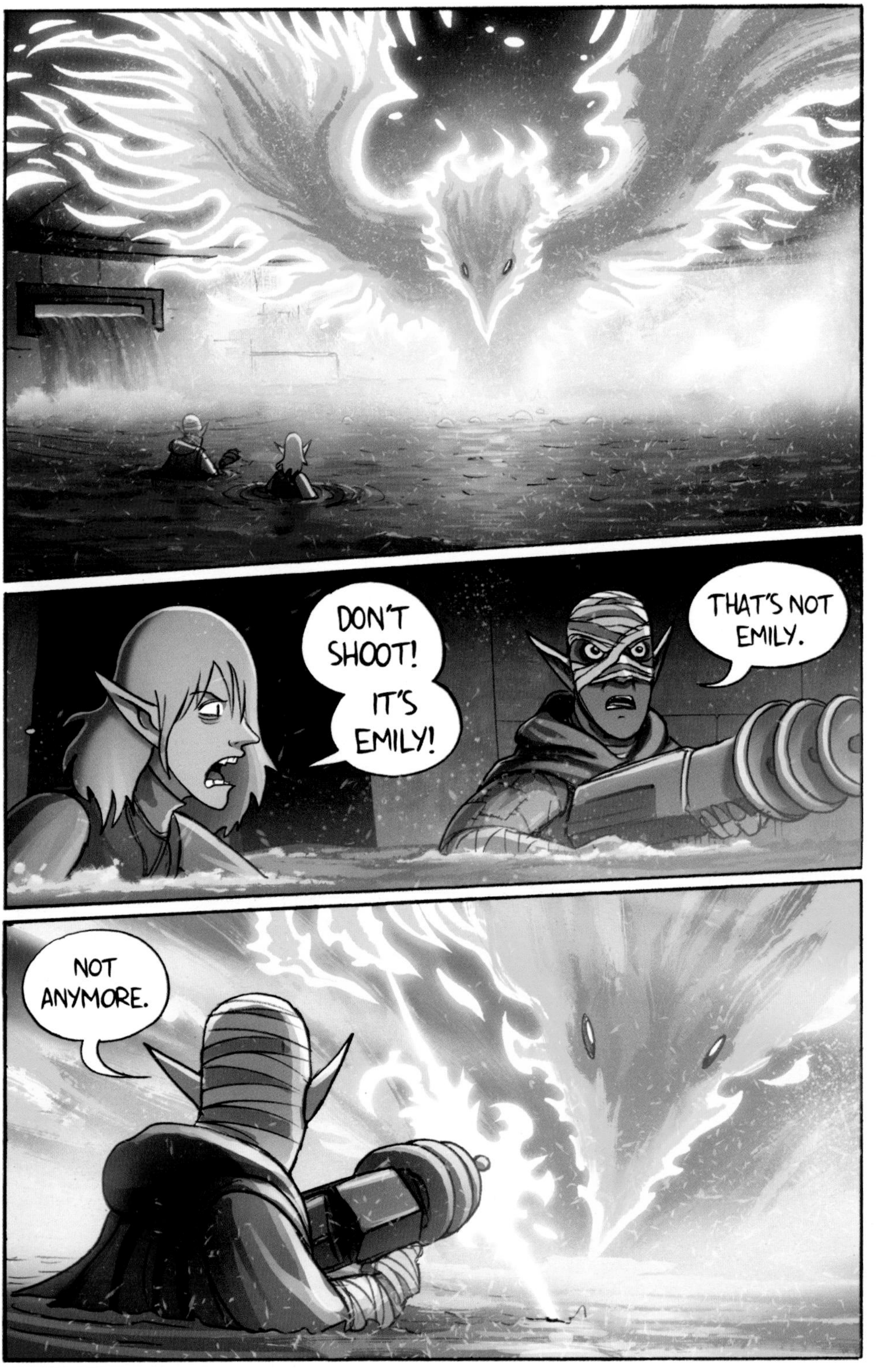
DON'T SHOOT!
IT'S EMILY!
THAT'S NOT EMILY.
NOT ANYMORE.

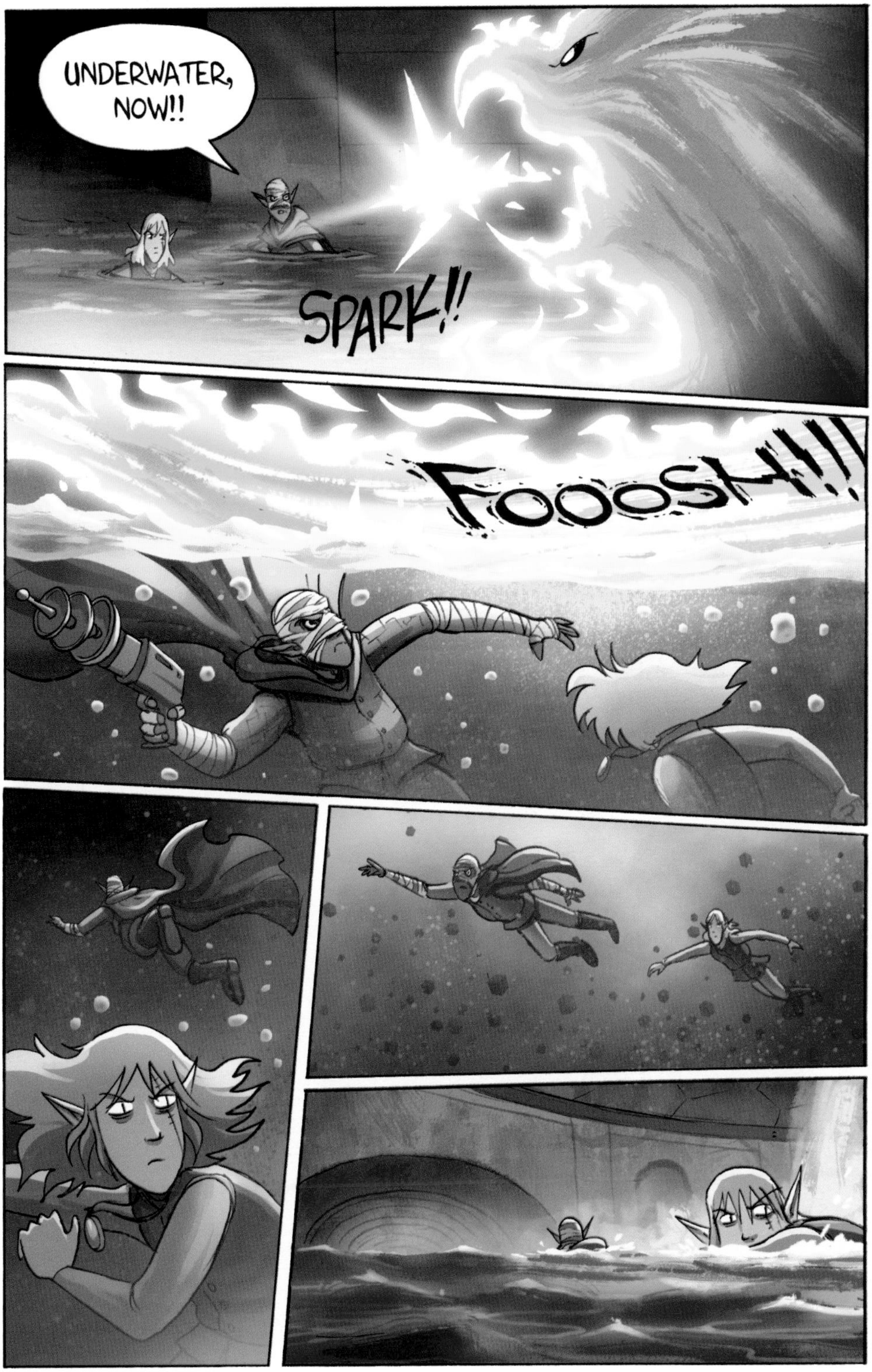
UNDERWATER, NOW!!
SPARK!!
FOOOSH!!!

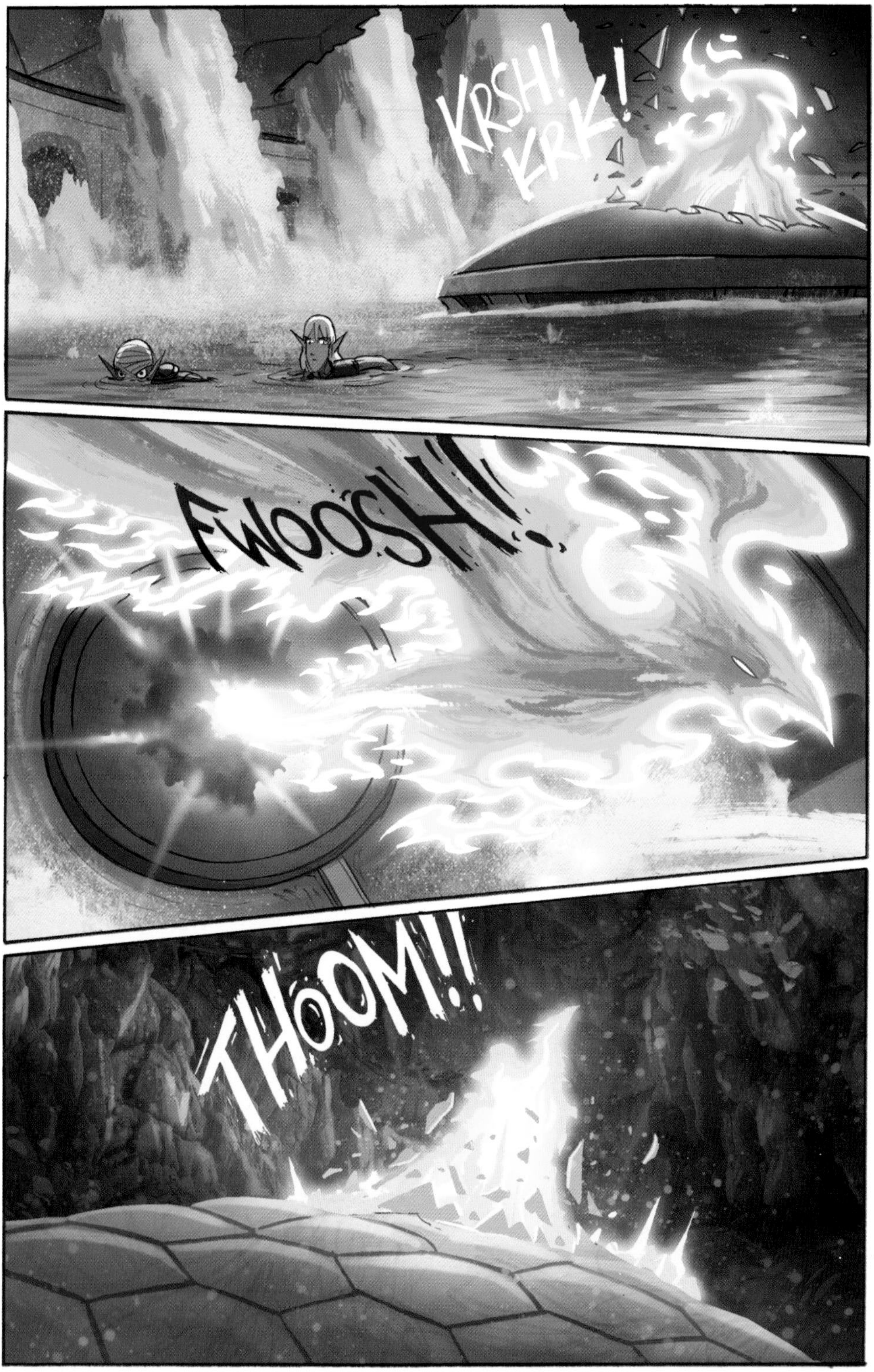
KRSH! KRK!
FWOOSH!!
THOOM!!

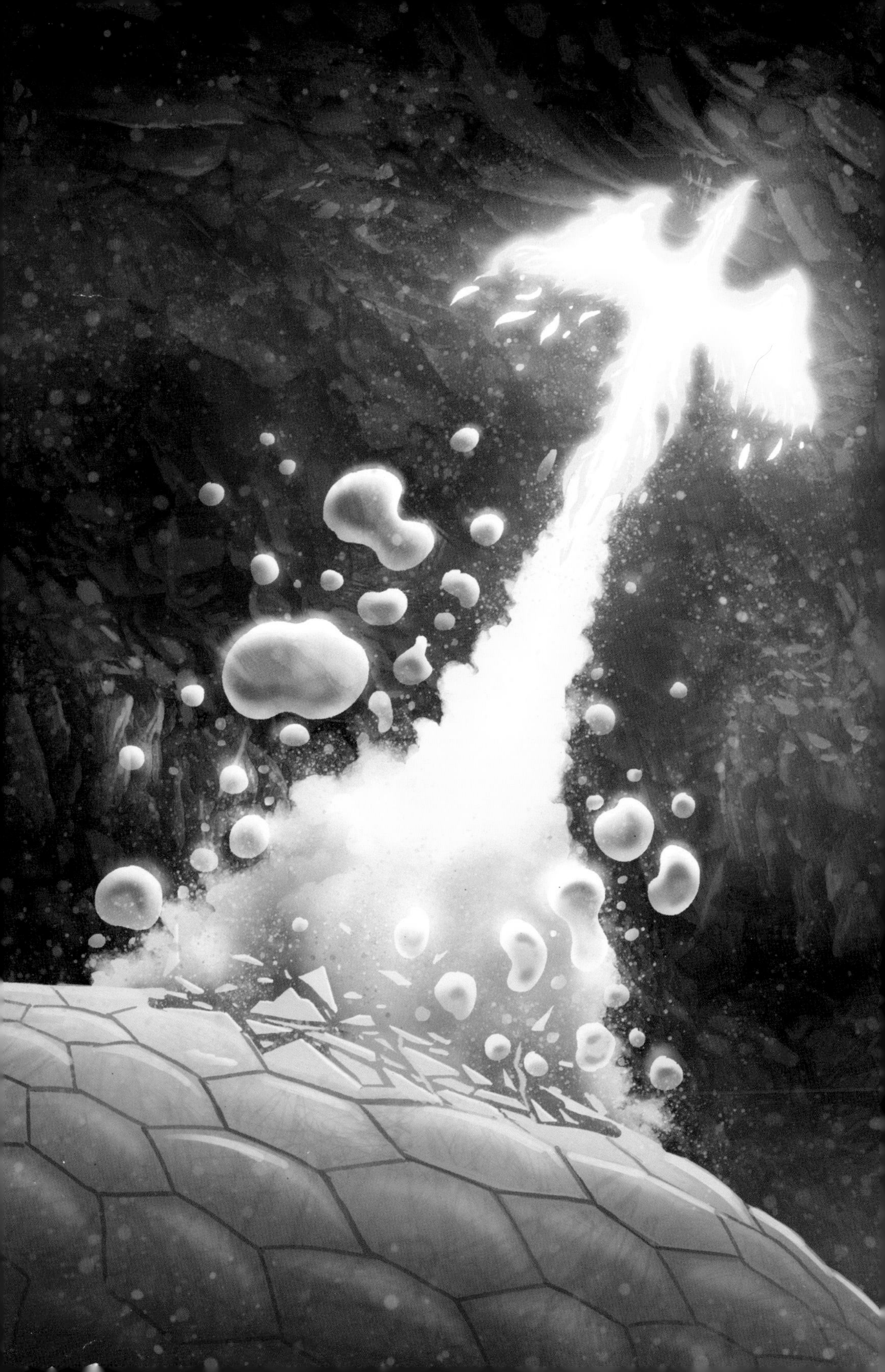

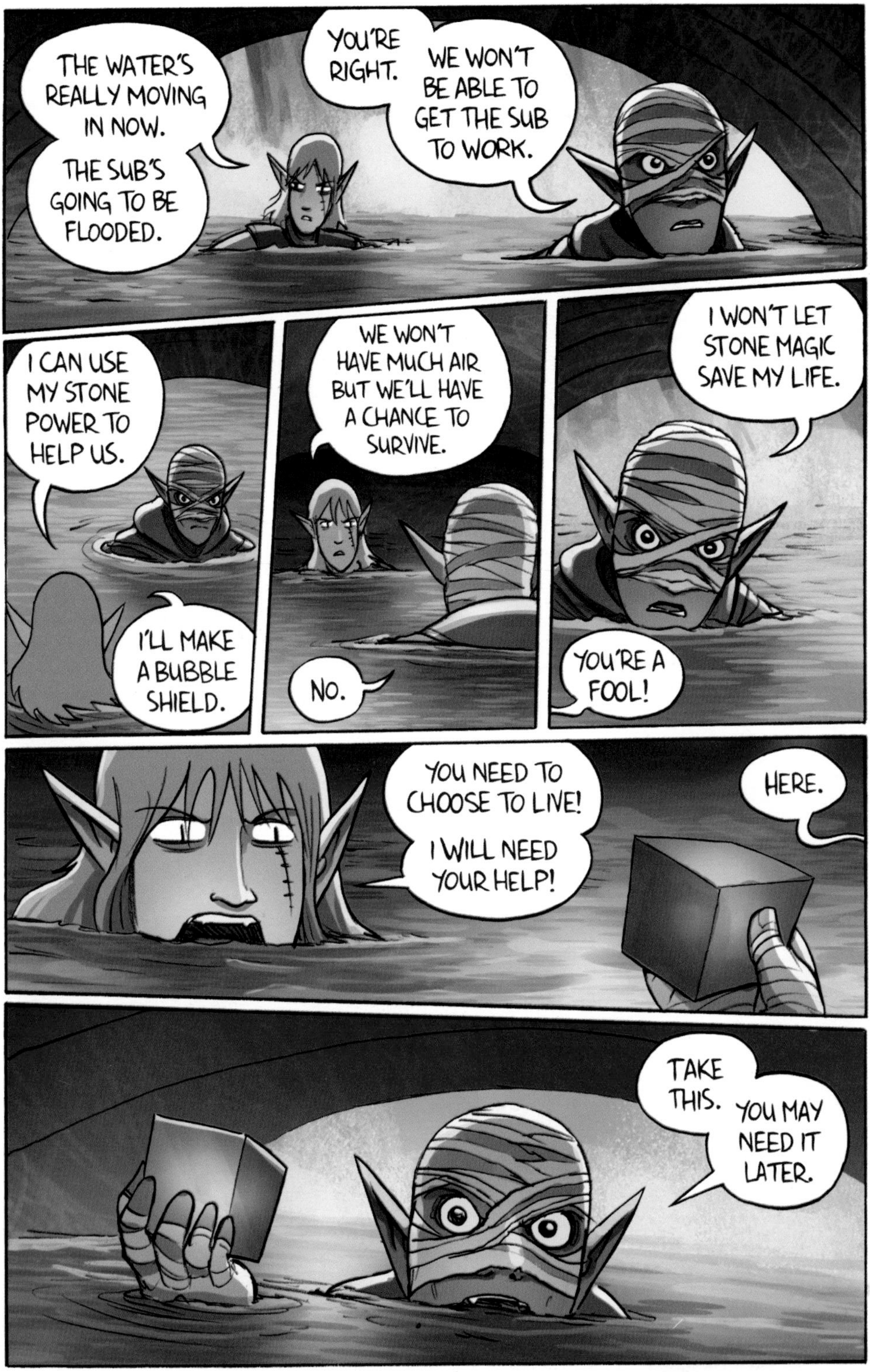
THE WATER'S REALLY MOVING IN NOW.
THE SUB'S GOING TO BE FLOODED.
YOU'RE RIGHT.
WE WON'T BE ABLE TO GET THE SUB TO WORK.
I CAN USE MY STONE POWER TO HELP US.
I'LL MAKE A BUBBLE SHIELD.
WE WON'T HAVE MUCH AIR BUT WE'LL HAVE A CHANCE TO SURVIVE.
NO.
I WON'T LET STONE MAGIC SAVE MY LIFE.
YOU'RE A FOOL!
YOU NEED TO CHOOSE TO LIVE!
I WILL NEED YOUR HELP!
HERE.
TAKE THIS.
YOU MAY NEED IT LATER.

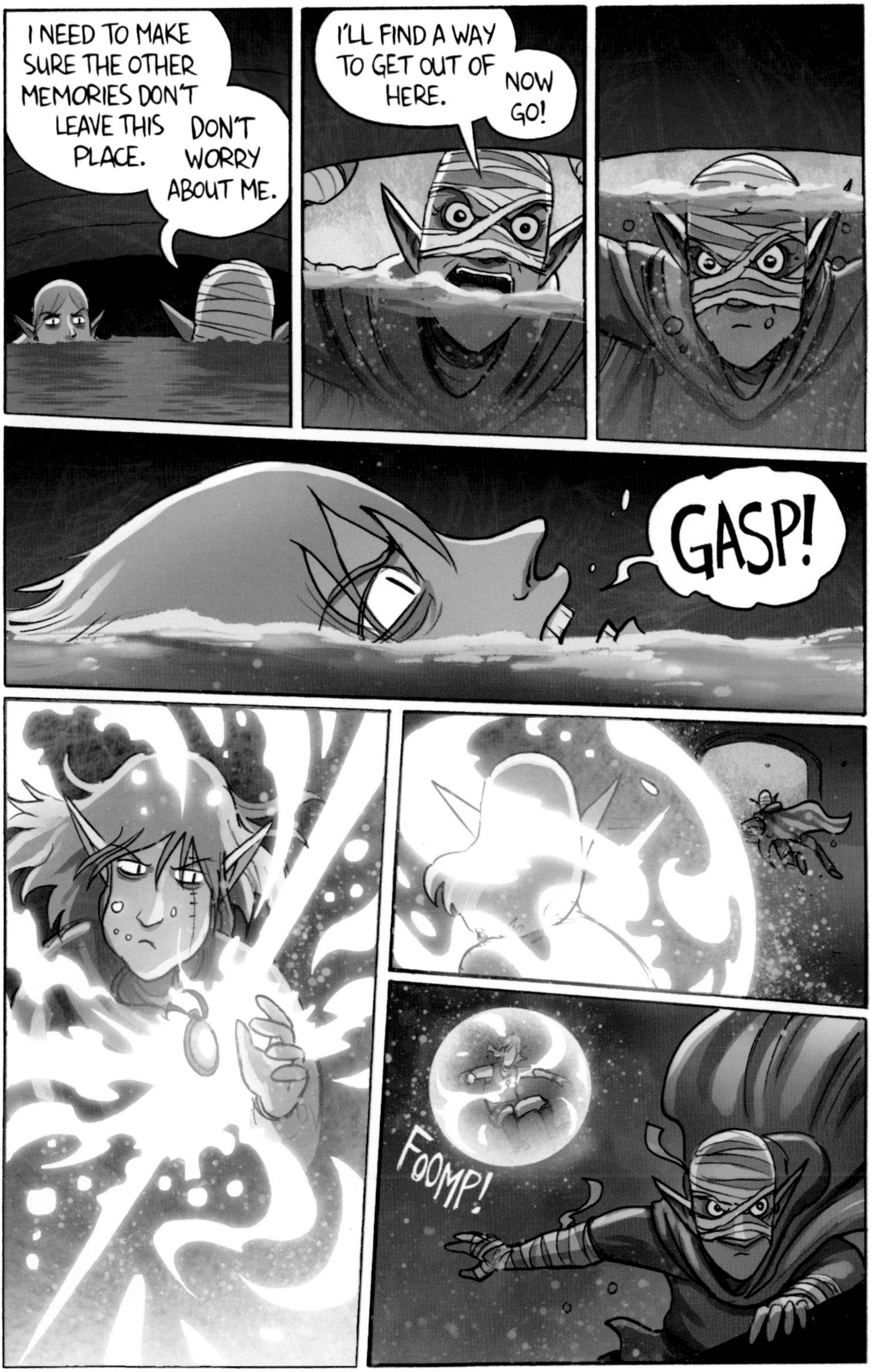
I NEED TO MAKE SURE THE OTHER MEMORIES DON'T LEAVE THIS PLACE.
DON'T WORRY ABOUT ME.
I'LL FIND A WAY TO GET OUT OF HERE.
NOW GO!
GASP!
FOOMP!

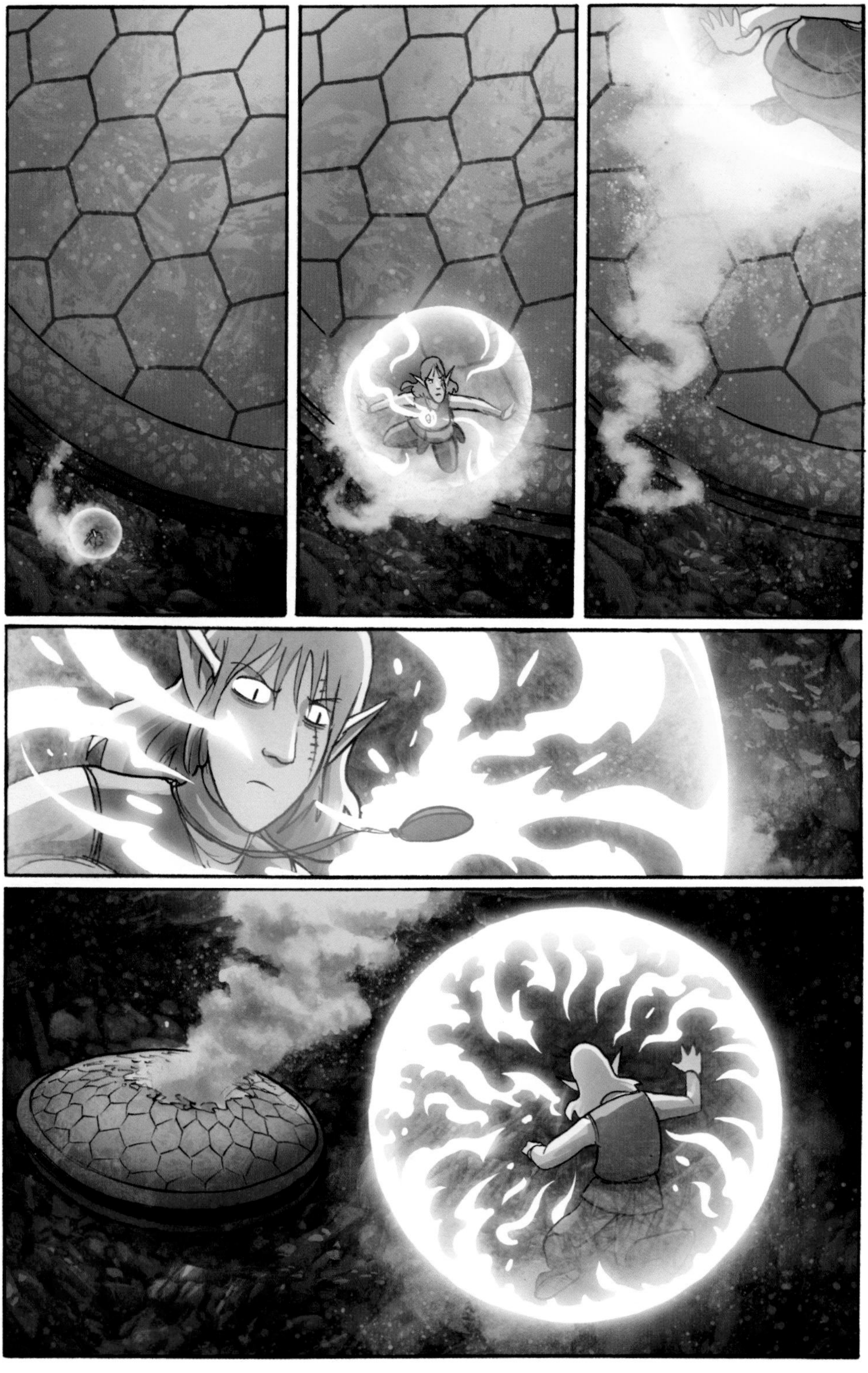

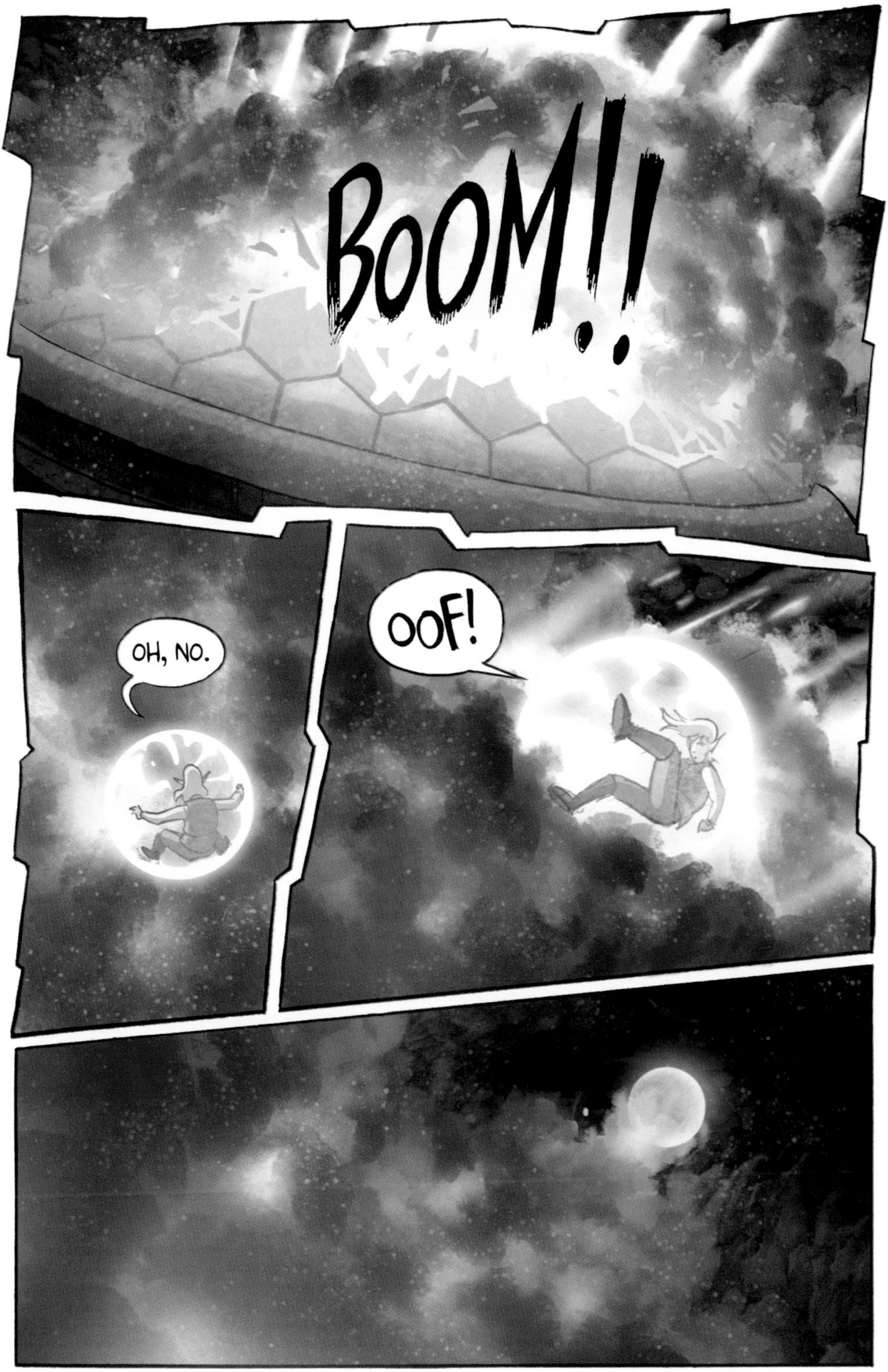
BOOM!!
OH, NO.
OOF!

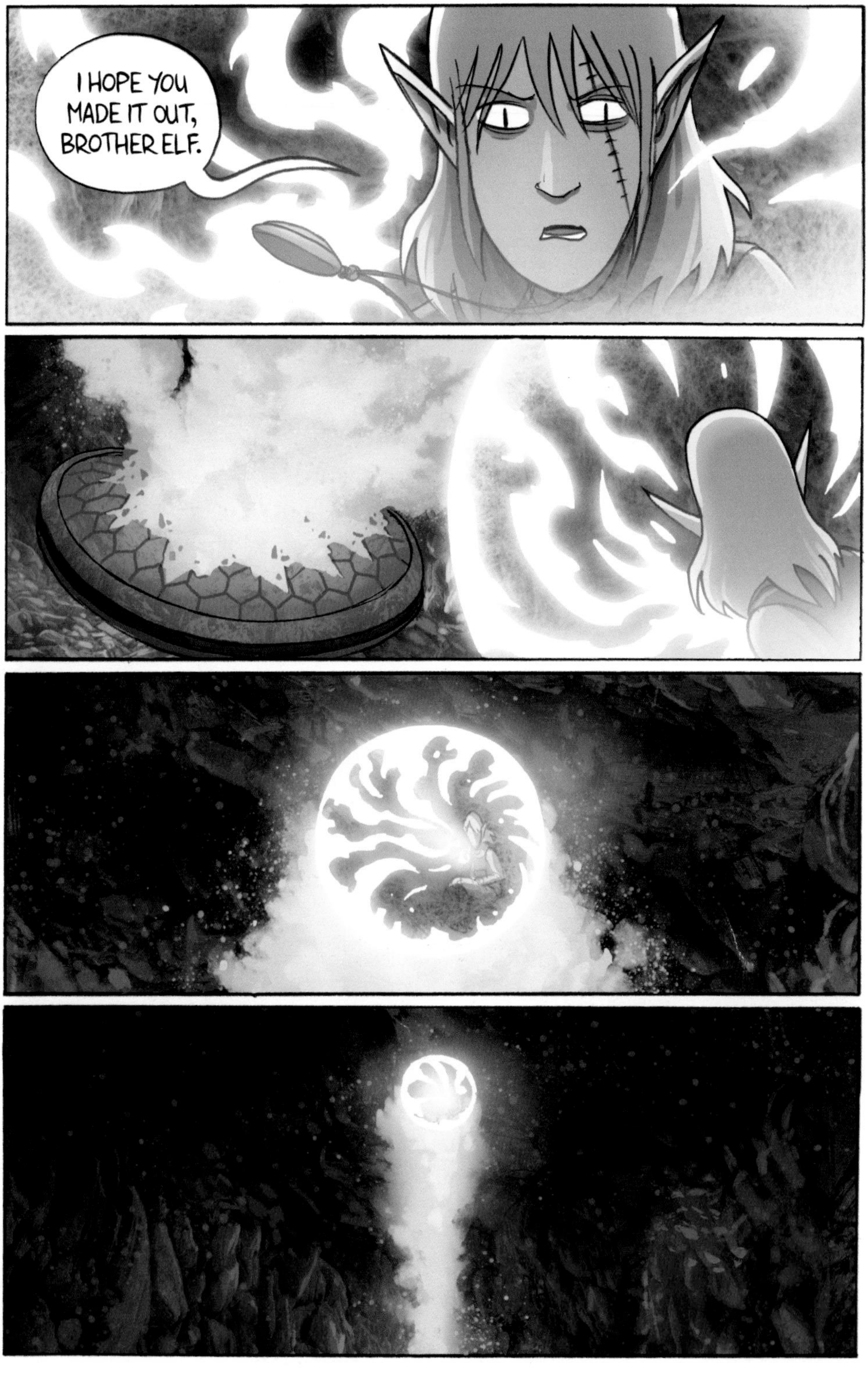
I HOPE YOU MADE IT OUT, BROTHER ELF.

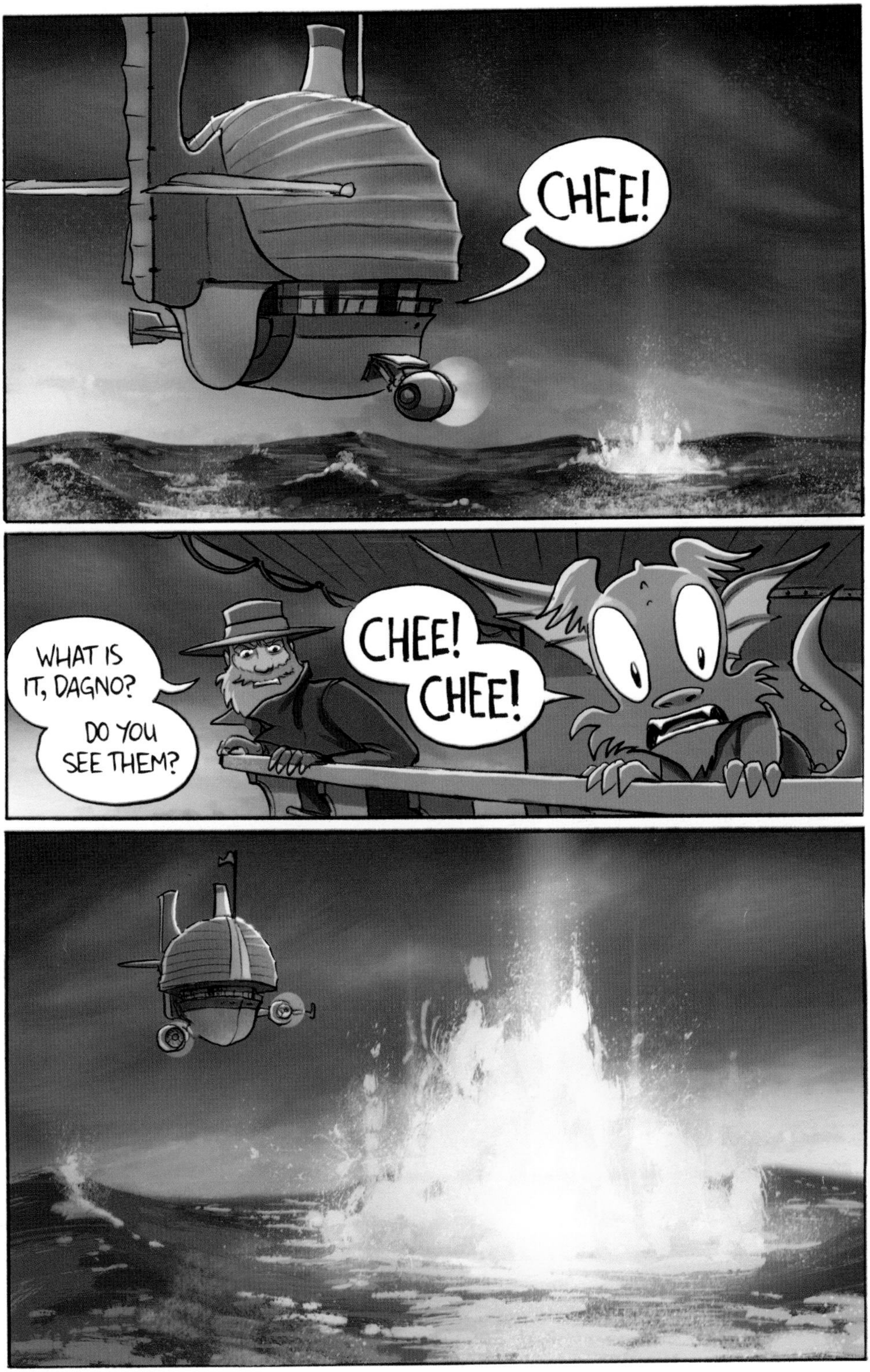
CHEE!
WHAT IS IT, DAGNO?
DO YOU SEE THEM?
CHEE! CHEE!

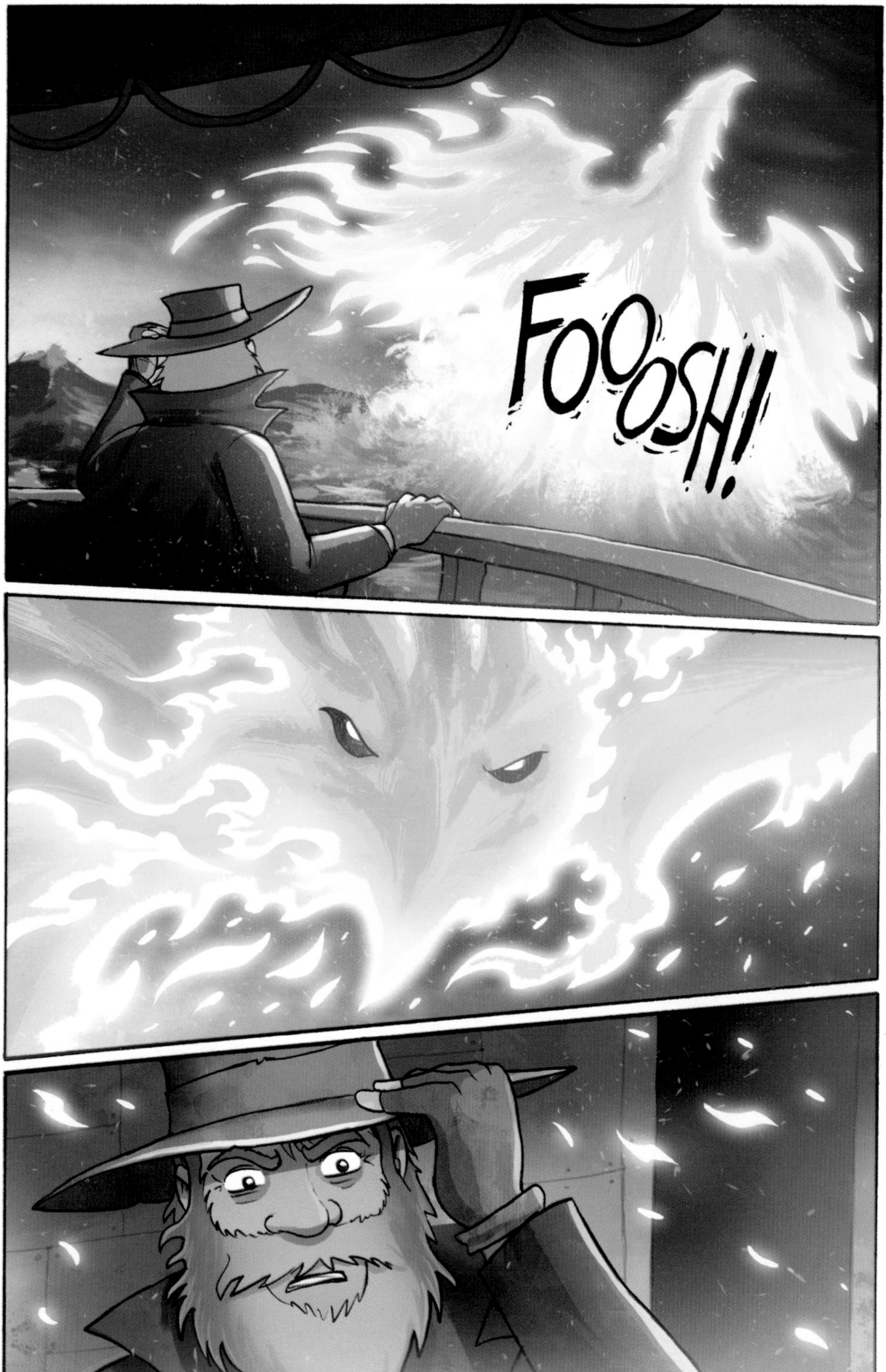
FOOOSH!!

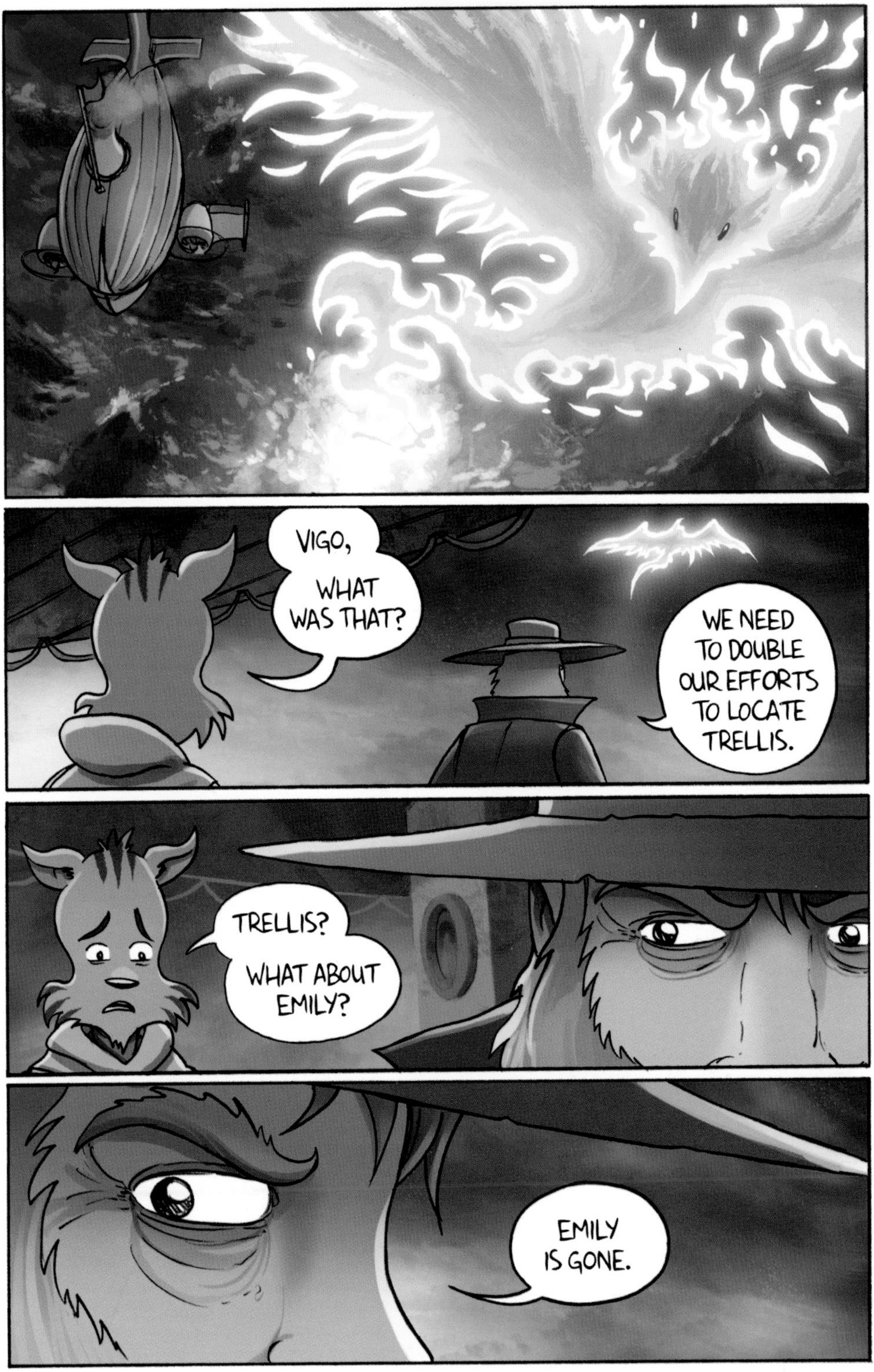
VIGO,
WHAT WAS THAT?
WE NEED TO DOUBLE OUR EFFORTS TO LOCATE TRELLIS.
TRELLIS?
WHAT ABOUT EMILY?
EMILY IS GONE.

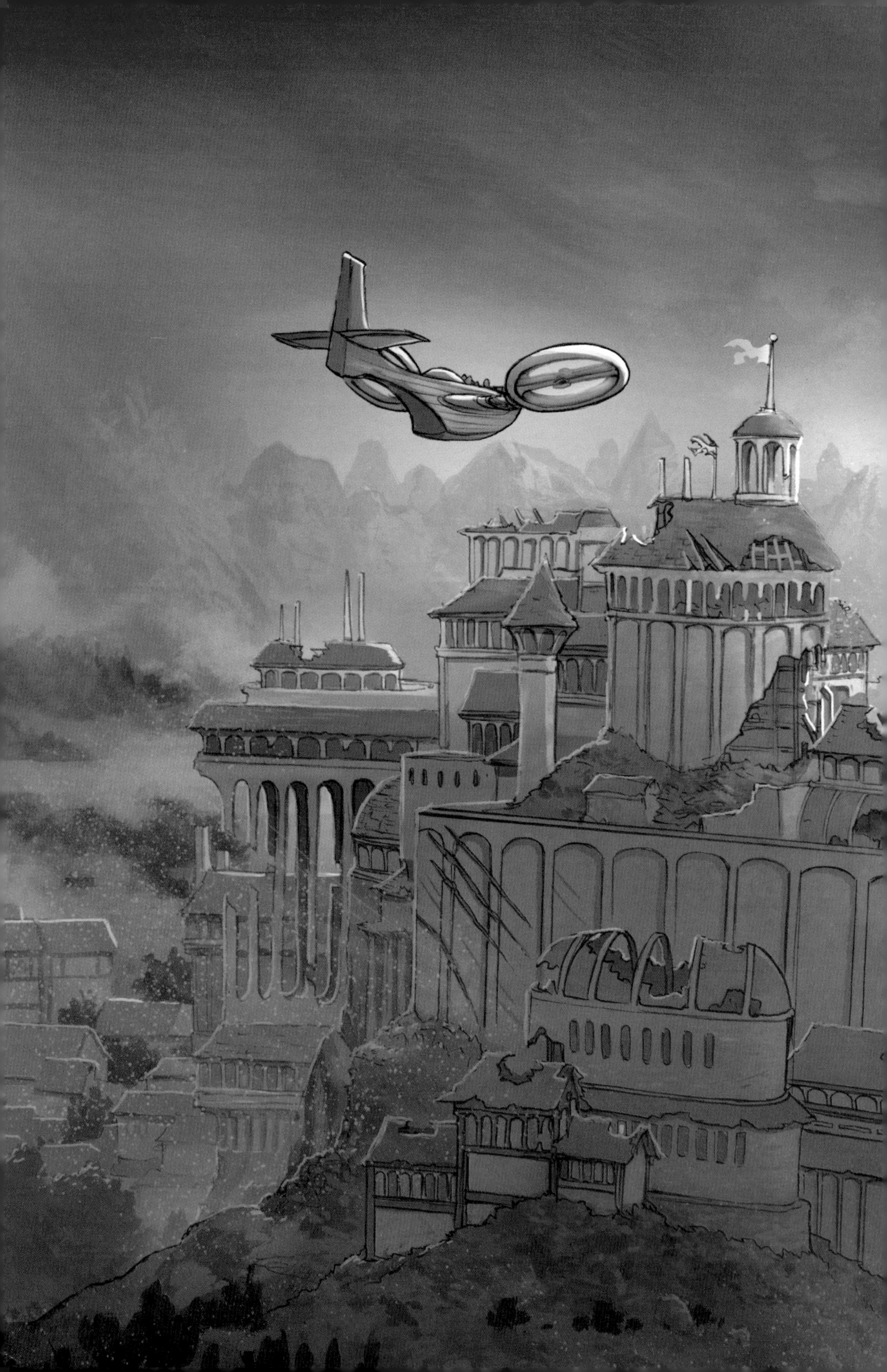

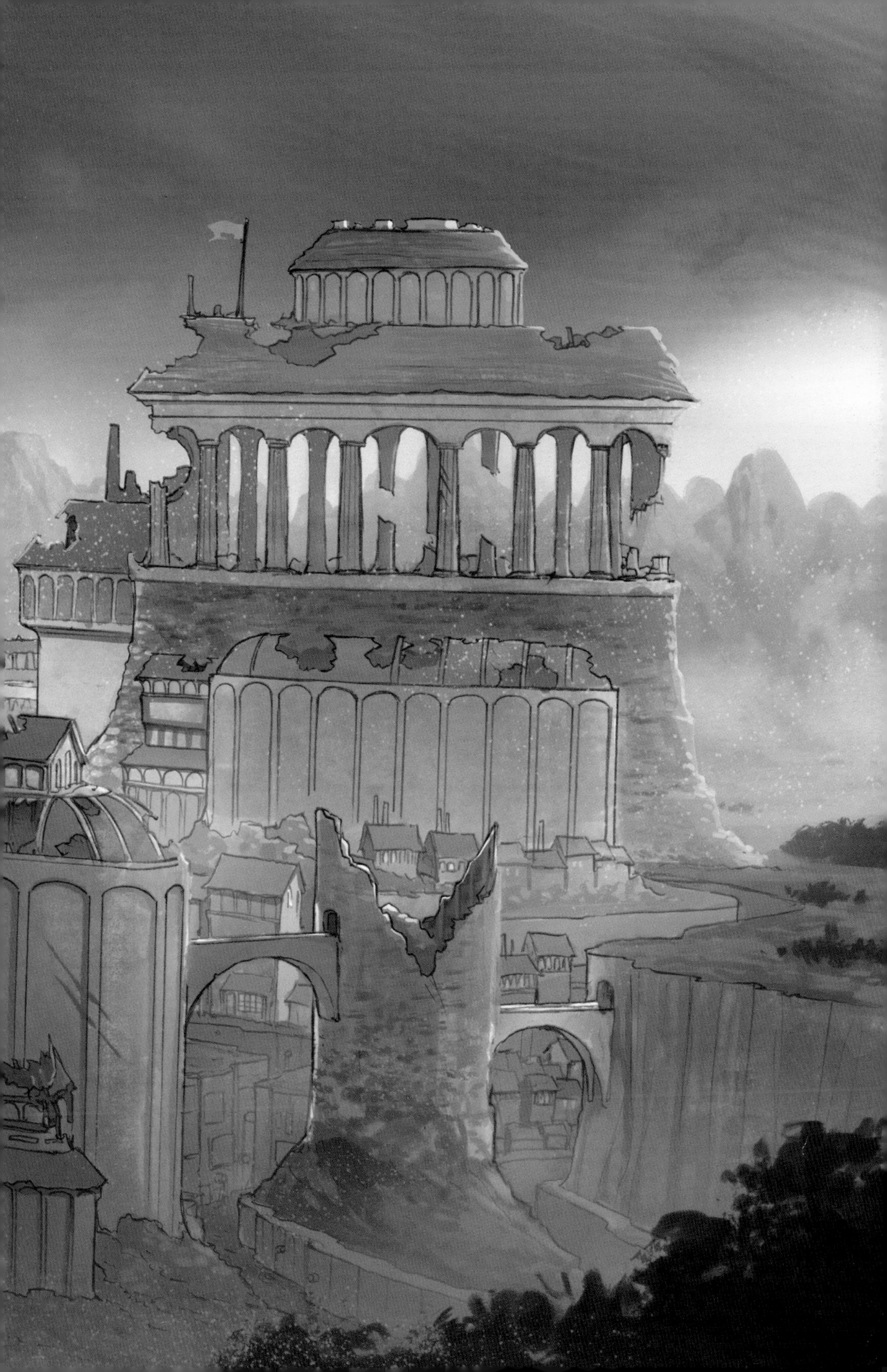

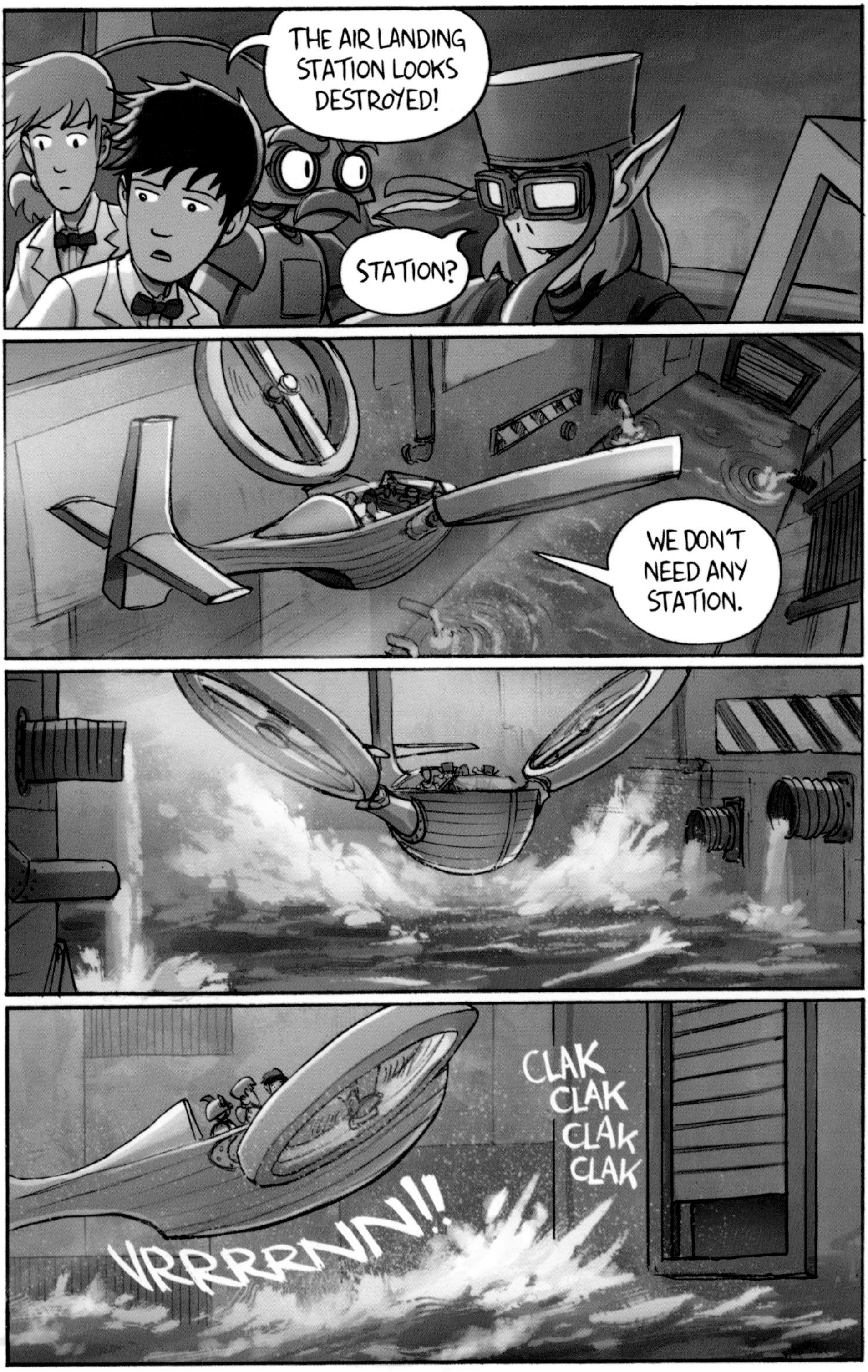
THE AIR LANDING STATION LOOKS DESTROYED!
STATION?
WE DON'T NEED ANY STATION.
CLAK CLAK CLAK CLAK
VRRRRNN!!

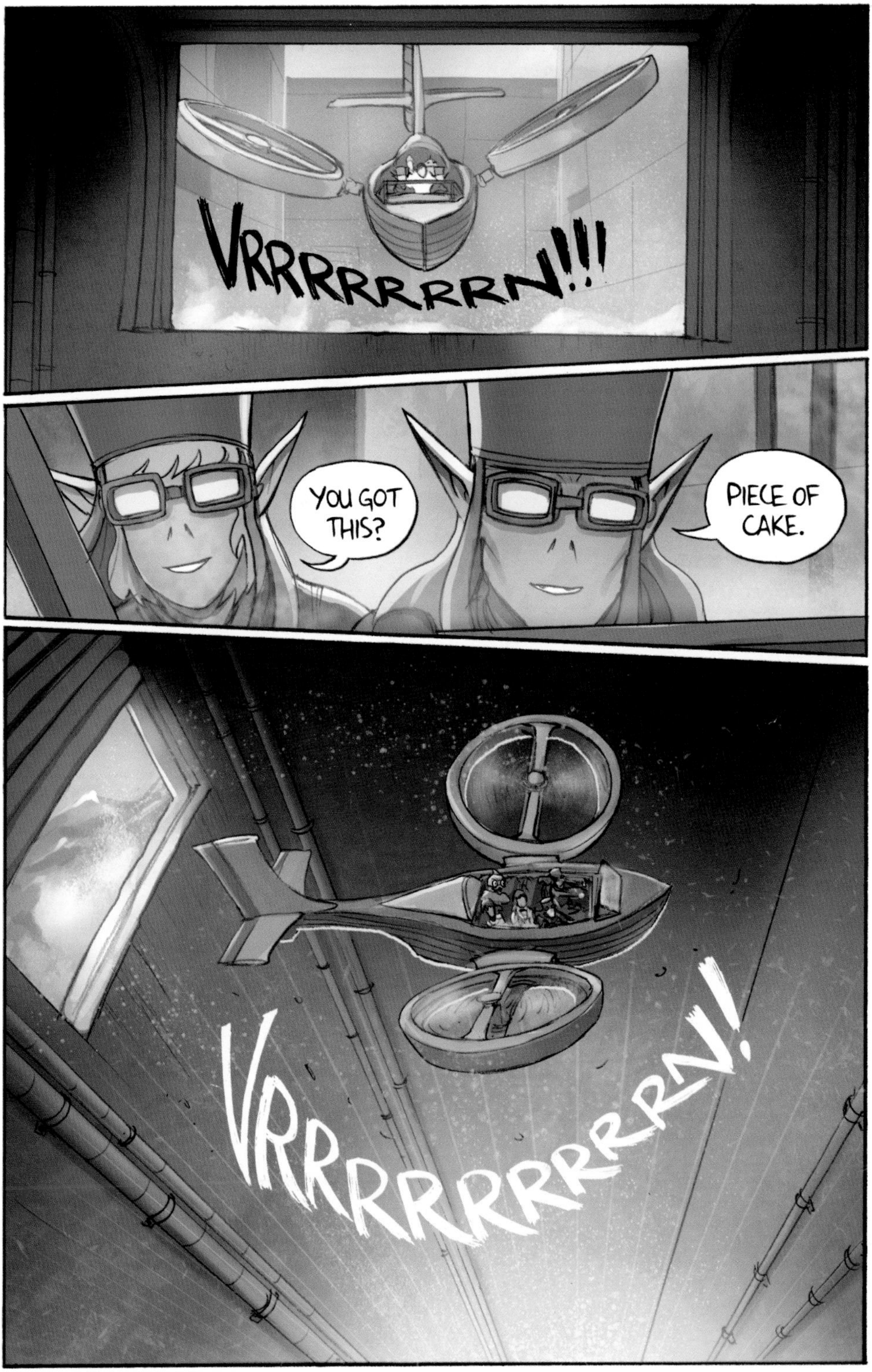
VRRRRRRRRN!!!
YOU GOT THIS?
PIECE OF CAKE.
VRRRRRRRRRN!

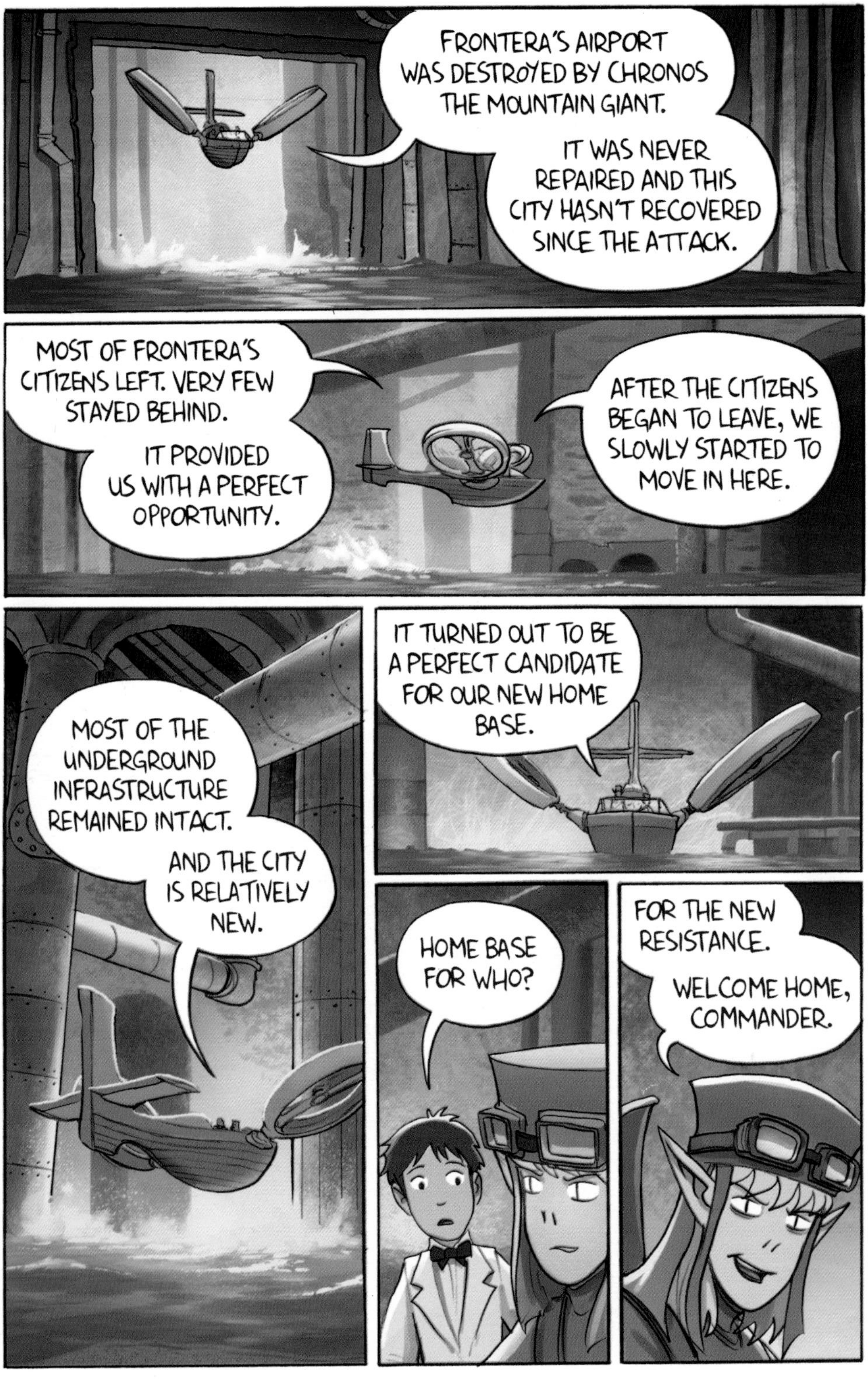
FRONTERA'S AIRPORT WAS DESTROYED BY CHRONOS THE MOUNTAIN GIANT.
IT WAS NEVER REPAIRED AND THIS CITY HASN'T RECOVERED SINCE THE ATTACK.
MOST OF FRONTERA'S CITIZENS LEFT. VERY FEW STAYED BEHIND.
IT PROVIDED US WITH A PERFECT OPPORTUNITY.
AFTER THE CITIZENS BEGAN TO LEAVE, WE SLOWLY STARTED TO MOVE IN HERE.
MOST OF THE UNDERGROUND INFRASTRUCTURE REMAINED INTACT.
AND THE CITY IS RELATIVELY NEW.
IT TURNED OUT TO BE A PERFECT CANDIDATE FOR OUR NEW HOME BASE.
HOME BASE FOR WHO?
FOR THE NEW RESISTANCE.
WELCOME HOME, COMMANDER.

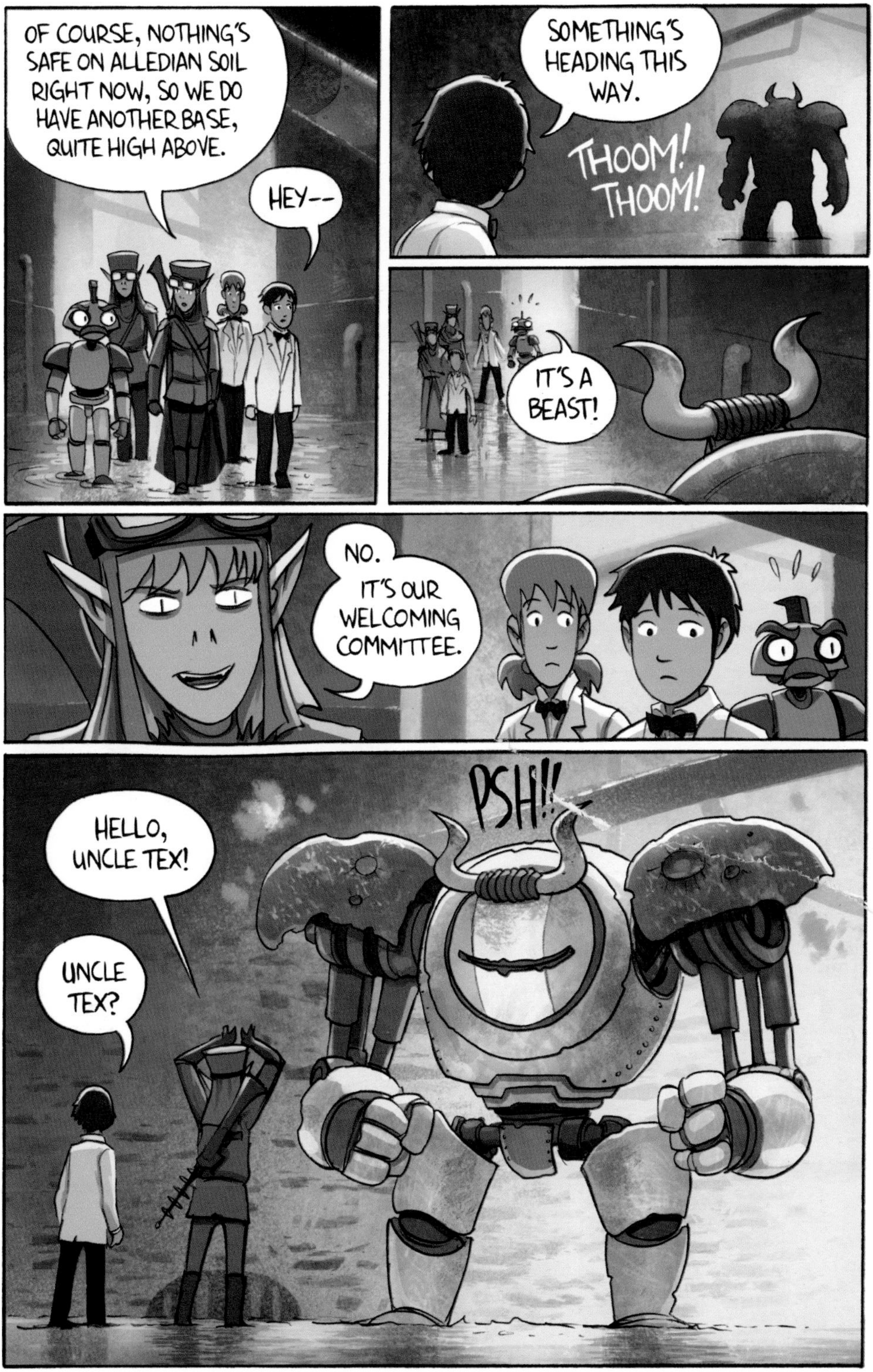
OF COURSE, NOTHING'S SAFE ON ALLEDIAN SOIL RIGHT NOW, SO WE DO HAVE ANOTHER BASE, QUITE HIGH ABOVE.
HEY--
SOMETHING'S HEADING THIS WAY.
THOOM! THOOM!
IT'S A BEAST!
NO.
IT'S OUR WELCOMING COMMITTEE.
PSH!!
HELLO, UNCLE TEX!
UNCLE TEX?

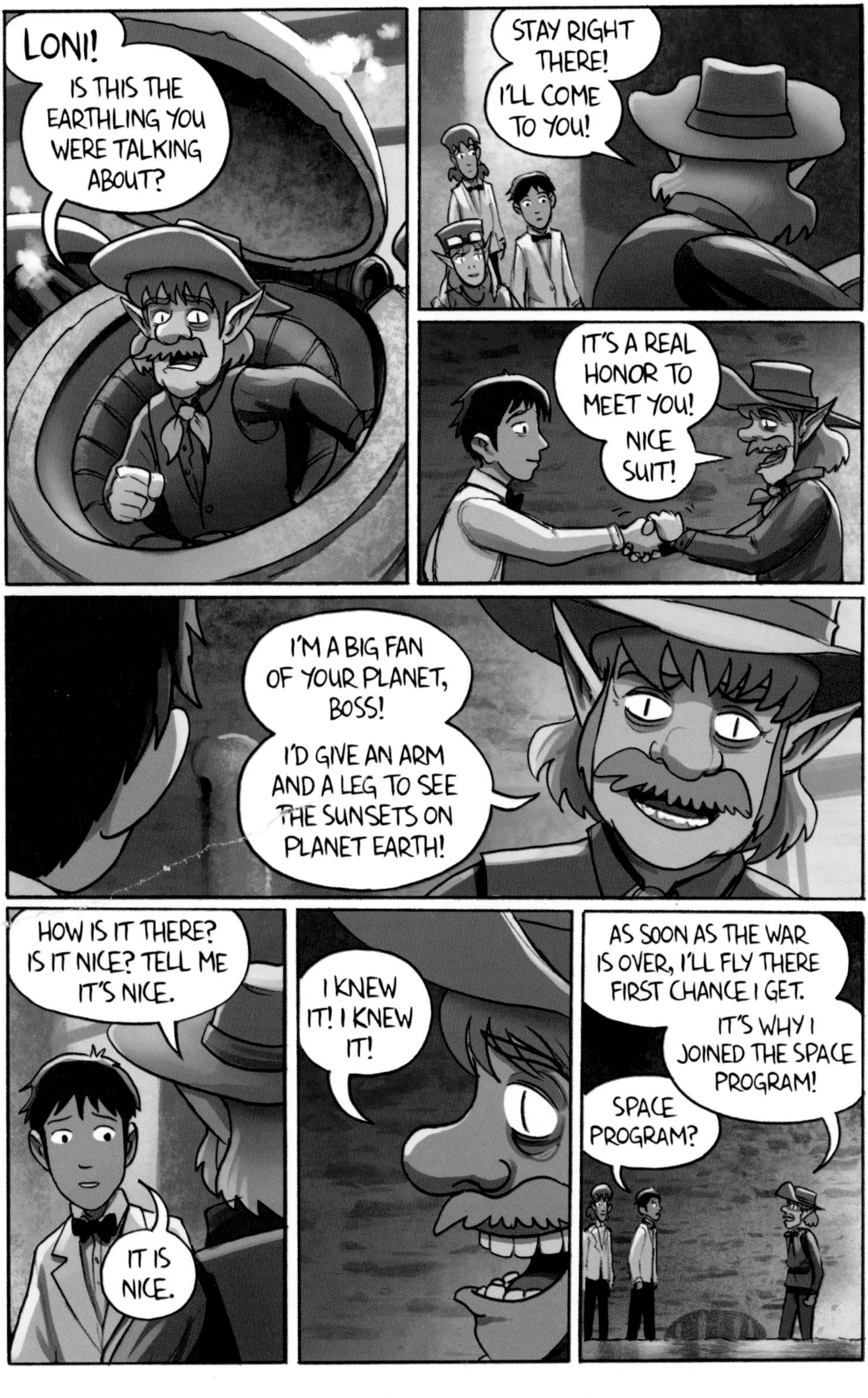
LONI!
IS THIS THE EARTHLING YOU WERE TALKING ABOUT?
STAY RIGHT THERE!
I'LL COME TO YOU!
IT'S A REAL HONOR TO MEET YOU!
NICE SUIT!
I'M A BIG FAN OF YOUR PLANET, BOSS!
I'D GIVE AN ARM AND A LEG TO SEE THE SUNSETS ON PLANET EARTH!
HOW IS IT THERE? IS IT NICE? TELL ME IT'S NICE.
IT IS NICE.
I KNEW IT! I KNEW IT!
AS SOON AS THE WAR IS OVER, I'LL FLY THERE FIRST CHANCE I GET.
IT'S WHY I JOINED THE SPACE PROGRAM!
SPACE PROGRAM?

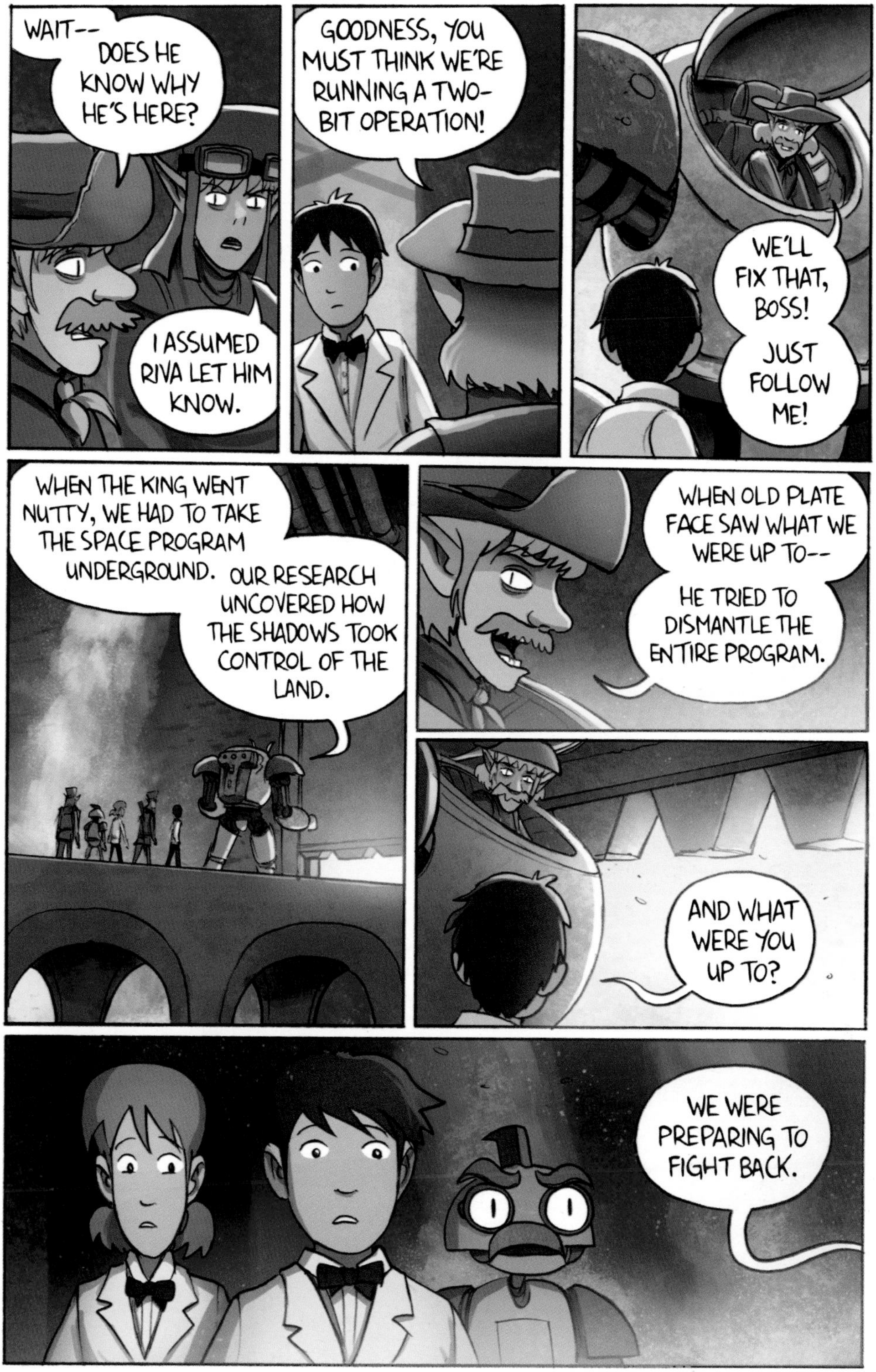
WAIT-- DOES HE KNOW WHY HE'S HERE?
I ASSUMED RIVA LET HIM KNOW.
GOODNESS, YOU MUST THINK WE'RE RUNNING A TWO-BIT OPERATION!
WE'LL FIX THAT, BOSS!
JUST FOLLOW ME!
WHEN THE KING WENT NUTTY, WE HAD TO TAKE THE SPACE PROGRAM UNDERGROUND.
OUR RESEARCH UNCOVERED HOW THE SHADOWS TOOK CONTROL OF THE LAND.
WHEN OLD PLATE FACE SAW WHAT WE WERE UP TO--
HE TRIED TO DISMANTLE THE ENTIRE PROGRAM.
AND WHAT WERE YOU UP TO?
WE WERE PREPARING TO FIGHT BACK.

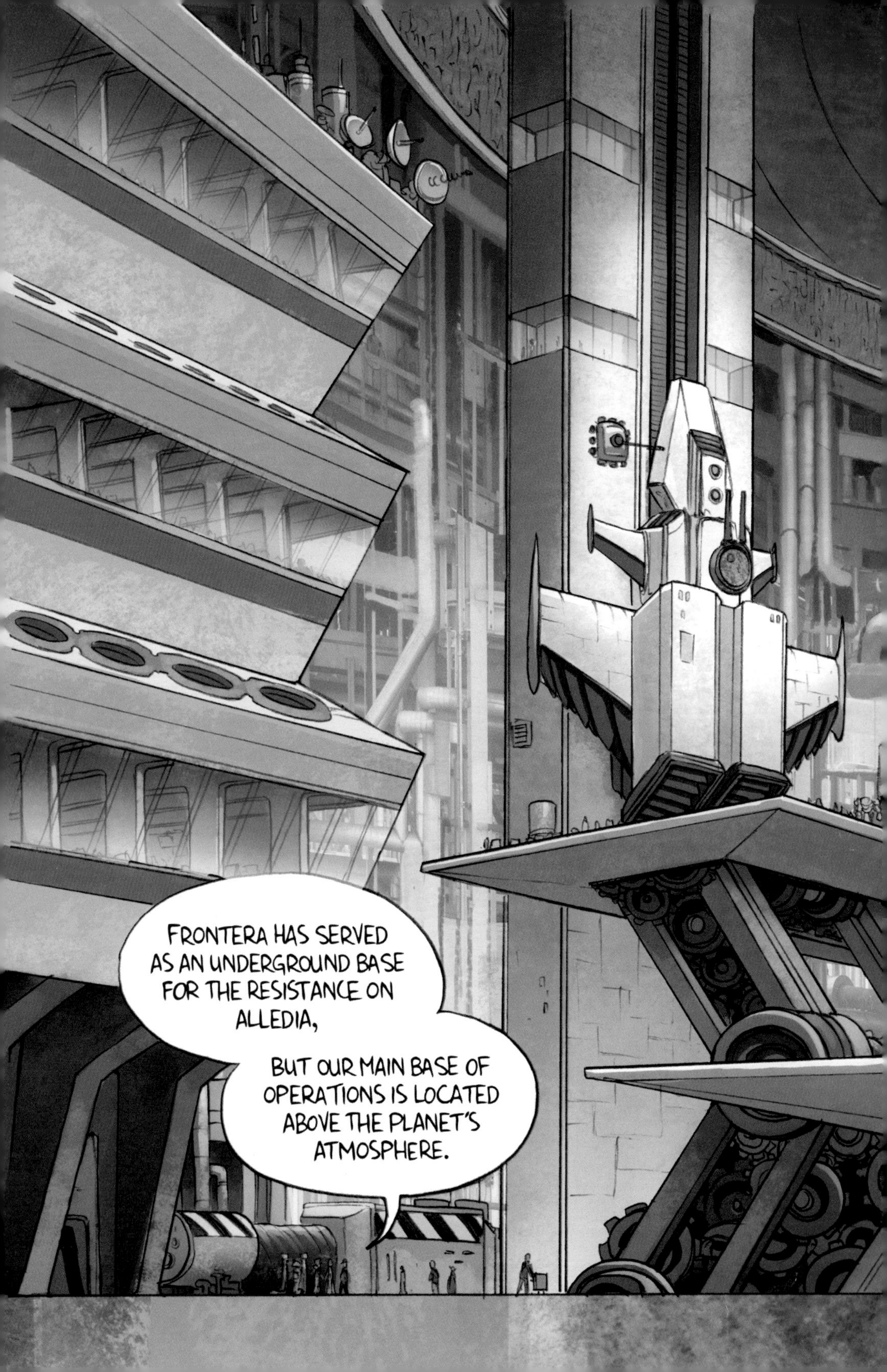
FRONTERA HAS SERVED AS AN UNDERGROUND BASE FOR THE RESISTANCE ON ALLEDIA,
BUT OUR MAIN BASE OF OPERATIONS IS LOCATED ABOVE THE PLANET'S ATMOSPHERE.

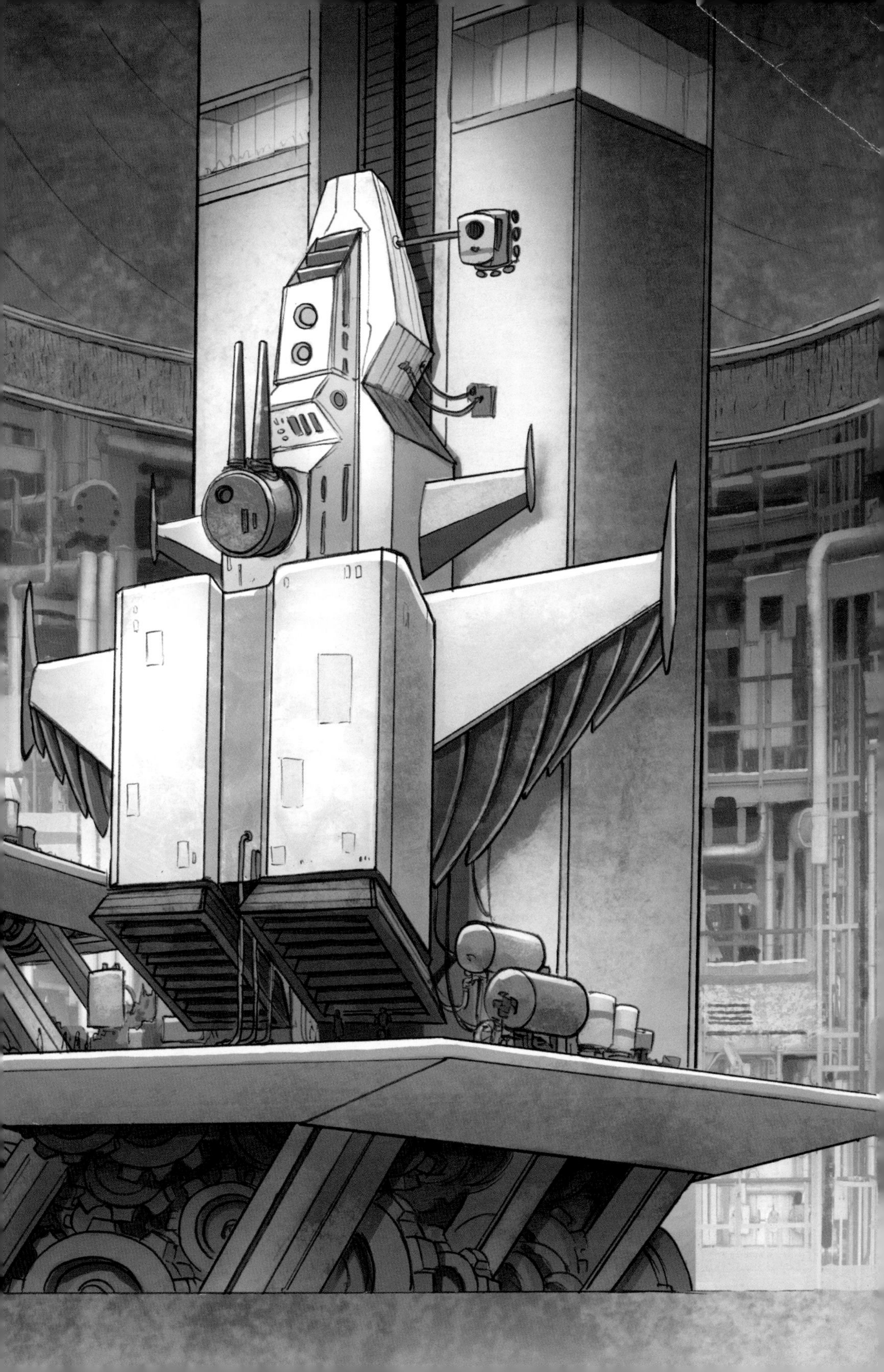

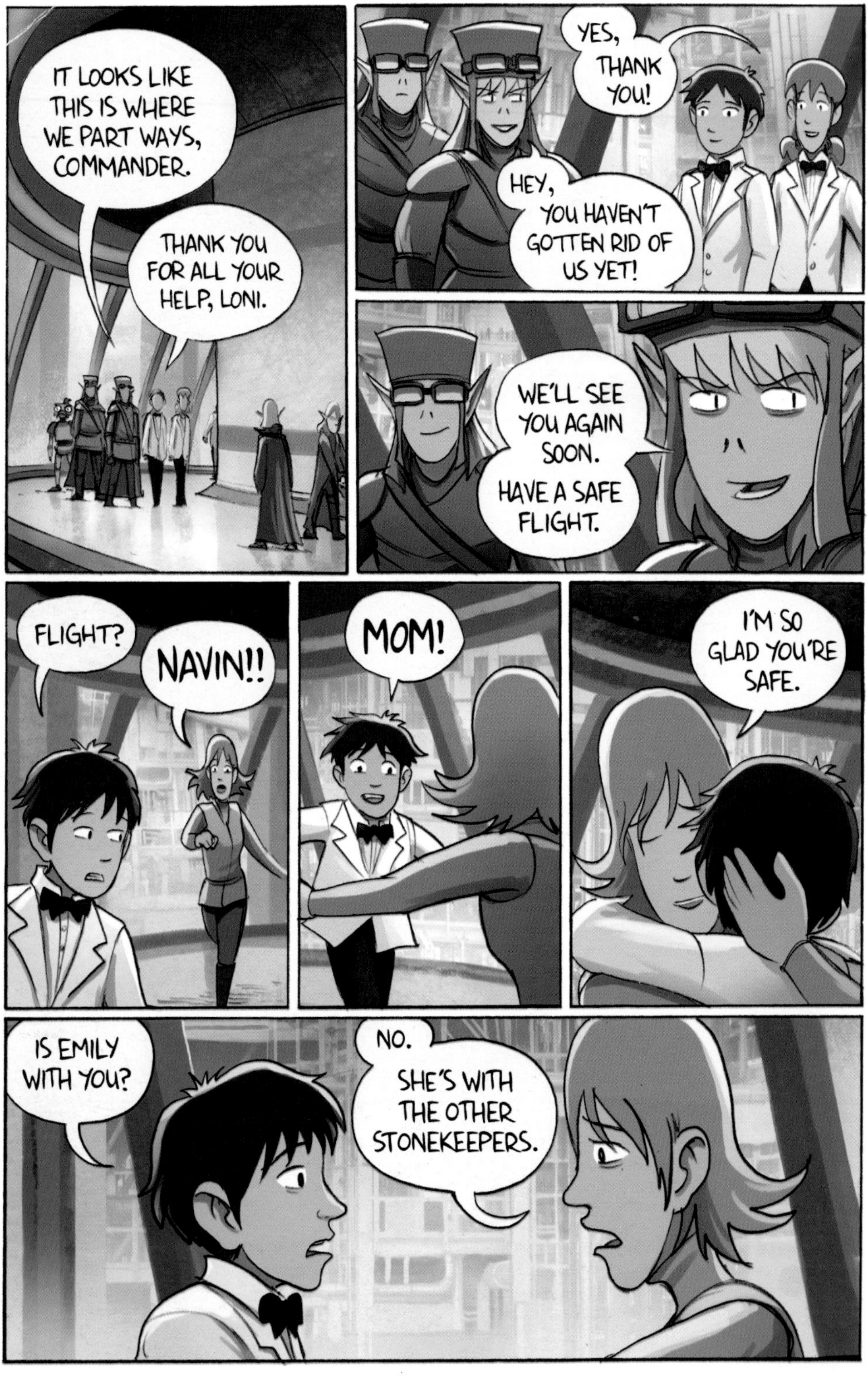
IT LOOKS LIKE THIS IS WHERE WE PART WAYS, COMMANDER.
THANK YOU FOR ALL YOUR HELP, LONI.
YES, THANK YOU!
HEY, YOU HAVEN'T GOTTEN RID OF US YET!
WE'LL SEE YOU AGAIN SOON.
HAVE A SAFE FLIGHT.
FLIGHT?
NAVIN!!
MOM!
I'M SO GLAD YOU'RE SAFE.
IS EMILY WITH YOU?
NO.
SHE'S WITH THE OTHER STONEKEEPERS.

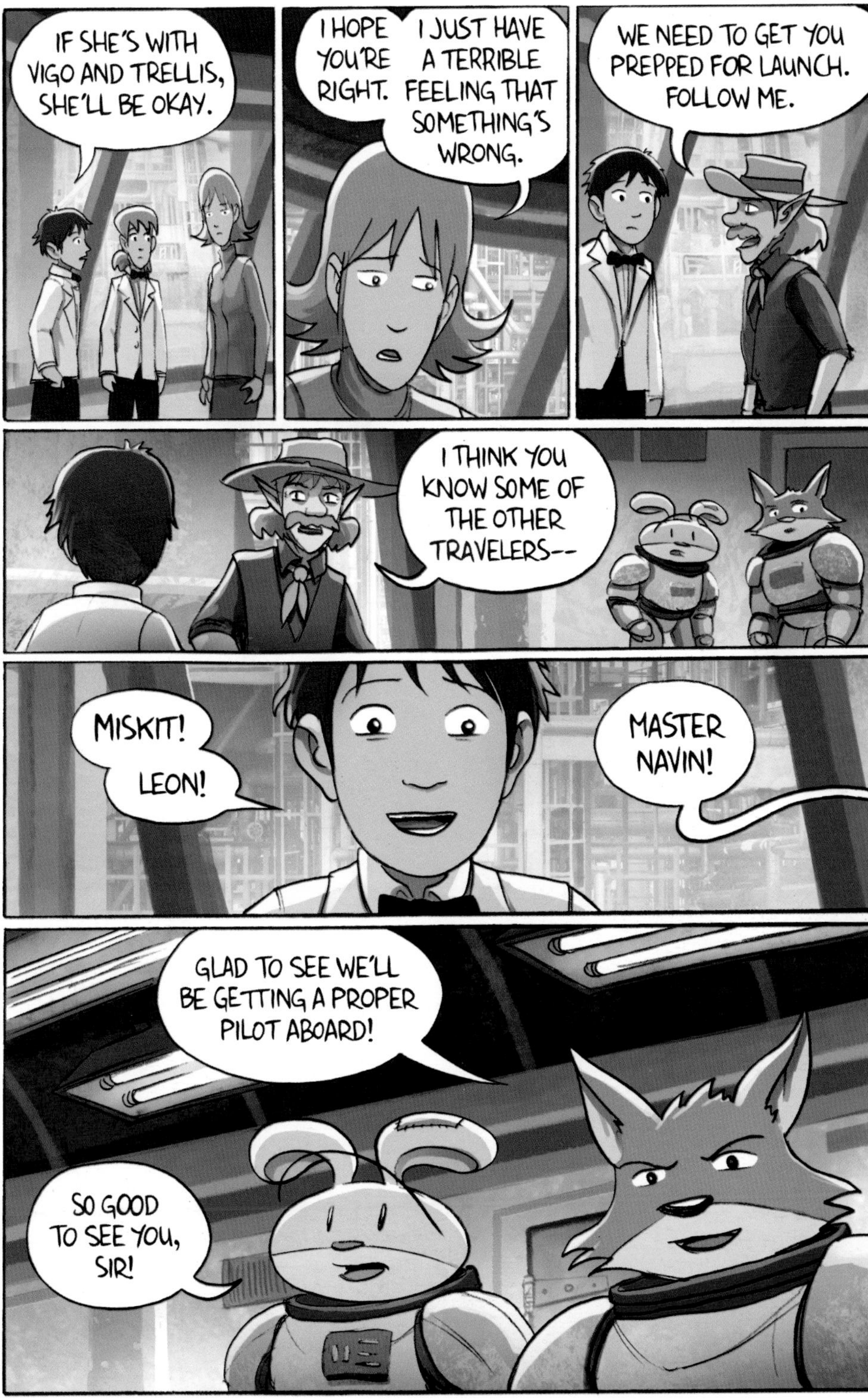
IF SHE'S WITH VIGO AND TRELLIS, SHE'LL BE OKAY.
I HOPE YOU'RE RIGHT.
I JUST HAVE A TERRIBLE FEELING THAT SOMETHING'S WRONG.
WE NEED TO GET YOU PREPPED FOR LAUNCH. FOLLOW ME.
I THINK YOU KNOW SOME OF THE OTHER TRAVELERS--
MISKIT!
LEON!
MASTER NAVIN!
GLAD TO SEE WE'LL BE GETTING A PROPER PILOT ABOARD!
SO GOOD TO SEE YOU, SIR!

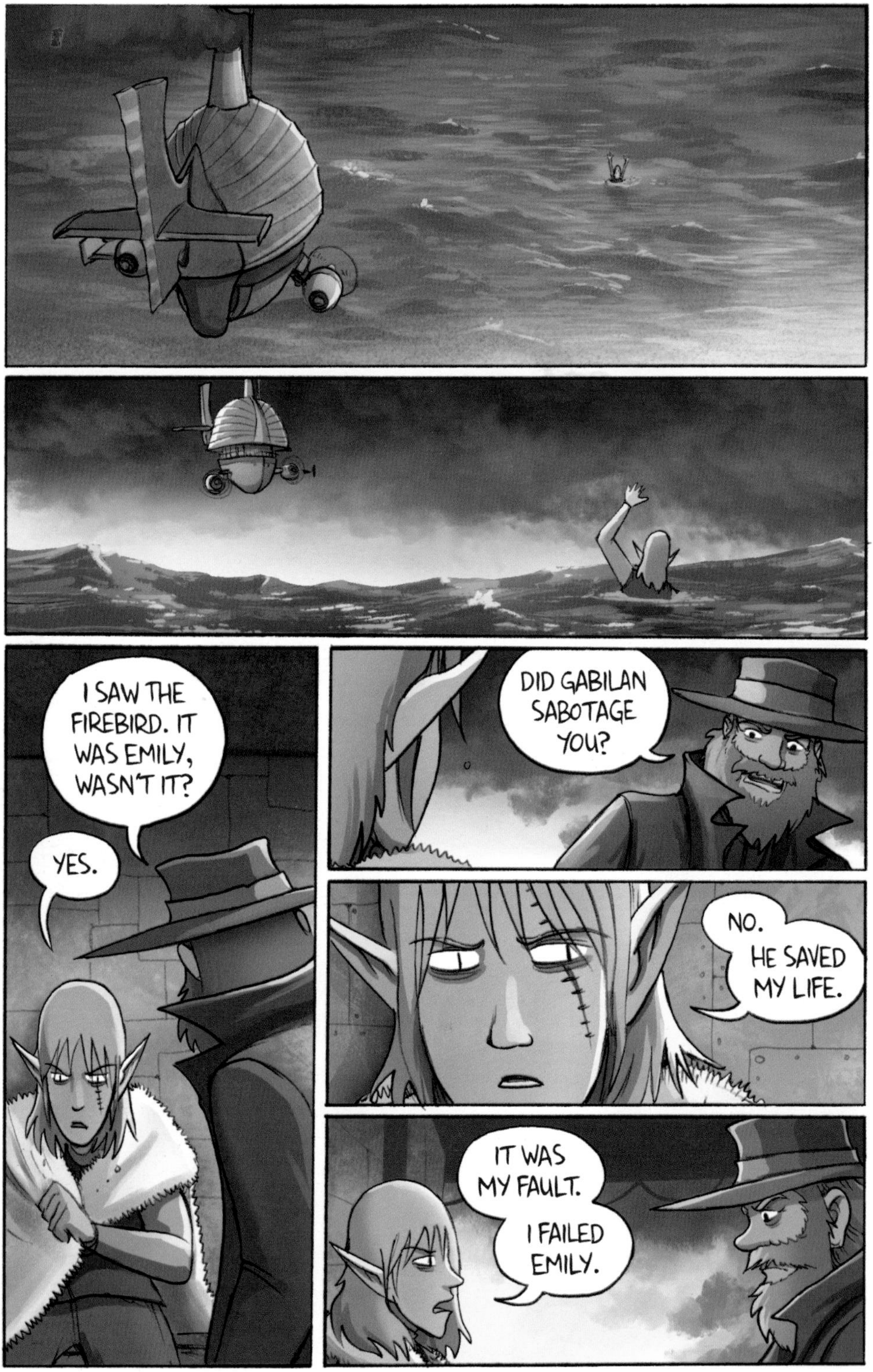
I SAW THE FIREBIRD. IT WAS EMILY, WASN'T IT?
YES.
DID GABILAN SABOTAGE YOU?
NO.
HE SAVED MY LIFE.
IT WAS MY FAULT.
I FAILED EMILY.

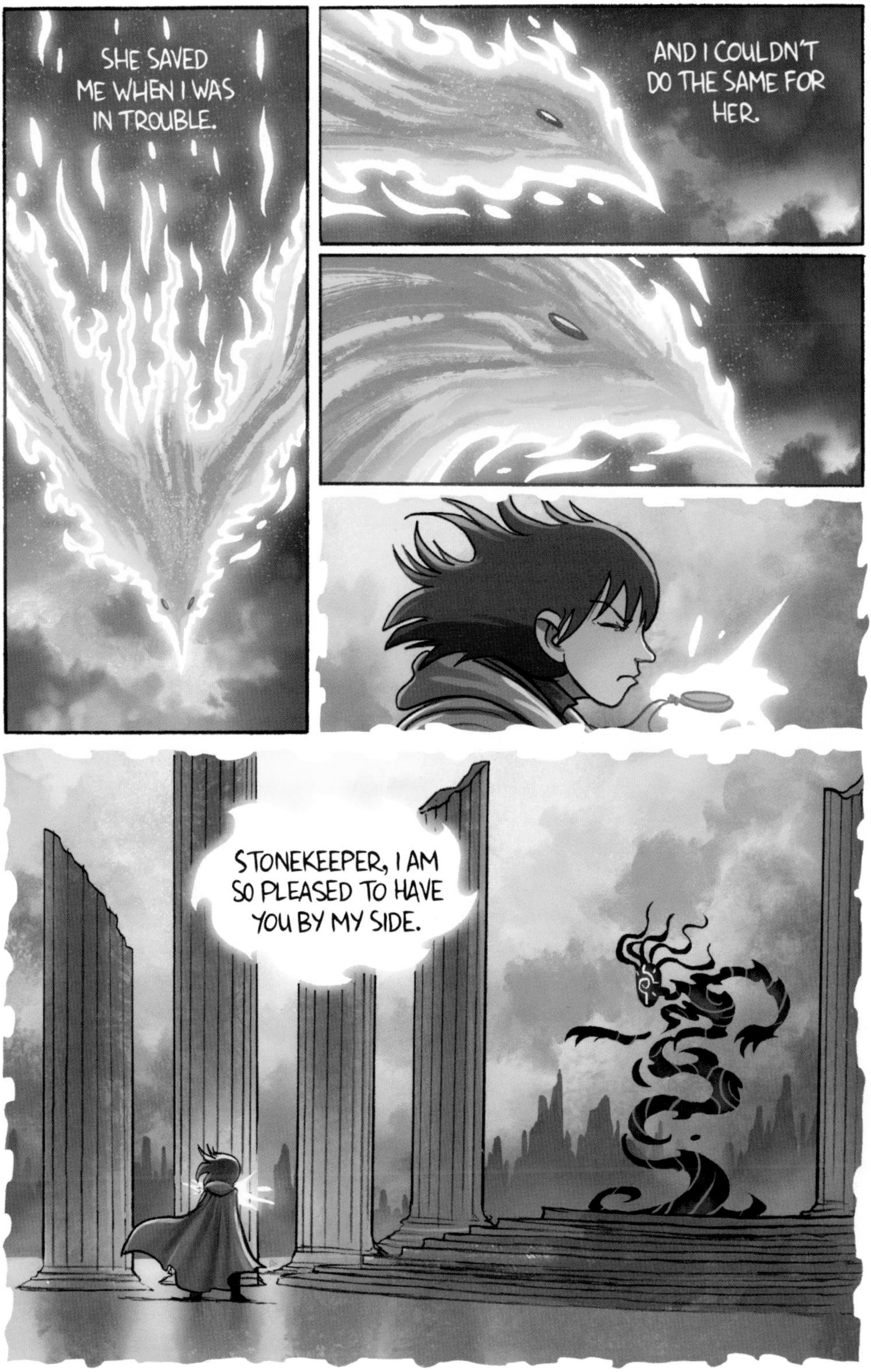
SHE SAVED ME WHEN I WAS IN TROUBLE.
AND I COULDN'T DO THE SAME FOR HER.
STONEKEEPER, I AM SO PLEASED TO HAVE YOU BY MY SIDE.

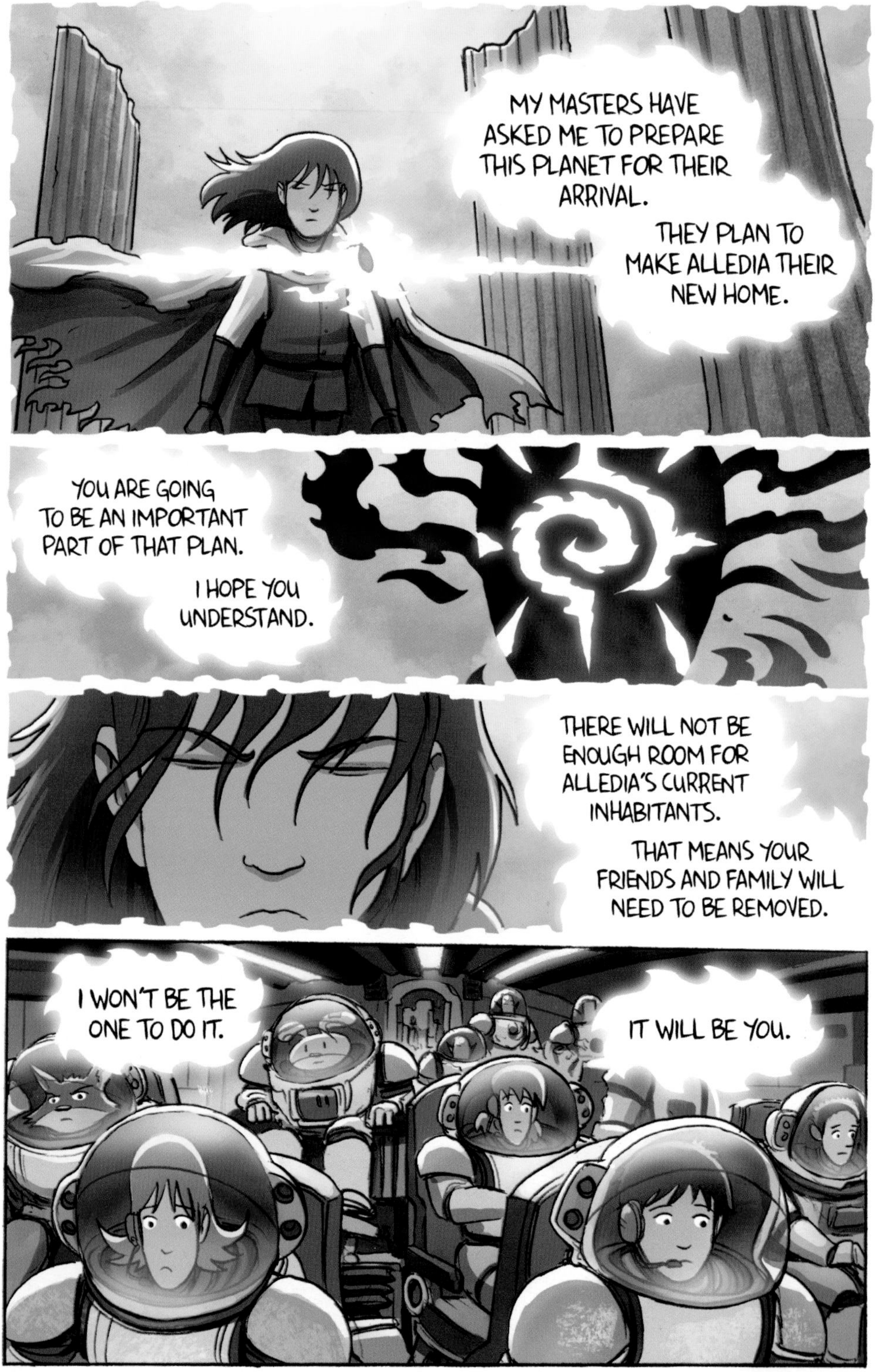

MY MASTERS HAVE ASKED ME TO PREPARE THIS PLANET FOR THEIR ARRIVAL.
THEY PLAN TO MAKE ALLEDIA THEIR NEW HOME.
YOU ARE GOING TO BE AN IMPORTANT PART OF THAT PLAN.
I HOPE YOU UNDERSTAND.
THERE WILL NOT BE ENOUGH ROOM FOR ALLEDIA'S CURRENT INHABITANTS.
THAT MEANS YOUR FRIENDS AND FAMILY WILL NEED TO BE REMOVED.
I WON'T BE THE ONE TO DO IT.
IT WILL BE YOU.

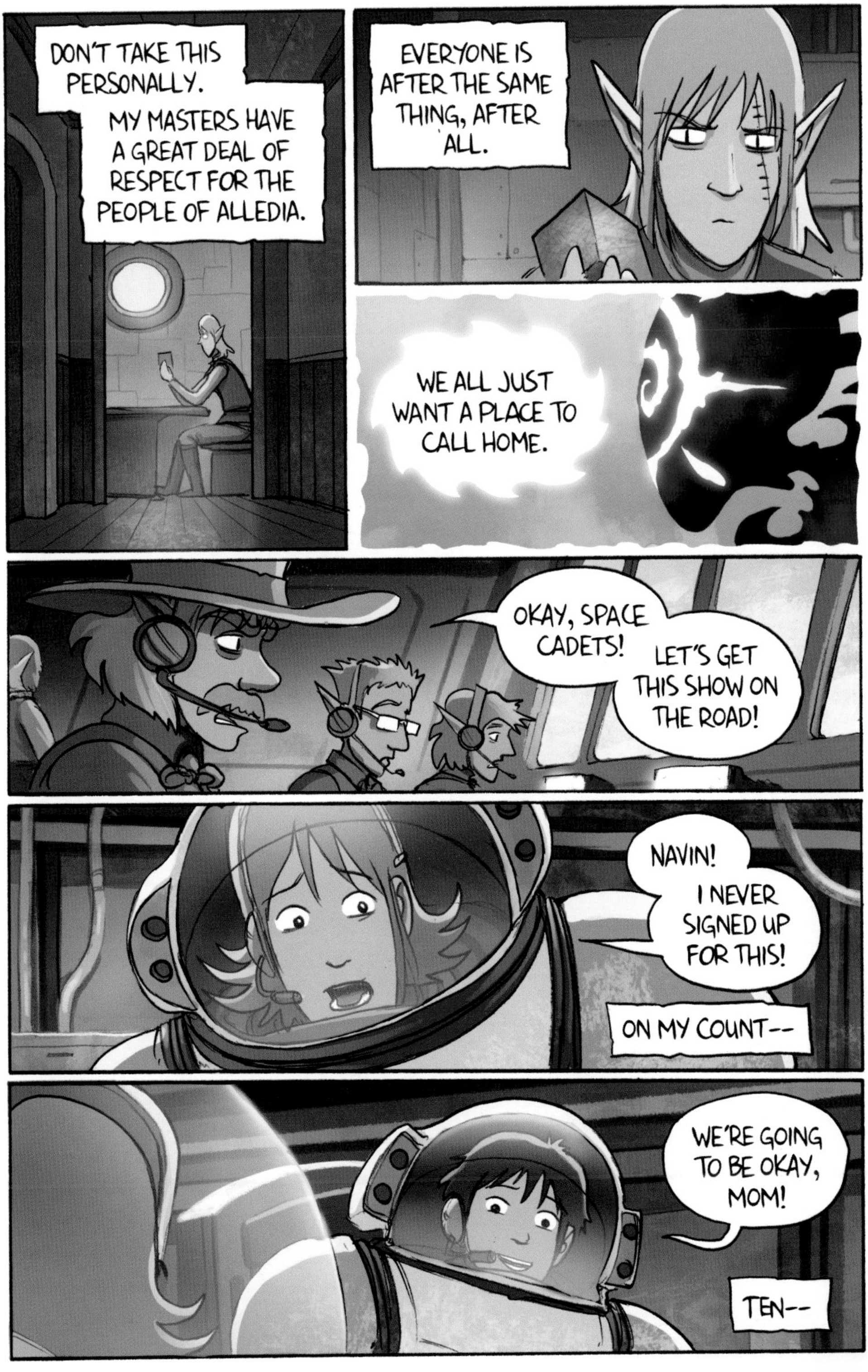
DON'T TAKE THIS PERSONALLY.
MY MASTERS HAVE A GREAT DEAL OF RESPECT FOR THE PEOPLE OF ALLEDIA.
EVERYONE IS AFTER THE SAME THING, AFTER ALL.
WE ALL JUST WANT A PLACE TO CALL HOME.
OKAY, SPACE CADETS!
LET'S GET THIS SHOW ON THE ROAD!
NAVIN!
I NEVER SIGNED UP FOR THIS!
ON MY COUNT--
WE'RE GOING TO BE OKAY, MOM!
TEN--

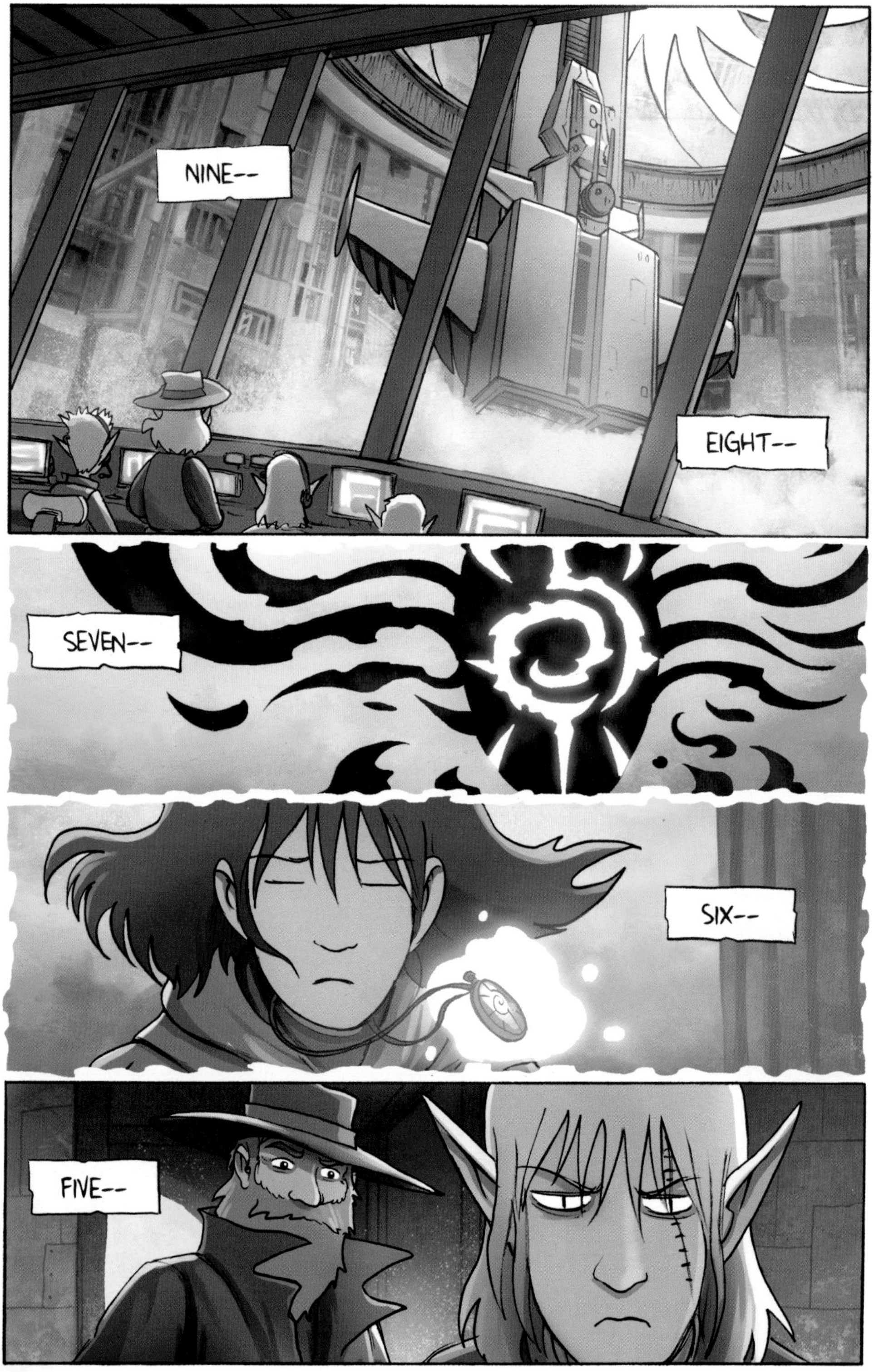
NINE--
EIGHT--
SEVEN--
SIX--
FIVE--

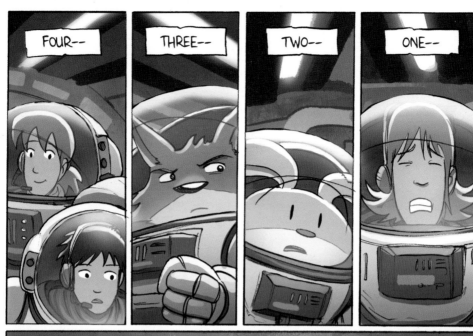

FOUR-- THREE-- TWO-- ONE--

IGNITION!

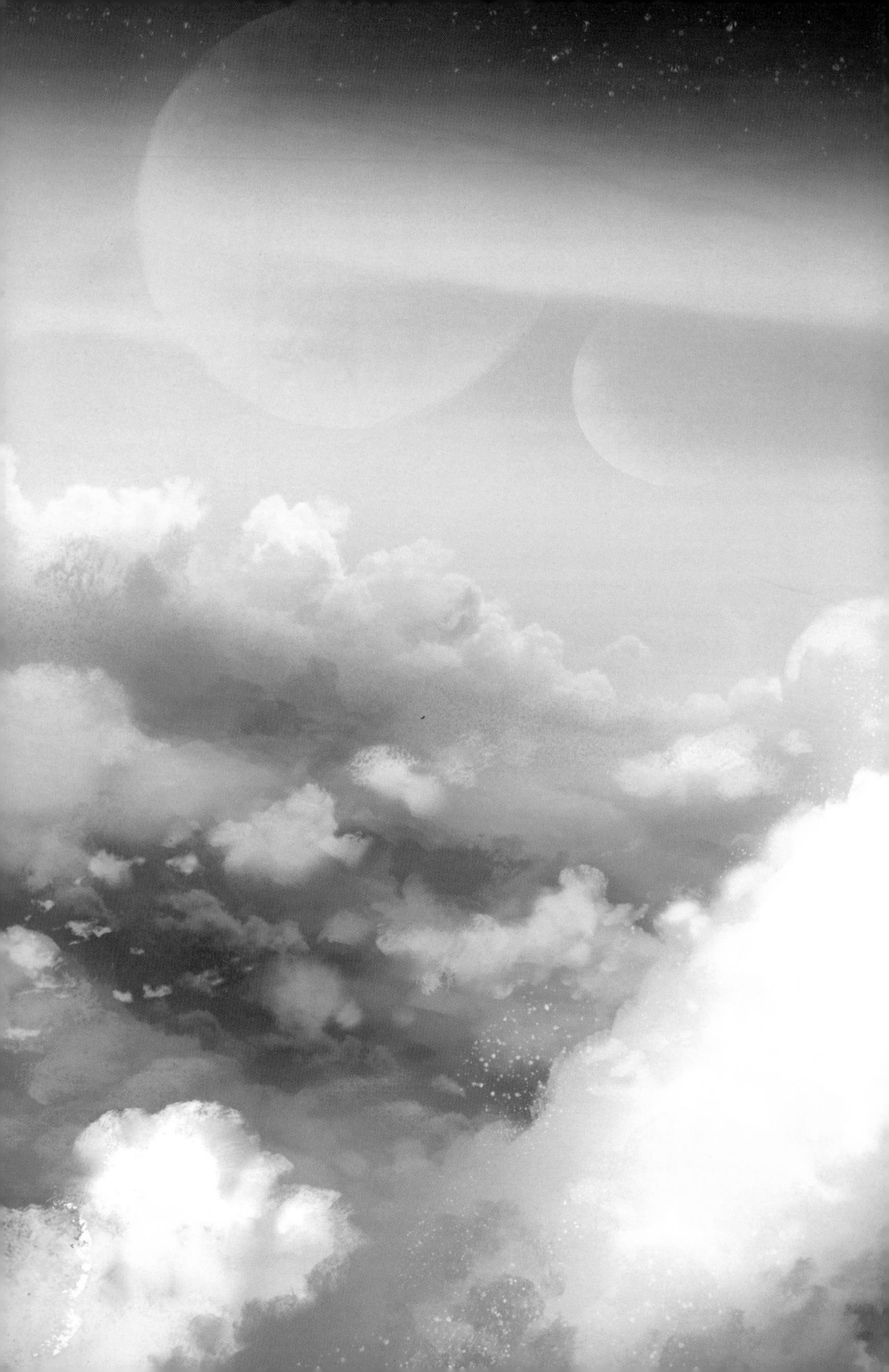

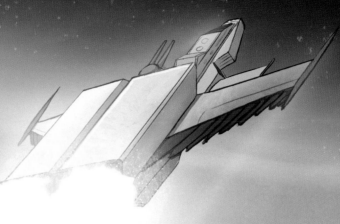

TO BE CONTINUED...

CREATED AT

BOLT CITY
PRODUCTIONS

WRITTEN & ILLUSTRATED BY
KAZU KIBUISHI

COLORS & BACKGROUNDS
JASON CAFFOE

COLOR ASSISTS
CHRYSTIN GARLAND
KAZU KIBUISHI

PAGE FLATTING
CRYSTAL KAN
MEGAN BRENNAN
NOLEN LEE

SPECIAL THANKS

Amy & Juni & Sophie Kim Kibuishi, Rachel Ormiston, Nancy Caffoe,
Judy Hansen, Cassandra Pelham, David Saylor, Phil Falco, Ben Zhu
& the Gallery Nucleus crew, Tao & Taka & Tyler Kibuishi, Tim
Ganter, Sunni Kim, June & Masa & Julie & Emi Kibuishi, Sheila
Marie Everett, Lizette Serrano, Bess Braswell, Whitney Steller, Lori
Benton, and Ellie Berger.

And the biggest thanks of all to the librarians, booksellers, parents,
and readers who have supported us all this way. You mean the world
to us.

ABOUT THE AUTHOR

Kazu Kibuishi is the creator of the #1 *New York Times* bestselling Amulet series. *Amulet, Book One: The Stonekeeper* was an ALA Best Book for Young Adults and a Children's Choice Book Award finalist. He is also the creator of *Copper*, a collection of his popular webcomic that features an adventuresome boy-and-dog pair. Kazu also illustrated the covers of the 15th anniversary paperback editions of the Harry Potter series written by J. K. Rowling. He lives and works in Seattle, Washington, with his wife, Amy Kim Kibuishi, and their children.

Visit Kazu online at www.boltcity.com.

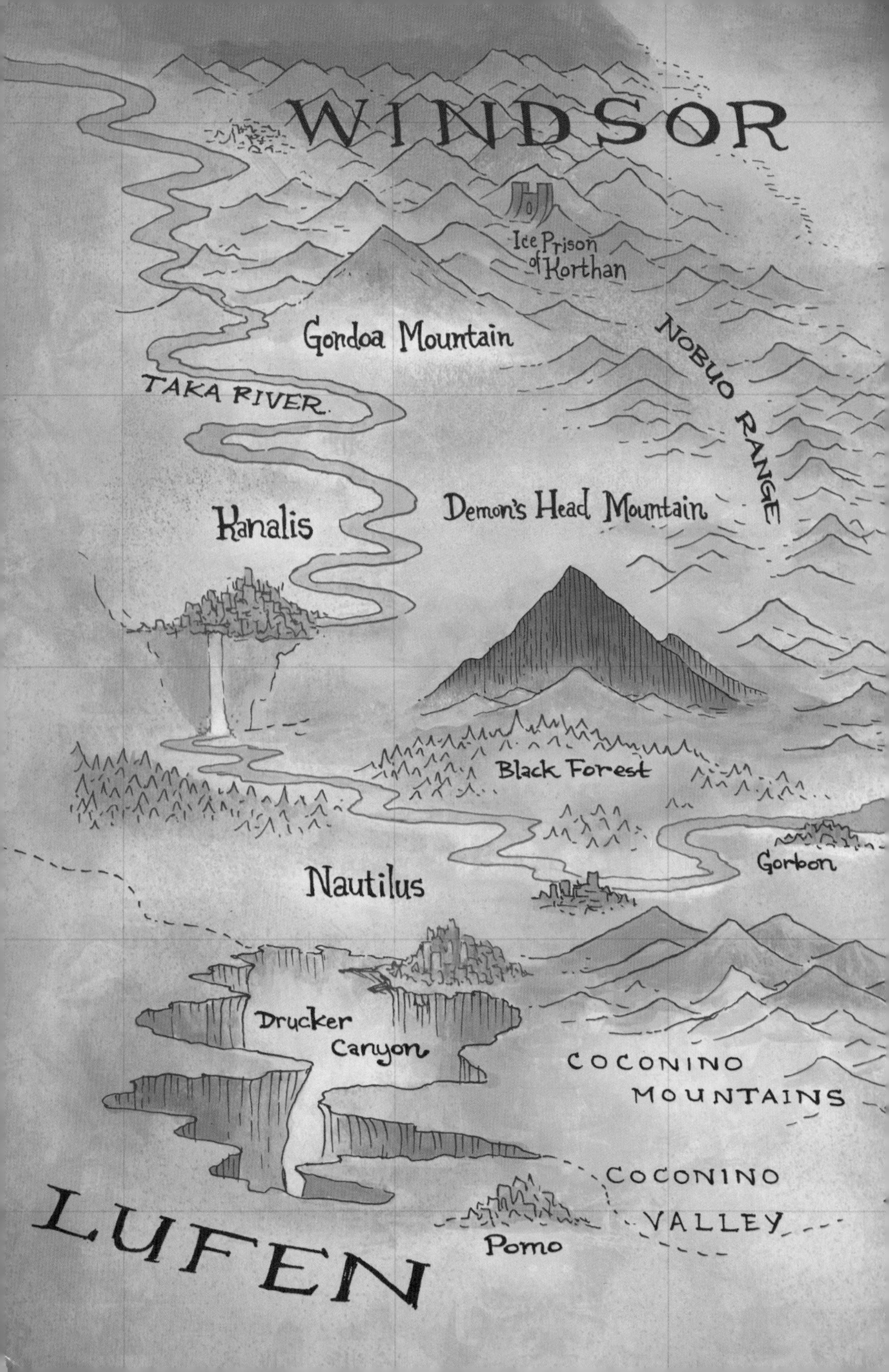
WINDSOR
Ice Prison of Korthan
Gondoa Mountain
NOBUO RANGE
TAKA RIVER
Kanalis
Demon's Head Mountain
Black Forest
Gorbon
Nautilus
Drucker Canyon
COCONINO MOUNTAINS
COCONINO VALLEY
Pomo
LUFEN

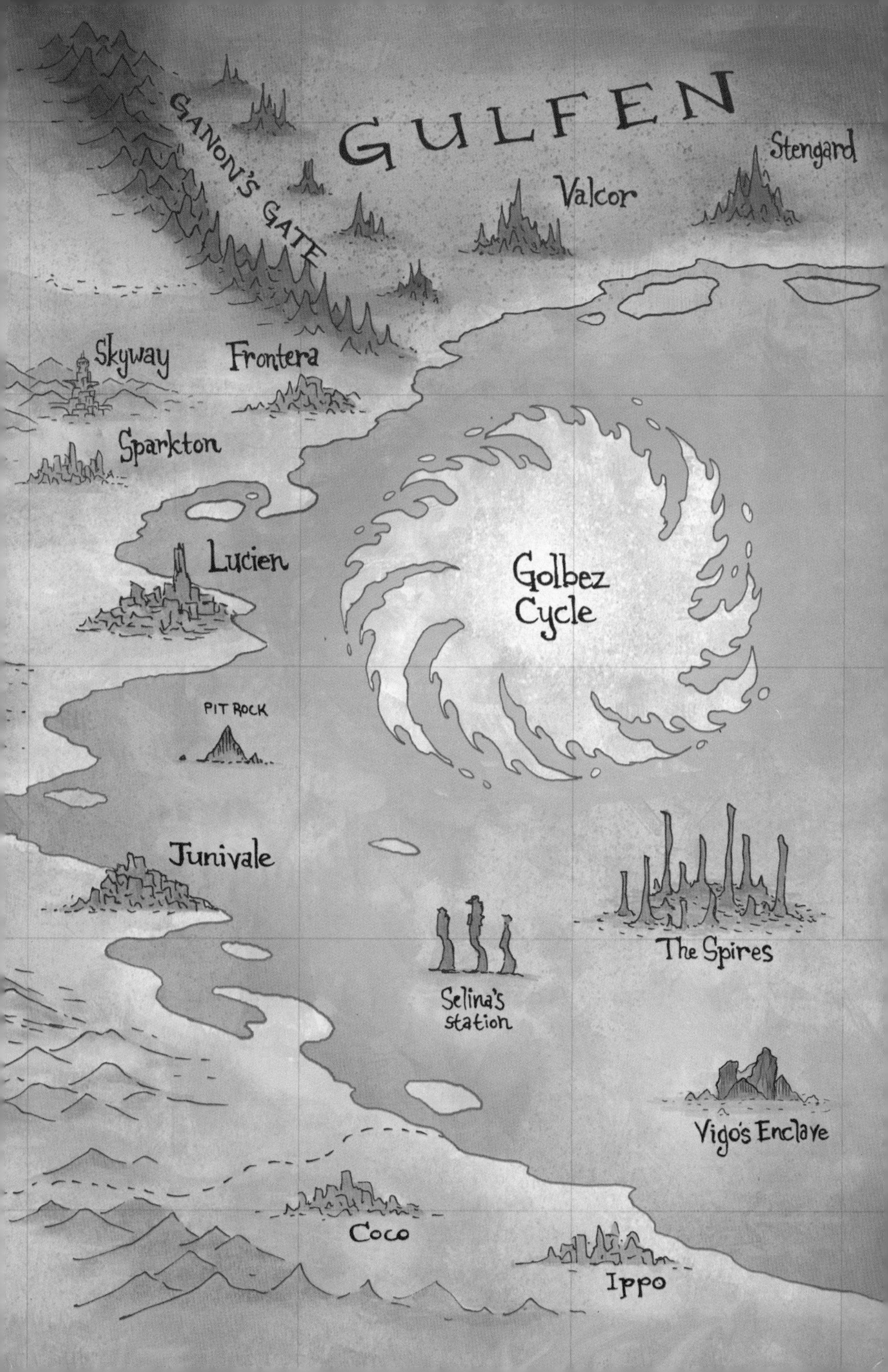
GULFEN
GANON'S GATE
Stengard
Valcor
Skyway
Frontera
Sparkton
Lucien
Golbez
Cycle
PIT ROCK
Junivale
The Spires
Selina's
station
Vigo's Enclave
Coco
Ippo

ALSO BY
KAZU KIBUISHI

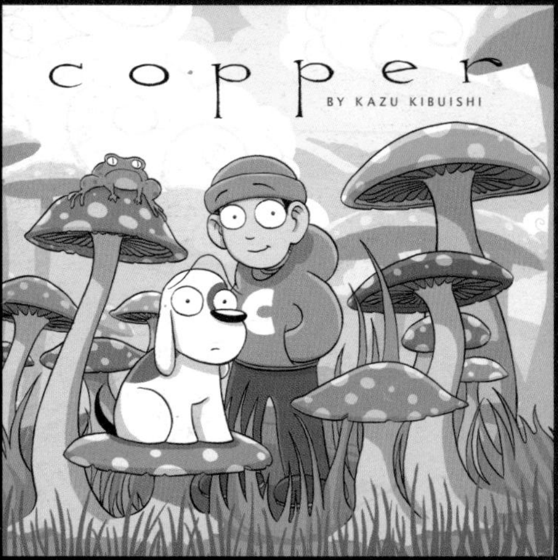
copper
BY KAZU KIBUISHI

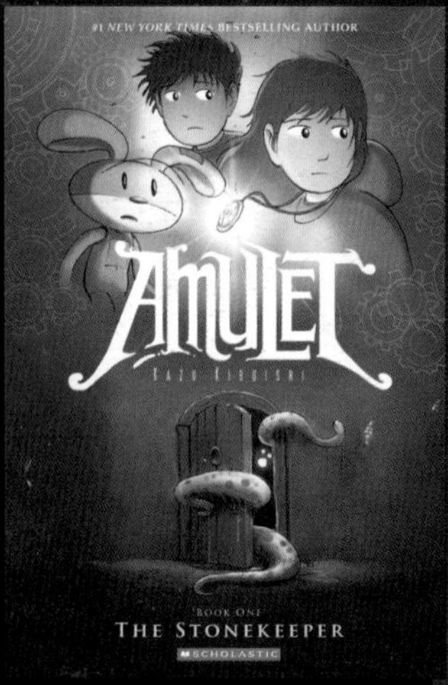
#1 NEW YORK TIMES BESTSELLING AUTHOR
AMULET
KAZU KIBUISHI
BOOK ONE
THE STONEKEEPER
SCHOLASTIC

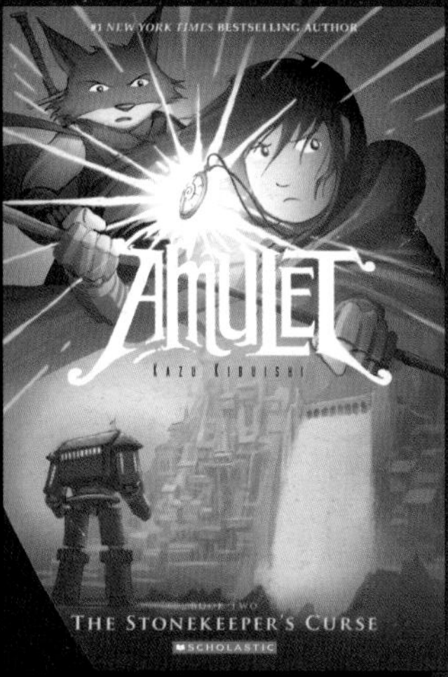
#1 NEW YORK TIMES BESTSELLING AUTHOR
AMULET
KAZU KIBUISHI
BOOK TWO
THE STONEKEEPER'S CURSE
SCHOLASTIC

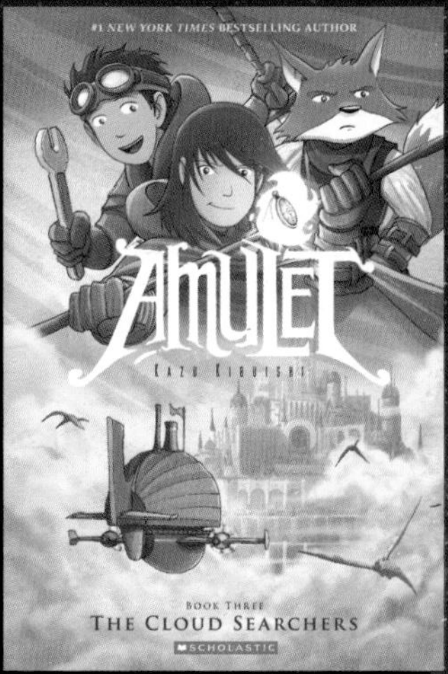
#1 NEW YORK TIMES BESTSELLING AUTHOR
AMULET
KAZU KIBUISHI
BOOK THREE
THE CLOUD SEARCHERS
SCHOLASTIC

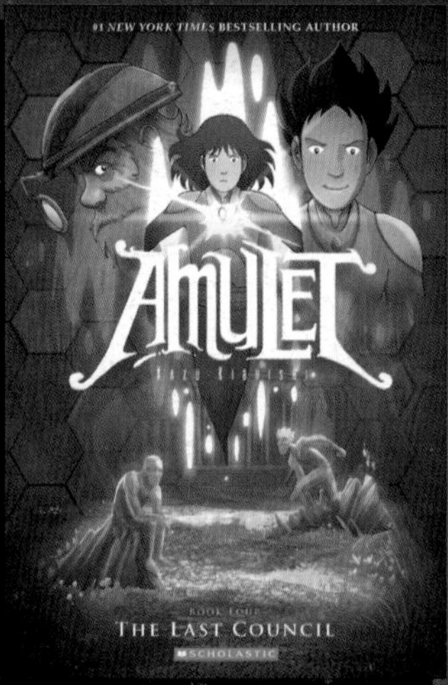
#1 NEW YORK TIMES BESTSELLING AUTHOR
AMULET
THE LAST COUNCIL
SCHOLASTIC

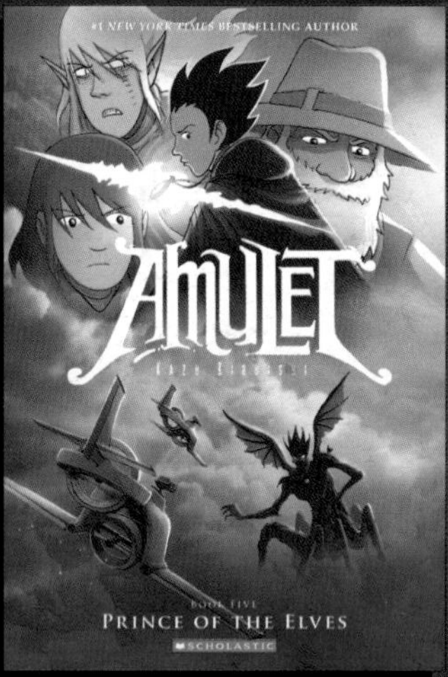
#1 NEW YORK TIMES BESTSELLING AUTHOR
AMULET
BOOK FIVE
PRINCE OF THE ELVES
SCHOLASTIC

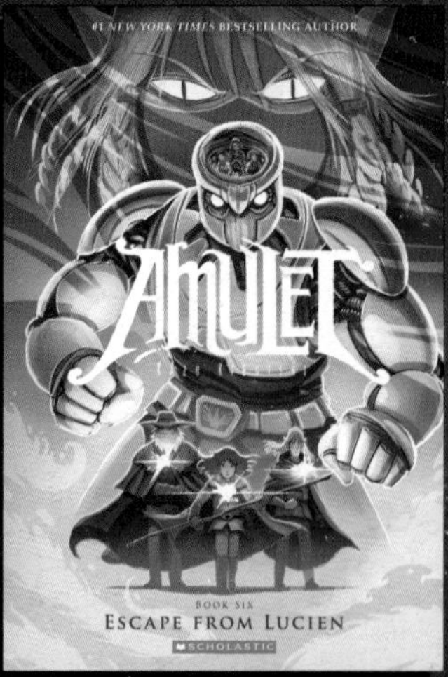
#1 NEW YORK TIMES BESTSELLING AUTHOR
AMULET
BOOK SIX
ESCAPE FROM LUCIEN
SCHOLASTIC